Tortoise

JESSICA GRANT

VINTAGE CANADA

Published in Canada by Vintage Canada, a division of Random House of Canada
Limited, Toronto, in 2010. Originally published in hardcover in Canada by
Alfred A. Knopf Canada, a division of Random House of Canada Limited,
Toronto, in 2009. Distributed by Random House of Canada Limited, Toronto.

Vintage Canada with colophon is a registered trademark.

www.randomhouse.ca

LIBRARY AND ARCHIVES CANADA CATALOGUING IN PUBLICATION

Grant, Jessica, 1972–
Come, thou tortoise / Jessica Grant.

Issued also in electronic format.
ISBN 978-0-307-39755-3

I. Title.

PS8613.R365C65 2010   C813'.6   C2009-905325-X

Text design by Kelly Hill

Printed and bound in the United States of America

6 8 9 7 5

Praise for
Come, Thou Tortoise

"Jessica Grant has an engaging, wry and forthright style, which echoes Miriam Toews, Don DeLillo, Lewis Carroll and Kurt Vonnegut Jr. (right down to the occasional and appropriate use of illustrations). . . . It's a delight. Pick it up, and prepare to see everything from Methusalan mice to palm trees in England. Pack a lunch. You may end up reading all day." *The Globe and Mail*

"The real success here is not the reptilian point-of-view or playfulness with language, but that *Come, Thou Tortoise* manages to be touching without excess sediment. Sorry, sentiment." *Toronto Star*

"A funny and sad and splendid first novel." *Winnipeg Free Press*

"A writer whose work twinkles with wordplay." *Ottawa Citizen*

"*Come, Thou Tortoise* is many things: a story about finding belonging, a paean to the importance of family, a commentary on relationships, and a kindhearted critique of modern life." *Quill & Quire*

"A funny yet poignant story of family frailty." *Edmonton Journal*

"*Come, Thou Tortoise* should be issued with a health warning: you will split your sides laughing, your eyes will leak, your heart rate will accelerate, and the abundance of wit will rewire the synapses in your brain. . . . A tortoise de force." Lisa Moore, author of *Alligator*

"In *Come, Thou Tortoise*, everything on the top shelf is now in the bottom drawer, and all the things you left in your backyard happen to be under your pillow. Mysteriously, this difference is all the encouragement you need to evict nonchalance from your heart. Please—I beg you dear reader—read Jessica Grant." Michael Winter, author of *The Architects Are Here*

Come, Thou

Contents

Part One

ODDLY FLOWERS

The plane is a row of gold circles and a cockpit. One of those circles will carry my head halfway home. I count back fourteen. That circle. In the cockpit the pilots are having a good time. Boy are they. Coffee cups have to be put down. They are really laughing. One puts a hand on the other's shoulder. Then the one with the hand leans over and kisses the other's cheek. A quick impulsive happy peck.

A fellow passenger joins me at the terminal window. Hey, I tell her. Our pilots just kissed.

No response.

I'm thinking that kiss bodes well for our safety.

She pretends she has a cup to throw away.

That is my plane. With the word NAP resolving on its tail. How do I feel about that acronym. Not great.

My phone rings and it's Linda.

What's up.

Winnifred isn't moving.

Never assume a tortoise is dead. Rule Number One of Tortoise Ownership. What's the temperature in your apartment. Remember it's winter. It's still dark. She's not nocturnal. These and other environmental factors have likely caused her to withdraw into her shell. Her heart beats maybe once an hour. Be patient. Wait an hour.

Still, I crouch down next to the window. Feel the heat coming up from the vent. Is my tortoise dead. Should I go back.

My own heart is all apatter. This is being alive. Can you feel the body worry before every beat. I can. Will this be the last. No. Will this be the last. No.

Should I go back.

I look up at the pilots who are possibly in love and I don't want to catch any other plane but this one. This is my plane.

Yesterday I peered down into her castle and she was beside the pool making the same journey I'd seen her start two days ago. I knocked on her shell. Excuse me, Winnifred.

No legs emerged. No little ancient head.

I picked her up and held her under my armpit. This usually worked. I did have a heat lamp, but paper castles tend to be flammable.

Finally she woke up.

There, I said. I put her in the pool.

I knelt down beside the castle with windows that look out onto my kitchen. Many times I have seen Winnifred poke her head wistfully through one of those windows. Many times I have seen her drop a piece of lettuce like a note.

She climbed out of the pool and creaked over to the window.

I have to go home for a while, I said.

Winnifred is old. She might be three hundred. She came with the apartment. The previous tenant, a rock climber named Cliff, was about to embark on a rock climbing adventure that would not have been much fun for Winnifred. Back then her name was Iris. Cliff had inherited Iris from the tenant before him. Nobody knew how old Iris was or where she had come from originally. Now Cliff was moving out. He said, Would you like a tortoise.

I would not say no to a tortoise, I said.

I was alone in Portland and the trees were giant. I picked her up and she blinked at me with her upside-down eyelids. I felt instantly calm. Her eyes were soft brown. Her skin felt like an old elbow. I will build you a castle, I whispered. With a pool. And I was true to my word.

Hold her under your armpit, I tell Linda.

Ugh.

Trust me.

And I hang up.

That was rude, but I am not myself. I am unslept. I am on automatic pilot. This image brought to mind by the pilots who clearly aren't. What does automatic pilot mean. I picture an inflatable pilot, but that is from a movie. Automatic pilot is just a computer. It is what flies the plane when the pilots take a nap or make out. It is what kicks in metaphorically when your dad is in a comma, sorry coma, and you are summoned home and you must make arrangements for your tortoise.

Last night I stepped outside carrying Winnifred in her castle and the sky was busy with stars.

Look, Win, I said. The past. Because the past is what you are looking at when you look at the stars.

Winnifred looked up.

That's where I'm going tomorrow, I said.

We drove out to Oregon City where the streets are all named after presidents in the order they were elected, so you can't get lost if you are American and know your presidents. Linda and Chuck live on Taft. When I pulled up, Chuck was outside smoking with his actor friends.

Evening, Chuck.

Hey.

As I climbed the steps, one of the actor friends said, Am I hallucinating or is she carrying a castle.

Yes, a castle.

Four people at my gate are knitting. Knitting needles are allowed on planes again. At security there was a new and definitive list of

Objects You Cannot Take in Your ~~Carrion~~ Carry-on Luggage.
All the usual weapons from the game of Clue were there, minus
knitting needles, and with the addition of snow globes.

I patted my pockets and said, Where's that snow globe.

The security woman in blue pinched the bridge of her nose
like I was causing her pain right there.

Move on, please.

In the little kiosk inside security there were knitting needles and
wool for sale. Christmas colours. So knitting is enjoying a revival.

I limped on to my gate.

Earlier, in the apartment, I had tripped over my carry-on bag
in the dark. I had lain in the dark and thought, I won't go, I've
been hurt. I lay there and looked up at the sloped ceiling, still
bumpy with Cliff's climbing holds. Cliff liked to refer to the ceiling as an overhang.

I had sent him an email saying, My dad is in a comma and
waiting for me to open his eyes. Must depart. Apartment avail-
able for your use. Tortoise with Linda and Chuck.

No reply.

I sent him a second email: I meant coma.

I lay on the floor. My cab with its little Napoleon hat was
puffing in the street.

Get up. Go.

When the right person arrives at the bedside of the comatose person, the comatose person opens his eyes. Everyone knows this.
This is Rule Number One of Comatoseness.

Yesterday Uncle Thoby called and said, Oddly. There's been
an accident.

Which word made me sit down on the kitchen floor.
Accident, I said.

Your dad received a severe blow to the medulla oblongata as
he was walking home. From, this is unbelievable, a Christmas
tree. Hanging sideways out of a pickup truck.

Uncle Thoby's voice was okay until he got to pickup truck. Then it broke down. I didn't understand. Hit *by* a Christmas tree. Or walking home *from* a Christmas tree. Or what.

Hit by. On his way home.

I thought about this. Finally I said, I have a question. Are you ready.

Okay.

Here it is. I've got it. What is a medulla oblongata.

A brain stem.

Oh. Right. So a Christmas tree stem had collided with my dad's brain stem. And now he was in a coma. I put my hand on the back of my neck. I had forgotten that the brain has geography. The human brain is 1,400 cubic centimetres of geography. Our heads fit inside airplane windows for Chrissakes. We are small and we can be pitched out of our geography.

I'll come home, I said.

The man in 14B is reading *Out on a Leash* by Shirley MacLaine and has not turned a page in fifteen minutes. I watch him in the reflection of my window. Shirley MacLaine is a good writer, so why isn't he turning. I am finding it hard to appreciate the sunrise going on behind his superimposed book stuck at page 59.

I turn and glance meaningfully at the book.

He smiles.

He is wearing a tweed jacket with a turtleneck and a pendant. The pendant looks like some Celtic business.

I turn back to the window. As a rule I dislike people who read.

We are cruising along at our cruising altitude. The sun is a red exit sign. It must be romantic in the cockpit.

I remain vigilant and concentrate on having a future. On a plane if you don't concentrate on having a future, you won't have one. Which is why, despite North American Pacific's injunction to do otherwise, I never nap on a plane.

I once saw a guy interviewed who wouldn't fly between popes. This was his Number One Rule of Flying. Never fly popeless. So after John Paul II died and before Benedict was sworn in, he wouldn't fly. Thus he missed the big funeral in Rome, which he would otherwise have attended, and the opportunity to touch John Paul II's brown leather slipper with his dead foot inside. Imagine.

I am not quite so superstitious as that. But ever since I was a kid (having spent many hours pretending to be a pilot, masterfully negotiating crises such as landing-gear malfunction), I have understood that planes are magic and one thing that keeps them afloat is belief in the magic and another is the web of goodwill among passengers. A plane with its passengers divided against themselves will crash. That is why I am curbing my irritation towards my Celtic neighbour. I am refraining from turning the page *for* him. Because this would signal hostility and the web of goodwill on board flight 880 would begin to unravel.

I prefer comma to coma. A pause. My dad will open his eyes and resume consciousness when I get there. I play out the scene in my mind. I will arrive. The hospital room will glow like a cockpit. There will be a bright medical dashboard of some kind. Keeping him aloft. Keeping him alive. His heart will beep. I will pull up a chair with wheels.

Dad.

No response.

Okay. I have to make a speech first. Yes, a moving speech at the bedside. Then he will open his eyes.

Compose that speech now. Compose it on the plane. Make good use of your time.

I do not make good use of my time. I study my neighbour in 14B. He reminds me of a Clue suspect who hangs out in the Billiard Room.

He is still on page 59.

I think it's time I force him to interact with his Shirley MacLaine. Excuse me. Certainly. He gets up. The book is dropped on the seat without a bookmark.

I very much suspect Mr. Tweed with the memoir in 14B.

I stumble into the aisle. Feet get bigger on planes. At least mine do.

Steady, says Tweed.

I'm perfectly fine. *Merci.*

Isn't it amazing that I can stomp around in here and do no damage. That a plane is a legitimate *room* with a ceiling, floor, and a few bathrooms. Here we all are in audience formation. While under our feet, 37,000 feet of nothing.

I head for the bathroom because where else is there to go. There's a lineup. Beverage carts en route. A ball of wool crosses my path. I return it to its owner. Thanks. Welcome. I rock on my heels and survey all the dishevelled heads. I've often wondered why the first passengers of commercial airplanes agreed to this seating arrangement. Why did they not put their feet down and say, Audience formation makes us look dumb. Then again, what arrangement of seats would not make us look dumb.

Someone joins the line behind me. Tweed has decided to make this a group outing.

He nods. 14A.

14B, I say.

The Celtic pendant is made of wire and looks like it could be manipulated into other Celtic shapes. Probably these shapes predict the future or reflect the inner self of the person wearing it. The present shape is a knotty oval. I glance at the face above it. Yes, a knotty oval. I cannot untangle that expression. Mr. Tweed is vaguely smiling but his eyes are sending a sinister beam over my head into the rest of the cabin.

I follow the gaze. Who. Who is he looking at.

So. *Out on a Leash*, I say. A real page-turner.

The gaze lowers. Sorry.

My dad read *Out on a Limb* to me when I was a kid. One of Shirley's first books. But isn't *Out on a Leash* told by her dog. Because my dad would not approve of that. Too Walt Disney. So is it.

What.

Told by her dog.

Tweed has been sharing some eye contact with the driver of

an approaching beverage cart. She is tall with a long neck and the word NAP across her breast.

Couldn't tell you, he says.

Interesting, I say. Yet you're on page 59.

No doubt Shirley MacLaine has made many speeches at the bedsides of comatose people and they have all woken up. Yes, they have all opened their eyes to see Shirley and her dog right there beside the bed, because who could resist a duo like that.

Well, my dad. But who else.

On the cover of *Out on a Leash*, Shirley is cuddling her dog and they have exactly the same eyes.

Out on a Limb had a very different cover, as I recall. A younger Shirley on a beach. In a sweatshirt. Arms akimbo. She was not holding a dog.

There might have been a dog running somewhere in the background.

We never finished that book.

A speech at the bedside of a comatose person should probably include:
- an apology for the late arrival at the bedside
- a lot of encouragement
- a question the comatose person will really want to answer, or
- a false statement the comatose person will really want to correct
- hand holding
- tears
- a walk down memory lane
- laughter combined with tears during the walk down memory lane
- a long look out the window
- a brief moment of forgetting the comatose person is comatose, followed by

- shaking of head, blinking, and disbelief
- an inspiring quotation
- an account of heroic acts performed en route to the bedside
- the solution to a great mystery

I am next in line for the bathroom. Here comes the beverage cart. I flatten myself against the door. Tweed scrunches himself into a row of seats. Christ he's a big man. He looks like Atlas carrying the world, except he's Atlas carrying an overhead bin. In this position his jacket falls open and the Celtic pendant swings like a pendulum. It is quite hypnotic, that pendulum. It seems to be gesturing. Look, it says. Look. Under the jacket. A gun.

A gun.

Which object I distinctly recall had *not* been removed from the list of Objects You Cannot Take in Your ~~Carrion~~ Carry-on Luggage.

The beverage cart rolls past. Tweed steps into the aisle. The bathroom door opens. It is my turn. And I have to make a decision. Am I going to disarm a hijacker. Or am I going to pee. Pray you never have to make this decision.

I jab a finger over Tweed's shoulder. Hey, here comes the pilot.

The idiot turns. It all happens quickly. I am very quick. The snap on the holster (a mere snap!) is already unsnapped.

It is remarkably easy to disarm a hijacker.

Me. With the Revolver—is it a Revolver—in the Lavatory. It is not a Revolver. It looks nothing like the Clue game piece I used to point at my dad when he said, You're going *back* to the Conservatory.

Tweed's gun is a capital L for loaded. Heavy, sinister. Nothing in this machine *revolves*. No, the bullets will burst forth from its dark interior in rapid and endless succession. This is what they call a *piece*. This is what they call *heat*.

I have a bad moment where I feel hot and in pieces. I put the gun in the sink. Imagine bullets ricocheting off all the metal in here. Holy.

Someone is pounding the door. Guess who.

I think of the two lovebird pilots and feel like crying with relief that they are safe. But are they. There could be other hijackers. Of course there are others. Who was Tweed looking at with that steely gaze. Will I have to engage in a gunfight to protect the pilots. Am I prepared to do that. Yes.

Are the pilots safe is all I can think about.

There is much commotion outside. A flight attendant identifies herself as Tuesday Miller and says, Ma'am.

I sit down on the toilet. Tuesday Miller sounds pretty calm. Has Tweed got a plastic knife to her throat.

That was an air marshal's gun you—

I find my voice. Oh oh oh. Is that what he's telling you.

Ma'am. He would very much like you to exit the bathroom.

I bet he would.

Now Tweed's voice: My name is Caesar Marshall. And I assure you I am a federal air marshal. Please exit the bathroom and return my weapon and you will not face prosecution.

I don't negotiate with terrorists!

Laughter. Now his mouth is very close to the door. Possibly his lips are touching the OCCUPIED sign. Do I look like a terrorist.

So I was right to despise him.

Okay. Say he *is* an air marshal whose last name is conveniently Marshall. Nevertheless he is a terrorist insofar as he has terrorized me and probably all the other passengers on board flight 880. Yelling and pounding the door. He has destroyed our web of goodwill!

Also, I am having trouble believing in my future.

He raises his voice and tells me again that he *is* a federal air marshal, and if I will kindly exit the bathroom he will show me his identification.

Slide it under the door.

Not enough room.

How convenient.

Tuesday Miller assures me that she is right now, at this very moment, looking at Caesar Marshall's badge and boy is it authentic.

An expert, is she.

As a matter of fact, yes. She is trained to be. Further, Tuesday has known Caesar personally for two years. They have been on several flights together—

Tuesday, would there by any chance be a plastic knife sawing into your jugular at this moment.

Pause.

Of course not.

Look, I don't care if Air Marshal Marshall is the director of Homeland Security. Guns are not allowed on planes, right. Rule Number One. I think I've just demonstrated why that rule exists.

Silence now on the other side of the door. Perhaps they are nodding, conceding my excellent point.

I *am* a federal air marshal, Tweed says again.

If you are, I'd wager you won't be one much longer.

More silence. More nodding and conceding my excellent point.

Imagine bringing something on board that could punch a hole in our snow globe. Imagine. I could shoot that Air Marshal Marshall.

Nothing has been said on the other side of the door for some time now. I check my watch—for five minutes. It feels like longer. Time passes slowly when you're alone in a small metal room with a gun in the sink. I check myself in the mirror, tighten my ponytail. Nope, I am not feeling a future of any kind.

Concentrate on your destination. Your dad is waiting for you to open his eyes. You have a necessary future. Try to envision it.

Can't. We are a plane divided. We are a plane with an air marshal.

The plane dips a little.

A knock on the door. Audrey.

A new voice from the OCCUPIED sign. Ms. Flowers.

What.

I'm co-pilot Keith Gordon.

Really.

Yes. And Caesar Marshall really is an air marshal. And we have not been hijacked. Nothing is amiss, I promise you. You have acted bravely. Even heroically. But you need to come out now and return the gun. Otherwise we will have to land the plane immediately. That is the rule. When we have a situation such as this on board, we have to land the plane.

Where.

We're looking at Cincinnati.

I have to get home, co-pilot.

Where is home. Toronto.

No. You've never heard of it.

Where.

St. John's.

Of course I've heard of it.

Oh.

Please, Audrey.

Yes, okay. But how do I know he doesn't have a gun to your head, or a very sharp white plastic knife.

You have to trust what I'm telling you, that everything is really okay.

If everything is really okay—

I promise you it is.

And you are a pilot—

I am.

Something happened in the cockpit before we took off. I saw something through the window.

Ah.

What was that thing I saw. Tell me and I'll come out.

You saw me kiss the pilot.

I thought that's what I saw.

Put her under your armpit.

No, you.

You.

A knock on my shell. Winnifred.

What.

Hello in there.

But I cannot move. When was the last heartbeat. If I have to choose armpits I choose Linda's.

I think she's traumatized, says Linda.

Shell-shocked, says Chuck.

Try freezing. Why am I beside the fridge so that every time Chuck opens the door and stares at its contents I get a blast of cold air through my castle. Why. Someone once said that there is no such thing as cold, only degrees of heat. That person was an idiot. A fridge proves that cold is a *thing*. A fridge is a rectangle of cold.

What I am thinking about is a warm dashboard.

It was weird, coming here last night, because normally in the car I ride the dashboard (hook my claws into the defrost vents and hang on!) but last night, since my castle and all its amenities, as she calls them, were being relocated, I was shoved, castle and all, into the back seat. Cold back there. And the castle floor was sloped. So crawling up to the window took even longer than usual. When I finally arrived I stuck my head out and the speedometer said 20 mph. Twenty! I can walk faster than that. She was saying, Which president comes after Harrison. Lincoln. No.

I looked around for a piece of lettuce to drop. Depends which Harrison.

Over the dashboard I could see little waves of heat, beckoning. Come hither, tortoise.

Here we are, she said. Taft Street.

Whereupon I was transported up some steps and transferred into Linda's custody. I watched her go with my head out the window. Don't planes have dashboards. Why not take me with you. Why.

Now they are fighting over whose armpit. Well spare me.

Linda says, Turn up the radiators full blast.

From inside my shell I can conjure the old flat because I have what is called internalized it. For instance, the red light of the fire alarm. I can still see that. The fire escape. The stove. The ceiling that became the overhang. The walls that grew teeth so that they might be climbed. Yes, if it weren't for the new voices and the rectangle of cold, I might be back in the old flat.

Chuck is saying, Don't tortoises carry salmonella.

Right. I will not be warming to Chuck anytime soon.

When was the last heartbeat. I think yesterday. But do not be sad for me. When the heartbeats do come, they are magnificent. Though of course they are followed by the ebb.

Let's capitalize Ebb. The Ebb is rather sad, I do admit. And when the heartbeats are few, the Ebb stretches on. The Ebb is like a path that becomes less a path the farther you travel along it. Until you are forced to stop because you are in some nondescript place and there is no path and what is the point of going forward.

The drafty, Tafty kitchen slowly heats up. I come out of my shell. I drag myself over to the window. Linda is on the phone.

Shit, she says. She's got her head out the window. That is so frickin cute.

Pause.

Yes, really. She's alive. She's watching me.

I break eye contact with Linda and make for the pool. So I was presumed dead. That hurts a little.

Water. I like putting my head right under to drink. The bottom of my pool has a recipe for Lemon Pie.

There is always a moment on the rim when all my legs are in the air and I'm balanced on my plastron. I like to pretend I'm coming in for a landing. Then I drop my front feet and pull myself forward. Splash.

The water is 65 degrees and rising.

Once, pre-castle, pre–heat lamp, Cliff assumed I was dead. I heard him calling out to her. It was only 60 degrees in the kitchen. What were they thinking.

He said, There's something wrong with Iris. I think she's dead.

I felt him lift me and carry me to the futon. I could hear her floppety feet following. Then I was on the warm expanse of Cliff's chest. I recognized his fast heart with the whoosh in it.

I heard her say, Rule Number One.

I looked out.

They were both very close. Her blue eyes. His grey ones. Their eyelids blinking down. I blinked up. You two look pretty happy, I said. Buy me a heat lamp.

She turned her face into his neck and closed her eyes. He closed his. Their hands linked over my shell. This was a good moment. I was warm. I felt my heart gear up for a tremendous beat.

But increasingly there were bad moments. Such as when he banged his head on the overhang and sat dazed on the futon. And she would look out the window and say, How can we be on the fourth floor and the trees are just getting *started*.

Well, this is Oregon, Cliff said.

Where I'm from the trees don't exaggerate, she said.

I know but this is Oregon, he said.

You already said that. What is a concussion, because I think you have one.

Possibly.

It was Cliff's country and Cliff's state and it didn't feel exaggerated to him. He liked to enumerate Oregon's amenities. He was always enumerating. Mountains, desert, ocean, rivers, plus the giant trees.

Good. Yes.

She got a job mowing grass under a table. She sometimes said to Cliff, I have to love you under the table. And he would climb the walls and say, You drive me up the walls. All this I watched through the roof of my Panasonic printer box, because this was, as I say, pre-castle.

Cliff had ropes hanging off his shoulders. He liked to rappel off the fire escape. He was always rappelling. Then one day he was gone.

Before he left they made arrangements for me. She held me close to her face and promised me a castle.

The castle was built of newspaper and made to stand tall and stately. She gave it a French name: Papier Mâché. She painted it purple. The Lemon Pie dish was filled with water and some of her tears too. The heat lamp arrived. Every day was for me bright and lemony. I was warm.

She said, You're going to be Winnifred, okay.

Okay.

We waited for Cliff to come back. We expected at any moment to see his hands on the fire escape. Followed by his head. Followed by his torso. Followed by his harness. To nutshellize, we waited. But he did not come back.

He became the previous tenant.

I became more and more fond of her. I learned that when the sun glinted off the stove she would soon be home. I waited with my head out the window. When it got colder, she came home earlier, still when the sun struck the stove, but now it hit the metal handle. She smelled less like cut grass and more like diesel and then fire. She ate cereal. Sometimes she brought home Taco Bell and fed me the shredded lettuce.

She decided the heat lamp was dangerous. The turrets of my castle had singe marks.

My heart rate got slower. The sun got lower. Winter came on. I memorized the recipe for Lemon Pie and dreamt it was a recipe for me. I had to plan trips to the pool days in advance because they took so long. I had to plan footsteps around heartbeats.

Then came the phone call. I didn't really think she'd go. Home. But it did get me thinking about where exactly mine is. Is it this shell or is it this castle or is it the old flat or is it somewhere bigger or smaller. Is it the place I call the Ebb.

The last leg of my transcontinental leap: Air Canada flight 696. The latest flight you can take to St. John's. No guns. No napping. Much laughter. My neighbour, even as the plane was taking off, held her catalogue in front of my face and showed me a digital belt buckle that could be programmed to scroll messages like HI MY NAME IS AARON or HAPPY BIRTHDAY. She wiped tears from her eyes. Sweet Jesus, imagine wearing that.

Imagine. I discreetly appropriated her armrest.

Frequent guffaws from the rear. I looked over my shoulder. There was a party going on. Chips, not purchased on board, were being consumed in large quantities.

The sound of Newfoundlanders on a plane: If sarcasm were generous, that is the sound.

When M. Latourelle, the flight attendant, came by with the snack cart, the man in 23D offered him, M. Latourelle, some chips and a beverage. Talk about funny. And nice.

M. Latourelle did not find the offer funny. Or nice.

He asked me three times, hand on shoulder, to please keep my *pieds magnifiques* out of the aisle.

What do you mean by *magnifiques*.

Catalogue Woman offered me her window seat.

I would not say no to a window seat.

M. Latourelle put on a newscast and told us—especially those of us in rows 21 and higher—to please settle down.

I tilted back my window seat.

When you're flying, the newscast is always cheery. Notice that. There are no plane crashes. If you could just keep flying forever, there'd be no plane crashes.

Tonight's broadcast is all about the merry-Christmas election coming up. And oh. The hostage-taking. Yes, it is still going on, but the hostages, the Canadian ones, are being fed candy.

What kind of candy, I wondered.

Probably Turkish delight, said Catalogue Woman.

Oh. Nice.

The non-Canadian hostages were not getting candy.

I am on the late flight due to prolonged questioning in Toronto where, immediately upon landing, I was escorted by two Greater Toronto Airport Authority (GTAA) guards to a room in Terminal 1 that you never want to visit. It is American with its own flag. I knew when I saw the flag that I would miss my connection.

The room was oval with an oval table and a window looking out onto a hallway. Tweed was already there, mysteriously sans pendant, leaning against the window. Also present were the two pilots and Tuesday Miller, long throat intact.

Enter the airport chief of security and various men with INS badges, all packing *pieces* and not bothering to conceal that fact.

Sit, said the chief.

We sat.

Keith Gordon and the other pilot sat together. I pretended to drop my passport so I could see if they were holding hands under the table.

They were.

I was asked about a lot more than my theft of Mr. Tweed's piece. I was asked: How long had I been in America. Why. With whom. Where did I live. Where did I visit. Where did I come from prior. Did I work.

I painted a careful picture of an extended love affair with America during which I spent freely but did not seek employment.

Then I steered the conversation back to Tweed, who was staring moodily into the hallway like it had a horizon and he was about to ride into it. I related how I was immediately suspicious of his failure to turn the page of a page-turner. How his pendant gestured towards his weapon. How absurdly quickly he fell for my here-comes-the-pilot trick. How he pounded the door and destroyed the web of goodwill on board flight 880. How he yelled. How it was unnecessary to yell, as is evidenced by the ease with which I could hear the soft-spoken Keith Gordon and Tuesday Miller when they spoke directly into the OCCUPIED sign.

At what point did I stop believing Caesar Marshall was a terrorist.

Not until I spoke with co-pilot Gordon.

You really thought Air Marshal Marshall had hijacked the plane.

I thought he was planning to. Frankly I could think of no reason besides an evil one for carrying a gun.

Silence.

On a plane, I added. And his violent reaction to being disarmed by me did nothing to persuade me otherwise, let me tell you.

Disarmed by you, repeated the chief of security.

We all looked at the air marshal. Christ he was a big man.

I am very disarming.

You are very something, said the chief, and he wrote that something down.

Look. I did what I was supposed to do, didn't I. I was vigilant. I thought there was danger so I acted.

Keith Gordon put both hands on the table and said, To her credit, she did exit the bathroom and return the weapon immediately upon my assurance that we were not being hijacked.

Why did you believe co-pilot Gordon and not Ms. Miller or Air Marshal Marshall.

Because co-pilot Gordon was persuasive.

In what way was he persuasive.

I hesitated. He knew my name.

Ms. Miller also knew your name.

If she did, she never said it. Also, co-pilot Gordon knew where St. John's was. Is.

How does that make him persuasive.

Okay, it makes him rare.

Rare how. I'm sure Ms. Miller knows where St. John's is. As does Air Marshal Marshall.

Antigua, Tuesday piped up.

I think we're done here, said Keith Gordon. Aren't we done here.

But the chief and his henchmen were not done with me. I must be delayed and put on the latest flight possible to St. John's. How to achieve this. They discussed it quietly in the corner. Finally one of the INS officers turned around and said, Relinquish your phone and any other electronic device you might be carrying.

Oh, well that's easy. I only have a phone. But I need that phone because I have a tortoise and a father *both* in comas.

I waited, but nobody said, What a terrible coincidence. How did that happen.

They said, Hand it over.

I handed it over.

Then two INS guys with surgical gloves searched my carrion bag right there on the oval table. Humiliating.

Why are you on the outs with me, INS men.

No answer.

Time marched on.

The chief disappeared and returned waving a boarding pass. Flight 696 for you, Ms. Flowers.

Flight 696. The one that gets in at 3:35 in the ante meridiem!

That's the one, he said. Then he gave me a voucher for the Skyway Bar and said to please, have a drink on him. And with that I was released into Terminal 1 on my own recognizance. Sans phone.

● ● ●

Terminal 1 had been refurbished. Boy had it. The ceiling was unlimited and everywhere Céline Dion was faintly singing "O Tannenbaum." Also there were moving pedways, which I would be riding momentarily.

I dragged my carrion bag with a bit of nightgown hanging out towards a pay phone. I made two calls, one to Uncle Thoby, who wasn't home, and one to Linda, who was. She confirmed that a living, breathing tortoise was right now basking in the warmth of an 80-plus-degree apartment.

So she's really okay, I said. Really. You swear.

Yes, really, said Linda. She's alive. She's watching me.

There. You see how important Rule Number One is.

I hung up, elated, and jumped aboard a moving pedway.

At the Skyway Bar I ordered coffee and remained vigilant. There were three ground crew workers on break. They wore bright orange vests and ignored their walkie-talkies. You can't help but admire people who ignore their walkie-talkies. Plus, one of the vests said LEAD. I asked who or what he was leading. He explained that he was a lead marshal and it was his job to lock eyes with the pilot out on the tarmac and wave him in with a come-hither look.

That's you, I said. With the pink light sabres and the come-hither look!

Yup.

The other two men were in charge of de-icing aircraft. We are known around dese here parts as De-Ice Men, they said.

Which made me laugh. I turned to the lead marshal. And is your last name conveniently Marshall.

No.

I nodded. We drank our coffees. Then, just to make conversation, I asked who was in charge of fuelling the planes.

They looked at each other, like, good question.

Independent company, said one of De-Ice Men.

Oh. And I guess that company is subject to some pretty rigorous background security checks. I mean, I would hope so.

Couldn't say.

Couldn't or wouldn't.

The lead marshal tipped back his coffee cup. Well, break's over.

Lead on, Macduff, said one of De-Ice Men.

So soon, I said.

Yes. But it was lovely meeting you.

Same.

And off they went to marshal a plane into gate 137 and spray pink foam on its wings.

There is so much in Terminal 1 to distract you from the word *terminal*. For instance, the store filled with chunks of exposed soap that smell so much like candy that you have to immediately run across the "street" to the fudge store and purchase yourself a big chunk of fudge.

As I was consuming said chunk of fudge on the moving pedway, I was approached by a fast-walking man in a blue suit and a GTAA badge that I could have made myself on my printer. I moved aside to let him pass, but he paused and leaned against the rubber rail. He said for what purpose had I been questioning three ground crew workers in the Skyway Bar. Excuse me, I said. Why had I wanted to know about the fuelling of planes, etcetera. Will my ordeal never end, I said. Pardon. Nothing. He asked why I had subsequently gone to gate 137 and waved at those workers from the window. What information had been transmitted.

None at all. It was a hi-how-are-ya wave.

We stepped together off the pedway and he put a hand on my elbow. Oh boy. *Noli me tangere*, I said.

What.

Give me a wide berth, friend. Or else.

Are you threatening me.

Remove your hand from my elbow. Yes I am.

Come with me, please.

I was pretty sure my three friends had not reported me, since they had been so congenial and forthcoming. Either the Skyway Bar was bugged, or one of the walkie-talkies had transmitted our conversation up the food chain.

Once again I was remanded into custody. The GTAA man escorted me through a door that otherwise blends completely into the north-facing wall across from gate 122. We descended some stairs. We descended some more stairs. You think the ceiling in Terminal 1 is unlimited. Try the basement. We walked for a long time through a maze of subterranean hallways. He was not touching me, lucky for him. Then we entered a room. This room did not have a flag.

The airport chief of security arrived soon after.

He flapped his arms and said, *Again,* Ms. Flowers.

Chief Dweck, how have you been.

He slipped another voucher into my palm and urged me to go, please, have a *drink* on him.

Merci.

Whereupon I returned to the Skyway Bar and ordered more coffee and observed that many of the children in the airport had wheels embedded in their sneakers.

Flight 696 is dark. The lights go out after midnight Toronto time. This is to encourage napping and quell boisterousness. Good luck. Someone calls down the aisle: Mister Lateral, could we have some beverage-cart action back here in the 21-and-highers.

M. Latourelle, over the intercom: *Non.*

Where's that little guy hiding.

Soon we are beginning our final descent into St. John's International Airport. Why do they always say final. The temperature is just above zero, says the pilot. Weather is moist. Local time is—

The plane banks steeply to the right.

—3:25 a.m.

Catalogue Woman pats my leg. Just the pilot checking his watch. Neveryoumind.

I look out the window. I can see ocean. I can see city. Is the landing gear down because I haven't heard any landing gear.

Don't you worry about landing gear. Catalogue Woman licks her thumb and turns a page. You want that, she says, pointing at a sumo wrestler garden ornament.

No. I look back out the window. Hey. I can see Wednesday Pond shaped like a skillet with a broken moon in it. And I can see the Piety pie factory with its sign glowing pink.

Is this the usual flight path. Because the last time I saw Wednesday Pond from the air—

Don't you worry about the flight path, says Catalogue Woman.

I press my forehead to the glass. I push the button on my armrest. You're already as upright as you can go. Fine.

We swing back out over the ocean and someone from the 21-and-highers says, Dropping fuel.

Catalogue Woman winks at me. Don't you listen to that. You're as good as home.

Uncle Thoby meets the plane wearing his bright orange gloves. I see those first. The airport has changed. It has learned what other airports look like. Who told it. The escalator takes forever. The old airport used to have low ceilings and heat.

We have time to look at each other, Uncle Thoby and me, as I make my slow and final descent into St. John's International Airport. His hands glow like a lead marshal's. His face makes me sit down. As a rule I am vigilant on escalators. I remain upright with nothing dangling. But I read Uncle Thoby's face and get wobbly.

Someone behind me puts their hands under my arms. Upsy-daisy my darlin.

Oh no.

Uncle Thoby is stepping up the sinking stairs. Oddly. I am
hugged into his noisy coat.

You said it was a comma.

I know, but it's over.

Period.

This is the wrong airport. The old airport had no escalators and we were all alive in it. It had a red brickish floor that made your luggage chatter. We used to arrive early and have a bite to eat at the Bite-to-Eatery. The Bite-to-Eatery was dark and had no windows. There were woodcuts on the wall but you could barely see them. You had to stand up on your seat. One woodcut was of a fisherman in agony. He looked like Han Solo in *The Empire Strikes Back* when he gets frozen by Darth Vader.

Outside the Bite-to-Eatery there was a rectangle of ocean. The lobsters inside the rectangle had claws like pigtails with elastics. They were harmless. You could put your hand in the rectangle and touch the pigtails. You could touch the bottom of the ocean and then fly into the sky all on the same day.

Or, if someone else was departing, not you, you could run outside to the chain-link fence and wave goodbye. If the departing party had a window seat, they could see you at the fence and wave something bright and cheery like the aircraft safety card or the sick bag. They could wave something bright as the plane took off. So you knew which window was theirs.

The day I left, I waved the sick bag from seat 21F. Uncle Thoby made a giant arc with his left arm like a windshield wiper. My dad waved smaller, with his fingers. They were all for it, this great safe adventure I was embarking on, so why did they look so sad.

I watched them from the sky. Long after they thought I was gone, I was still watching. I saw them drift back across the parking lot. I saw my dad sit down on the pavement. Because this is what he does when something bad happens. Because he is wobbly like me.

Uncle Thoby has been waiting at the airport since three o'clock.

Ante meridiem.

No.

You've been here for twelve hours.

Don't picture him. Standing at the bottom of the escalator. Unshaven. Alone. I hold on to his coat.

It's okay, he says.

He picks up my bag and we head for the exit.

The revolving door is new. Don't push it. It revolves by itself. If you touch it, it will stop. It is like one of those dessert displays. You are the dessert. At the centre, encased in glass, is a small artificial Christmas tree.

Uncle Thoby steps in. Looks over his shoulder. Coming.

Yeah.

He is outside now, waiting.

I rush into the door's open mouth. I guess I touch the glass, because the whole mechanism grinds to a halt. I am stuck inside a revolving door that has stopped revolving. With a fake Tannenbaum. Do not look at the Tannenbaum. I press the glass. Uncle Thoby lifts an orange glove. I look past him to the taxi queue. Past the taxi queue to the parking lot. Past the parking lot to the small black trees, just about my size, overlapping. Maybe this is Antigua. I have arrived in St. John's, Antigua. My dad is still in a comma in the other St. John's. The real St. John's.

Except that, on the other side of the glass, Uncle Thoby is definitely himself. Asymmetrical. Pirate patch of hair.

The door starts to move. Spits me out. Uncle Thoby hugs me like I've been in there for years.

We walk past the taxi queue. A Clint's cab pulls up. I check to see if it's Clint driving. It's not. Uncle Thoby says Clint is running in the election.

Oh right. There's an election.

As we pass the line, I recognize M. Latourelle, the flight attendant. He feels like an old friend.

Bonsoir, mademoi—

Then he notices Uncle Thoby's arm.

Now is probably a good time to mention that Uncle Thoby's left arm is very long. Like a whole foot longer than his right. The orange gloves don't exactly downplay this discrepancy. He usually puts on a show that whatever he's carrying is really heavy. But tonight he forgets to put on the show. So as we walk by the taxi queue I point at my bag and say, One hundred pounds. Then make a gesture like wiping sweat from my brow.

Nobody laughs. Usually people laugh.

At the front of the line there's a couple with a stroller. They've got a rear-view mirror rigged up so the baby can see them, and they can see the baby, at all times. What a great idea. I crouch down. I predict this baby will be an excellent driver, I say.

We hope so, says the dad.

Crouched there, I have an escalator moment. This is when the body remembers having been recently on an escalator. You could also call it a sinking feeling. I put my fingertips on the wet pavement. Steady.

The short-term parking lot is full of winter topography. I am no longer used to winter topography. Uncle Thoby says to watch my step. I breathe deep. It smells like home. It smells like Atlantic Ocean with jet fuel mixed in.

Why didn't you take a cab, I ask. Or let me take a cab.

Because it's an emergency.

Oh.

The topography is melting. It rained yesterday, he says.

Weird to think that the raindrops on the car landed before I did.

He asks if I will drive.

Of course I will drive.

How can there be only two of us. I keep looking over my shoulder.

Uncle Thoby has this rule that he will not chauffeur someone he loves. Ever since he came to live with us, this has been his Rule Number One. He said he was bound to someday forget which side of the ocean he was on, and when that happened the child (me) would not be in the car. He would only drive himself, he said. In an emergency. Okay, he might, in the most emergent of emergencies, drive an adult he did not love. But both of these (emergencies and adults he did not love) were few and far between. So he did not drive.

My dad, who could always remember which side of the ocean he was on, drove. And later I drove. And of course there was Clint.

Clint's is the Qantas of cabs, Uncle Thoby liked to say. Because of that airline's impeccable safety record.

Uncle Thoby once witnessed Clint avoid a head-on collision with a hydroplaning minivan by driving his cab lickety-split up a concrete staircase. The driver of the minivan had applied her anti-lock brakes, which, according to Clint, just let you aim at what you are already crashing into. You might as well have death built into your braking system, Clint said.

Uncle Thoby, who was in the cab at the time, nearly choked on his free mint. Later he said he had never seen such vehicular prowess.

Vehicular prowess, said my dad. Do I have that.

Of course, said Uncle Thoby, patting his shoulder. But Clint has a superabundance of vehicular prowess.

A Clint's cab will not crash. Has never crashed. In more than three decades, not one cab in Clint's entire fleet has been involved in an accident. Sorry, collision. Which is pretty remarkable when you consider that Clint's fleet consists of sixty-five cars.

Clint's cabs are bright black and say CLINT WON'T COST YOU A MINT on the sides. All the cabbies are trained at a secret boot camp in our twin city, Mount Paler. Which boot camp I attended, even though I had no immediate plans to become a Clint's cabbie. Special allowances were made because I was Uncle Thoby's niece, and Uncle Thoby was Clint's most loyal customer.

Here is the secret of the boot camp. It has an ice rink. I learned to drive on an ice rink. At Clint's boot camp I learned to write my name with my tires. I also learned to palpitate my brakes, which is not the same as pumping them, not the same at all, but I can't explain brake palpitation to you, it is something you must feel and coordinate with your own heart.

Don't brake, Clint always said. Palpitate. Which is one of those phrases you find yourself saying in all sorts of slippery situations, not necessarily automotive.

None of this is to disparage Young Drivers of Canada. Which I also attended. My dad thought I should attend YDOC since I was both young and of Canada. Uncle Thoby thought I should attend the boot camp. So I did both.

Herein lies the formula of my childhood: My dad plus Uncle Thoby equals Qantas. Which in our family means safe. Be Qantas. Be safe.

What I learned at YDOC was to never say accident. Say collision. Look in your rear-view mirror every ten seconds. Filter out Ambient Vehicle Distraction (AVD). Assume every other driver on the road is drunk, or putting on makeup, or both. Give everyone a wide berth. Make *Noli me tangere* your motto.

The parking lot attendant can't get his sliding glass window open. So we wait, the car idling, while he struggles. The bright light in the booth and the man trapped inside make me sad. I look away.

Uncle Thoby puts a toonie in my palm.

Oh, I had forgotten toonies. They are so lovely. I turn it over and over. Will they ever make a three-toned coin. Or a four-toned.

I eagerly await more complex concentricity in our Canadian coinage.

Uncle Thoby says, That poor man.

He's like a bug in there, I say. Don't look at him.

Uncle Thoby's legs in their brown cords are shaking.

I have another escalator moment.

Uncle Thoby presses his hands down over his knees to stop the shaking.

Finally Bug Man gives up. I show him my toonie. He waves us on. Forget it, he mouths. Just go.

So we have short-term parked for free.

The little LeBaron's dashboard glows a pale brown. This car is old. You can tell it is old because it is brown on the outside and brown on the inside. Most new cars have a different but complementary colour on the inside. For instance, burgundy inside grey. Grey inside black. Blue inside cream. This reminds me of how my favourite fruits also have different but complementary colours inside and outside. I'm thinking of apples, pears, plums, oranges, and lemons. Yes, even oranges and lemons. Their exteriors are not as bright as they pretend to be.

A Clint's cab is black on the outside and black on the inside, but a Clint's cab can get away with it because the dashboard is spectacular and the blackness is leathery.

You're driving a bit slow. Am I. Am I going the right way. Not really, says Uncle Thoby, but it'll do. The speedometer is in kilometres. That is my problem.

Only it isn't.

I shift into fourth. And I remember how, all those years ago, when my dad and I went to pick up Uncle Thoby at the airport and he wasn't on the flight, my dad could barely shift out of third on the way home.

This looks a lot like Mount Paler, I say.

Only it isn't. It's a new subdivision.

Oh.

I don't recognize this latest permutation of the Trans-Canada. It is wide and makes a wet sound. On either side there are pastel houses with their backs to the highway. They have that hunched look like, yuck, is that a highway behind us. Why yes, it is. And I am on it. And why did you get built out here on your fancy treble-clef streets if you did not intend to embrace your location.

All the houses have tiny upstairs windows that open sideways. I imagine trying to open one of those windows, unsuccessfully.

It would be frustrating to live in one of those houses. To see your house from the highway and know that you are only two minutes away as the crow flies, but still you must drive for twenty more minutes to get there. You must take an exit and perform a short sonata on the streets leading to it. Meanwhile, the person waiting for you in one of those upstairs windows has seen you coming but still has time to watch a sitcom before you get there.

Holy. What happened to the blue lights.

What.

I jab my finger at the Christmas lights around an upstairs window. Look how big the blue is compared to the other colours.

The road, Oddly.

It's so spacious, that blue. I can feel the mind that invented it.

It is impossible, as we enter the city proper, that my dad is not here to enjoy this confluence of Election and Christmas, his two favourite things. The city is bedecked with election signs and Christmas lights, the combination of which creates much Ambient Vehicle Distraction. For instance: Up ahead there is a giant election sign for Noel Antle. Someone has changed his name to Noel Antl*er* and given him a pair. Pretty funny.

'Tis the season.

We pass a Byrne Doyle sign. Byrne Doyle! He is looking very Jacob Marley.

Poor Byrne Doyle, says Uncle Thoby, his usual refrain.

I want to see a Clint sign.

Coming up.

We are approaching the dispatch office. It is really just a shack with a car on the roof. But boy does that car surprise you, every time. A Clint's cab! On the roof! And you wonder, why did you not become a cabbie when you had the chance.

The shack glows like a spaceship. The Christmas lights are dazzling. The lonely-inventor's blue has nothing on the green. You are like Superman in the presence of kryptonite. You are getting weak. You gear down. And gear down again. It's like the green is alive and all the other colours are dead.

We turn the corner and come face to face with a giant picture of Clint. He's got an orange scarf wrapped doubly, Bob-Cratchitly, around his neck. ORANGE YOU GLAD CLINT'S RUNNING IN ST. JOHN'S CENTRE, says the sign.

There's another sign: DRIVERS WANTED.

Much AVD.

As I pull away from the shack, the road gets very dark. I think my retinas are damaged. Is that a red light ahead.

That's the pond.

Okay. Well, I can only see red.

Did you look directly at the green.

Should I not have looked directly at the green.

Well.

The car skids a bit. Don't brake. Palpitate. Is that the pond.

Yes. You might want to stop.

I'm blind.

Give them a moment, he says. Meaning my pupils.

We live on the other side of Wednesday Pond. We're almost there. But now I can't see, so we'll have to wait. I guess we could get out and walk. Uncle Thoby could lead me. We could stumble together like orphans over the winter topography. There is enough sidewalk today that a sideways tree might just miss your medulla oblongata.

The day my dad was struck down there was snow, lots of it, and no sidewalk.

I rub my eyes. We flew over the pond tonight.

Mundy Pond.

No it was Wednesday. Also, I had a flight attendant called Tuesday.

Uncle Thoby leans over and wipes the windshield with his long arm.

Are there decorations up at home, I ask.

No.

You took them down.

He nods.

Don't picture him doing this.

There's a rumour (more than a rumour, a theory) that Wednesday Pond has no bottom. My dad found this theory ridiculous. Bollocks, he said. Of course it has a bottom. Uncle Thoby, who did not find the theory ridiculous, said, Well, Clint said. Oh boy, said my dad. What. Nothing. Please continue. Clint said a man disappeared in that pond once, and the police tried to dredge it, but lo and behold, there was no bottom to dredge.

The discussion proceeded like a tennis match.

Just because the police do not, or did not at the time, possess the proper equipment to dredge—

How do you explain that it never freezes, Walter.

It did freeze once, said my dad.

When, said Uncle Thoby.

Before you came.

That's sweet of you to say, but—

What are you talking about. Sweet of me to say.

—but it has never frozen in my or Clint's or Oddly's memories, Uncle Thoby finished.

True enough, I said.

It did freeze once when you were a baby, said my dad. We skated on it.

Doubtful looks exchanged between me and Uncle Thoby.

I put you in your stroller and we went out onto the pond and I pushed you at great speed across the ice.

Jesus!

You loved it.

. . .

As far back as I can remember we have lived on Wednesday Place. The pond is our backyard. We are number 3. All the houses on Wednesday Place are odd numbers and the best houses are prime.

The porch wraps all the way around the house. All the way. You can go into orbit if you're not careful. The boards bounce when you walk. That bounce can be felt inside the house and possibly inside all the houses on Wednesday Place. It is quite a bounce. The porch has also been known to support upwards of 5,000 watts of Christmas lights. You haven't lived until you've seen our house with all its lights reflected in the pond. But tonight there is no wattage. What is the wattage of a full moon. Because that is the wattage as we approach the house. Maybe 25 watts.

Our front door does not lock but seems locked to people who don't have a special relationship with it. It can only be opened with the Northwest Shove.

I bypass the front door and carry on around the porch.

Oddly, says Uncle Thoby. But he follows me, my bag bouncing behind him.

There are forty-seven ducks (native) and two swans (not native) living on Wednesday Pond. When the swans put their heads underwater, they look like baby icebergs. When they lift their heads, they look surprised. Did you see the bottom. No. Did you. No. Let's check again. They have been checking for years and continue to be surprised.

Come inside.

In a sec.

He parks my bag.

I have a question, I say. Are you ready.

Okay.

Remember the bracelet.

Because I am remembering a bracelet my dad had, like a medical alert bracelet except that it had instructions for accidental death. It said ABSOLUTELY NO EMBALMING. There was an 800 number to call. A SWAT team was supposed to arrive by helicopter and take my dad to a facility in Arizona where his brain would be kept on ice until the necessary technology for, say, repairing a damaged medulla oblongata was developed.

The bracelet was a joke, Uncle Thoby says.

How do you know.

I gave it to him.

You did. When.

On one of our birthdays. Your dad called cryonics the domain of Disney.

He would. But whatever. Is it too late to call the SWAT team. Because let's call them.

Let's not, he says.

Let's. And I Northwest Shove the door open.

Five minutes later I'm on the phone with Phoenix, my dad's bracelet in hand. The CRYNOT representative, Darren Lipseed, or maybe Lipsey, says my dad's subscription expired back in 1996.

Okay. Minor setback. Let's renew it.

There are forms to fill out, Ms. Flowers. Many many forms.

Please call me Audrey.

Okay, Audrey. Your dad's going to have to sign some forms.

Well, that's going to be a problem.

Why's that.

And I explain to Darren Lipseed the details of my dad's accident. Sorry, collision.

Are you pulling my leg, he says.

Oh Darren Lipseed.

Yes.

I am not pulling your leg. Um. I don't think my dad signed any forms the last time. I look at Uncle Thoby.

Uncle Thoby taps his chest.

Apparently my uncle forged his signature last time.

Well, that would nullify the contract, says Darren.

Look. Let's just get the SWAT team en route and we'll work out the details later.

Uncle Thoby pours some sherry into a glass.

I'm afraid we can't send a SWAT team to Canada.

But you have subscribers in Canada.

Yes, we do. I'm going to put you on hold now, Ms. Flowers.

Why.

Just 'cause.

This is bad, I tell Uncle Thoby. This is unbelievable.

He anchors his hand, with the glass, to the counter. Aren't you tired, sweetheart.

No.

I think you really are.

I turn my back to him. I read the silver bracelet again.

Push 50,000 U Heparin IV. Do CPR while cooling with ice to 40°F. Keep pH 7.5. Call 800 544 7000. ABSOLUTELY NO EMBALMING.

I shake my head. Such a simple formula. And we failed to follow it. Well, one of us did. At least we haven't embalmed.

We haven't embalmed, have we, I ask.

No.

What is embalmed.

Darren comes back on the line. He explains why he, or rather the CRYNOT SWAT team, cannot transport a dead, or rather vitrified, body across the border. You would not believe the hoops at customs—

Oh I would believe the hoops, Darren.

Not to mention the fact that the body is already dead.

Don't refer to my dad as the body.

Sorry.

S'okay.

Of course, there are degrees of dead, says Darren.

I consider this. I can hear a clicking sound. Are you knitting, Darren.

Darren says, A baby blanket. I have to put you on hold again, Ms. Flowers.

Why.

Dead air.

I'm on hold again.

Uncle Thoby takes the phone. Hangs up. We need sleep, he says.

But I'm still in a different time zone.

Nevertheless. He puts his glass in the sink.

I jingle the bracelet. Remember in *The Empire Strikes Back* when Darth Vader freezes Han Solo. How he's unfrozen in the sequel. Remember.

That wasn't cryonics. I don't know what that was.

It was George Lucas. Not Walt Disney. And therefore possible.

Here is something to do if you are unslept and have a ponytail: Bring that ponytail around under your nose like a moustache. This will calm you down and make you sleepy. Also it will force you to let go of the table. Where I have been sitting since Uncle Thoby went downstairs to bed.

See you anon, he said.

I had forgotten the word *anon*.

The SWAT team might still come, I said.

He creaked down the basement steps. Go to bed, sweetheart.

I nodded. Instead I went to table. Drummed my fingers. Eventually stopped drumming and started holding. Forced myself to stop holding.

Hey. My ponytail smells like Air Canada.

And I remember something. How, on the plane, on the news broadcast, the word *disappeared* was used in a way I'd never heard before. How did it go. Some people have been disappeared, said a reporter. Not disappeared. *Have been* disappeared.

It was as if that word, which had always sat in a dark corner like a piece of furniture, had got up and started to move.

I pick up the phone. Dial Linda's number. Chuck answers. I've woken them up. Sorry about that. I was just wondering how Winnifred is—

Who.

Can I talk to Linda.

Oh the tortoise. She's great. We're the ones who're sweltering. It's a hundred degrees in here.

Can I talk to Linda.

Rustle of sheets.

Hi Audrey. She's fine.

Could you get up and check.

It's 2:30 in the morning.

Please.

Sigh. Hang on.

And I hear Chuck say, What, the armpit wasn't enough. We're supposed to sleep with the Jesus tortoise.

Linda, from far away: Shut up.

A minute passes. Another minute. Finally, she comes back. Tortoise alive and well. She woke up when I turned on the light and knocked on her shell.

So she seems okay.

She seems pissed off actually.

Oh. Good. Okay.

I drum my fingers.

Audrey.

Yeah.

Oh. I thought you'd hung up.

No.

How're things there, she asks.

Um. Smaller. The trees are smaller.

But otherwise—

Fine. I'm sorry I woke you.

No sweat.

Speak for yourself, I hear Chuck say. I'm sweating like a—

Bye.

Bye.

I sit there for a moment thinking about how Winnifred is fine, just fine. How it is hot, very hot, in that apartment. Then I pick up the phone. Chuck answers. Sorry to bother you again, I say.

Jesus Christ this is not acceptable.

I was just wondering if you have a fire alarm. And what kind of heaters. And where the castle is in relation to those heaters.

Click. Dial tone.

Right.

I read the CRYNOT bracelet, now around my wrist. How can the directions be to keep a person cool. Surely you should keep him warm.

Outside the pond is silver. It is almost dawn. The all-year-round swans bounce by. The trees on the other side look small and friendly. Make that small and fierce. And where does the pond go. Where. I used to think about Wednesday Pond when I mowed the grass around the reservoir in Portland. There was a high spiky fence around the reservoir so you couldn't poison the city's water supply. At least I assumed that was the reason. I mowed the grass and looked through the spikes and thought about how a reservoir has no bottom. How maybe if you swam down and down through the pipes and took all the right turns you'd splash up somewhere totally unexpected, like, say, Wednesday Pond.

Were the two bodies of water connected, is what I wondered.

I'm sorry I didn't climb the fence and swim through the maze of pipes and try to come home, Dad. I'm sorry my great safe adventure kept going and going. I lost track of time. I was afraid. I don't know why I didn't make the cross-continent leap sooner.

There's a sound behind me so familiar, like the heat coming on, that at first I don't notice it. A squeak and whir coming from the living room.

Wedge!

I drop my ponytail.

Not that I assumed he wouldn't be here. I just forgot. I skid across the kitchen floor. Stop in the arch. By the wattage of an incomplete dawn I see Wedge glowing white on the mantelpiece. His wheel flashing.

Mr. Sam, I whisper. Mr. Wedge Man.

He stops running.

I approach the cage, sorry terrarium.

Hey, look at you.

He fluffs up his forehead fur. How do I look.

Good.

He carefully dismounts his wheel. There's a half-eaten Licorice Allsort in his bowl, along with the usual pellets.

So who are you running from today, I ask. Or chasing.

Wedge has a wicked imagination, so likely it's a mountain lion or the Russian mafia.

I remove the metal grid and pick him up.

He is hot and fluttery. His little heart makes me catch my breath. I'm not used to mammals anymore.

He touches his nose to mine. My wheel could use some WD-40.

Right.

I take him into the kitchen. He explores the table. When he gets too close to the edge, I put my finger on his tail. He looks over his shoulder. Someone's stepping on my tail. I lift my finger. He scurries off in another direction. We play this game for a while. Finally, as the sky gets brighter, he settles down. Nocturnal creatures do. He sits in the enclosure I make with my arms and grooms himself. I put my head down and watch the sun come up between his ears. From behind, with the light streaming through, the tattoo on his ear says 81.

Assume life, my dad says, can go on indefinitely.

We are in his lab, watching the mice swim. I'm small. My lab coat drags on the floor. He puts a hand on my head. Barring accidents, he says.

Right.

Indefinitely means forever.

I know what it means.

He is wearing a stopwatch like a necklace.

It is mouse vacation. Each mouse has his own pool. There are five pools. Twenty mice. There are cages like hotel rooms stacked against the wall. Each hotel room has a room number. Each mouse has a room number tattooed on his left ear.

The left ear is the key.

Five mice go swimming for ten minutes. Then five more. Then five more.

In the water their fur puffs up with worry. Are they swimming or are they trying to climb out. They are trying to climb out. I do not see one mouse do the breaststroke or the butterfly or float around on his back. They swim in circles, scratching the sides of the pool.

It is not really mouse vacation. It is a Forced Swimming Test. The pools are garbage cans from Canadian Tire. But don't tell the mice that.

According to my dad, we are made up of little circles called cells. As we get older those cells get dirty and bent out of shape. Then we die. But cells, even the oldest and most wrinkly, *remember* how to be young. The knowledge of how to be young is still in there. And so all you have to do is jog their memory. Jog, jog. Remember how to be young. Recall your youth. It sounds easy, but no one has figured out how to jog a cell's memory.

Well, that is not quite true. A man at Cambridge University has made a frog remember how to be a tadpole.

Light, which is made up of circles called photons, also has a memory. No one really understands how that works, but light sometimes makes a choice based upon its past. So does water. If you boil water, it remembers being boiled and will boil faster the second time. I mean, *after* it's back at room temperature. Hey, I know how to boil. Whereas the first time it had to ask, What is boil.

So how does the Forced Swimming Test jog a cell's memory. It doesn't. This is just a sidebar. We are just talking. There is no connection whatsoever, says my dad. Oh.

There is a brain in the lab. A human brain. It sits on a shelf in a Tupperware container filled with formaldehyde. Now think about this: That is a person up there on that shelf!

Who is that. What's his name.

I have no earthly idea.

Could you find out.

My dad looks reluctant to find out.

Can I name him.

No.

Can I hold him in my lap as long as I don't open the lid.

Okay.

Hello there cauliflower brain. Mr. Cauliflower. You are so small and meaty. And yet you are also a person. I don't know if I can love you if you are not cute. Yes I can.

It makes no sense to me how small a brain is.

Consider the distance between a mouse and a person in my dad's brain. It is very long. There are miles and miles of words between them. Just look at one of his articles. You will probably not see the word *mouse*. But the mice are in there. And so are the people. And the word *mouse*, cleverly disguised, eventually leads to the word *person*, also cleverly disguised. But the mouse never equals the person. My dad would not write: The mouse hated swimming and longed to be back in his hotel room.

He would write . . . I don't know what he would write. Something about how much the subject drank afterwards. In grams.

My dad doesn't like it when I pretend a mouse equals a person. Or when a story does. For instance, those Beatrix Potter books Grandmother sent had to be thrown out because of the way my dad's voice sounded while reading them. Beatrix Potter makes a mouse equal a person. She has a small stupid brain, apparently.

Now we only read books about real people. True books that don't make my dad's voice lie.

But here is a secret about my dad's brain. Say you followed the path all the way from the word *mouse* to the word *person*. It is very long. Say you walked for days along that path. Finally you reach *person*, but if you look beyond, you see that the path keeps going. It gets narrower and narrower, until it's thin as a mouse's tail. And there, at the very end, what do you find. You find the word *Audrey*.

Assume life can go on indefinitely. Translation: Yours.

On the day of the Forced Swimming Test, the book waiting for us at home is a biography of Andrew Toti, inventor of the life vest. He also invented the automated chicken plucker. My dad says the automated chicken plucker is just as important an invention as the life vest and not celebrated enough. So now we must celebrate the ACP every time we eat chicken. Which is a bit gross.

Anyway, as we conduct the FST, I am designing a life vest for mice in my head. I imagine little hooks outside each hotel room where the life vest could hang to dry. The mice could be taught to put the vests on themselves. They have such nimble fingers. Imagine the mice looking down while they do up their life vests. Imagine how cute they'd look from behind.

Heads up, Audrey.

Sorry.

My dad is drying the mice. It is my job, when he's finished, to carry them back to their hotel rooms. They are damp and all aflutter but I never scream or drop them. I put them back and secure the metal grids. Their pink hands press the glass. Their chests rattle.

Dry me some more.

They love being dried. My dad has a super-soft, super-absorbent towel that makes them go all dreamy and close their eyes.

Now we are ready for the final heat, numbers 16 through 20. The stopwatch starts. In they go, one minute apart. They have to be dropped in quickly or they might run back up my dad's arm. Once, a mouse got as far as his shoulder.

In the water it's like their fur explodes. Poof. I feel a pang. But it's only ten minutes. Chin up, little guys. And they do keep their chins up. I have never seen a chin go underwater. Never. Until today.

Dad.

What.

I point at the third pool.

That's funny, he says.

No it's not. He's drowning!

Give him a sec.

So we give him five. He lands on the bottom of the pool. Doesn't move. I would not say no to a life vest. Bubbles fly up.

He can't swim.

All mice can swim.

I splash my arm into the water, but I'm not tall enough. Dad! Okay. He plunges his own arm in.

I turn away. Is he alive. Don't look at him.

He's fine, Audrey. Look.

So I look. Some very rapid mouse breathing. Some very wide mouse eyes.

Little frigger, my dad says. His sleeve is wet up to the shoulder.

And so number 18 gets dried, but not as gently as the others, and for not as long.

I guess he's no good for a Forced Swimming Test, I say as I carry him back to his room.

Well, no. Not if he can't be forced.

My dad's lab is in the B-4 building, which I call the Before Building. In the basement of the Before Building is the Animal Care office. We stop by on our way home. Verlaine has her feet up on the desk. She is the animal caregiver. She is from Switzerland and she always wears short sleeves, no matter how cold her office is.

My dad knocks on her desk.

She has her big arms bent at the elbow like she is holding reins, but what she is really holding is a magazine with a horse on the cover and a rider wearing a top hat.

Bonsoir. And she lifts an imaginary top hat.

Is it *soir* already, says my dad, checking his stopwatch.

It is always *soir* in the bowels of the earth, she says.

Verlaine looks after my dad's mice and Dr. O'Leery's cats, as well as some pigeons, chickens, and rats. She says the situation is saddest for the pigeons because they have to watch their free *confrères* parading back and forth on the third-floor window ledges.

All four walls of the Animal Care office have pictures of horses on them. There are no pictures of mice, cats, pigeons, chickens, or rats.

My dad tells her there is a problem with number 18. He won't swim.

Of course he will swim.

My dad lifts his wet sleeve.

She shakes her head. Cheeky *souris*. She drops her feet and rolls her chair across the room. Jots something down. TantaMouse, she says. Shall I not order from them again.

When she writes a muscle high up on her arm twitches.

What's going to happen to number 18, I ask.

I feel like a mouse sandwich, says Verlaine, still writing. That is what's going to happen.

I laugh. Obviously people do not eat mice. Then I stop laughing. What do giant people from Switzerland eat. Verlaine pats her stomach. No trace of a smile.

Don't tease her, says my dad. Number 18 will be youthenized.

I nod. That's what I thought.

Verlaine seems surprised. She tilts her head in my direction and says, Chip off the old block, *non*.

When we step outside the wind knocks me over. This is not the first time I've been blown down on campus. The university was designed with wind speed in mind.

Whoa, says my dad, picking me up. Where's your rock.

I'm supposed to carry a rock when it's windy. Forgot it, I say and tighten my ponytail by one notch. Dad.

He skips down the steps. I hold on to the door of Before.

Dad!

He turns. The wind is loud.

I don't trust Verlaine as far as I can throw her, I yell.

What, he yells back.

His hair flaps around. His sleeve is instantly dry. He holds it up like, look, dry, amazing. Then, since I'm not moving, he comes back up the steps. What.

I don't trust Verlaine as far as I can throw her.

He smiles. Which wouldn't be very far.

I want to do an experiment with number 18. My own experiment. I want to youthenize him myself.

My dad says nothing for a moment. Then he lifts his chin. Oh Audrey—

Like the frog who turned back into a tadpole. Why not. Why not.

You don't understand.

Yes I do.

We can't bring lab animals home every time—

Verlaine wants a mouse sandwich!

We can't bring lab animals home. Period.

I say nothing. I keep holding the door.

My dad pretends to carry on home. Then looks over his shoulder. Comes back. Okay. Tell me your experiment.

I wasn't asleep. I was resting my face. On the table. Like in kindergarten when the teacher said, Settle down, *enfants maudits*. Heads on desks.

My head is where Wedge should be. Did I squish Wedge. I sit up and pat my head.

He's not in your hair. He's back in the terrarium. Uncle Thoby puts coffee in front of me. Poor little guy was about to rappel off the table.

I wipe away drool. Did I sleep, I mean rest my face, through the coffee maker.

Yeah.

Wow. The coffee maker is pretty loud.

Uncle Thoby is not wearing a bright sweater. Uncle Thoby always wears bright sweaters with one sleeve stretched. Today's sweater is black. Sleeve not stretched. One of my dad's.

When was the last time you ate, he says.

I try to remember. I recall some fudge in Terminal 1. Which might have been soap.

He opens the fridge.

Don't make me anything.

How about an Orange in a Castle, he says.

And some Piety pie, I add.

Outside it is dark and windy. When did that happen. I look at the clock. Noon.

· · ·

If I put my head back on the table in the same *enfant-maudit* position, I will remember my montage. Which is code for dream. My dad was against dreams. Well, against their prolonged discussion at the breakfast table. Dreams are of interest only to the dreamer, he said. So spare the rest of us.

This from a man who used to be a psychologist.

Actually I mostly agreed with him. I did not much like hearing about other people's dreams. Unless of course I was in them. But discussing my own, at great length, over breakfast—one of life's great pleasures.

Uncle Thoby agreed. He suggested we refer to our dreams as montages.

What is a montage.

Something fast and true and mixed up.

I nodded. That'll fool him.

My dad was fooled for all of two seconds.

I saw this montage.

Where.

I glanced at Uncle Thoby. On the news, he suggested.

Right, on the news. About this girl who found a secret compartment in her arm. And inside that secret compartment was a message. And guess what the message said.

Do tell.

It said DNA.

Now when I put my head back on the table, I remember that it is four and a half days earlier in Oregon. Oregon is still in the comma. In my montage, my dad was making a W with both hands in the air.

Heads up. Uncle Thoby puts an Orange in a Castle on the table. More coffee.

I would not say no to more coffee.

 An Orange in a Castle is the prettiest thing you will ever see. It is an orange sitting in a castle made of its own peel.

I saw this montage on the news that my dad was alive and waving from the west coast.

Me too, says Uncle Thoby.

You had the same montage.

Similar.

I notice you have ignored my request for pie. But that's okay.

He sits down across from me. Drops two tablets of Alka-Seltzer in a glass. Look, the Tycho crater. Our old routine. There is a point at which every tablet of Alka-Seltzer looks exactly like the moon.

Thank you for the castle and the coffee.

Welcome.

The orange is bright against his black sweater. I remove one piece. I have a question, I say. Get ready.

Okay.

Did you make a moving speech at the bedside.

He looks up from his drink.

Did my dad know I was coming home. Did you tell him.

I told him.

And did he wake up.

No, sweetheart.

I see. I chew. It is all a bit sick-making. Do not throw up. If you throw up, Uncle Thoby will throw up too. If you even talk about throwing up, he'll gag. He is very sensitive that way.

I chew carefully.

I have a theory about sympathetic throwing up. It is a naturally selected trait. If one person in a group throws up, it is likely (or at least possible) that others in the group have ingested the same poisonous thing as the thrower-upper. Therefore, as a preventative measure, the others throw up too. The sooner you all throw up the ingested poison together, the more likely you are to survive.

I look over his shoulder at the pond. Which is what you are supposed to do if you feel sick. Look at the distance. The swans are really bouncing. Boy are they.

I don't feel so good.

Want to lie down.

I shake my head. But I can't eat all the ramparts.

That's okay.

I rest my cheek in my hand.

He notices the CRYNOT bracelet. I heard you on the phone, he says.

Yeah.

Not to Darren Lipbalm again.

Lipseed. No. I called Winnifred.

Winnifred. Uncle Thoby's eyebrows fly up. He had forgotten Winnifred. And there is a glimmer, not quite a smile but almost. She's got her own phone, of course, he says.

Cell.

Ah.

And for a moment it's like everything is going to be funny and good. But then his face collapses and he says, Oh Odd, I know how hard it must have been to leave—

No, it wasn't hard. It wasn't. It was a piece of pie.

Did I say how good it is to see you. Did I say that last night.

I think so.

I can't remember. I can't think.

S'okay.

So Winnifred, he says after a moment.

I tell him that she's with Linda and Chuck. I tell him that she was in a comma too. But she woke up.

Dark clouds build like fists over the pond. Look, I say.

We're getting a Weather Bomb, he says, turning.

A what.

He explains that this is a new meteorological term. It means what you'd think.

A Weather Bomb. Coming here. Sounds like a term my dad would have loved.

Oh yes. He'd been using it, ad nauseam.

I nod. And experience a wave of nauseam.

Sorry, says Uncle Thoby, hand over mouth.

S'okay.

My dad used to stand by the range hood when the wind whistled through it and rub his hands together and say, Is that a B-flat I hear.

Because if the wind whistled a B-flat, bad weather was coming.

I think it's A-sharp, Uncle Thoby would say.

And my dad would say, You say potayto. I say potahto.

Let's call the whole thing off.

And I would say, What the.

Ssh and listen to the wind, Audrey. It's music.

Uncle Thoby gets up to clear the table. Speaking of weather, he says. I hope Toff's flight gets in okay.

Toff. And isn't *that* a punch to the castle-filled paunch. What.

Innocently he looks at me. I thought I told you last night.

Let me think. Um, no.

I must have seen a montage on the news that I told you last night.

No.

I had a montage that I told you Toff was en route from London and you took it really well.

You didn't tell me!

Don't yell.

Was I yelling. Does Uncle Thoby think he can just slip Toff in under the radar like this. This is not the way to introduce a major new development.

How does one introduce a major new development. I tried the montage.

Fuck.

He'll be here in a few hours.

Why. *Why.*

Because I called him.

When.

After the accident.

Collision, I correct him.

He pauses on his way to the counter. He is unshaven and pathetic in my dad's too-small sweater. Don't look at him.

Also, do not think about the collision. Because if you do it will have a new embellishment. Such as: The tree is now decorated. Which of course it could not have been. The tree that hit my dad was en route to decoration. So technically not a Christmas tree. Yet. But in this new version, the tree has lights, and they are lit up with that lonely inventor's blue.

Oddly.

I scrape my chair back. Call him and tell him not to come.

He's over the ocean.

And just like that, I wish the plane down. Wow. It's easy. I imagine the plane nose-diving into the Atlantic. Toff, engrossed in the incomprehensible section of the newspaper with the smallest font, has not bothered to figure out his flotation device. Oh dear. Oh well.

Toff is, or was, my dad's "best chum" from Cambridge. He is also Grandmother's whipping boy, and let's see what else. A lawyer. And, as Uncle Thoby now informs me, my dad's executor.

Oh oh oh, is that what he's telling you.

Please sit down. Yes that's what he's telling me, because that's what he is.

My dad would not hire an executioner.

Executor.

Toff the Lord High Executioner!

Try to understand, Uncle Thoby says quietly, that I can't do everything that needs to be done here. I can't.

I'm here.

There are things only Toff can do.

Well he can do them from a distance. Because he's not staying here.

Uncle Thoby looks disappointed, not that Toff won't be staying with us, but that I could be so inhospitable. He didn't ask to, Oddly.

So Toff's plane will (probably, unfortunately, safely) land. At which time he will assume command. Toff the cartoon assassin. He is coming to make my dad really dead.

But when you called Toff, my dad was alive. Why would an alive person need an executor.

Because there was no hope.

I stare at him. You didn't tell me there was no hope.

Yes I did, sweetheart. But you didn't hear.

Chuck rehearses with a book propped open on his bare chest. The book is called *Lowering the Bard: Shakespeare for the Uninitiated*. He's wearing boxer shorts and that's it.

Pool: 75 degrees, approximately.

Chuck does this thing where he opens *Lowering the Bard* at random and drops his finger on the page. Then he rehearses that passage. More often than not it's by someone called Antonio. If this happens he keeps dropping his finger until he gets someone important.

Linda left for work at the crack of dawn. She mows the same mountain Audrey used to. So it's just me and Chuck. This will be the new routine.

One of Linda's long blond hairs floats on the surface of my Lemon Pie pool like a golden bridge. A bridge for a termite. Linda does not keep her hair tidy. I spent three hours this morning extracting a single strand from my throat. Three hours. I was so tired afterwards I had to take a nap.

And how did this hair mishap occur. It occurred because last night Linda bent over my castle and said, Hanging in there, Winnifred. And her hair touched my pool. Hasn't she heard of a ponytail. Then she knocked on my shell even though I was clearly awake. Just checking, she said.

Jesus Christ this had better not be a nightly occurrence.

Later I took a drink from my pool. Big mistake.

At least it is warm. The radiators chatter constantly in Morse code. When Chuck walked by my castle earlier, he said, I hope you're happy. Now we live in an oven.

Yes, well. That is the price you pay for a tortoise you will not pick up and hold under your armpit. Not that you are really paying any price, since I overheard Linda say heat is included in your rent. So why complain. Enjoy the air boiling over the radiators like a highway mirage. Enjoy.

Will Audrey come back. That is the question. Or is an allegiance switch in order. And is an allegiance switch even possible, considering my options. Linda the Unkempt or Chuck Stanch. Stanch is Chuck's last name. This I learned last night when a Red Cross representative came to the door and referred to him as Mr. Stanch.

Which Linda found for some reason very amusing. Would you like to donate some blood, Mr. Stanch.

Shut up. You're going to be Mrs. Stanch soon.

Over my dead body.

Later he threw his book on the floor and said there was an Antonio in every play and it was always him.

Linda said, Well, some of us are bricks.

What the hell does that mean.

It means we can't all be the entire edifice.

To which he replied, Fuck that.

Chuck wants to be Prospero, not his brother. He wants to be lord of everything and then fall on his own sword. Or staff. Or whatever. He is sick of bit parts, he said. They make him want to fight.

On the floor, *Lowering the Bard* was slowly closing of its own accord.

Chuck is what is called a pugilist.

As Linda explained it once to Audrey: You know those actors who put on Shakespeare in the Park. Yes. Well, Chuck is not one of those actors. Chuck finds one of those parks and stages his own production with his own actors. So on any given night there might be two Shakespeares happening in the same park. Often the two casts fight each other. These fights bring in a whole other audience. Which is where the real money can be made.

It is a dangerous business. Last summer Chuck broke a rib. If you look closely at his torso, you can see the dent.

It is not that they are unlovable, Linda and Chuck. Well yes, it is that they are unlovable.

I have switched allegiances many times—many many times—but it is never easy, and I always think, This time I won't be able to do it.

For instance, the Panasonic salesman. He was the tenant prior to Audrey and Cliff. How I loved the Panasonic salesman. He was not often home, but I lived for the moments when he was. He would come through the door, tie askew, and say, Phew, what a week. He had a region to tend to. It was a big region. I lived in a Panasonic printer box, sans heat lamp. I slept a lot.

He called me Iris after the Panasonic Iris Reader, one of the new biometric security devices in his sales portfolio. Actually tortoises don't have irises. We have nictitating membranes. But nevermind. The Panasonic Iris Reader, as he explained it to me (or rather rehearsed it to the bathroom mirror), verified the identity of (hopefully) authorized persons before admitting them to, say, a Highly Infectious Disease Research Area, by scanning their eyes. Each iris has a unique pattern, he said. An iris is more unique than a fingerprint. Can something be "more unique," I queried. I hope you don't say "more unique" when you're giving your sales pitch, Mitt. Which was his name. In any case, he became a very successful salesman. So successful that his own irises got pale from so many successful PIR demonstrations.

Then one day out of the blue he said he was being transferred to Dubai, where they have more money than you can shake a stick at and bright, beautiful irises just waiting to be leached of their colour. Dubai, I said. Wow! I'll pack my bags.

Um, said Mitt.

I looked up.

Bringing a tortoise to the United Arab Emirates, Mitt said. That would not be happening.

Oh.

The new tenants need you, Mitt said.

Oh.

And so they did. But I didn't love them, not at first. And then slowly I loved Cliff. And then I loved her too. They spent a lot of time reminiscing about the country where they had met and been happy. This other country had a lake, a tram, mountains called the Yelps, and high ceilings. They liked to remember the tram and how Cliff never bought tickets and mostly got away with it.

They had slept together secretly in the house of a woman who did not find Cliff very *sympa*. This did not matter. They were on the brink of togetherness. Which is apparently better than togetherness. The bedroom had high ceilings with wood beams and a skylight. Cliff stood on a chair to carve their names into a beam. He never banged his head.

They went into the mountains and engaged in extreme sports. This was the clincher. When they came down from the mountains they were sore and in love. They had to make a decision. Would they live in his country or her country or the country with the Yelps. They chose his country. Which in retrospect was maybe not the best decision. In any case, they came to this country and this state and the flat where I was waiting in the Panasonic printer box. Cliff picked me up. He passed me to Audrey. Look, he said. A tortoise. I would not say no to a tortoise, she said, and not for the last time either.

After Cliff left she started climbing the walls, going round and round in sad circles, circumnavigating, as she called it, the flat that did not have Cliff in it anymore. Watching her was enough to penetrate any tortoise's plastron. Especially when she fell and crashed. Not that she had far to fall, but still.

She had strong arms from mowing grass under a table, but strong arms are not what you need to be a good rock climber. Strong legs are what you need.

Big hands are an asset. Big feet are not.

Later we travelled together and I started riding the dashboard. That was the clincher.

She is not the *previous* tenant. She is *the* tenant.

But I do wonder, how long before she meets a Canadian tortoise she cannot say no to. And builds that tortoise a new fireproof castle with a state-of-the-art heat lamp. But oh. Wait. The Canadian tortoise will not *require* a heat lamp because Canadian tortoises *embrace* the cold. Oh yes, I can see it now. The new castle flies a Canadian flag from an unsinged turret. Audrey and the new tortoise frolic in the snow. Make snow angels. Yes, the new tortoise is more dog than tortoise.

Uncle Thoby has been gone for three hours. He went off in a Clint's cab in the middle of the Weather Bomb to meet Toff at the airport. Amazingly the flight was on schedule. Glad I'm not on that flight, I said. Glad Toff is.

Why did Uncle Thoby have to risk his own life in a Weather Bomb, I wanted to know. Couldn't Toff find his own way to his hotel.

Uncle Thoby pulled on his bright orange gloves and looked tired.

Sorry, I said.

Here is a lesson I never seem to learn: Whenever you say something unkind about anybody, it is as if you have said something unkind to Uncle Thoby personally.

I followed him onto the porch. The wind flapped our hair. Toff has to be told, he said. In person.

Told what. Oh. That the comma is over.

Poor Uncle Thoby. A repeat performance of last night. Toff's slow and final descent via the escalator. Walter is dead. Period. Would Toff wobble. Or would he simply open his briefcase and say, That's what I thought.

I'm taking a Clint's cab. There's no risk to my life.

You don't want me to come with you.

Do you want to come.

Um. No.

He kissed my forehead. A black cab pulled up. It wasn't Clint, but it was someone with a moustache who looked a lot like him.

Be Qantas, I said.

Back inside I felt like: What if this is the future.

And I realized I could smell the house. You can only smell your own house if you have been subtracted from the smell. Or if someone else has been subtracted. Or if you have not taken out the garbage. We used to have a family smell that I could not smell.

I decided to do something useful. I would grease Wedge's wheel. A little WD-40 would be just the thing. He was asleep in a corner of the terrarium. Soon he would be up and running, and what a surprise to find his wheel all greased and soundless!

I took the wheel to the kitchen table. I was not prepared for the force of the spray. Shit. WD-40 all over the place. All over the metal treads of the wheel too. So now Wedge would have a toxin on his hands and feet, and when he bit his nails he'd be poisoned. Jesus Christ. My dad used to take care of this. How did he do it.

What you should have done is sprayed a piece of paper towel, then greased the axle of the wheel *only*.

Yes, well, I'm none too swift.

Clean it up.

In a while. Suddenly I felt like crying. I put my elbow on the table and it slid out from under me.

The range hood sang its ominous B-flat. Outside there was no pond. The Weather Bomb had erased it. Was it a Weather Bomb when he walked home that night. Don't picture it. But I do. And I realize there are many more pictures to come and each one will hurt more than the last. It's a Weather Bomb and he's leaving the Before Building and he says *bonsoir* to Verlaine, who offers to drive him, but he declines because he has this policy of never taking the weather personally. And there are no sidewalks. But off he goes. And the last word he said was probably *bonsoir*.

Uncle Thoby said Verlaine had come to the hospital and was not in good shape. I can't picture Verlaine not in good shape. I'm glad I can't picture it.

.   .   .

The last time I talked to my dad, I had an agenda written out. I like to write out agendas before important phone calls. They keep me on track. And this was an important phone call because I had just received my old student file from GOLEM (God of Light and Eternal Mercy) and I had good news. Or I thought I had good news.

It was the kind of file that you, the subject of the file, were never supposed to see. Other people (teachers, employers, friends, neighbours) might petition the school to see your file. But not you. You were supposed to be protected forever from its contents. Probably the accident of my receiving such a file had something to do with the collapse of the Catholic school system and the soon-to-be-demolished building that was GOLEM.

On my agenda I had the following items:

1. Growth of grass in Oregon, astounding rate of.

2. Smoke detector vs. fire alarm, differences between.

3. Mercury in canned tuna, dangers of.

4. French submersion, value of.

5. My IQ!

We moved through the first four items pretty quickly. (No more tuna for you, Win.) Then I broke the news. That manila envelope my dad had forwarded. Yes. Well get ready. Because inside were the results of those tests all the Frenchly submerged students had had to take, to make sure we could all still speak English and recognize basic geometric shapes, and guess what.

What.

Guess what my IQ is!

Pause. What.

I told them the number.

No response.

I should mention that Uncle Thoby was also on the line.

Isn't that great, I said. I mean, wow.

It's bollocks is what it is, said my dad after a moment.

Why. Why is it bollocks. You don't think I'm that smart.

We think you're off-the-scale smart, said Uncle Thoby energetically.

So—

Listen to me, Audrey. You know what those tests measure. They measure how similar your brain is to the brain that made up the test.

Yeah, I said. So. And then it dawned on me. Slowly. That what I had assumed was a high score was *not* a high score. It just sounded like a high score. It sounded like a not-bad grade, the kind of grade I never got in school.

Oh. It's low, isn't it.

IQ is not even a real acronym, Uncle Thoby was saying. GOLEM is a real acronym. SCUBA is a real acronym. You can't even pronounce IQ. Don't take it personally.

You can too pronounce it, I said. You can pronounce it Ick.

Okay. True.

I had always been good at acronyms. Acronyms were for smart people with secrets.

My dad said, What in Christ was GOLEM thinking. How enlightened. How merciful.

I have to go now, I said.

Audrey.

You knew, I said. You knew my Ick was low and you didn't tell me.

Oddly—

This is why I hate the phone, my dad said. I can't see her face.

Why couldn't we have just bantered as per usual, Uncle Thoby complaining that the dramatis personae of Portland was very confusing—who is Chuck again—and my dad saying, Dramatis personae, do we have one of those, and Uncle Thoby saying, Of course, but we are easier to remember. And me saying, Ha ha.

I hung up the phone and said, Low IQ. *Ce n'est pas possible.*

Winnifred dropped a piece of lettuce.

It's not possible, I translated.

The problem was, it felt a little bit possible.

From across the room, Uncle Thoby says, Are you there. The phone is ringing. Do you feel like answering. Are you there. No pressure to answer.

Except Uncle Thoby is not in the room.

I drop Wedge's wheel.

My first thought is: Uncle Thoby is dead, and that is his ghost. Or ghosts, plural. Because I can also hear his voice coming from upstairs.

Are you there. The phone is ringing.

And then I remember. It's the new phone. The Hear Ye 3000. Which I had yet to hear "ring." So this is the ring.

The Hear Ye 3000 was a gift from Uncle Thoby to my dad on their last birthday. I remember my dad telling me about it. He said finally a phone that did not torture him. He had always likened the sound of a ringing phone to being stabbed.

When have you been stabbed, Dad.

He said okay, he had a sinking feeling every time he heard a phone ring.

So Uncle Thoby had bought a phone that played a Bach fugue. My dad said the "fugue" was just three notes repeating and was clearly a ring. Next Uncle Thoby bought a phone with a purr setting. The purr, my dad said, was just a ring on low volume. A dagger as opposed to a butcher knife.

But now, behold the Hear Ye 3000! Wherein you can record your own summons. Now you can be coaxed to the phone by the voice of someone near and dear to your heart.

The Hear Ye's keypad glows gold. I lick the grease off my fingers. Pick up.

Hello.

One disconcerting effect of the Hear Ye 3000 is that you expect the caller to be the person whose voice summoned you. It is not the same voice.

Can I speak to Walter Flowers.

No.

Silence at the other end while the caller awaits an explanation. There is no explanation, caller.

He coughs. Well, I represent Christmatech. We're recalling our D-434 model Christmas lights. We've sent you several notices in the mail.

Recalling. As in withdrawing from circulation. Or as in fondly remembering.

Long pause. As in withdrawing. We'd very much like to exchange those lights for the D-534 model. And give you a ten-dollar coupon.

I'm sure you would. But you'll excuse me now because I think I just ingested poison.

Oh. Of course. By all means. Do—

I hang up. Spit in the sink. Wipe my mouth on my sleeve. Jesus Christ I can't believe I just licked WD-40 off my fingers. Now would be the time to throw up. If I could.

Outside the LeBaron is dwarfish under a mushroom cap of snow. The air is deep dark blue. The snow sparkles. Why does snow sparkle. Because snowflakes are prisms.

The Weather Bomb has detonated. It's all over. Uncle Thoby is still not home. True, the roads are deep. But he has been gone too long. What if Toff has done something to him.

Like what.

Kidnapped him. Disappeared him.

Don't be ridiculous.

I decide to do something useful. I will shovel the driveway. I head out to the shed for my old Flower Shovel. The Flower Shovel has an imprint of a flower on the bottom so you can make floral patterns in the snow. Really it works best if you whack the snow rather than shovel it.

I had the idea for the Flower Shovel after noticing the vertical stripes left in the snow by run-of-the-mill shovels. Why not *decorate* your snow while you shovelled it. Say, with a flower! Uncle Thoby said I was a genius. So he had the Flower Shovel custom-made for me at Murph's Turf, Lock, and Key. Uncle Thoby said I should patent the idea. I didn't know what patent meant. It means you own the idea, he said. I already own the idea, I said. But not in the eyes of the world, he said. Oh, in the eyes of the world.

He said Murph's eyes had sparkled entrepreneurially when he'd handed Uncle Thoby the Flower Shovel.

Sparkle entrepreneurially, said my dad. Do my eyes do that.

Of course they do.

I think Uncle Thoby might even have ordered the patent forms for me. Possibly the shovel is already patented in my name. It wouldn't surprise me. For someone so law-abiding, Uncle Thoby is weirdly lax about signing other people's signatures. Anyway, I must remember to ask him if he did patent it. Because that would make me an inventor.

At the time, we thought up other shovel designs. Uncle Thoby said snowflakes would be popular. Hearts for Valentine's Day. You could also have words, I said. They'd have to be spelled backwards on the shovel so they'd come out right on the snow. Like MERRY CHRISTMAS or BURIED ALIVE.

My dad said porn would be a big seller.

Walter.

I'm just saying.

You want your daughter to patent porn shovels.

It would be lucrative.

That's naked people, right.

Of course my shovel had to have a flower because Flowers are what we are.

I have been out here all of fifteen minutes, fluffing up snow with the Flower Shovel™, when Byrne Doyle and Jim Ryan converge, Byrne from number 11 across the street, Jim from next door. They are both brandishing shovels as tall as they are.

They are sorry. God, they are both so sorry. Byrne Doyle hugs me. How you holding up. Good to see you.

Byrne looks more like Jacob Marley than ever. He's wearing a long wool coat and a button on the lapel that says VOTE FOR BYRNE DOYLE. The button is a bit rusty, like it might be from a past election and he never bothered to take it off. The lines around his mouth have deepened.

Jim Ryan indicates the Flower Shovel™ and says, Fisher-Price make that shovel.

Of course not. Murph made it.

Oh. Apologies.

I remember that shovel, says Byrne fondly.

I hoist it in the air. I've whacked some pretty patterns in my day.

So, Byrne says. Some WMD, what.

What.

Weather of Mass Destruction.

I'd heard Weather Bomb.

Both are acceptable according to the Weather Network.

I like when the Weather Network says Ceiling Unlimited, says Jim. That is a good day.

Byrne Doyle puts a hand on my shoulder and asks where my uncle is.

At the airport, meeting someone.

No flights today, surely.

I tell him that actually, yes, there are flights today and they are all on schedule.

Byrne shakes his head. Pilots are braver than they used to be, what.

Pilots are too big for their breeches is what, says Jim.

Don't listen to him, says Byrne.

Jim Ryan's driveway is already shovelled. Byrne Doyle's is not. I can smell sweat, which I deduce is Jim's. Please, I say as they both hunker down to tackle the driveway. Please don't bother.

They wave me back.

Byrne Doyle's coat is totally impractical. It's a wool straitjacket.

Your uncle, he says, already breathing hard. Has shovelled my driveway on more occasions than I can count.

Wish I had a shovelling arm like that, Jim says.

Which I think is bordering on inappropriate.

For years Uncle Thoby has been shovelling Byrne Doyle's driveway to make up for my dad not voting for him. Politics in the

Flower household is complicated. Or I guess it became complicated after Uncle Thoby got to know Byrne Doyle. Before that, it was simple. We voted orange. Orange was how you voted if you cared about other people. But now here was a problem: How did you vote if you cared about a blue candidate.

I remember meeting up with Byrne Doyle on the Wednesday Pond path when he was running in an election—a provincial one, I think. He liked to walk around the pond, deep in campaign thoughts, accompanied by a little dog who was not deep in campaign thoughts. Uncle Thoby was walking me home from school and we stopped to chat. Or rather Uncle Thoby stopped to chat while I played with the dog, Bellhop. Bellhop had solid black eyes that you could only see if you parted his bangs.

Anyway, Byrne Doyle had said something about the Poles not liking him, and afterwards Uncle Thoby said he felt bad. He was sure Byrne could tell we didn't vote for him by the colour of Uncle Thoby's gloves. The orange gloves were a recent gift from my dad, and boy were they bright against the igneous rock.

Byrne Doyle's gloves were, naturally, blue.

We carried on around the pond and Uncle Thoby said, Poor Byrne Doyle.

Why is he poor. Because the people in Poland don't like him. What.

Scrooooooooge, I bellowed.

Ssh, Oddly.

But he looks just like Jacob Marley.

I know. But keep it down. Then he sighed and said, People with dogs. As a rule. Are sad.

Sad! But I could still feel the wagginess of Bellhop in my arms. He seemed so happy.

Oh, Bellhop was happy.

Then I understood. Byrne Doyle kept his happiness outside him. Because he was so busy on the inside with worry about elections and whether the people in Poland liked him. All his happiness was stored outside him in a woolly dog.

Later that night my dad said, You want me to vote for Jacob Marley.

It might be the orange thing to do, I said.

Which infuriated him. Out of the way, he said. Even though I wasn't in the way.

We were making supper. Macaroni and cheese. Not from a box. The real thing with three different kinds of cheese you grate yourself (or Uncle Thoby grates himself) and bits of lobster mixed in.

Why are lobsters freckly like my shoulders.

No answer.

I arranged my alphabet magnets: VOTE FOR BYRNE DOYLE AND BELLHOP.

My dad opened the fridge. He paused. Who is Bellhop. Does the man have a porter.

I thought this was a democracy, said Uncle Thoby.

He had a point. We were supposed to be a democracy within a democracy. Uncle Thoby couldn't vote in Canada, and I was too young, so my dad's vote was supposed to be *tripartite*.

Tripartite, I said to the fridge.

Outside, snow had started falling heavy and gold in front of the street lamps. The wind was blowing through the range hood. My dad made his usual comment about the B-flat and waited for Uncle Thoby to counter with his A-sharp. Uncle Thoby didn't counter.

Uh-oh.

Supper went on longer than usual. My dad had already put his knife and fork in the eight o'clock position, which signalled that he was ready to read, but he did not reach for the book. We were supposed to be reading a biography of Marconi, the man who received the first passenger seagull on Seagull Hill.

This Marconi is some good, I said, stabbing a noodle. I mean macaroni.

No response.

Fine.

From what I gathered, our voting options were as follows:

a) Vote for the blue candidate because he's your neighbour and he looks like Jacob Marley and the Poles have not been kind to him. Plus, he has a dog called Bellhop.

b) Vote for the orange candidate, but stop wearing orange gloves in front of your blue neighbour.

c) Make it clear to the blue candidate that only *one* person in the Flower household is eligible to vote, and although his vote is supposed to be tripartite, it no longer is. Democracy in the Flower household is dead.

d) Vote for the orange candidate because you care about other people, but shovel the blue candidate's driveway when he's up late at night burning the midnight oil, as is his wont, trying to get elected.

We eventually settled on the last option. Well, Uncle Thoby did. And he even managed to get the whole Flower family out there on several occasions, shovelling (or whacking flower prints) in Byrne Doyle's snow.

Jim Ryan is waxing on about his driveway. How it's a crescent, of which he is very proud, but it's a bitch to shovel. There's a *lot* of crescent. Still, he would not go back to a linear driveway for all the world. Crescent is where it's at. Never have to back in, never have to back out. Pull in forward, pull out forward.

We get it, says Byrne Doyle.

The amount of time you spend mowing your lawn, says Jim, pointing his shovel at Byrne, is not equal to the additional time I spend shovelling.

What, says Byrne. *What.*

I ask Byrne about the election.

Oh my child, he says.

Yes.

There's no end to it.

God help us, says Jim.

No end to the *work*, he amends. The election itself will of course end.

I whack a few flowers.

Down the street there's a low rumble. We all stop and look.

Oh shit, says Jim.

Aha, says Byrne.

What, I ask.

The plough.

Fuck, says Jim. And he vaults across our lawn into his crescent.

He's going to defend it now, says Byrne, amused. That's the trouble with a crescent, see. You can't defend two entrances. And when you're ploughed in, you're ploughed in doubly.

The plough comes slowly down the street, pushing its frozen wave. I love how Jurassic it is. Also how cosy. The guy inside smiles benevolently down. He's wearing a T-shirt in there! He toasts me with a Tim Hortons coffee. Did you see that, I yell over my shoulder to Byrne Doyle.

Stand back there love.

Next door Jim Ryan is whacking a snowbank, and not to make pretty patterns but to release negative energy.

Uncle Thoby Northwest Shoves the front door open, and I try not to hug him but I can't help it. Hi, he says. He smells cold and sweet.

You've been gone for hours. *Hours.*

He bends over to untie his boots and spends a long time untying them. When he straightens his face is flushed. Hey! Did I see some flowers in the snowbank.

You did, you did.

I'm holding on to his sleeve. He looks at me, touches my ponytail—Odd—and then he wobbles. Reaches out for the banister.

Steady.

I'm going to take off my coat now.

Right. I unclench my fingers. How did he take it, I ask.

Who.

The executioner.

Uncle Thoby rubs his forehead. I wish you wouldn't call him that.

Was he mean to you.

No.

We heat up some chicken soup Byrne Doyle brought over. Uncle Thoby leans against the counter and says he thinks he has a fever. Me too, I say, stirring.

He looks skeptical. Since when.

Since you said you had one.

That was just a second ago.

I didn't know that's what I had until you said it, but fever, yeah, that's what I have. Feel. I tilt my head back.

Have you eaten since the orange, he says.

A little WD-40.

He nods and gets two bowls out of the cupboard, a regular bowl for me and the fly bowl for him. The fly bowl has a fly painted on the rim.

So Byrne Doyle, bless his heart, brought soup, he says.

I nod. And he helped shovel the driveway, I add.

Man's a saint.

I serve the soup. This is from scratch, I say. You can tell.

It's delicious.

Imagine making soup from scratch.

Man never sleeps.

Byrning the midnight broth. Hey, you've got a fly in your soup.

We are speaking our secret family language. I love our secret family language.

Uncle Thoby's glass slides a few inches to the left. Why is the table slippery, he says.

Bread, I offer.

Please.

And then from the wrong side of the room Uncle Thoby says, Are you there. The phone is ringing. Do you feel like answering—

I smoosh the loaf to my chest.

I know, says Uncle Thoby, getting up. I feel the same way. But your dad loved it. Hello.

It's Toff.

I watch Uncle Thoby's face remain neutral and his eyes refuse to meet mine.

If you want to know how kind someone is, here is a little experiment. Try to make eye contact with him while he is on the phone. If he is kind, he will avoid your eyes. Because eye contact is a betrayal of the person on the other end, who can't see. It is like having a blind person in the room. Would you make eye contact with a seeing person while talking to a blind person. Not if you are kind. Not if you are Mr. Earnest. If you are Mr. Earnest you turn off your eyes when you are on the phone. Because you are intent on the person you can't see. You never show irony with your eyes unless everyone has an equal chance to be in on it.

Can irony exist in a world where everyone has an equal chance to be in on it. I don't know. Food for thought.

Uncle Thoby confirms lunch for the next day. Then he turns to me and says, Yes. Do you want to talk to her. I shake my head and shove a wad of bread in my mouth. For a second he looks into my eyes. Then he says, earnestly, Actually she's chewing. It could be awhile.

After he hangs up, and I swallow, I say, Do we have to see him tomorrow. Can't we wait.

For what.

A long time.

He smiles at me. I do not smile back. I put the bread, smooshed, on the table.

I don't think you understand how much has to be ironed out, he says.

Let's not talk about ironing yet.

We're going to talk about it tomorrow at lunch, okay.

I nod and disappear my spoon into my soup. Has Uncle Thoby heard the new usage of the word *disappeared*.

What new usage.

As in, some Canadian aid workers *were disappeared* in Iraq, I say. It's pretty scary. Just try it in a sentence.

I can't think of—

Okay. Here's one. My dad was disappeared.

His spoon stops.

It's worse than murder, I say quietly. Isn't it.

He doesn't answer. So I nod for him.

In cartoons, you can tell the bad guys by their eyebrows. If the eyebrows make a V on the forehead, you know you're in trouble. Conversely, if the eyebrows make an *accent circonflexe*, all will be well. Just look at the word *bientôt*. Look how happy and hopeful those eyebrows.

This is a beautifully simple formula and why should it not apply to the world beyond cartoons.

For instance, Uncle Thoby has *accent-circonflexe* eyebrows. Even when he's sleeping. My dad also has, sorry had, *accent-circonflexe* eyebrows, except when he first woke up. When he first woke up he had a grognard face and who knew how long it might last. He didn't want to hear about your dreams anyway. Can we be quiet while I finish my coffee. But his eyebrows never made a V. I guess they were sort of straight like Bert's. Whereas Uncle Thoby's are like Ernie's. That's a good analogy. I mean, you trust Bert, you love Bert, but you're careful around him in the morning.

A grognard is someone who has just woken up and is not yet happy about it.

I used to marvel at how different my dad's grognard face was from his later-in-the-day face. Sure, I was a grognard in the morning too. My eyes were smaller. But my dad's eyes were smaller and his eyebrows were darker and his whole face was harder to break open in a laugh. And when he did laugh, the laugh looked tight, like it hurt.

Every morning we walked to school together. No matter the weather. The car was for heavy car-go loads only. He said I should never take the weather personally. You sally forth, he said. Remember you're waterproof.

I am.

You could stand in the rain for hours and you wouldn't fill up with water, would you.

My hair would.

Cut it off then. Like me.

My dad had short, straight, stand-up hair. I had a ponytail, which I loved, and which I would never cut off. My dad called my ponytail my question mark. Cut off that question mark!

Whereas Uncle Thoby *did* take the weather personally. If there was snow or freezing rain, he said, Why don't we call Clint. And quite often Uncle Thoby, whose job it was to collect me from school, would arrive in a Clint's cab. But my dad, never. My dad walked me to school, and then he walked himself to the university. Always. Rain or snow. Sidewalks or no. That was his rule.

No Clint for me, my dad said.

No Clint for me, I echoed.

If the wind picks up, you just hold on to a rock, he said.

Right.

Or me, if I'm there.

When we said goodbye at the GOLEM gate, he still had the grognard face. *A bientôt,* I said hopefully.

A bientôt.

My eyes get bigger at night and look prettier. This is because we are mammals and once upon a time we had to do all our business at night while the dinosaurs slept. It was important to look our best for these transactions.

My favourite moments were at night when we were all around the table and there was candlelight because it was a special occasion—say Christmas or my dad and Uncle Thoby's birthday—and all our eyes were big black dots.

Or maybe it was a power outage and Wedge was allowed on the table because my dad had rigged up a light bulb to his wheel. The light bulb glowed faint brown and flickered like a candle. It did not give off much light, but hey, we were eating by the light of Wedge!

Then my dad would read from a biography about someone with the good eyebrows. Although sometimes he read about someone with the bad. And then the book became a whole other kind of treat because we had an enemy we could all share, even Uncle Thoby, who didn't believe in sharing enemies unless the enemy had been dead for a long time and was in a book.

All of which brings me to Grandmother and Toff and my first encounter with real-life eyebrows of the bad variety. They arrived the summer after Uncle Thoby had come to live with us. From the moment they got off the plane they were sporting big Vs on their foreheads. They did not like our airport. They did not like our cheerful baggage carousel which was called a BAGGAGE CAROUSAL.

Does that sign say what I think it says, said Grandmother, squinting.

Hello Mum.

Grandmother kissed my dad. Then she kissed me, hard, on both cheeks. You're taller, she said.

You're sharper, I said.

It was the second time I'd seen her. The first had been in England for my grandfather's funeral. She had been blurrier then.

Her bag had gone astray. She looked like she would very much like to kick that bag. No doubt it's off carousing, she said.

Uncle Thoby, who used to be a baggage handler at Heathrow Airport, said (eyebrows maintaining triangularity) not to worry. It would turn up on the next flight from London.

Which is when, said Grandmother. Next month.

Behind her, wolfish Toff made eye contact with my dad and said he needed a cigarette.

. . .

Toff's beard got caught in the car seatbelt buckle. His beard was incredibly long. So was he. He had to fold himself into three sections to get into the car. Grandmother crammed herself into the back seat with me and Uncle Thoby. I perched on Uncle Thoby's knee and he made his long arm a seatbelt. I stared at Grandmother's floppy hair, which stayed in place like a hat. She lit a cigarette. So did Toff. They did not stop smoking after that. When they smoked, they tilted their heads back and their eyebrows assumed an even steeper slope.

Our house was different with Toff and Grandmother in it. Smokier. But something else. Downcast. Or maybe I was just tired. I'd given up my room to Toff and was sleeping in a cot at the foot of my dad's bed.

It is exhausting, watching your dad sleep. I don't recommend it. You should not have to witness your dad's absence while he is in the room. I tried very hard to fall asleep before he came upstairs to bed, but invariably I would only have had a quick montage before he opened the door.

Still awake, old goat.

Goddamn it. I sat up in my cot. It was red metal and it squeaked.

Can I turn on the light.

Yes. I put my hands over my eyes. Dad.

Hm.

They're not staying forever, right.

Audrey—

Because Uncle Thoby stayed forever.

I peeked out through my hands. The room was bright yellow.

My dad sat down on the edge of the bed. But you're not sorry Uncle Thoby stayed, are you.

No! No. I couldn't explain. Okay. For one thing, I didn't like sleeping in my dad's room with his bare feet pointing at me. I didn't like seeing his bare feet. He never had bare feet. Could he wear socks to bed please.

Why.

Could you!

Yes, okay.

It was summer. But we sat outside on the porch and got goose-bumps. Even my face got goosebumps. My dad tied helium bal-loons to the porch because it was his and Uncle Thoby's birthday. We sat and shivered. The pond bounced like black coffee. Everyone drank black coffee. Toff and Grandmother were assigned (by me) their own mugs. Toff's had a rude cartoon of the Queen on it. Grandmother's said London. I hoped they would feel homesick.

My eyes felt small and stayed small even at night.

When I said my face was cold, Toff said his beard was like a blanket. Then he picked it up and said, Want some.

That freaked me out.

And then: Hadn't Toff and Grandmother come for my dad and Uncle Thoby's birthday. But this morning they hadn't said Happy Doozoo even after I'd said it, loudly, three times.

I'm sorry, Toff said. The Doozoo is—

Today, I said.

August twelfth, Uncle Thoby said.

Toff continued to look mystified.

Le douze août, I said slowly.

Oh right. Of course.

And why hadn't they brought presents. Grandmother seemed confused. She said the presents were in her runaway bag. If you say so, I said. Audrey, said my dad. At least there were the helium balloons (from me) because Uncle Thoby loved helium. And a new phone for my dad (from Uncle Thoby). And a bowl with a very realistic fly painted on the rim for Uncle Thoby (from my dad). And a bottle of sherry for Uncle Thoby (from my dad).

Pour, oh pour the pirate sherry, Uncle Thoby sang in the kitchen, his pirate hair falling over his eyebrow.

His mug was replaced by a little red glass.

. . .

That night we had chicken lasagna for dinner. I stood up and gave a toast to Andrew Toti, inventor of the automated chicken plucker.

Grandmother and Toff lifted their eyebrows.

And the life vest, I added. Amen.

Amen, said my dad.

The lasagna had three layers and each layer could be cut into a twelve-car parking lot and each parking space eaten separately. Occasionally I took a break to play with the corkscrew.

Sometimes she has hairy armpits, I said, lifting her arms.

And sometimes hairy shoulders.

Don't interrupt, said my dad.

Which would you rather have, I asked the table at large.

Silence. Then Uncle Thoby said, I've got both.

I patted his arm. Your shoulders aren't hairy.

They sort of are, he said.

I returned to my lasagna.

Now there was a lull (for which they should have been grateful) in Toff's story about his formative years as a choirboy. I glanced up to see some eye contact happening over my head. I was the only one still eating.

What, I said.

Take your time, sweetheart, said Uncle Thoby.

Before dinner I had been dispatched to my room to look for the corkscrew, which I had hidden in my bottom drawer. I was very fond of that corkscrew. I liked how it was part ballerina, part weapon.

Where is the goddamn corkscrew. Audrey!

Oui. I danced into the kitchen.

The corkscrew is not on the board.

Non.

Where is it.

Use Uncle Thoby's knife one.

Where's the proper one.

Am I allowed in my bedroom.

Of course.

So I clumped upstairs. I had not been in my own room for two days. Because now it was Toff's room. And boy was I in for a rude awakening. First of all, it smelled really bad. There was an ashtray (full) and a wood brush with beard hairs in it on my dresser. And the tree painted on my wall seemed to be withering. Poor tree, I whispered and touched a leaf. Then I said it again, loudly. Poor tree, I wailed.

Uncle Thoby poked his head in. What's going on.

My tree is dying.

It can't die. It's not a real tree.

Yes, but it is.

The tree was Uncle Thoby's creation. The branches were long and bent onto the adjacent walls and ceiling so that they seemed to embrace the bed that lay under it. On the branches were little brown Velcro buds. Since it was summer, each bud had a green felt leaf stuck to it. Come the fall, those leaves would be replaced by red and yellow leaves. We had a ceremony, Uncle Thoby and me, called the Changing of the Tree, which occurred on the equinoxes and solstices.

I unstuck a leaf from a branch and sniffed it. Smell, I said.

He made a face. It's not that bad.

Yes, but it is.

I know. But there's nothing we can do about it right now. Come on. Why are you in here.

For the corkscrew.

He was unsurprised. Well get it and come on.

· · ·

After dinner, Uncle Thoby and I went outside to untie the balloons. I stomped on the boards and said, Toff is trying to make my dad smoke.

Uncle Thoby sighed. No he's not.

He's trying to kill my dad. He's like the man in the book my dad is not reading after dinner because we have guests.

Say that again.

I stomped back and forth. Like the man from Russia who also had a beard that disappeared under the table. Rumples*toff*skin.

Rasputin.

I nodded. Rasputin had proved (so far) unkillable. He had not been killed by poison or by gun. Let's poison Toff's coffee, I said.

Let's not, he said. He was bent over the railing, untying a ribbon. You want to give me a hand, he said.

I put my hand on his arm.

Ha.

The balloons tugged at their ribbons and leaned out towards the pond.

I'm going to make a loop, I said. And I set off, boards bouncing. As I passed the dining-room window, I heard Grandmother say, What on earth.

When I got back to Uncle Thoby, he was waiting with his arms open. This was a thing we did. I did a loop and he was waiting. He lifted me up and sat me on the porch railing. What a workout, I said, wiping sweat from my brow. I leaned back. He held my ankles. I leaned back until I saw the pond upside down.

I have a question for you, he said.

I have a question for *you*.

Okay, let's hear yours.

I sat up. I looked around. Behind him the balloons were bobbing in the kitchen.

You don't really have a question, he said.

Yes I do. And here it is. Are you ready. Okay. My question is. Did you have a Happy Doozoo.

He smiled. I had a very Happy Doozoo.

I put my face close to his. I pushed his hair aside so I could look into his eyes and see if he was lying. He was. I gave him a hug. I wrapped my arms around him tight. He picked me up and we walked the full orbit of the porch together. What's the matter, he said in my ear. You've been acting very oddly.

I smooshed my face against his. I don't like having guests.

I was a guest once.

Not the same, I murmured. These ones are *très méchants*.

Très méchants.

They have mean eyebrows.

He didn't say anything. I asked him what his question was.

Oh yes. My question. Are you ready. Here it is. Did I see you drinking coffee earlier.

No.

I think I did. And I think that may be the source of some of the trouble. Are you tired.

No.

I think you really are.

No.

I think it's time for bed, he said.

You mean cot.

In cot, I compiled a list of grievances:

1. It bugged me the way Grandmother watched me eat. Even when someone else was talking, she was focused on my plate. I also didn't like the way she and Toff made eye contact against me like I was blind. Uncle Thoby explained later that they were agitated because they wanted to smoke, and it's rude to smoke at the table when someone is still eating. Well, even if I wanted to, which I didn't, I couldn't just speed up. I ate slow. My dad ate fast. And Uncle Thoby ate medium-fast. When my dad finished, he read out loud from the biography. He read until I was finished

eating. That was the rule. And just because he didn't read at the table when we had guests, that didn't mean I should throw a perfectly good habit out the window. Because what if I did. What if I did throw a perfectly good habit out the window and then got into the habit of eating fast. What would happen to our biography time. Dishes would come sooner. Bedtime would come sooner.

2. I did not like the way Toff talked on and on about Cambridge. It was ridiculous. He was always trying to get my dad to walk down memory lane. He needed to be interrupted more. That would be my job. I had already used the corkscrew to that purpose. Also I had asked him, How deep was that river you fell overboard into. Only up to my waist, he said. I laughed. Our pond has no bottom, I told him. Maybe you should go for a swim in it. Audrey, said my dad. But it was mean to Uncle Thoby, this memory-lane business, when Uncle Thoby had not gone to Cambridge, but had stayed in London to be a baggage handler and the black sheep of the family.

3. Grandmother didn't kiss Uncle Thoby at the airport.

4. Uncle Thoby wasn't included in any of the memory lanes.

5. I didn't like how exasperated Grandmother sounded when she talked about my dad's experiments. For instance, when he was little my dad used to rescue hurt insects and keep them alive, even if they only had three legs. There was a three-legged beetle he kept in a jar for years. You exaggerate, said my dad. Grandmother seemed equally exasperated (disgusted) by Wedge.

6. Wedge wasn't allowed on the table while they were visiting. Not even to light a light bulb.

7. When I asked Toff what his favourite game was, he said Spite and Malice. What's that, I asked. A card game. And then he showed me how you played. You had to stack the cards in their proper order, jack, queen, king, over and

over. It was incredibly dumb. Then I asked Grandmother what *her* favourite game was. Solitaire, she said. What's that. A card game. And she showed me how you played. You had to stack the cards in their proper order, jack, queen, king, over and over.

8. Jesus Christ doesn't anybody love Clue.

My dad opened the door and said, Still awake, old goat.

Goddamn it.

Etcetera.

And just when my eyes had adjusted and I was fully alert and ready to explain, or try to explain, all my grievances, he got into bed and turned off the light. I couldn't see his feet yet, but when I did, they'd better have socks on them or be under the covers.

My dad usually started out on top of the covers and ended up under them. He liked to say he didn't know how he got there. Well, guess what, that mystery was now solved because I'd *seen* him pull the covers over himself in the middle of the night. It wasn't like they magically moved.

I'm blind, I said.

Give them a moment, he said. Meaning my pupils.

I turned over. My cot squeaked.

Tell me the story of the two men and the lion.

Why. Have you had a bad dream.

Yes.

And you're just mentioning it now.

I just remembered it, when I got back into the same position on my cot.

Audrey, I'm really tired.

Oh, I said.

Oh what.

I'm not.

On nights when I'd had a bad dream, I was allowed to wake

up my dad and relate—very briefly, sans embellishment—my nightmare montage, and then my dad would tell me the story of the two men and the lion.

Can't I tell you about my dream.

Was it about a plane.

No. Guests.

I can't guess.

No. *Guests.*

Go to sleep.

My eyes had adjusted. I could just make out his foot. I poked it lightly. It had a sock on it. I poked it again.

Stop.

I had wanted to play Clue since Toff and Grandmother arrived and finally the next night I was granted my wish. We gathered around the table. I would be playing Miss Scarlet. I made that clear from the get-go. And my dad would be Professor Plum and Uncle Thoby would be Mr. Green. All *comme d'habitude.* But now we had two more characters in the mix. Mrs. Peacock and Colonel Mustard. So all the Clue characters were accounted for. Except Mrs. White.

The plot thickens, I said, nodding.

What plot, said Toff.

You look like your character, I said. It was true. He was mustard-coloured, especially the fingers that held the cigarette.

Aren't you going to sit down, said Grandmother.

No. I play standing up.

Since when, said my dad.

Since today.

Someone has had C-O-F-F, Uncle Thoby began.

That's rude, I said, pointing at him.

Pointing is rude, he said.

I unfolded the board. I remarked on how much it resembled Grandmother's house, only rolling-pinned flat. Silence while they pondered this.

Not really, said Toff.

Yes it does, I said. But actually, when I tried to remember Grandmother's house, all I saw was the Clue board.

The Candlestick game piece was missing, so we replaced it with the Corkscrew. My suggestion.

I like to carry the Revolver on my person, I warned Toff and Grandmother.

Okay, said Toff.

And so we commenced.

Toff and Grandmother used the words *accuse* and *suspect* interchangeably, which was a bit confusing.

I paced back and forth with my cards in one hand and the Revolver in the other. I said, Very interesting, even when it wasn't. After my turn I sometimes left the room on business.

Audrey, get back here. I thought you wanted to play.

I do.

Come back or it's game over.

I clumped back. It was four turns until mine. I went into orbit around the table.

She's looking at my cards, said Mrs. Peacock.

I pointed at my chest. *Moi*.

Then I stood behind Toff and pointed the gun at his head for a long time without him noticing.

Uncle Thoby pulled out my chair. Sit, he said. Now.

So I sat. For a while.

Toff said why didn't they make a Clue board with an upstairs. Bedrooms. A bathroom with a hot tub.

An adult version, said my dad. With a whole new set of weapons.

Long silence.

Walter, really, said Uncle Thoby.

Something that infuriated my dad: How I hardly ever rolled the dice. There was no need. Once you got to a corner room, you could leap across the board to the opposite corner without rolling. So my strategy was to just keep leaping back and forth.

Have you ever been to the Billiard Room, Toff asked.

Nope.

So you just keep jumping back and forth between the Conservatory and the Lounge.

Yup.

How do you figure out the room.

I have my ways.

Are they above board.

Bien sûr.

Grandmother now suspected Mr. Green with the Candlestick in the Kitchen.

You mean Corkscrew!

Sorry, Corkscrew.

The Corkscrew was too big. It didn't fit in any of the rooms.

It is pure laziness not to roll the dice and walk to a bloody room, said my dad, studying his cards. Can't help you, he said to Grandmother.

Well then, she said. I'm going to accuse.

Wait wait wait, I said. Are you really going to accuse. Or just suspect.

I'm going to accuse, she said. I accuse Mr. Green with the Corkscrew in the Kitchen.

I pointed the gun at her. Wrong, I said.

Grandmother reached for the envelope that contained the answer.

Stop! You have to wait till the next round.

Someone isn't acting her age, Grandmother said.

Who, I said, looking around the table.

Mum, said my dad.

Walter, I just think—

I'm only one year old, I said.

You are not one, she said.

I've had one birthday, I said, holding up a finger. Put that in your pipe and smoke it.

Well, said Uncle Thoby, standing up. I think it's time for cot.

She means one leap birthday, my dad said.

I know what she means, Grandmother said. You're *seven*, Audrey.

I did not like the way she leaned on the word *seven*.

Uncle Thoby took the Revolver out of my hands. Upstairs, he said. Nightie. Now.

The next morning I came downstairs and the coffee was not made. I could not smell coffee. My dad was unloading the new fly bowl from the dishwasher. This should not have been put in the dishwasher, he said. And his eyebrows were like Bert's.

I pointed at the coffee maker. Where's Ernie.

Audrey. Come back here a moment.

I was halfway down the basement steps. I looked up. He's not down there, my dad said.

Why.

Come here.

Slowly I climbed the steps. Uncle Thoby always made the coffee. He was always the first one up.

My dad explained that Uncle Thoby had checked into a hotel. Temporarily. This would solve the problem of rooms. I could now move back into mine. And Toff would move downstairs into Uncle Thoby's. As he said this, he was trying to separate a coffee filter from the stack. Fuck, he said, and put the stack down. He pointed at it. Could you, he said.

Was this my fault. Because I'd pointed a gun at Toff and Grandmother. Because I wasn't acting my age, whatever that meant.

This was my worst fear. That I would wake up one morning and Uncle Thoby would be gone and we would be unable to separate the coffee filters. Life would unravel. It was like *A Christmas Carol*, but the reverse. Imagine Scrooge wakes up and is not happy but devastated because he fell in love with one of the ghosts. And now he hates the real people around him even more because they're all bastards. Except his dad.

My dad was pretending to be cool, but he would not normally say fuck over filters. Now you'll have your room back, he said again.

But this was not how I wanted my room back. So that Toff could move into Uncle Thoby's new basement apartment and stink up the green walls.

Upstairs a toilet flushed. Fuck, I said and glanced at my dad.

Okay, he said. Meaning, enough.

But it didn't make sense. If this was about sleeping arrangements, why had Uncle Thoby left in the middle of the night after I was in bed, sorry cot. What was the hurry.

Well, here is maybe a clue. The Grandmother-Toff reaction to the news that Uncle Thoby would not be joining us for breakfast this morning or any morning because he had checked into the Civil Manor: They lifted their eyebrows. For two seconds. Then put them back down again.

Wow. Don't look so sad, I said.

Which was the straw that broke my dad's back. Go to your room, he said.

I don't have a room, I said and sipped coffee filtered through five filters.

Audrey, so help me.

Toff got up and said he would move his stuff downstairs. And okay, maybe he did look a little bit sad as he stroked his beard and left the room.

The Civil Manor was in the *environs*, I was told. And I was allowed to visit Uncle Thoby any time. Yes, okay, right now. I could even take the helium balloons to cheer him up.

So he needs cheering up!

I didn't say that.

Yes you did.

Get the balloons and come on.

What are *environs* and is Uncle Thoby happy to be in them. Jesus Christ. I want to bring Wedge in his ball.

No.

Please.

Put your raincoat on.

Apparently Wedge and the helium balloons qualified as a heavy car-go load because we took the car. The balloons bobbed in the back seat. No more smoke, they bobbed. No more smoke. Wedge looked groggy. He had been conducting his mammalian business all night and now we were waking him up for diurnal exercise. He pressed his hands against the plastic. What is going on.

I pointed at some beard hairs caught in the seatbelt. Ugh, I said.

You know what, Audrey. I don't want to talk about Toff's beard or Grandmother's eyebrows.

You noticed her eyebrows!

No you did.

No *you* did.

My dad would not be playing the no-you-did game today.

In any case, he said after a little while. Let's try to be civil.

Ha. I get it. I get your joke.

The Civil Manor was around the corner on Blackbog Drive. Why had I never noticed it before. Probably because it was across the street from the Piety factory, and whenever we passed the Piety factory, I had eyes only for it.

Actually the Civil Manor looked a lot like the Piety factory turned on its end. The factory was a rectangle lying down. The Civil Manor was a rectangle standing up. Both were white and rusty around the eyes.

Of course there were some key differences:

The Piety factory had five little chimneys puffing pie smell into the air. This smell was delicious, and if the wind was blowing the right way, you could smell it on Wednesday Place. The Civil Manor did not have any chimneys. The Piety factory had five pink letters on the roof that spelled PIETY. The Civil Manor had a small sign with a butler on it. The butler was holding a tray and on that tray was the word VACANCY.

As I got out of the car, I had the feeling that the Piety factory and the Civil Manor were in love. But they had this busy road between them.

My dad carried the balloons. I carried Wedge. There was no one at the front desk. The lobby was small and damp. Hi Doreen, my dad said. Who. I stood on tiptoes. Behind the desk, through a door, a woman was watching soaps. I knew it was soaps by the music. Go on up, she said. She looked pretty cosy in her wing-back chair.

Who the hell is Doreen.

Ssh. She is.

That made me nervous. How did my dad know someone I didn't.

Also behind the desk was a board with hooks. All the hooks had a key except one. Room 203. That was Uncle Thoby's room. So he was the only guest at the Civil Manor. That was a bit heartbreaking. Although Doreen seemed to be holding up pretty well.

My dad said he wouldn't be staying. He was just going to show me to Uncle Thoby's room and then go back to our guests, so they wouldn't feel bereft. Bereft, I said. Lonely, he said. I don't think they'll feel lonely, I said.

Why not.

No comment. Which is what you say if you have a secret, which I didn't, but no harm practising for when I did.

We were walking down a hallway with orange carpet and a part in the middle. Follow the part. We arrived at 203. Go ahead and knock, my dad said.

No, you. I clutched Wedge's ball to my chest. My dad knocked. This was my first real hotel. It seemed impossible that Uncle Thoby, *our* Uncle Thoby, could be behind that door. Sure the Civil Manor was close to home, but it was another universe. I mean, Doreen. Who was she. Just someone in a wingback chair. And all of a sudden she mattered.

No answer.

I began to feel braver. I gave the door a kick.

There you go, said my dad.

And the door opened. And it really was Uncle Thoby. And I forgot to feel nervous because it was him and he was wearing his bright yellow sweater with red diamonds. He did a little jig of happiness at the sight of me and Wedge and the balloons. What is this, a party, he said.

I half joined in the jig, but really I was looking around the room. Holy smallness, I said. Small in a good way, I added.

Someone is distressed, I heard my dad say as I investigated.

Room 203 had a table with two chairs under the window. We sat down. I put my feet on Uncle Thoby's lap to make a bridge. Then I heard the car start. I jumped up and waved goodbye to my dad. Then I sat back down. Remade the bridge.

Someone is hyper, Uncle Thoby said.

Someone is distressed, I said.

Uncle Thoby crossed his hands behind his head.

I did the same.

Okay, Miss Sarcastic.

Wedge rolled by in his ball on his way to the bathroom. He likes it here, I said.

Seems to.

Do you.

Sure.

There was a loud pop. A balloon hit the floor. I looked up.

The ceiling is *sharp*, I yelled.

Stucco, said Uncle Thoby. Shit. He got up and tied the other balloons to the doorknob.

So I was not very fond of the ceiling in room 203, but the rest of it was not bad. I liked how small and neat and portable it was. Well, not really portable. But it reminded me of the dream I'd had of a portable room. The portable room could be attached to a train or a truck. Everyone had a portable room they could attach. You could take your portable room anywhere. It had a bed, a bathroom, and blue carpet. That was all.

When I'd told Uncle Thoby about my portable-room montage, he'd said, That's called a camper, Oddly.

No. It was not a camper. Jeeze. I know what a camper is. This was a *portable room*.

We decided to murder one balloon, a white one. This was something we did, secretly. We punctured a balloon and sucked the helium. We'd been doing it since the day we rescued six balloons from a wedding party outside a church. All the guests were holding pink balloons and when the married couple appeared in the doorway, they let their balloons go. Uncle Thoby and I were walking by and we couldn't believe our eyes. Free helium balloons! Uncle Thoby leapt like a ballerina in the air to catch as many as possible. The bride and groom looked puzzled, like, who invited the long-armed man.

We brought the balloons home and Uncle Thoby showed me what helium will do to a voice. How it will turn a voice into Wedge. Or how I always imagined Wedge would sound.

We didn't tell my dad because he would not approve of using a scientific thing like helium to make a scientific animal like Wedge talk.

Now, as Wedge came rolling out of the bathroom, Uncle Thoby squeaked, Bathtub needs regrouting.

I giggled.

Wedge looked so cute when he came rolling towards you with his hands in the air talking about regrouting. Come to think of it, his plastic ball was a portable room. I wished I had a plastic ball to roll around in. You could hit walls and not be hurt. The only thing that could hurt you were stairs.

Uncle Thoby passed me the balloon, and I asked him, in Wedge's voice, why he had come to stay at the Civil Manor.

Somebody has to, he squeaked.

Why, I squeaked back. There's room at home.

No. I mean, poor Doreen. Somebody has to.

For some reason hearing Wedge say Poor Doreen killed me. I mean, who was Doreen. And now she was practically family.

I have some more questions for you.

Shoot.

I took a breath from the balloon. What's Doreen like.

I have no earthly idea.

Okay, here is my real question. Are you ready. Is it because of *me* that you left number 3 Wednesday Place. Or is it because of *Toff* and *Grandmother*. Say Toff and Grandmother.

Uncle Thoby got serious. It's not because of anybody.

I think it really is.

No, sweetheart. His Wedge voice was petering out. Which was a very sad sound.

More balloon, I offered.

Thanks.

Is it because Grandmother and Toff were *très méchants* to you.

They weren't mean to me.

I nodded to myself.

What does that nod mean.

It means they were mean to you.

Some rain hit the window. Splat. It felt sent by Toff and Grandmother.

They're worried, Uncle Thoby said after a moment.

Worried about what.

They think I'm living off your dad.

Living off.

Because I don't have a job.

So. Neither do I. Neither does Doreen.

He smiled.

Living off, I said. What crap. Why can't Toff stay in the Civil Manor. The ceiling matches his beard.

We both looked up. All the little mountains on the ceiling had brown peaks.

Because Toff is a guest, he sighed.

Guests stay in hotels. That's what hotels are *for*.

Oddly.

He's a goddamn pollutant.

Uncle Thoby lifted his eyebrows even higher than usual.

Okay. Moving right along. I know you're in the *environs*. But *environs*. What does that really mean.

It means nearby. Or thereabouts.

I know what it means.

Uncle Thoby's voice was all grown-up again. He asked me if I remembered how, when he moved from the guest room into the basement, I'd complained that the basement was too far away. And what had he said. He had said to think about how all the heat vents in the house were connected like secret passages. How my room was connected to his room. And his room was connected to my dad's room. And my dad's room was connected to mine. Remember that idea, he said.

I nodded. I loved that idea. It was one of the best ideas in my head.

Okay then. Well, the secret passages still hold. Even when I'm in the basement. Even when I'm in the Civil Manor.

He drew a triangle on the table with his finger. Between the room you're in and the room I'm in and the room your dad's in. Secret passages.

Splat went the rain.

They want you to go back to England with them, don't they.

He leaned back in his chair. They would probably not say no to my going back to England with them.

Hatred welled up. Those bastards.

I would say no, I told him. I am saying no.

He walked me home in time for supper. He'd devised a little carrier for Wedge's ball. You take a towel and put Wedge at the centre and then tie the four corners of the towel together. Ta-da. A breathable bag.

It was still raining. Uncle Thoby was wearing his green raincoat that matched the lichens on the rocks. He called it his Chlorophyll Coat. Uncle Thoby loved green. He had painted the basement the colour of iceberg lettuce with a sunset behind it. One night he had been standing at the kitchen sink and he'd held up a piece of lettuce and said, That's the colour I'm going to paint the walls.

Now Toff was turning those walls brown.

Come away from the edge, Oddly.

We were on the Wednesday Pond path, approaching the house.

The whole way home I had tried to rally him, to get him to say one mean thing about Toff and Grandmother. But he wouldn't. All he would say was that they were worried. And that was not a mean thing to say. That was a nice thing.

But I couldn't picture Grandmother and Toff being worried any more than I could picture them being lonely. Worried people have *accent-circonflexe* eyebrows. No, they were scheming. They were plotting to take over the house and then kidnap Uncle Thoby, and who knows, maybe my dad too, back to England. And who would be left behind. Me. The Canadian.

Mr. Green.

Yes.

Are you coming for dinner.

No. But I will be in the *environs.*

I went up the porch steps and waved goodbye. He had his hood up. I watched him go down the path. Wedge shifted inside his breathable bag. I leaned against the house and counted to sixty. Then I went back to the path.

I followed him. He was not going back to the Civil Manor because he walked past Blackbog Drive. Instead he went down Manche Street. Oh. He was going to Bebe's on Manche Street.

I hid behind a parked car. Then I approached with much stealth and looked through the window. Bebe's had a fireplace. The fire burned in the stomach of my reflection and reminded me of that antacid commercial. I looped Wedge's bag over my elbow and made blinkers around my eyes and saw the pool table. Clint was bending under the cone of light, lining up a shot. Uncle Thoby came in and pushed back his hood. Clint straightened and said something. He was smiling, but then he saw Uncle Thoby's face and he stopped smiling. He called out to someone and pointed at Uncle Thoby.

I moved away from the window.

There was a Clint's cab parked on the street.

Room 205 was like room 203, only with fresh vacuum tracks in the carpet. I opened the window. The rain had stopped. The bridal veil curtains billowed. Across the street, the E in PIETY was flickering.

I turned on the TV and tried to find the channel Doreen had been watching downstairs, but there were only two channels and no dinosaurs on either. Doreen had more channels down there.

It had been so easy. I'd walked in. I'd pushed off my hood. I'd said, Hi Doreen. Doreen had leaned forward in her wingback chair. Oh hi, hon. And then she'd leaned back again. I thought about how a wingback chair is like a little room with one wall missing. On the TV someone said: The dinosaurs learned to fly by falling slower and slower out of the trees.

Which struck me, even in my heightened state of nervousness, as something remarkable and important. File that away. I did not dawdle. I went behind the desk, reached up on tiptoes, and grabbed the key to room 205. Simple as pie.

It is really not hard to become a guest at the Civil Manor.

Did I have a plan. Sort of. My plan was to wait for Uncle Thoby to return from Bebe's, whereupon I would:

a) spring out into the hallway as he was opening his door and say, Aha!, or

b) wait until he was settled and then say his name into the heat vent, or

c) just sleep next door to him and be on his side.

In the meantime I was a guest and should behave like one. I hung up my coat and took off my sneakers. I let Wedge out of the bag. I bounced on the bed. I unwrapped the soap in the bathroom and tasted a bit. I went to the window and sniffed. The smell of pies was over for the day.

Wedge rolled by.

Wow, this room is familiar.

That's because it's just like the one next door.

Oh.

I looked around. I had never been by myself before, really by myself, with no one knowing where I was. It was exciting. But also a bit scary. I reminded myself I was totipotent. Totipotent is what my dad called me when I got a bad grade in school. It means: Potentially anything within a repertoire.

Repertoire.

Well. For instance. You can't be a mermaid. That is outside the repertoire.

Apparently a guest at the Civil Manor was not outside the repertoire.

For a while I stood at the window and waited. I thought he would arrive any moment. It was dark now, except for the PIETY sign. You have not seen pink until you've seen the PIETY sign. I think Piety invented that pink. And when the sky behind the sign is dark, and when there are three stars overhead, you will feel very hungry for something. Probably pie.

Hungry, Wedge.

Wedge was in full nocturnal business mode. He had rolled under the bed. I crouched down and gave him a nudge. He rolled out. He had peed and pooped in his ball so I took him into the bathroom and let him run around the bathtub (needs regrouting) while I washed the ball.

All clean.

I bounced on the bed some more, something I was not allowed to do at home. I bounced but kept an eye on the window. I imagined Uncle Thoby coming up the drive and seeing my head bouncing up and down in the window. That was a fun picture to keep in my head.

I held on to that picture when I started to feel afraid. The stucco ceiling was ugly. Uncle Thoby had said that stucco was for soundproofing. Sounds got stuck up there in the stucco mountains.

Stucco mountains, I said out loud. Yucco mountains.

And I remembered what the voice on Doreen's TV had said about flying. How you flew by *falling* slower and slower, not by *taking off*.

Was flying within my repertoire then.

And so I stood on the end of the bed in room 205 and practised falling backwards slowly. I did this over and over, slower and slower, until one time I stayed fallen. I hadn't had any coffee in twelve hours.

We are meeting Toff for lunch at his hotel. Where's he staying, I ask Uncle Thoby, lacing up my boots. Not the Civil Manor, I bet.

The Fairfont.

He would be.

I check the mailbox and there's a recall notice. Christmatech. This guy called, I tell Uncle Thoby. This guy fondly recalling his Christmas lights.

He nods. I think he's called before.

It is 12:35 and there is no colour except Uncle Thoby's gloves. His face is the colour of snow. He gets in the passenger side. Closes the door.

Don't worry about scraping, I yell.

I grab the scraper from the trunk and clear the sleep from the LeBaron's square eyes. Always clear the eyes first. Cars don't have square eyes anymore, do they. No. They have wraparound eyes like embryos. And daytime running lights. But I don't mind turning on your lights myself. I don't mind one bit. I scrape its forehead.

Sorry I didn't scrape, Uncle Thoby says when I get in. I didn't think. I'm not thinking.

I don't mind.

To scrape is the job of the long-armed man, he half sings. Which is the first line of a song I made up when I was small and scraping meant climbing onto the hood.

He looks tired and it's my fault. Because last night I was test-ing one of the fire alarms at the table, and it went off for a rather

prolonged period, prompting him to come bolting up from the
basement while I frantically dislodged the battery.

Just as I thought, I said, showing him the nine-volt. Faulty.

What are you doing. It's three in the morning.

Sorry. But this fire alarm was blinking.

It always blinks.

It does.

Yes. It's when it chirps that you have to worry.

Oh.

Oddly. He sat down across from me. His pirate patch of hair
was standing straight up.

Can I borrow this, I asked.

What. The fire alarm.

I mean, there are three others on this floor.

Why—

I leaned over and patted down his hair. That's better. I set the
nine-volt upright on the table. The king of batteries. You know
what I heard on the news, I said. I mean really on the news. Not
a montage.

What. He wiped his eyes.

Quadruple-A batteries. They're making quadruple-As now.
Smaller than triples. They're like this big. And I marked off a tiny
space between my thumb and forefinger. Pretty cute.

If you needed company, all you had to do was say my name
into the heat vent.

They last forever. Longer than lithium.

Don't you want to sleep in your old bed.

I thought about my room with the horses on the bedspread,
the bare tree on my wall, the Charlie Brown pillows. This table
is my new headquarters, I said, giving it a pat.

Yes, he said. But why.

I shrugged. Because the rest of the house hurts.

He nodded. Okay, he said. I know.

•   •   •

Behind the wheel, I am brave. The roads are white tunnels. I sing "The Ballad of the Long-Armed Man."

> To scrape is the job of the long-armed man,
> 'Cause he can reach farther than me.
> He puts the leaves on the highest branches
> When we do the Changing of the Tree!

> To change the battery in the fire alarm
> Is also the job of the long-armed bloke.
> He doesn't need a chair or a ladder to get up there,
> He just needs his arm and a fresh nine-volt!

One thing I love is how the fire hydrants have their own little alcoves carved out of the snow. They look so cute, sitting there waiting for something bad to happen. I love how good we are at thinking ahead and preventing bad happenings. I love that about us.

What else. I love that NEIGHBOURHOOD WATCH sign with the yellow duct tape over the word WATCH and the word TRUST written on top. This seems to me a wonderful thing.

According to the Young Drivers manual: Sometimes you will see a wonderful thing by the side of the road, and you will find yourself drawn towards that wonderful thing, and you will inadvertently turn the wheel in its direction—

Um, says Uncle Thoby.

Sorry. I adjust the wheel. Ambient Vehicle Distraction.

There's really nothing ambient but snow, he says.

Well, but the few things that *aren't* snow are very distracting. Don't worry. I'm in my element.

The only other cars on the road are Clint's cabs. Every time we pass one, I give a little staccato honk. None of the cabbies is the real Clint.

Uncle Thoby's legs are jiggling. Not shaking. A shake has a higher frequency than a jiggle and is harder to stop. So the jiggle is, I guess, an improvement over the last time we were in the car together. It occurs to me that he is dreading this meeting with Toff even more than I am. Or possibly he is just reacting to our near collision with the NEIGHBOURHOOD TRUST sign.

Toff is not the enemy, he says after a while. Okay.

I nod.

He looks at me closely. What does that nod mean.

It means Toff is the enemy.

Oddly.

Enemy Number One. Toff is.

The left windshield wiper is stuck in a chunk of ice. I roll down my window to free it. The wiper feels thin as an insect's leg.

If Toff does anything or says anything, you just give me the word and I'll take him out.

Uncle Thoby looks alarmed. You'll take him out where.

To the curb.

What does that mean.

I don't know. But picture it. It's a good picture.

The wonky wiper continues to need my help. We stop at a red light. I get out. Free the wiper. There you go. Get back in. I feel tender towards the wiper. I feel tender towards everything that is not Toff. That is how you feel when you have an enemy. It is a good feeling.

Last night after supper I looked out the window and realized that no one on Wednesday Place had their Christmas lights up. Uncle Thoby said he'd noticed that too. I said, They had lights up before, didn't they. He said, I don't remember but I think so. Maybe they had all been recalled. By the Christmatech guy.

But that wasn't it. The reason there were no Christmas lights on Wednesday Place was because my dad was, sorry is, dead. And because of how he died. And I love our neighbours for that. I love them and I enlist them in my army against Toff, my dad's executioner.

· · ·

Uncle Thoby likes to say fear is the mark of insufficient curiosity. Maybe. But fear is also the mark of insufficient people to protect.

We come to a slippery slope. Don't brake. Palpitate. At the bottom, the road is blocked by a sideways police car. A power line is down and the police car is protecting the fallen line, its lights flashing. That gives me a warm feeling. Let's park here, I say. It's not far.

And so we park and trudge. As we pass the police car, I stop to ask the cops, do they have coffee in there, is there anything they need, because I'd be more than happy.

Uncle Thoby looks at his watch.

Thanks my darlin. We're good.

Yes you are.

We carry on to the hotel. The roads are deep. I say, Did you see that screen on the dashboard. They were playing a video game.

That was a map of St. John's, says Uncle Thoby.

It was not. Was it.

The Fairfont Hotel greets you with signage so cursive you curse your inability to read it. There is a *valet*, or a *waltz*, on the premises. There is a hair salon called *Hair to Stay* or *Heir to Shag.* Everything is slanted and gold.

Uncle Thoby and I sit in the lobby, sorry atrium. It is jungly. There are terraces. Water meanders through. Upstairs there's a waterfall like hair in a shampoo commercial. Underwater lights. A grand piano on a lower terrace.

Also there's a twenty-foot Christmas tree with maroon decorations.

I knock my boots together and shed a little snow. That tree cannot be real, I remark.

It can if it's imported.

Would they do that.

Uncle Thoby shrugs and blows his nose. He's wearing a black suit and he's unshaven. He looks like a chauffeur. Or like someone whose brother just died. His coat lies across the arm of his chair. Orange gloves stick like roosters' combs out of the pockets.

He retains the aura of outdoorsedness. What is this aura. Say you were faced with a lineup of people, and one had just come in from outside and the others had all been standing around in that room for an hour, could you pick out the one who'd just arrived. Yes. But how. Is it just rosiness. Moistness in the eyes. Blowy hair. Or is there some other quality. And how long before that quality vanishes. At what point will Uncle Thoby look acclimatized. I touch my own cheek, which is still cold. How long before we look like we belong in the Fairfont.

Toff said one o'clock. It is three minutes to. I feel dread. Which is a form of fear. Which is a mark of insufficient curiosity or people to protect.

Which direction will he come from. The tree. From behind the tasteful tree. There is a point where tasteful (i.e., maroon) becomes distasteful. What is that point. The tree has passed it.

I scan the jungle for someone to feel curious about. No one. No one. No one. I look up at the waterfall. Hey, did I just see a goldfish jump over the waterfall!

I jump up. I have an important phone call to make.

Oddly, don't run away.

Save my seat.

One terrace up I find the pay phones. I rummage through my pockets. All I have is the toonie from short-term parking. Will that be enough. No. But hey, right here is the fountain. And look at all the coins. Thousands of them. Not just pennies either. Quarters. A loonie, even. People have expensive wishes at the Fairfont. I push up my sleeve and reach in. The water is warm. Probably from all the underwater lights. Winnie would love this fountain. Hang on, Win.

I do not see any goldfish. Did I imagine the goldfish. I grab the loonie. Someone with a cursive Fairfont badge walks by and curses at me.

This is an emergency, I say.

Back at the phones I plug in all the money and dial Linda's number. Two rings. Three rings.

To my right is a bar called the Sans Serif and inside I can see two Air Canada pilots in full uniform. They are sitting at a low table and drinking from tall glasses.

Four rings.

They are laughing. One punches the other in the epaulette.

Linda's machine picks up.

Hi Linda. Guess you're at work. I just thought of something. Protein. Winnifred needs some fishy protein in her diet. Every so often. Kelp. Did I give you that mixture. I did, right. Just wanted to remind you.

A computer voice cuts in and says, Please insert two dollars and seventy-five cents.

What.

You have ten seconds remaining.

Ten seconds. A tortoise cannot live by lettuce alone! I blurt. But no tuna. Kelp—

Dial tone.

I stand there with the phone to my ear for a while. When one of the pilots looks in my direction, I wave, but he doesn't see me.

On the lower terrace wolfish Toff is in my chair. His beard is shorter and spade-shaped. And he's wearing a purple scarf. Sorry, cravat. Some silk business tucked into his shirt. Uncle Thoby is nodding. There's a briefcase beside my chair.

My dad used to have an expression for a flamboyant dresser: Christmas on a stick. I'm sorry but a purple cravat is flamboyant. It is Christmas on a stick. Especially when your "best chum" has just died.

I take a few steps down to their level.

Toff unfolds himself. Oh, he says. My goodness. Hugs me. Steps on my foot. I'm so sorry.

S'okay. Steel-toed boots.

About your father. He continues to stare at me and says, You've grown up.

Yes and no.

Uncle Thoby pretends to have a crick in his neck that requires him to roll his head around so he doesn't have to look at us. Really this moment is too awkward. Toff's hands are still on my shoulders. Like he's taking a mental photograph. So I put my own hands on his shoulders. Pat, pat. They are high and ridgy, Toff's shoulders.

His pale eyes blink in time with my patting. This is sort of fun. But then, it is disconcerting to see tears in the eyes of a wolf. Is he to be feared or pitied. I don't know. Stop looking at him. Back away.

The restaurant is not the kind you bring a briefcase to. It is champagne-coloured and crowded and festive. There's a harpist. We proceed like a small chain gang to our table. The harpist is in the corner behind Toff. She doesn't so much pluck the strings as blur them. It's fascinating.

How does Toff like having a harpy right behind him like that.

You mean harpist.

That's what I said.

The harpist plays "What Child Is This," which at any other time of year would be called "Greensleeves."

Uncle Thoby asks Toff about his room—is it satisfactory— and Toff says, yes, it's very nautical. It has a porthole and a balcony and a picture over the bed of some men in a boat capsizing.

Lovely, says Uncle Thoby, studying the wine menu.

I pick up my bread knife, the handle of which is a Victorian figurine wearing skates. She can be moved along the edge of the tablecloth, like so, so that she appears to be skating around a pond.

The waitress arrives and smiles down at me. You're not the first one to do that, she says.

I put the knife down.

What can I get you to drink.

Uncle Thoby orders a bottle of the house wine. Toff looks briefly discomposed, touches his cravat, then says, Okay.

Coffee for me please.

I have missed the moment when Uncle Thoby's face acclimatized to the Fairfont. It must have happened when I was on the phone. It probably happened the moment he saw Toff. His face went pale and lost its memory of outside. I put my hand to my cheek. Room temperature.

What a pointy beard he's got.

Sitting down like this, cut off at the chest, Toff looks like the jack of spades. Especially when he turns his head in profile to better hear the harpy. Who is now playing "Away in a Manger," the version I hate. I wish she would stop pretending this is heaven.

Toff decides to take a walk down memory lane with me. And because our shared memory lane is short, more a parking space than a lane, he naturally alights on my legendary decampment, the night I ran away and checked into the Civil Manor. All by myself. Only yay high.

Yes, just a wee two of clubs I was then. But now, Toff. Behold a queen. Well, if not a queen, at least a full-fledged joker.

He becomes really quite grotesquely animated as he describes the torture I put them all through, the phone calls, the search party.

I glance at Uncle Thoby whose eyes are getting pointy and sad with the memory. Right. I'll be nipping this in the bud. Let's not do the memory-lane thing now, Toff.

Which pulls him up short. He glances at Uncle Thoby, then nods and studies his menu.

I ask how Grandmother is. He says not good. She knows about the comma being over, then. Yes. He called her this morning.

Should we have done that, I ask Uncle Thoby.

Uncle Thoby's neck seems to be bothering him again.

She was prepared, Toff says.

Was she. That's interesting. You prepared her.

She knew about your father's condition, yes.

It was hardly a condition. I mean, we all have a medulla oblongata that could be whacked.

Awkward silence filled by the harpy. Okay, moving right along. So you are here on Grandmother's behalf.

I wouldn't say that.

But you're her lawyer.

I'm here as your father's friend and executor.

Interesting. So you knew when you left England that my dad would need executing.

Oddly, says Uncle Thoby. What are you doing. I explained all this.

Did you. I don't remember. Let's hear Toff's version.

Toff reaches for the briefcase and explains that several years ago my father asked him, or rather his firm, to draw up a will.

Which makes me laugh. A small, all-by-myself laugh.

What, he says.

Come on. I nudge Uncle Thoby. My dad would never. *Never.*

Apparently he did, Oddly.

Toff's soup arrives. And there is my dad's supposed will on the table next to it—I think it's a bisque. Meanwhile Toff is talking. I watch him turn pages with one spade-shaped hand and levy a spoon with the other. Stocks. Bonds. I'm barely listening. My dad would never. I look at Uncle Thoby. I try to make eye contact with him against Toff. This is what I need more than anything right now. Only common-enemy eye contact will empower us. Let's acknowledge, together, that Toff is Satan and he is here brandishing a contract and therefore we should beware.

But Uncle Thoby just sits there, listening politely.

May I.

I reach for the will.

Toff drops his spoon.

I hold the will out of reach and scan one paragraph:

d) to transfer and deliver to my daughter, Audrey Flowers,
   if she is living on the tenth day following my death—

If she is living!

That is a standard clause, says Toff.

That's just it, see. My dad would not have approved of that standard clause. His whole life was about *not* approving a clause such as that.

Toff looks at Uncle Thoby. There are a few things we need to iron out, Toff says.

Uncle Thoby shakes his head. Not now. Then he says, Give the will back, Oddly.

I continue reading. My dad would *never*. Then I stop. The harpist is playing "O Tannenbaum." Like the branches of a Christmas tree will ever delight me again.

I push back my chair.

Uh-oh, says Uncle Thoby.

Chuck sometimes takes me to the window and says, Doesn't the Willamette look inviting. I don't know what that means. Maybe he is trying to rename me. Tenants do this. If not right away, eventually. They get to know me and decide my name is wrong. Outside the rain pours down.

He is picking me up now.

Do I look like a Willamette and not a Winnifred to him. Maybe. Up close his cheeks are painfully razor-burnt. He shaved this morning because last night Linda said he looked like a common thug. He made a joke about growing a bard, and she said, Well, don't come near me with your half-grown bard. So this morning he shaved it off, and while he was shaving I heard him rehearse in the mirror something about the loss of a dukedom.

We stand at the window together. He's got me in one hand, *Lowering the Bard* in the other. He looks down at the book, then closes his eyes and says something about breaking his staff and drowning his book. I take it I am the staff in this scenario.

He fumbles his words. His shoulders sag. I drop to hip level.

Going out for a smoke, he says.

He leaves me on the coffee table holding open the *Bard*. This is what I've been reduced to. A bookmark. Shakespeare's bookmark.

Chuck is not allowed to smoke in the apartment. Although last night, as he was grabbing his cigarettes, he paused to look at me with my head stuck out my castle window and asked Linda why he couldn't just be like the bloody tortoise and stick his own head out the window to smoke.

Since when do I smoke, I wondered.

Linda said, Let's not frighten the neighbours.

Anyway, Chuck puts on his long coat over his boxer shorts and goes out for a smoke while I play bookmark. And then the phone rings.

The phone rings and there is no one to answer it. I count the rings. Four. And then the machine picks up and it's her.

I lift my head.

It's her and she leaves a message and I can actually hear her voice because Linda and Chuck do not have secret voice mail that stays in the phone but real voice mail that broadcasts openly to the room at large. Which room I happen to be in.

Hi Linda. Guess you're at work.

It's really her. She says my name. She says something fishy. Then she says the word *kelp*. Something fishy happens to her voice when she says *kelp*. It starts to break up.

Then: A tortoise cannot live by lettuce alone!

You're telling me. Come back.

Kelp. And then nothing.

The bard's words blur beneath my feet.

She sounded the same but different. Was the difference because I am getting so used to Chuck's Shakespearean that he is becoming the current tenant. Oh perish the thought. Oh woe is me.

Methinks I need a plan. I need a plan to get to Canada. I could walk. I have crossed the country on foot before. Part of it anyway. I could do it again. Or I could find a dashboard travelling east.

I look at the door.

After she had climbed the walls for a while, we started taking impromptu "vacations," which involved setting out for places where you might expect to see cliffs. And therefore Cliff. We covered Oregon first. We went to the desert. Amazing that Oregon has one. We stopped in a town called Bend and stayed at a motel called the Swerve Right Inn. The Swerve was being renovated and she got a reduced rate in exchange for helping out with some bathroom tiling. Our room looked out onto the three mountains called the Three Sisters. While she tiled, I admired the view and wondered if it was possible that Cliff was hiking up or down one of those sisters. The next day we drove through a lightning storm to the mountains but saw no trace of him. I rode the dashboard and she said that when lightning hit the horizon it looked like it was hitting my shell.

Well, that was a fun vacation, she said when we got home.

Then we went to the ocean. It was all downhill to the ocean. We passed bicyclists who never had to pedal. We arrived and there was a beach with many dogs on it. She fell in love with a basset hound and later said she thought she would get a dog. Something with long ears that flapped in the wind.

Okay, I do not have those.

A basset hound puppy, she said.

She was off her rocker. A puppy would bite off my legs and drink up my pool.

On the beach there were cliffs with tunnels that led to other beaches. But there were also signs that said DO YOU KNOW WHEN HIGH TIDE IS. We didn't. We went home. She never got the puppy.

What I am thinking now is that when things are very bad, maybe you climb the walls and go in circles and that is normal, but then gradually you widen the circles until you are out the door. You widen and widen until you cross state lines. Because we did eventually hit California. Nevada. New Mexico. Arizona. We were slowly working our way east—looking for Cliff, yes, but also widening the circle—and eventually, maybe, we'd have cleared the continent.

But a leap became necessary instead. A cross-continent leap at untortoisian speed. And now she is in another time zone and she needs kelp.

Still perched on *Lowering the Bard*, I look over my shoulder at my castle and think: Hey, I am not in it. And it occurs to me that this is step one. Step one is get out of your castle. Step two is locate the door. Step three is the dashboard travelling east.

Later, when Linda comes home, she plays Audrey's message and looks at me while she listens. I put my head underwater at the word *kelp.*

I think we're fresh out of kelp, I hear Chuck say when I come up for air.

Jesus Christ, Linda says. Can't you hear it in her voice.

Hear what.

I climb out of my pool and head for the sad corner of my castle. The sad corner is the one farthest from the radiator.

We do so have kelp, Linda is saying. She left us some.

Where.

She opens the fridge. Here.

Please don't tell me that's kelp, Chuck says.

Some kind of kelpish paste, yeah.

I thought it was hummus.

Uh, nope.

Oh shit. And Chuck spits in the sink and gags in an exaggerated fashion that I find very insulting.

You tortoise, Linda says.

Also very insulting.

She reads the label and says, You don't want to know.

What I really want is some lettuce. Fresh lettuce of the iceberg variety. Crisp as paper. I can almost live by that alone.

In the obituary, written by yours truly, the deceased is referred to as *Water* Flowers. Pretty punny if you ask me. Uncle Thoby thought it was punny too. This morning, before the funeral, we were laughing so hard we had to hold on to the kitchen counter, which is a sign of real laughter. Rule Number One of Real Laughter: Are you holding on to something. Say the counter or someone's shoulder. Do you have to put down your beverage. Then you are really laughing. Or maybe crying.

We were really laughing until Toff showed up with his own newspaper folded in that special Toffish way and said, You don't. You just don't. His face was as purple as his cravat. Smack went the newspaper on the counter.

Don't what, I said.

Make a mockery of a man's name.

Calm down, said Uncle Thoby.

Yes you do, I said.

What.

Make a mockery.

Oddly.

It's going on the headstone too, I said, my voice spiralling. So there, so there.

Uncle Thoby stepped between us and said, She's kidding. It was a mistake. But one that Walter would have loved.

He would not have loved it, Toff said.

Whereupon I stepped between Toff and Uncle Thoby and

said, I think *we* know what my dad would have loved better than *you*, executor. You come here with your Hellvetica font.

My what.

Oddly. Hand on shoulder.

My dad's will was in Hellvetica. I know hell when I see it.

Toff was briefly silent. He picked up the newspaper. "Far from peacefully," he quoted. Was that necessary.

Yes.

Collision. Say accident for God's sake. Or better yet, say nothing at all. And why name the medulla oblongata.

Why not name it.

Okay, why *capitalize* it.

Rule Number One of Capitalization, I said. If it matters hugely, capitalize. You might need it for an acronym later.

Toff just stared at me. Then he went on: It makes him—it makes Walter sound like a brain on the sidewalk.

Which image made me laugh. I nudged Uncle Thoby. But he was not joining in. Why aren't you joining in, I said.

I've tied a black ribbon to Wedge's wheel so he can't run today. He looks miserable, hunched in the corner of his terrarium, his back to the room. Funny how everyone gravitates towards him. As if it's Wedge they must pay their respects to.

The house creaks under the weight of people I don't know. Colleagues, grad students. Of course there are islands of people I do know. Clint has his own island. So does Byrne Doyle. Never the twain shall meet. Except on our front lawn, where Uncle Thoby has put a Byrne Doyle sign and a Clint sign shoulder to shoulder.

Somehow I have lost Uncle Thoby. In our own house. And where is Toff.

There is election talk. Someone in the Wedge queue says, Byrne Doyle, bless his heart. The Poles have not been kind to him. They are unreliable.

Yes, an actual queue has formed beside the mantelpiece.

A hand touches my arm.

Patience is not in the queue. She is not one for mice, generally. Although she looks a bit like one. She is short with white hair and round black eyes. She puts a small box in my hand.

What's this.

I made it myself.

Inside, wrapped in tissue paper, is a bar of soap with the words WALTER FLOWERS IS DEAD carved on the surface.

Oh.

It's called a Grief Bar, she says. You wash with it, and when those words disappear, so too will your grief.

I exhale slowly. Bollocks, Patience.

She pats my arm because I am such a chip off the old block.

Patience has been my dad's secretary for as long as I can remember. She department-hopped with him, from Psychology to Biology, Biology to Neuroscience, Neuroscience to Biogerontology. I think that's the right order. Biogerontology comes last anyway. It is, or was, a department of one. Just my dad. Who somehow persuaded the powers that be that he needed his own full-time secretary.

Sometimes, if my dad was in class, I was allowed to put my feet up on his desk and hold office hours. No one ever showed up except Patience. She'd sit in the student chair and ask me why she'd done so poorly on her last test.

Look, Patience. You are totipotent.

How do you mean.

You are potentially anything but a mermaid.

I see.

Go away and try harder.

I loved her for that. And I loved how she saw my dad from the outside. How to her he was boyish. Silly but endearing Walter. Up to no good in that lab of his. With his long-lived mice. You couldn't help, at the end of the day, but fall a little in love with him. Which Patience did. And she showed that love by not taking him too seriously, and by protecting him like a Rottweiler. She always took his side. It didn't matter that there weren't sides. She took his side against the psychologists (who had no souls), against the biologists (who had no backbones), against the neuroscientists (who had no hearts). My dad was right to leave them all. He was right to start his own little operation.

My own little operation, said my dad. Is that what I have.

If you build it, they will come, she said.

Who will, asked my dad, not catching the reference. And do we want them.

She wagged her finger.

My dad's heart was in the right place, she liked to say. And at the end of the day—something else she liked to say—at the end of the day, my dad was harmless.

Which was apparently a good thing.

But for me, sometimes, at the end of the day, the question I found myself asking was, How harmless is Patience.

Because one Christmas she gave my dad one of those pink Energizer bunnies, except instead of holding a drum, it was holding a sign that said ENGINEERED NEGLIGIBLE SENESCENCE. That was pretty funny. Wasn't it.

I don't know because I didn't get it. I told Patience, We prefer Duracell. We are Duracell people.

But my dad thought the bunny was funny. Or he said he did. He kept it on his desk. It was the first thing you saw when you came into his office.

But I had a bad feeling about the bunny. And sometimes, when I had my feet up on his desk, I kicked it. Not hard. I mean, I loved Patience, but my dad was not just a pipe-dream smoker, or whatever the expression is. He was not just a bunny beating a sign.

And quite often, walking home with my silly, endearing, harmless dad, I would have hurt feelings. On his behalf. I would ask to be lifted. Piggybacked. Forgiven. On account of his brain being light years deep and Patience not seeing that. Because he would have *us* live forever, Patience. Not a stupid battery.

There was something so wounding about the bunny.

And there is something wounding about the Grief Bar. Was it a bar of Irish Spring in a past life.

Notice I spelled his name right, Patience says. A reference to the obituary.

I nod. You know what would be really amazing, Patience. If, when the words WALTER FLOWERS IS DEAD disappeared, my dad stopped being dead.

More patting of my arm. More chipping off the old block.

What I am thinking now is that some jokes are okay and some are not. The Energizer bunny joke is not. But Patience is, I suspect, offended by the obituary. As is Toff. Maybe people who loved my dad can be divided into two categories: Those who mind the obituary and those who mind the bunny.

I swim through the crowd and find Uncle Thoby on Clint's island. This is good. This is a safe place to be. Where's Toff, I ask him.

He looks around.

Nevermind, I say. Let him be lost.

He asks what's in the box. I show him the Grief Bar. He looks upset until I tell him it's from Patience. Oh. That makes sense then.

It's Irish Spring, isn't it.

He sniffs, then sings softly: Manly yes, but I like it too.

Clint puts an arm around me. Oh my darlin, oh my duck. I am hugged into a dark grey armpit. There's a Clint's cab on his breast pocket. Clint is very meaty and warm. Can I get one of these shirts, I mumble.

Not unless you come work for me. I'm hiring.

Since when are you a politician, Clint.

Since this election.

You won't really go to Ottawa, will you.

Don't think there's much chance of that, sweetheart.

Just this morning, though, one of Clint's campaign flyers came in the mail, and on the front was a picture of a Clint's cab driving off into a sunset with a long orange scarf blowing out the window—and where was that cab going if not Ottawa.

That sunset was local, Clint says.

Still, it is an odd image for a campaign flyer. And I was thinking of it earlier at the cemetery when the sun slanted through the bare trees at two o'clock. The sun was already setting. I'm going to slip away early today. Stuff on my plate. So down it went, eggy, into the snow.

And my hand curled around the flyer in my pocket and I thought about how sunsets are for people to drive off, or die off, into.

I had checked the mail before we left for the funeral, because checking the mail is something I do, and why should today be different. Toff had tried to check it and I'd yelled at him. Which made Uncle Thoby wince and Toff step back from the mailbox like it had a bomb in it. There was no mail except the campaign flyer.

I held on to the flyer all through the funeral.

My dad would have voted for Clint, and if Clint is deprived of an Ottawa sunset by one vote, it will be because my dad is not here to cast his ballot.

Do not look at the hole in the ground.

I did not look at the hole in the ground. I looked at the prison, which borders the cemetery. How do I feel about my dad's feet pointing for all eternity at a prison. Um.

I had always assumed this cemetery was for convicts. But no, Uncle Thoby assured me, this is a cemetery for anyone, it just happens to be next to the prison. Oh. So the prisoners can look out their windows, sorry slots, and see a slice of burial. Or a slice of Quite-a-Bite-of Lake. (The cemetery, the prison, and the lake make a triangle.) Imagine watching the Regatta through a window so skinny you cannot see a full boat. Just sections of boat. Bites of boat.

Poor prisoners. The backside of the prison is baby blue. Do they know the back of their prison is baby blue.

The sun was setting and my nose was running. I had no Kleenex so I had to use the campaign flyer. Whereupon ten people at the graveside thrust tissues at me. Thanks, thanks. Too kind.

They think I am crying.

Am I really going to be able to leave my dad here with his feet pointing at the prison for all eternity and go back to the house for a post-part-him party or whatever it's called.

Uncle Thoby's orange glove touches my shoulder.

Concentrate on the baby blue backside of the jail and the windows designed for shooting arrows. Because what else could fit through such a window. Well, a paper. A message. And the moment I think *message* I see one. I get one. I see a note falling from a window. The wind actually picks it up and carries it in my direction. I lift my hands. A note, a note. But alas, it snags on the barbed wire atop the prison wall.

So naturally I run over to the wall. I run towards the note, which is not a note. And which, even if it were a note, is not one I could ever reach because the wall is five people tall. I run over to the wall and my shadow is tall enough to reach the note but I am not. Still, I leap like a ballerina in the air. A note, a note.

Then I see. It's the wrapper from a Piety pastry. Goddamn it. I used to love Piety pastries. I ate one every day for ten years in the GOLEM cafeteria.

There are no messages to be had.

S omeone in the Wedge queue says, Should those flowers be put in Walter.

Or maybe I mishear.

I am standing at the window, my own island, when a familiar car pulls into Jim Ryan's driveway. Bold little Lada (still running!) and Verlaine leaps out. Wow, she is parking in Jim Ryan's crescent without permission. She's not wearing a coat.

She does an extended trot across the lawn.

I run to the door to greet her. She hugs me. Bare arms. Hair all alert. Audray. She kisses me Swissly. Right cheek, left cheek, right cheek.

I think the reason the Swiss kiss like this is to delay for as long as possible looking into the eyes of the person they are greeting.

She says she was not at the service because there was a pigeon crisis at the Before Building that required her immediate attention.

Still not looking at me.

A pigeon crisis.

She is wearing a white polo shirt with a black horse on the breast. Almost all her shirts have horses. She buys them for the horses. But if you ask her who is Ralph Lauren, she can't tell you.

You look unslept, she says.

Now she is looking at me. It just took her awhile.

In the living room we skip to the front of the Wedge queue.

Ah, there he is, she says. My little sandwich. My little Wedge of sand. She pats her stomach. I am feeling a bit peckish, Audray.

That old joke.

Speaking of jokes, she says. The biography in the paper.

The obituary.

Yes, that.

Behind us, the queue disperses. Clearly we aren't moving on. Wedge looks at me over his shoulder, like, bloody hell what is this.

Verlaine gives me a thumbs-up on the obituary. Were you behind it, she says.

Yes and no.

Oui ou non.

Oui.

Walter would approve.

We are joined at the mantel by Jim Ryan (Are you the proprietor of that adorable Russian antique parked in my crescent), Byrne Doyle, Dr. O'Leery, and a stranger. Hey, we are our own island.

Dr. O'Leery admires Wedge's shiny coat. What are you feeding him.

Licorice Allsorts.

Much laughter.

Seriously.

Byrne Doyle asks whatever happened to that ball Wedge used to run around in. Remember when he ran into the street in his ball and Byrne had to rescue him because Jim Ryan was pulling (frontwards, yes) out of his driveway at great speed.

It's still around, I think. We used to call it Wedge's crystal ball.

They don't make Ladas anymore, of course, Verlaine is saying. And the Americans don't know they ever existed. An American will tell you there is no such car.

Dr. O'Leery says he is working with mice now. Which does not give me a warm feeling. He sticks a finger through the grid roof of Wedge's terrarium.

Um. Don't do that.

My dad was not a fan of Dr. O'Leery. In fact, my dad was partly responsible for Dr. O'Leery's "long sabbatical." So what is he doing here.

Working with mice and, what, rhombuses, I say.

He gives me a blank look.

Because, as I recall, one of Dr. O'Leery's experiments involved electrocuting cats in the presence of circles (ostensibly to prove something about psychology, not geometry), and my dad had filed a complaint.

Like I said, I am not getting a warm feeling.

The stranger says, And this mouse was your father's pet.

He has an accent—German maybe, or Dutch—and a lion's large face. He is drinking out of a goblet I don't recognize. There are a lot of dishes around that I don't recognize.

Ours, I say. We've had him since I was a kid.

Apparently this is amusing. He winks at Dr. O'Leery.

What, I say.

The Lada conversation has petered out and Verlaine says, Well, Audray, where is the wine.

You must be much younger than you look, says the lion, sipping slowly. His eyes are dead serious over the rim of the goblet.

I glance at Wedge. Why.

Verlaine interjects. The rest of us age four years for Audray's every one. She is like a horse that way. Where is the wine.

She grabs my elbow.

I've had six birthdays, I tell the lion. Put that in your pipe and smoke it.

Sorry.

Figure that out.

Verlaine is leading me towards the kitchen.

He tilts his big head, scratches his ear. Ah. You are a leapling.

A what. Do you know that man.

Verlaine prowls along the counter. Reading bottles. Shakes her head. But I think he is Belgian. I have a sixth sense about Belgians.

I nod. A leapling sounds like something you might have for dinner in Belgium.

I sit down. Rub my eyes. The day feels so crowded. Every interaction is a blow. Sudden, fast, and over. And holy hell. Look at all the students smoking on the porch.

And look, there is Toff.

So that's where he is. Hanging out with the students, smoking. Actually no, he is not hanging out. He has a corner to himself. He's got his collar turned up. Purple cravat flapping. An outfit loses flamboyancy after a couple of days. Then it becomes merely sad.

He brought one outfit.

Don't look at him.

Verlaine pours me some wine in a goblet I don't recognize. I slide it away. She slides it back.

You look unslept, she says again.

I've been sleeping here.

Where.

At the table.

Why.

I have my reasons.

But maybe tonight I will sleep in my own room. Under my tree. This suddenly feels possible. Maybe I am acclimatizing to this house that doesn't have my dad alive in it. All these strangers are helping. They will strip the house clean of associations and then debark.

Don't think about where my dad is right now.

My aunt called this morning, says Verlaine. She wanted me to tell you how sorry she is.

This requires a shift of gears. I prop myself up. Madame Mourou called.

She asked about the American. I told her I thought it was over with the American and you would not be going back. Am I right.

I stare at her white shirt. It's weird how Ralph Lauren's horses always look like they're tipping over. And for a moment the only American I can think of is the tiny one galloping out of her chest, wielding a mallet.

• • •

The doorbell rings. I am supposed to be on door duty, but Verlaine says no, she will go. So I am left alone in the kitchen. With Toff on the other side of the glass. The students have dispersed and he is standing with his pointy shoulders up near his cravat. Why isn't he wearing a coat. I press my lips together. He does the same. Everyone has a special smile of pure unhappiness. This is mine. What's odd is that mine is the same as Toff's. We purse our lips and lift our eyebrows. What's next, our eyebrows say. What can possibly be next after this.

I forgive you for the obituary, say the eyebrows. I forgive you for throwing your father's will in the Fairfont fountain. I forgive you for forcing me to smoke outdoors in this Weather of Mass Destruction. I am just as miserable as you.

But why are you, Toff. And why did you have to accuse me of making a mockery of my dad's name. Of making him a Medulla Oblongata on the sidewalk.

Okay. I apologize. But why did you have to disrupt the burial by flinging yourself at the prison wall like a lunatic.

Okay. But why do you care so much, Toff.

Okay. But why do you hate me.

Okay. But why did you have to bring up the Civil Manor at lunch the other day like it was something fun to reminisce over. Like all that turmoil and worry I put my dad and Uncle Thoby through that night was something fun to reminisce over.

Okay. But why did you do it.

Because I hated you and Grandmother. And because I love Uncle Thoby.

Okay. Hang on a sec while I light my four hundredth cigarette of the day. Why did you hate us.

Okay. Let's go down that memory parking lot since Uncle Thoby is safely out of the room. There were many reasons why I hated you. Many many reasons. Only some of which I know. But it was because of *you* that Uncle Thoby checked into a hotel. You and Grandmother, with your disapproving eyebrows. And that was what led *me* to follow suit. So that I could protect him from you. Who wanted to disappear him back to England. And the unfortunate consequence of *that* action was to cause my dad to be frantic and to subsequently blame Uncle Thoby for losing *me*. Even though I wasn't lost. Or drowned. Or run over. But they didn't know that.

I'd fallen asleep in room 205 of the Civil Manor and woken to the sound of the phone ringing next door in room 203. And guess who that was. My dad. Phoning Uncle Thoby to ask, Where is Audrey. But Uncle Thoby was still at Bebe's, so no one was answering. I knew it was my dad calling. I could tell by the worry in the ring. I sat up in the dark. It was horrible. The phone kept ringing and ringing. And I sent feelers out into a world that had my dad worried in it. My dad was calling me from the other side of a wall, and I couldn't answer.

So I got up and stood by the wall.

Finally it stopped. Dad, I said into the heat vent. I didn't mean to not come home.

Then I got smart and realized I had a phone in my room. Hey! *I* could call *him*.

But *you* answered.

Where are you, you said.

At the Civil Manor, I said.

Your father's frantic.

Well, put him on.

He just left.

Uh-oh.

I hung up. I sat on the bed. Now I was in trouble. Would he come here. Yes. He would come here first. He would talk to Doreen. Oh yes, your little girl was here in her raincoat when the dinosaur show was on.

And my dad would try very hard not to yell, When was the dinosaur show on.

Then he would glance at the board and notice that the key to room 205 was missing. Ah. And he would nod to himself and say, Thank you, Doreen.

Or he would check the pond first. Because what if I'd fallen in. Yes, he is walking around Wednesday Pond right now, calling my name. And when I don't answer, he jumps in. The police come to dredge the pond, but lo and behold, there is no bottom to dredge. And my dad is gone, never to return. But where. Where does the pond with no bottom go. Will he splash up somewhere else.

All because he expected me to come home and I never did.

But this was not what happened. What happened was that my dad, not getting an answer in Uncle Thoby's room, went directly to Bebe's.

This must have been a bad moment. Don't picture it.

I brought her home.

No you didn't. She never came home.

Uncle Thoby drops his pool queue. Sorry, cue. In slow motion. Also his pirate sherry.

Poor Uncle Thoby.

I can picture them, wobbly, thinking where oh where is she. They search the streets around Wednesday Pond. Calling Oddly.

I waited for a long time to be found. I watched a whole episode of *The Love Boat*. Which is a show you don't need to watch because it is clear from the moment the faces appear in the ship's steering wheel who is going to fall in love. I watched and imagined my dad and Uncle Thoby looking for me. I cried a little. Then the news came on and I turned it off, because what if I was on it.

I dragged a chair to the window. The PIETY sign said PITY because the E was out.

Finally the LeBaron pulled up. My dad and Uncle Thoby got out of the car.

Dad!

He froze in his tracks. Looked up.

Uncle Thoby put a hand on his shoulder. My dad closed his eyes. In two seconds they were in the hallway. I stepped out of 205. Hi.

My dad swept me up.

When we got home, you and Grandmother were playing cards. Remember. And I clumped upstairs to my room. My bed smelled like smoke, so I got the Lysol spray from the bathroom and disinfected the entire room (and some of myself by mistake). Then, on my way back to the bathroom, I heard Grandmother's voice downstairs. She was leaning on her words again. I stopped.

I heard her say, Do you know what you're doing with that child.

And my dad said, Of course not.

I had a very bad taste in my mouth (Lysol). I went into my room and closed the door. I got into bed. My eyes smarted.

Do you know what you're doing with that child.

I knew what she was getting at. The other parent. Where is the other parent. And clearly you do *not* know what you're doing with that child, Walter. Families are supposed to have a king and a queen and a jack. Not a dad and a pirate and a child who doesn't know her own age.

But my dad had explained this to me. That sometimes there is only one parent. Sometimes there are two. Sometimes there are three. But what it comes down to is who wants to be. And if someone doesn't want to be, they shouldn't have to be. And if someone does want to be, like my dad, who really really wanted to be (and hopefully still wanted to be, despite my running away to the Civil Manor and putting him through torture), or like Uncle Thoby, then that person should be allowed to be. Was I on board with that.

I was wholeheartedly on board with that.

But what I now saw through my Lysol tears was that not everyone was on board with that. Our guests from England were not on board with that. They would make us like a deck of cards. They would shuffle us apart. And so it was more important than ever that I protect us.

England had kings, queens, and jacks. But we had the jokers. We *were* the jokers. Outside the deck, across the ocean, dancing our little jigs of happiness.

V erlaine puts a hand on my shoulder. There's a young man at the door looking for your father.

What.

I told him to wait.

It is a bit like hearing Uncle Thoby's voice on the Hear Ye 3000. You persuade yourself it's really him calling. And you answer with hope. Just like you want to believe the person on the porch who thinks your dad is alive might really have a ticket to a world that does not have your dad dead in it. Maybe he knows something you don't.

And so I walk down the hall, slowly, to prolong the moment. My fingers touching the wall. Steady. He's standing at the edge of the steps, his back to the house. I open the screen door. He turns. Dark red hair. Wool sweater. Boots like castles. In the street there's a red van with the hazards flashing.

I step onto the porch in my socks.

I'm looking for Walter Flowers, he says.

He's big. His sweater has that braid pattern down the front, five ropes of it. His stomach pushes out the sweater.

I'm his daughter.

He extends a hand. Judge Julian Brown.

He is impossibly young to be a judge. Judge of what. A skate-boarding competition.

He corrects me. Judd.

Oh. Judd, period.

Yes.

Julian Brown.

Hyphenated.

Of the Julian-Brown furniture dynasty!

It's not a dynasty, but sort of.

Okay. Got it. How can I help you.

Your father purchased some Christmas lights. Which have since been recalled. We're here to collect those lights.

Behind him the flashing van says Christmatech. You're that guy.

We've sent you several recall notices.

Yeah, we noticed. This is beyond customer service, isn't it. This is intrusive.

We prefer conscientious.

We.

We would very much like to exchange your father's D-434 model for the D-534 model.

Clearly.

Those lights would not be in use, would they, he says, peering over my shoulder into the house.

No. What's in those lights, Judd. Plutonium.

We make a deal that Judd will give me the new model now, and I will inform my dad about the inadvisability of using the old one. I will have my dad bring the old model to Judd's place of business. Tomorrow. But now is not a good time, since we're having a party, as Judd can see from all the cars, and I don't want to disturb him with this untimely, albeit urgent, recall. But we are not in any danger because we are not using the lights at this time. And surely the lights are not dangerous if they are not plugged in, are they.

They are not entirely undangerous if they are not plugged in.

We look at each other. He has twinkly eyes.

I laugh.

How did my dad meet this guy. Okay. Well. We'll take our chances for another day.

Judd says he's got the new model in the van.

Okay. Off you go then.

As he negotiates the driveway I call after him, Who is the we.

He turns, walks backwards. Points at his chest. Me. Bangs into a car's side mirror. Ouch.

His hair is unbelievably, solidly red against the blue background of snow. The van blinks a syncopated rhythm.

I hug myself. I do a little dance in time with the van. Cold.

The porch bounces with other footsteps. Toff comes around the corner. Collar up. Lips the colour of his cravat. Judging from his expression, he has overheard all or part of my conversation with the Christmatech representative. Whom I have not disabused of the belief that my dad is alive.

I try to smile a smile of pure unhappiness. Only it is not pure. Toff walks past me into the house.

My dad always was courageous in the Christmas light department. Capitalize Christmas Light Department. Certain rules must be followed in the CLD:

The house must be dark—no ambient light—before the switch is flipped. Two Flowers (Oddly and Thoby) must walk to the other side of the pond and watch the switch-flipping from there. So that the lights of number 3 Wednesday Place are reflected in the pond's surface. More bang for the buck. Double the wattage. Etcetera.

Oddly and Thoby stamp their feet, dance a little jig, while they wait. Come on, Walter, says Uncle Thoby. Come on. Then bam. They're on. And holy wattage. We gasp every time. Because they are even better than last year. There is always some new technology in the CLD. Remember when Christmas lights were hot and bulbous. Remember that. So hot they melted nearby ornaments. Then they got smaller. Brighter and braver. If one went out, the others kept going. They deepened to jewel tones. They were stained glass. They were a church in your hand. They didn't burn. You could put them in your mouth and make your cheeks glow. (Don't do that, Audrey. Why. What's Rule Number One of Things That Are Plugged In. Oh right.)

The two Flowers now wait for the third to join them. Uncle Thoby hums the "Hallelujah Chorus." The all-year-round swans glide through the dazzling reflection. Finally we hear the sound of footsteps and Walter arrives with one hand cupped over an eye so he can't see the house and says, Well.

Oh Walt.

Yes. Say it. Go on.

You've outdone yourself.

Have I. And he unblinkers himself and turns around to take in the full view. And if he were prone to doing jigs, he would do one now. Yes, he has outdone himself. I won't tell you the wattage, he says.

Why.

Shocking.

Ha.

And the swans put their heads underwater and say, Can you see the bottom. No. Can you. No.

And Oddly says, Somebody somewhere is looking into *their* pond-with-no-bottom and seeing our lights!

What a nice thought, says Uncle Thoby. Orange glove on Oddly's head.

Except that the pond *has* a bloody bottom, says Walter.

But how do you explain that it never freezes.

It did freeze once.

When, says Uncle Thoby.

Before you came.

That's sweet of you to say, but—

What are you talking about. Sweet of me to say.

Judd's van crawls away. I imagine it from above, a red rectangle in a white maze of streets. I feel not terrible. I sit on the porch steps with my box of D-534-model Christmas lights. The box might be a recycled pizza box. When Judd handed it to me, he remarked how odd it was that no one on our street had Christmas lights up.

Promise me you won't turn on the old model, he said.

I hugged the box. I promise.

Imagine being a Christmas light inventor. I lift the lid. Inside is a coiled vine of green wire with dark promising buds.

A heavy coat drops over my shoulders. I look up. Toff. He goes back inside. Yeah. I'm not ready to go back inside.

Verlaine's Lada will not start. Jim Ryan is casting aspersions. Around the car he stomps. His crescent is plugged at one end with an ancient Soviet eyesore. What colour was it originally. Dark beige. What colour is it now. Dark beige. Weirdly, it has not rusted.

Let me try.

Verlaine gets out. Jim gets in. The engine turns over but will not catch. You can hear that it will not be catching any time soon.

I put my hands over my ears.

As a kid this sound—the sound of a car not able to start—could make me cry instantly. It was the sound of pain, of fever, of wanting to throw up and not being able to.

Clint passes me on the steps. He sees my box of lights and says, Hey, Christmas Boy was here.

I take my hands off my ears. What.

Christmas Boy.

You mean Judd, period. Julian-Brown hyphenated.

You seen my dispatch office recently.

Holy. That was him.

Yes, God love him.

There's a crowd around the Lada now. The moon is up and on. They look like they're in a play. Jim Ryan cannot stop himself from turning the ignition one more time.

Finally Mrs. Ryan comes out of her house and screams, Jim Ryan stop flooding that G.D. engine.

Hear hear.

Jim gets out. Slams the door. Except it doesn't slam. It sort of sticks. He pokes it. She's made of cardboard, he says with disgust.

Clint and Uncle Thoby poke around under the hood. Clint points. What were the Russians up to, I wonder, with this business.

Verlaine chews a fingernail and spits it in the snow.

Oddly, can you bring us some duct tape.

I slump my shoulders. Part of me wants to go over there and console the Lada. Which is an old friend. The other part wants to stay right here on this step. Forever. No part of me wants to get up and look for duct tape.

I'm not wearing boots, I call back.

Uncle Thoby looks over his shoulder. That can change, can't it.

Yes it can bloody change. This is the worst feeling. I need coffee.

Uncle Thoby unwinds duct tape by the metre, and I stand at the ready with scissors. I am Scissors Girl.

Byrne Doyle and Clint are actually chatting. So the twain shall meet after all. Clint wears a short leather jacket that says CLINT WON'T COST YOU A MINT on the back. Byrne Doyle wears his wool straitjacket. They stand shoulder to shoulder in a posture not unlike that of their respective signs on the lawn behind them.

Some shockin those antlers on Noel Antle, what.

Sign on Empire says JOYEUX NOEL ANTLER.

They chuckle. And continue chuckling. Oh my. Byrne Doyle wipes a tear from his eye.

Sure he can't complain. If anything it's helped him.

He should have been wearing antlers all along.

He's up in the poles.

Up in the north poles.

More laughter.

Backstage Jim Ryan says, This car is making a political statement that I am not comfortable with.

Verlaine tells him to *va t'en*.

Pardonnez moy.

I peer into the back seat. Hello old friend. What political statement are you making with that hole in your floor, two Piety pie boxes (one half-full), and an old hoof pick.

The hole's getting bigger, I remark to Verlaine.

She is lying prostrate on a snowbank. Either she is making a snow angel or a political statement.

I used to think the hole was on purpose. Those daredevil Russians.

Do not put your hand or foot in that hole while the car is moving, Verlaine would caution me.

What do you take me for, an idiot.

I open the back door. I grab the hoof pick. Look. I hold it up for all to see. Who knows what this is.

The Byrne Doyle–Clint conversation pauses briefly, then resumes. Funny how people will not see something they don't recognize. I'd bet my bottom dollar that neither Clint nor Byrne Doyle has ever seen a hoof pick before. But do they pause to say, What an interesting implement, Audrey. What is that. No.

Not the sharpest antler in the rack, Clint is saying.

Uncle Thoby is still under the hood.

Jim Ryan says, A silver question mark.

I look at him. That is unexpected.

It's a hoof pick.

Oh.

I run my tongue over my front teeth. Rule Number One of Hoof Picking. Do not bend over the hoof with your mouth open.

Do not sing, O Tannenbaum, O Tannenbaum, your branches green. Because if the horse shifts his weight, if he lifts his hoof so much as an inch, hey, where'd your front teeth go. Oh, they are down your throat.

It is surprisingly easy to lose your front teeth.

Examining my bleeding gums all those Christmases ago, Verlaine shook her head and said, Yes, well, you never were exceedingly bright.

I was about to cry when she winked at me. Because we both knew I was one sharp antler.

Verlaine thinks the Lada could be jump-started if it were pushed by a few burly men, a strong young woman, and two political candidates. Jim Ryan quickly agrees. And if by chance she won't start, she can be pushed into Byrne Doyle's driveway.

Uncle Thoby has duct-taped God knows what under the hood. Yup, he says, nodding, like, my work here is done, but I hope no one will ever look closely at my work. Righto. And he slams the hood.

I slide the hoof pick into one pocket, the scissors into another. I feel competent. We arrange ourselves like so along the back bumper: Byrne Doyle, Clint, me, Uncle Thoby, Jim Ryan. The idea is to push the car the rest of the way around Jim's crescent and out into the street, thus making a big, and hopefully momentum-building, loop. Then we keep pushing on the straight, at which point Verlaine pops the clutch.

There is much jostling. Clint says, You gonna be able to run in that sleeping bag you call a coat, Byrne Doyle.

Maybe I should take it off and leave it on the bank.

Yes, why don't you.

When we start pushing, Jim Ryan says, By Jesus she's light.

Bottom's gone right out of her, says Clint.

Is that Verlaine Russian, Jim says.

"That Verlaine" can hear you. Her window's open.

Well is she.

Why.

I'm just wondering why anyone would buy a car of this persuasion.

What persuasion.

Eastern European, shall we say.

That's enough now, Jim, says Uncle Thoby.

Byrne Doyle is of Polish descent, I announce.

He is.

I am.

We are picking up speed. In the crescent it is not hard work. In the street it's a little tougher, because the street has snow in it. Unlike Jim Ryan's pristine driveway. We put everything we have into it. How fast are we going. Ten, twenty, forty, sixty kilometres an hour! No, a cheetah hits sixty. Maybe ten. Just as we pass Byrne Doyle's house, the car hiccups to life. We feel it leaving our hands. What an amazing feeling. Verlaine gives us the thumbs-up out the window. The car turns at the end of the street, just like a regular car. Indicator blinking. Like dum-de-dum, I have not just been humiliated by Jim Ryan's slurs about my homeland or by five people heaving my ass down a quiet cul-de-sac. Back to business as usual.

I am the last to stop running, the last to let go. I feel a pang. I want the party to be over but I don't want anyone to go home. Or at least I don't want certain people to go home. I turn around. The others are under a streetlight. Byrne Doyle looks like a ghost in his shivery shirtsleeves. Jim Ryan puts his hands on his knees because everyone knows this helps you catch your breath.

Uncle Thoby is beaming. He looks like himself for the first time since I got home. Group hug, he says. Everyone just stands there. So I run up and throw myself into his arms.

Part Two

ODDLY THE BIOGRAPHER

M y name is still Winnifred. Chuck has not changed it. The Willamette, I have discovered, is a river. Of course I knew that. I remember seeing said river from the dash-board on at least one occasion. We crossed a bridge. Look, Win. The Willamette. Right. The Willamette pays tribute to the Columberer, which lumbers wider and gentler than that chas-mic business beneath the bridge.

The other day Linda said there was a movie about loan sharks being filmed on the Willamette and why didn't Chuck go down and see about being an extra. Which word, *extra*, was like a red flag to a bull. Chuck is no extra.

Linda the Unkempt said she'd seen people firing soundless guns on the bridge. Pretty cool.

Chuck was unimpressed. He said the gun soundtrack came later.

But to return to the Willamette. Now that I know it's a river, Chuck's frequent remark, that it looks *inviting*—what does that mean exactly. He holds me up to the window and faintly, yes, I can see a bridge in the distance.

As I recall it was a long way down to the river from the bridge. A *long* way. Also, apparently there are sharks in it.

There's a knock at the door. Chuck looks at me. Would you, he says, gesturing.

I blink at him with a piece of lettuce hanging out of my mouth.

Fine.

He hauls himself off the sofa.

It's a UPS guy. Wow, he looks so dapper compared to Chuck. Let's do a quick comparison. The UPS guy, whose name is Julius, is dressed in a crisp brown jacket with yellow accents, brown shorts (in December!), and brown boots. He's carrying a package and an electronic device that will record the signature of Chuck Stanch. Chuck is wearing the usual. Nothing. Well, boxers. He's carrying *Lowering the Bard*. Julius eyes the book. Chuck eyes the package. Sign here, says Julius and looks around the apartment. Wow, is that a tortoise.

Unfortunately, says Chuck.

Julius hands Chuck the package.

Gramercy, says Chuck.

Sorry, says Julius.

Godspeed.

Chuck closes the door and turns the package over. It is small and disc-shaped. Well, he says. Guess who this is from.

I drop my piece of lettuce.

That's right, he says. He sits down on the sofa. You know what it looks like.

And not until he says it do I realize that, yes, the package is about my shape and size.

If this is another tortoise, so help me.

My blood runs cold. A Canadian tortoise. But that is ridiculous. You cannot *mail* a tortoise. Can you. And why would she send a new tortoise here, instead of having her old tortoise sent there.

Chuck is slowly unwrapping. I watch with my head out the window.

It is not a tortoise. It is a fire alarm.

When Linda gets home, she does what the note says, which is to please install the fire alarm above my castle.

Chuck says this is ridiculous. They already have a fire alarm in the other room. Linda says an extra one won't hurt. Chuck says it's because Audrey thinks they have electric heat. But they have hot water radiation. The castle might warp, but it will not catch fire.

Nevertheless, says Linda. You smoke.

Not inside.

You smoke in the vicinity.

Would that I were not required to smoke in the vicinity, he says.

Later, when they are asleep, I climb into my pool for a nocturnal dip, and when I look up, I see the red light of the fire alarm, like a plane crossing the sky. It reminds me of the old flat, because there was a plane in the sky there too. And if I keep very still, the red light makes a bright dot on the surface of my pool, which I can then try to eat, unsuccessfully.

She sent the fire alarm to keep me safe, and to make this place feel more like home. That is thoughtful. But sending a fire alarm also suggests a long-term tenancy on Taft Street, doesn't it.

It is not fire I need to worry about.

Methinks Chuck has been preparing me in his ungentle way for a long fall from a bridge. Doesn't the Willamette look *inviting*. How long before he decides the tortoise is better off in her "natural" habitat.

What scares me more than the sharks is the thought of being dropped. I mean, I love water as much as the next tortoise, but if you hit it with enough force, it's curtains. Especially if you have a flat plastron like me. You can skip me like a stone, so flat is my plastron.

I was once dropped from a great height, though not from a bridge. A previous tenant (quite previous, perhaps thirty years previous) threw me in the trash on the assumption that I was a doorstop left by the tenant before him. *That* tenant, who left in a hurry ("credit" problems), had not bothered to inform the *subsequent* tenant of the pre-existing tenancy of a tortoise. Dark days for yours truly. I found myself in a paper bag with a few other miscellaneous scraps left behind by the in-debted tenant (shaving brush, hair dye). I was not, however, in the trash more than an hour when the bag was torn open—alas, not by human hands, but by seagull feet, which might as well be hands, so dexterous are they—and I was carried to a great height, for which purpose you can well imagine. To be dropped. And, were it not for a child's inflatable pool, which had been inflated that very morning by the new tenant's daughter, I would have been shell-smashed, food for birds. But fate intervened, lucky for me. Because splash. Into the pool and, more precisely, into the plump lap of the child, whose legs were just beneath the surface, fell I. She screamed bloody murder at first, but then—calm down, calm down—yelled to her father, who was leaning out the window: A turtle just fell into my lap.

Tortoise, please.

A turtle, a turtle. Can we keep him.

Her.

And the rest is history, as they say.

But that fall. I will never forget how it felt to fly at such a speed. How death approached fast in the form of *ground*. It was as if the path that I call the Ebb had turned vertical, and I was rushing headlong towards the End. My heart stopped. The body *knows* when it's falling. And understands the outcome before the brain does.

Which is why, as Audrey once pointed out, people scream on roller coasters. Their bodies think they are dying.

We were driving through the Mojave Desert and we heard the screams before we saw the roller coaster. We had seen nothing for miles. Nothing, nothing, nothing. Then Audrey said, I think I hear a theme park. It was the end of a long day and I assumed she was hallucinating. We had both hallucinated Cliff on that particular stretch of highway. But no, I could hear screams too. And then I saw it: a giant roller coaster that spelled *hell* across the sky.

A dry wind blowing. She pulled the car over. We watched the little coaster inch its way up the H and then drop, tracing the cursive script. Who would want to fall like that, she said. On purpose.

Good question.

After a moment I realized she was talking about Cliff the Unmentionable, who, as an amateur stuntman, aspired to do precisely that. Fall on purpose. But let's not discuss Cliff. And hadn't she fallen for him, as they say, in the country with the Yelps. Hadn't they been skiing and hadn't she windmilled down the hill, possibly on purpose. And that was it. True love. *Coup de foudre,* as she always said. But what do I know.

The sound of screams on a desert wind. That is quite a sound. I sipped some water from the Yoplait container stuck to the dashboard with gum.

Wanna see it, she said. Up close.

I lifted my head.

She put the car in gear. She had on a red T-shirt with the sleeves rolled up over her shoulders. It had been a hot day for humans, though not for dashboard tortoises. No air conditioning in Cliff's car. The arm that had been stuck out the window was burnt and freckled. Her hair was damp around the edges. Now she wants to go to a theme park. Because she thinks he might be there. People who love to climb and fall do tend to gravitate towards such places: theme parks, airports, bridges. Cliff would love that roller coaster, sure, but he will not be on it, Audrey. He is not right now tracing the tracks of hell. He isn't.

We turned off the highway. The sky was pink. We pulled into a parking lot the size of Oregon. We found a space in the Tortoise section.

The park was all sparkling lights. I was tucked under her burnt arm. The temperature dropped, as it will in a desert at night, and all around us *people* dropped. A ride called the Plummet was just a broken elevator that continued to break, over and over. A ride called the Triple Bypass had, for many, contributed to their sooner-rather-than-later need for that operation. So the sign said. And then of course the main attraction, the roller coaster we'd seen from the highway, was far steeper and bulkier than its lower case script had suggested. It was called the Defibrillator because there was one waiting for you at the exit. Ha.

We stood under the Defibrillator and watched its passengers make the slow climb up the H. They were not yet screaming. But soon, soon.

When they dropped, Audrey hugged me close.

The reason a ride like the Defibrillator is quote unquote fun, she explained later, when I was safely back on the dashboard and she had her seatbelt securely fastened, is because you survive. Surprise, you survived. That is the fun.

We backed slowly out of our Tortoise spot. There were goosebumps on her arms. Outer space will suck the heat right out of a desert.

Later, back on the highway under the stars, I recalled my own heart-stopping fall into the lap of a child, and how I loved her for catching me and for never once begrudging me the tortoise-shaped bruise I left on her thigh.

My first memory is of the plane crashing. I say *crashing* because we were, for a while, crashing. And I say *first* because my memory of everything before the plane is fuzzy, while everything after the plane is sharp, bright, of the highest resolution it is possible to have in a brain. In this brain, anyway.

I was somewhere between my first and second leap birthdays. Closer to my first than my second. We were flying home from England. A line was crossed up there in the air. Or no, to be precise, a line was crossed back on the runway at Heathrow. Yes, on the runway. Because I remember the beginning of the flight too. I remember the plane girding its loins, as my dad liked to say.

What are loins.

He pointed vaguely at his stomach.

I did not like the sound of the plane. I did not. It girded, it gathered, it heaved itself into the grey sky.

We had gone to England for my grandfather's funeral. I remember almost nothing of the flight over. I remember very little of England, except that the house was a Clue board out in the country and there were giant bees in the garden wearing sunglasses like a private security force. There were men with beards who asked me about Newfoundland dogs. My dad was sad because his dad had died. I was homesick. The house felt like we might be murdered in it. That is what I remember.

And before that. Can I go back in my brain to before my first birthday. I have one fuzzy memory of a towel. I remember getting out of the bath and putting a towel over my head and asking my dad if he could tell which way I was facing. You're facing me, he said. How can you tell. I can see your feet, he said. Oh. I looked down at my bare feet. They were at the bottom of a long tunnel of towel. Of course. My dad could see my feet.

So I spun around a few times (to confuse him) and then quickly arranged my feet in what ballerinas call the first position, an almost horizontal line, toes pointing out. *Now* which way am I facing. Come on, Audrey, my dad said. Come on where. At which point, dizzy from the spinning, I fell forward and whacked my chin hard on the edge of the bathtub. My dad swept me up and said, Oh Wobbly. Which is what he called me when I fell over. Wobbly Flowers.

That is an early memory. But it is not of the same calibre as the plane memory. It is as if, in the first memory, I was protected from knowing I was crashing by the towel over my head. And in the second, someone had yanked the towel off and said, *See* yourself crashing. *Know* you are crashing. And oh, it will take awhile.

My seat was 12A. My dad's was 12B. We were in the first row, right behind the first-class curtain. I noticed that the stewardess fixed her hair before stepping through that curtain.

We did not have flip-down tables like everyone else. We had tables that unfolded like robotic arms from our armrests. At first I could not find my robotic arm. I looked in my armrest and it was empty.

I am without table!

No, it's over here, on the right, said my dad.

So why does this armrest open if there's nothing in it.

Must be a mistake.

I had a sinking feeling. A plane could have a mistake in it.

Nevermind. After a while my hollow left armrest seemed intentional and designed especially for me. I liked how the top flipped up. I liked the rectangle of darkness inside. It was a secret compartment. I loved secret compartments. I took a picture of my dad with my Polaroid camera and put the photo in the armrest to develop.

Okay, he said. Meaning, enough.

Earlier I had gone to the bathroom and taken pictures of all the passengers en route, many of whom were sleeping. I couldn't understand how people could sleep on a plane—I mean, we were flying!—with their arms all overlapping like that. I went to the bathroom and took pictures of the miniature sink.

Want to see my plane pictures, I asked my dad.

I've seen them.

The stewardess brought us meal trays. I told her how nice her hair looked. She smiled and said, Aren't you a cutie. Outside my window, a conveyor belt of clouds rolled steadily by.

The meal trays had compartments. I love compartments, I told my dad.

So you've said.

In fact, I would not say no to keeping this meal tray.

I would say no, he said. Adamantly.

Who's Adam Antly.

No response.

Fine. I also love tinfoil.

When the stewardess came by, I said, Excuse me, can I keep this tray.

Sure, honey.

I beamed at my dad.

I ate everything. My dad not too much. I asked him what he was reading.

"Slow Mortality Rate Accelerations During Aging in *Mus musculus* Approaches That of Humans."

Is it a biography.

No.

Oh.

I looked down into my armrest. I don't like people who read, I said.

My dad sighed.

Without me, I amended and started making a ball out of tinfoil.

Sleepy, my dad said hopefully.

I wasn't. But I must have slept because I woke up with a sore back and my right arm overlapping with my dad's left. We were beginning our descent. The pilot over the intercom sounded jaunty. The weather in St. John's is what you'd expect, he said.

The plane's engine changed pitch. I yawned. The pitch changed again. I hummed along. I looked out the window. We were stepping down wide invisible steps. When we broke through the clouds I saw Seagull Hill with its parking-lot top. And the harbour. I saw Quite-a-Bite-of Lake. Then I saw the ocean.

Then I saw them all again. And again. Then I saw Wednesday Pond.

Look, Dad!

I could even see the two swans with their bums in the air. Can you see the bottom. No. Can you. No.

The plane tipped so far to the left that my window became the floor. Then it tipped the other way and became a skylight. This was fun. At first.

We're making circles, I said.

Figure eights actually, said my dad, peering across me and out the window.

Why.

Not sure.

That's when someone behind me said, Problem with the landing gear.

What is landing gear! I yelled.

Shh, Audrey. Sit back down.

What is landing gear, I whispered.

My dad was buckling my seatbelt. He tore off the first page of his article and said, Why don't you draw a picture of Wednesday Pond from the air.

I need my table for that, I said.

We'd been told to put our tables away, but my dad extracted mine. He was breaking the rules. We're crashing, I said. Aren't we.

No, sweetheart. He gave me a pen.

I drew a map of Wednesday Pond on the back of the page. I put a house where our house was. I put a big arrow pointing at that house. *Home*, I wrote.

The plane continued to tilt.

I decided to add a secret message to my map. I would leave a secret message in the armrest. Then the plane would not crash. Because a plane carrying a message in its armrest could not crash. Rule Number One of Secret Messages in Armrests.

How do you spell *crash*, I asked my dad.

He spelled it for me. He was looking up at the ceiling.

How do you spell *landing gear*.

No response.

How do you spell *Wednesday*—

Which is when he leaned forward and threw up in the Aim Your Vomit Here Bag.

I had never seen my dad throw up before. I took a quick picture.

Audrey, what the—

I waved the picture to develop it. Then I put it in the armrest. I could feel my own vomit coming. I could also feel my heart. Of course I'd felt my own heart before, when I'd pressed my palm against my chest. But now I could feel my heart without touching it. It was knocking.

My dad wiped his mouth. Why did you take a picture.

Because I'm scared.

Someone behind us said, The wings are stuck.

I looked out my window. Weren't the wings *supposed* to be stuck. A plane's wings were not supposed to *flap,* were they.

Someone else said, We'll soon run out of fuel.

I finished my message and "mailed" it to my armrest. Please please please someone answer.

We were still figure-eighting. The pilots were not speaking to us. They were not saying, Ladies and gentlemen, we are *not* crashing. Therefore we were.

All the stewardesses had disappeared. Someone said they were distributing parachutes in first class.

I undid my seatbelt.

What are you doing.

Getting my life vest.

No Audrey. Get back in your seat.

There was nothing under my seat but someone else's briefcase. I am without life vest!

It's under your cushion. But you don't need it.

I do. I do. We're crashing into the pond with no bottom.

Bollocks. Sit up straight. Put this on. Click went the seatbelt.

There was no future. I was not feeling a future. There was no *next.* There was nothing, nothing, nothing.

And then something.

The plane remembered its dinosaur past. I must fall *slowly,* not quickly, out of the sky. Sorry about that. Sorry, sorry. I was just jogging my memory. Allow me to right myself. And the plane righted itself. Allow me to fall slowly. And fall slowly we did. Slower and slower. Home arrived in slow motion. We disembarked. We shook and wobbled on terra firma. My dad carried me to the car in long-term parking. Home was foggy but luminous. I squinted. I could smell ocean. I could smell rock. I could smell small trees overlapping.

No bees with sunglasses. No murderers. I looked up at the sky. What had happened up there.

When my dad put me down I rushed to kiss the car between the eyes.

Come on, old goat. Get in.

No long-term parking ever again, I whispered.

A few weeks later we brought Wedge home from the lab. My dad could not say no to me wanting to keep Wedge alive forever.

U ncle Thoby is on the porch with Toff. I can hear their lower case voices. Something has happened to Grandmother. She fell. A stroke of bad luck. Toff got a call and now he is talking to Uncle Thoby. I lean out the front door. I just called you a Clint.

Sorry, Toff says.

I just called you a cab. Get ready. They're fast.

Oddly, this is serious—

You've got two minutes. Wrap it up.

And I go back inside.

Toff is the last to leave the post-part-him party. Why are they talking outside. Because they don't want me to hear or because Toff can't think without a cigarette. Both, probably. Should I be concerned about Grandmother. Maybe, but I'm not.

Someone is distressed, Uncle Thoby is no doubt telling Toff.

And Toff is no doubt telling Uncle Thoby that I am not as distressed as I should be, because he overheard me perpetrating a fraud on the Christmatech representative.

Yes. Well.

Toff is leaving tomorrow. Back to the land of Eng. He was supposed to stay two more days but Grandmother's fall has prompted him to move up his departure date.

I am dropping. When was the last time I actually lay down. I consider the stairs. Upstairs is a bed with my name on it. But also upstairs is my dad's empty room. Am I ready to leave the ground floor. I've been circling—kitchen, living room, hall, bathroom—for days. Time to veer off. Or up.

On the wall, halfway up the stairs, is an adorable picture of me with a five-dollar bill taped over my eyes. I think I'm being the Queen, but really I'm being Wilfred Laurier. Uncle Thoby took that picture one Christmas after we'd watched the Queen's address, which always made my dad chuckle and me say *Chawles* and *Flip* and make a tiara out of tinfoil. That Christmas I got the idea of making a Queen Elizabeth mask out of money. My dad kept calling me Wilfred, and I didn't get it until he pointed out that not *all* bills have the Queen on them. They don't! No. But honest to God I couldn't tell the difference between the Queen and Wilfred Laurier. They're identical, I said.

Not really, said Uncle Thoby.

I get halfway up the stairs. I reach the picture and sit down on a step. After a while I feel the porch vibrating. Someone is walking away. It had better be the right person.

I slide slowly back down the steps on my bum. Look sideways out the screen door. Uncle Thoby is on the porch. A car is pulling away. The headlights light him up. He lifts his hand. When the car is gone, he bends over the railing like he's going to be sick. Is he going to be sick. He is without an Aim Your Vomit Here Bag.

But no, he isn't sick. He is supporting himself on the railing. His shoulders are shaking. I have a sinking feeling on fast-forward. Get up. Go out there.

He seemed okay when we pushed Verlaine's car. He seemed so okay. I jumped into his arms and he lifted me up.

He is not okay.

I know. And the moment I think the word *crash*, he starts to. His legs buckle and he sinks down.

I jump up. I've got my hand on the door handle. He is folded up on the porch. Crying. And I'm paralyzed. I'm watching him behind his back. I'm not supposed to see this. Back away.

In my room I don't turn on the light. I climb into bed. My eyes won't adjust. They have adjusted enough. There is no more adjusting. Just close us. So I close them. And see nothing. Just the thought of him crying makes my throat tighten. I turn on my side and corkscrew my arms. Now I see the syncopated red lights of the Christmatech van on my eyelids. I see a red rectangle moving through a maze of white streets. My dad is alive in that van. My dad is alive in that van. I feel myself running after it. Then it turns into the Lada. My arms are so strong. I can lift this car.

It was my dad who saved Uncle Thoby. Who went back to England to rescue him. Who persuaded him to come here. Don't ask yourself what you can do for your country. Ask yourself what you can do for Uncle Thoby. No. I mean, don't ask yourself what you are going to do without your dad. Ask yourself what Uncle Thoby is going to do. Wake up and ask yourself.

I will protect him.

You are already in montage mode.

That was so sweet of you, Judge Julian-Brown. To perform a house call to protect my dad from your faulty hardware.

We just assume our customers are alive. We assume life.

Thank you for assuming that.

On the kitchen table is the maze my dad built for Wedge one Christmas. We plunked Wedge down at the centre, but he just sat there and washed his ears.

He likes it, I told my dad. Really.

Uncle Thoby put a hand on my dad's shoulder. Is that Hampton Court.

As a matter of fact, yes.

You built Hampton Court, Uncle Thoby marvelled.

Still no reaction from Wedge, despite the cheese at the exit.

Where's Hampton Court, I asked.

London.

Your dad and I got lost in Hampton Court maze once.

Lost together or lost apart.

Lost together.

When you were little, I said.

No.

We sat around waiting for Wedge to smell the cheese. He didn't. He just leaned against the wall and groomed himself. Finally Uncle Thoby got up and replaced the cheese with a Licorice Allsort. That'll do the trick.

And sure enough, Wedge stood up on tiptoes, hands atop the wall, and sniffed the air. He figured out the maze in six minutes.

I can still do it in my head. I can do it in two minutes. I can do it in my sleep even faster. The thing about mazes is, there is always a solution. There is always a way out. Because who would build a maze without an exit.

A ssume life can go on indefinitely. Barring accidents. Barring plane crashes. Yes, well. My dad and I had been living indefinitely for almost a year since the plane crashing—I was still having plane crash dreams—when he said he had to go back to England for a while.

We had just finished a chapter of *Out on a Limb*, a biography about Shirley MacLaine by Shirley MacLaine. Shirley was getting on a plane and going to London. And oh by the way, so was he.

He stood up to clear the plates.

What!

He had to go out on a limb for his brother, Thoby, who was in crisis.

What. Stop talking Shirley.

Sorry, he said. I have to go to England to see Uncle Thoby, who's in a spot of trouble.

My dad used to talk about his brother every so often, but lately it was Uncle Thoby this, Uncle Thoby that. When I'd said I remembered Uncle Thoby from Grandfather's funeral, my dad had said, No you don't.

Yes I do. Long beard.

That was Toff.

Oh.

Uncle Thoby wasn't at the funeral.

Why.

My dad said it was a long story. Uncle Thoby was the black sheep of the family.

Interesting. I thought you were the black sheep of the family.

If you'd seen Uncle Thoby, you'd remember him, my dad said.

Okay, fine. But was a black sheep worth risking your indefinite life for. I didn't think so. And I noticed I was not invited on this trip. Why was that. Not that I was in a hurry to get on a plane again.

This was not an Audrey kind of trip.

Jesus Christ what was an Audrey kind of trip.

Not this one.

I have about a thousand questions, I said.

Okay, he said. So we retired to the living room for a serious talk.

The living room at number 3 Wednesday Place was for:

1. Serious talks.
2. My dad's annoying papers (scientific articles scattered all over the sofa and stacked in columns on the floor).
3. Wedge.

My dad used to call the living room the *drawing* room, which is short for *with*drawing room, but not short enough to be useful in my opinion. After we got Wedge, we agreed that we should start saying *living* room. Since that's what Wedge would be doing in it.

On my way into the living room I kicked over a column of articles and said, Oops, there goes a Lionel. I called all my dad's annoying articles Lionels after Lionel de Tigrel, who had written most of them, and who was my dad's arch-enemy.

My dad said Lionel de Tigrel was *not* his arch-enemy. But I remember him getting so mad once that he threw an article in the pond with no bottom, and when I went out there to fish it in, the name on the first page—the biggest name anyway—was Lionel de Tigrel. I nodded to myself. It was Lionel de Tigrel who had successfully turned a frog back into a tadpole. Lionel de Tigrel was a big shot at Cambridge. Well, we would show him.

My dad didn't like it when I called all his articles Lionels. He said, Can we not exaggerate the man's output.

Now he cleared a space on the sofa. Have a seat, he said.

I walked behind the sofa and sat in the window.

Fine. He sat down and twisted around. He said Verlaine would be staying at number 3 Wednesday Place and taking care of me while he was away.

Verlaine, the Swiss troll who eats mice!

My dad glanced at the mantel where Wedge was just now waking up and arranging his hair.

She'll make a sandwich out of Wedge, I whispered.

She will not.

Well. I'll be hiding him under my bed.

Fine.

I walked my feet up the window jamb. What am I going to do without a biography for years and years.

Not years. A month. Maybe Verlaine can read Shirley MacLaine to you.

I gave him a look.

Or not. Or you can read Shirley yourself.

I can't read.

Shirley you can. You can write. If you can write, you can read.

Not true. Whenever I tried to read, I turned the pages backwards. This was from watching my dad read so much. His right page was always my left. So when I got over to the other side of a book, *his* side, I kept turning the left pages and got confused. Also, the other side of a book was a lonely place when my dad wasn't on it.

My dad said it was important to read books and not just watch movies like *Star Wars*. He said the reason it was important to read was so I'd get all the jokes out there in the world.

What jokes.

You're only getting about twenty percent of the jokes, he said. And that is a low percentage.

Twenty percent!

Now my dad poked my leg and said, I have an idea. Why don't you *write* a biography while I'm away. And when I get back, I'll read it. How would that be.

I nodded to myself. Very clever.

Biographer is within your repertoire, he said.

Who would I write a biography about.

Outside, Jim Ryan was getting into his car and pulling out of his crescent.

How about him.

We were both quiet a moment. Then my dad laughed. He thought he was pretty funny.

We talked some more. I asked a lot of questions. They were all dumb. Finally I asked the important one, the not dumb one: How can you go back to England when it tried to murder us the last time.

My dad reached across the back of the sofa and pushed my bangs off my forehead. His hand was warm and dry. Nobody tried to murder us, Audrey.

I think they really did.

I have to help Uncle Thoby, he said. And that was that.

The night before he left, Verlaine came for supper. She stabbed her baby potatoes and gobbled them up whole while my dad gave her the scoop on the house. He had a checklist on the table. He told her about the sump pump. He explained the Northwest Shove. Audrey knows how to do it. Then he said, Wedge's food—

I kicked him under the table. *Which* food do you like best for dessert, I amended. All we have is *ice cream* sandwiches, so say them.

Them, said Verlaine.

So I went to the freezer. Shirley MacLaine was propping open a window, arms akimbo.

There's nothing I can do, I told her.

My dad was telling Verlaine about my routine. Actually Audrey doesn't have a routine in the summer. Except bedtime at ten o'clock sharp.

I'm writing a biography, I said, dropping dessert on the table. In the mornings. That's my routine.

Oh right. Audrey's writing a biography of our neighbour, my dad said. In the mornings.

Verlaine unwrapped her sandwich. A biography of your neighbour.

Yup.

How interesting.

But he doesn't know I'm his biographer, I said. So mum's the word, okay.

Verlaine buttoned her lips.

Now it was time to hear about *her* routine, which I, Audr*ay*, would have to be *folded into*. Great. I folded the chocolate roof of my ice cream sandwich into a fan. Then I ate one fan segment at a time.

There was the Before Building, of course. And there was a horse to be tended to.

A horse of course, I said.

Would I mind going out to the stable every day for a few hours to help look after the horse.

I gave my dad a look, like, I think that sounds a bit dangerous, don't you.

I think that sounds fun, he said. Don't you.

Um.

You've got ice cream here and here, he said, pointing.

I wiped my mouth on my shoulder. What's your horse's name, I asked.

Rambo.

Whereupon my dad laughed. So I did too.

•   •   •

The next day Verlaine and I waved goodbye to my dad's plane from behind the airport's chain-link fence. My dad had promised to wave something bright and white, like the sick bag. He would wave the sick bag.

But promise you won't need it.

I won't need it.

I had put a secret note in his carry-on luggage that said, Dear Plane. Do not crash. I love you.

A little car pushed the plane back from the gate because planes can't back up by themselves, which seems to me a serious design flaw, but what do I know. The car looked too small to be able to push such a fat pigeon as that plane was. I tried to see the pilots, but the cockpit was dark. They were not waving sick bags.

I felt sick. My dad was flying without me. I climbed the fence and Verlaine held on to my shirt. She didn't pull but her grip said that's far enough. I stuck my hands and toes through the fence. Held on tight. The wind was flappy.

The plane rolled slowly down the runway on its pigeon legs. I let go with one hand and waved but nobody waved back. He's on the other side, Verlaine said. Wait until the plane turns around.

Pigeons can barely fly. At least the ones I know can only stay in the air for about a minute before they fall down. And then they're out of breath for an hour.

At the end of the runway, the plane turned around and stood for a long time, gathering its thoughts. Then it girded its loins.

Now I could see him waving. Something white flashed in the fourteenth oval.

Dad!

I jumped off the fence and waved big. With both arms.

Verlaine waved too.

The loins girded louder. The plane rolled forward. Faster and faster it rolled on its tiny legs. And then, instead of taking off, the ground just let it go. The ground let go of the front wheel first, and then the back wheels. The plane climbed steeply and slowly. Too steep and too slow. It's going to fall back. I covered my eyes. Then uncovered them.

Remember in *The Empire Strikes Back* when Yoda is training Luke to be a Jedi. He lifts Luke's plane out of a swamp using only the Force. He points at the plane and holds it in the air.

I pointed at my dad's plane. Stay in the air.

The plane's legs folded up.

The plane got so ridiculously small that there was no way my dad could still be inside it.

This was the first time I'd been away from him. Ever. Verlaine took my hand. We walked back across the parking lot. I kept looking back. We got inside the Lada. We shut the doors and the wind came up through the hole in the floor.

What if this is forever.

Rambo's eyes are so big that you can actually see *inside* them. I mean, right inside the pupil. What do you see in there. You see a dark blue world with an upside-down mountain. You remember your dad saying that the eye flips things over and the brain flips them back, and you wonder, are you intercepting this process. Are you witnessing the first flip.

Verlaine says to go ahead and pat his neck.

So you do. And it is love. And before long you will know that he likes his neck scratched under his mane, where it gets hot. And when he's in his stall with his head down, he doesn't mind if you kiss the small dent over his eye. And he likes to rest his nose on your shoulder and chew a bit of your hair. And he likes carrots. And if you pull down his lower lip you will find bits of carrot left over, in storage.

His teeth are fat and not very frightening.

Why did she name her horse after that sweaty, bullety Sylvester Stallone.

Verlaine says a horse walks on his middle fingers. After I get to know Rambo a bit better I'm not surprised he's giving me the finger. He can be grumpy.

No, actually by middle fingers she means that a long time ago horses had paws with stubby fingers, and all the fingers except the middle one crawled back up the leg and are now buried inside, under the fur, except for one that still peeks out and is called the chestnut. So the hoof is really an old middle finger.

The hoof when you pick it up has a triangle inside called the frog. The frog is a shock absorber so that Rambo's toothpick legs don't shatter when he runs. The frog is also a second heart that pumps the blood back up those incredibly long legs.

So he has five hearts.

Sort of. Verlaine puts down the hoof.

I march up to Rambo's flippy eye and stare right in. You crazy cat. He seems to me a perfectly magical creature.

Verlaine takes me downtown to a shop with a sideways sign that sticks out like a flag. It says THE SADDLERY.

The Sad Larry, I pronounce.

Downtown is a bit smooshed. It takes Verlaine five tries to park the Lada. The stores all touch shoulders and tell pretty much the same story. Food, clothes, books. Food, clothes, books. But the Sad Larry tells a different story. A bell rings hoarsely when we step inside.

Horse stuff!

The guy behind the counter is called Larry. He has a long black braid. The braid starts out thick and gets thinner and thinner until it is only three strands. The braid doesn't lie straight down his back but comes over his shoulder to say hello. Verlaine says we are in the market for a hard hat.

I discreetly bring my ponytail over my shoulder and look around.

There is a lot of brown leather. On the floor there are tubs of bright-bristled brushes. Some of the brushes are hard. Some are soft. Some are in between. I use a soft one to fluff up my bangs. Whoa, static. There is also a tub of silver question marks. I twirl one around my finger and slide it into my back pocket.

Sad Larry does not seem sad so much as not very excited. He disappears into a back room and returns with a box. I'm guessing, he says (glancing at my bangs), that she's five and seven-eighths.

If Larry is guessing how old I am, boy is he Saddlery mistaken.

Larry fumbles with the box. Five out of ten of Larry's fingers, count them, have purple blotches from being careless with a hammer or a car door.

On the box there's a picture of a girl riding a white horse over a jump. She's wearing a black velvet hat and her brown hair makes a beaver's tail down her back. She is looking over her shoulder at the next jump. The next jump is red and white like a sideways candy cane.

Larry lifts a black velvet hat from the box. He passes it to Verlaine who holds it over my head like a crown.

Lower that ponytail, Larry instructs.

The ponytail is lowered.

I look up. The inside of the hat is red satin and says 5⅞ in gold.

The hat fits snugly. Verlaine adjusts the strap under my chin. Then she whacks two fingers down on the visor. It doesn't budge.

Merci, Larry, she says.

I can feel my hair trapped in a wave under my new hat. I am different in this hat. I am older. I check out my reflection in the car window. Before I open the door, I look over my shoulder for oncoming pedestrians. None. Okay.

The way I looked over my shoulder just now. Exactly like the girl on the box.

I slide into the car. I have stolen a hoof pick. Oops.

Verlaine asks if I'm going to keep the hat on in the car and I say yes.

The road rushes by under the hole in the floor. The city is different now that I have a hard hat. Now that I know there is a Sad Larry downtown. Now that there is a horse in the vicinity who can be driven to. I could probably drive the Lada myself if I were wearing a hard hat.

I turn the box around in my lap and ask Verlaine how the girl makes her hair go into a beaver's tail.

A hairnet, she says. Much simpler to have short hair like me.

Verlaine's hair sticks up like she was just electrocuted. No thanks.

Can I have a hairnet.

So we stop at the drugstore on the way to the stable. Who knew drugstores sold hairnets. Everything I need is everywhere I need it.

The city is new. I have a black visor and I don't squint into the sun. This new city does not have my dad in it. And I don't expect to find him in it. So I don't miss him. Which, I know, is the plan. But there is still nighttime. I still miss my dad pretty bad at night when my bare head is on the old Charlie Brown pillow.

I try, not very hard, to work on my biography of Jim Ryan. I have a notebook that says The Life and Adventures of Jim Ryan, but all I've written so far is: Jim Ryan is brave. Jim Ryan is stupid.

Because the other day he went up a ladder with a broom and swatted a wasps' nest. Of course they all swarmed him and he had to run away. Later, when everything had calmed down, Mrs. Ryan went up the ladder in a flowery dress with long sleeves and a can of something. No more wasps.

I am surely lucky to have a bedroom that looks out directly onto my biographee's house. Most biographers would kill for such a location. Verlaine suggests I go out there and interview the man. Come clean about being his biographer.

Well. I have already gone out there with my camera and taken some pictures for the cover.

The cover of the biography he doesn't know you are writing.

Right.

Jim Ryan, over his shoulder, says, Nice hat.

Thanks.

Should I be posing.

No. Don't mind me.

Possible covers:
1. Jim Ryan coiling a hose.
2. Jim Ryan running from wasps.
3. Jim Ryan doing a cartwheel in his crescent. (If only Jim Ryan would do a cartwheel in his crescent!)

When I'm not being a biographer, I'm being a rider. When I ride Rambo, the stirrup leathers have to be looped around twice because my legs are too short. Hold on to the mane for balance, Verlaine says, not the reins. She assures me Rambo has no feeling in his mane.

No feeling. I give his mane a tug and lean forward to look at his face. No response. I pull a bit harder. He sighs. And begins to walk in the direction of the barn.

The walk is a four-beated gait, Verlaine says. The trot is two-beated. The canter is three-beated. There is usually at least one hoof on the ground.

Oh good, I say. Good. Then I think about it. I look down at Verlaine.

Yes, there will be moments, split seconds, when no hoofs touch the ground at all. When you are galloping.

Holy Lada, I say.

The stable is not far from the airport, and sometimes planes fly so low that the landing gear scrapes my hard hat. Just about. When the planes fly low, I duck and Rambo swirls and Verlaine has to hold on to him tight. All four hoofs leave the ground.

Is he afraid of the noise. Or the plane crashing. Or what.

Verlaine says he is not really afraid. He's just faking.

Faking!

Planes, she says, are old hat to him.

Slowly I unlearn the old Verlaine. She is not a basement troll. She still eats Swissly, but her arms no longer seem dangerous. I drag

Wedge's terrarium out from under my bed. She laughs. Did you think I didn't *know* that mouse was somewhere in this house.

We eat ice cream sandwiches after every meal, including breakfast.

She takes Wedge out of his terrarium and handles him like an expert. Hello my little sandwich. She rubs the ear that says 18 and Wedge goes all dreamy and closes his eyes.

I watch her. Do you love Rambo.

Of course.

What about the mice in my dad's lab. Do you love them.

Non.

Why not.

Because I have decided not to.

But do you secretly and pretend to yourself that you don't.

What.

Do you secretly love them.

Non.

Secretly.

Non.

Wedge's whiskers twitch. He sits up.

Well, I love *all* animals, I say, grabbing him. He squeaks in protest.

Even a fly, says Verlaine.

I'm about to say yes, but then I recall killing one that very morning.

You love pieces of yourself.

My dad calls. I tell him all about Rambo. I gush.

He says, Do I hear Wedge in his ball.

You do, you do! Wedge is rolling by on the kitchen tile.

Verlaine hasn't gobbled him up, then.

No, I snort. Of course not.

I hand the phone to Verlaine and follow Wedge into the living room.

Fine. Yes. Good. *Non.* Do you think I would put that child on a horse without a helmet. She won't take the thing off. She's a natural.

I feel myself getting hot with happiness. Wedge, did you hear that. A natural. *Moi.*

Wedge puts his hands in the air and runs towards me.

I bend my arms like I'm holding reins and check out my muscle.

Three weeks without my dad and I am what Verlaine calls a gutsy rider. I no longer crouch when the planes fly low. I swat Rambo's neck and tell him to chill out. I can do a posting trot and keep the beat. We go for a hack. Verlaine walks beside me while I ride. The trails are rocky and Verlaine complains about this goddamn rock always giving birth like a bitch to more. We cross a river. Verlaine hops from rock to rock. So I guess they are useful sometimes. Rambo takes a long drink and I lean forward and hug his neck. I can feel the gulps travelling up under my arms.

At the end of a trail we reach a familiar chain-link fence. There's a field on the other side, then pavement.

That's the runway, Verlaine says. And the airport. She points at an itty-bitty building.

Holy Lada.

Will you stop saying that, you cheeky *souris*.

We wait for a plane to show up. Finally one does. Rambo pricks his ears. It's a dot that keeps getting bigger. It drops and gets bigger, drops and gets bigger, until it probably has people inside it. I watch from under my black velvet visor.

Soon, Verlaine says. That will be Walter.

The night before my dad is scheduled to come home, I can't sleep. My legs ache. Verlaine says it's growing pains, but it's not. It's waiting pains. The only thing that will make my legs stop hurting is to go out to the airport and run up and down the run-way until my dad's plane lands.

Well, that is out of the question, Verlaine says over breakfast. She studies me a moment. You look *dépeignée*. What. Uncombed. She reminds me that a hairnet is not a substitute for combing my hair.

I think it really is.

I think it would be nice to be well groomed for Walter's homecoming.

I concede that, okay, maybe it would.

Here are a few things I did yesterday to welcome my dad home:

1. Cut out a picture of Sylvester Stallone all sweaty and taped it over his bed (originally intended for Verlaine but she'd said, *Non, merci,* and suggested current location).
2. Made a new bookmark for *Out on a Limb* that says WE SHIRLEY MISSED YOU!
3. Arranged the alphabet magnets on the fridge to spell OUT ON A CRESCENT: THE JIM RYAN STORY (new working title).
4. Combed Wedge and fluffed his bangs.

We finish our ice cream sandwiches in tandem. For once I am as fast as she is. Three bites it took. Let's go to the airport!

She looks at her watch. We have five hours.

Five hours! But we have to go early for a Bite-to-Eatery.

Verlaine points out that we just had a bite-to-eatery. You've got ice cream here, she says. I wipe my mouth with a Lionel de Tigrel article. This is something else I've been doing for my dad. Using his arch-enemy as a napkin. I'm sure he'll be pleased.

She says she has a few things to do at the Before Building, then we'll go to the airport. Okay.

Okay. I guess.

And so we hop in the Lada and the whole way to the university I keep my head out the window. The sky is bright blue.

What are you doing.

Keeping an eye out.

He won't be here for hours, Audray.

What about a tailwind.

What do you know about tailwinds.

I know about tailwinds.

It is far more likely that he'll be late, she says.

Which words are like a knife to my heart. I sink back in my cardboard seat.

She glances at me. I didn't mean that, she says.

Verlaine usually takes me with her on her rounds. I fill up water bottles and have a chat with my dad's cauliflower brain. But today she says that if I want her to hurry I should wait in her office. I tend to slow her down, she says.

That is a bit insulting, but okay. Today I am all about hurrying. Hurry, hurry.

I sit in her chair and roll around the office. I flip through her calendar and find today's date. She hasn't circled it. I draw a tiny picture of a plane with my dad inside, waving.

Time marches on. My legs start to hurt. Where is she.

Her car keys are on the desk.

Now here is the thing. Even if I wanted to go find her and tell her to hurry up, I couldn't, because you need a special key to get into the animal part of the building, and she has that key with her. What if she has forgotten all about me and my dad. What if one of the pigeons has escaped and she has to spend hours trying to catch it.

I crouch down. Get up. Grab the keys. Run. It feels good to run. Smack, smack go my sneakers on the shiny floor. Up the stairs. Outside, I head for the Lada. Then stop. Look up. There's a plane overhead. Is my dad in that plane. Dad! I wave hugely.

I jump in the Lada and put the key in the ignition. Turn the key. The car jumps up in the air. All four tires leave the ground. Which scares the bejesus out of me. Holy Lada calm down. I do this a couple of times. The car keeps jumping, but we aren't moving forward. Why aren't we moving forward.

I slide down and put my feet on the pedals. Push, push, turn, turn.

That's when I see Verlaine coming out of the Before Building. Jaw set. Uh-oh.

Turn the ignition. Turn, turn, turn.

She lifts a hand to stop. I stop. I roll down my window.

What in hell are you doing.

I just saw my dad's plane.

Do you know how dangerous—

My legs hurt, I tell her. They really really hurt.

She opens the door. I look up at her from under my visor— because, oh yes, I am wearing my black velvet protective head-gear. With hairnet. I am beautifully groomed.

Why—

From waiting.

Get out.

I get out and run around to the passenger's side.

Verlaine turns the ignition and the car doesn't lurch, but it doesn't start either. Well, she says. You've drained the battery.

What battery! I didn't touch a battery.

She slumps. We're stuck here for a while.

Which is too much. I start to cry. But I saw my dad's plane.

She turns in her seat. What is this about, Audray. For a whole month you've been fine.

Yes but I haven't been.

She puts a thumb on my cheek. Smears a tear. Your legs hurt from *waiting*, she says.

I nod.

She nods.

We are late for my dad's plane. He is already outside in a pale yellow shirt. His hair looks lighter. Verlaine pulls up to the curb.

I jump out. I am swept up.

Did the landing gear come down okay, I say into his neck.

Yes.

He hugs me for a long time. Verlaine puts the Lada's hazards on. I hear her say, *Mais c'est incroyable*.

Thank you for the note in my luggage.

My dad seems different. His accent is stronger. But then, I am different too. I have a hard hat. And even when my hard hat is off, it is still on *in spirit*, because I have a tan line across my forehead and strap marks down my cheeks.

Also, there is the hairnet.

My dad doesn't know what to make of my new hair accessory. He says, what, am I in the food industry now. Am I making Piety pies.

Don't you love how my hair is caught in a swirl, I ask.

Well, sure.

I ask him about Uncle Thoby. Is he off the limb.

What.

Is he off the *limb*.

I am holding the fridge door open, pretending to look for cheese.

Out on a Croissant, my dad pronounces slowly. The Jim Ryan Story.

I peer over the edge of the door. It's supposed to say crescent!

You funny bunny.

He is making a lot of phone calls. This is new. To Grandmother. To Uncle Thoby. He sits on the basement steps and talks on the phone for hours. Sometimes he half-closes the door so I can't hear what he's saying.

His voice on the phone is soft and drippy. I want to kick him when I hear that voice. Sometimes I spring open the basement door and it whacks him on the back. Aha! I say, like I've caught him. But caught him doing what.

He looks up at me. Gotta go, he says into the phone. The girl with the swirl is eavesdropping.

Shirley MacLaine is back on the table but she's falling a bit flat. She's a doofus, I say one night.

Doofus, says my dad, nodding.

Do you know what a doofus is, I ask him.

Of course.

He says he has a biography of his own to tell me, the biography of Uncle Thoby, but he's waiting till we're finished with *Out on a Limb*.

But why are we waiting. This is dumb. Clearly he is not enamoured of Shirley's biography of Shirley. Clearly Uncle Thoby is not a doofus.

That's true, my dad says. He isn't.

Okay then. Shirley can hold up the window.

When do I get to read about Jim Ryan, he asks.

I hold up eight fingers.

Eight days.

No.

Eight weeks.

I shake my head. Eight is the number of words in Jim Ryan's biography.

Does that include the title.

No comment.

Here is something I have noticed about biographies: They all start off with a guy no one would write a biography about. All the odds are against this guy's biography being written. But you know it *has* been written because you're reading it. Or hearing it. So his luck is about to change. Plus, there are early signs that he's special. There are early signs of his destiny. Watch for them.

OFF WITH A LIMB: THE UNCLE THOBY STORY

Uncle Thoby was a baggage handler at Heathrow Airport until one day, through no fault of his own, a plane's cargo door closed on his arm and that arm was flown to Dublin by mistake.

What!

At first they didn't realize the arm had gone to Dublin. Uncle Thoby was rushed into the airport and an ambulance was called. He was faint from the loss of blood, which his co-workers were attempting to staunch with a bathrobe from a nearby suitcase, but before passing out he asked after his arm. Go. Stop. My. Arm. Unfortunately, by the time his co-workers reached the tarmac, the plane had already departed. Imagine the surprise of the Irish baggage handlers.

It was all a big debacle but not Uncle Thoby's fault. The two metal rods that hold the cargo door open had snapped in two. Both of them. What are the chances. It was a mechanical failure. And yet, because Uncle Thoby had a history of clumsiness, his employers decided that he was responsible for his own amputation. Further, they would not be needing the services of a one-armed baggage handler in the future. He was dismissed without pay.

Does Uncle Thoby have a history of clumsiness.

Well, so what if he does. He's been known to trip over a level threshold. And once he fell out of a moving car on the highway and broke his leg. Then he went sailing with that broken leg and fell overboard and almost drowned because the cast was so heavy. And once, when he had a cold, he tried to heat Vicks VapoRub on the stove, in order to produce a real "vapour," forgetting that the vile stuff is made of *grease*, whereupon it splattered and burned his face. But was he to blame for the cargo door of a Boeing 727 slicing off his arm. Hardly.

So now he was without an arm and in hospital. He had been in touch with Dublin airport authorities, but they had already taken certain "measures" with regards to his arm that prevented it being returned to him. What measures were those. Incineration. But what had he planned to do with his old arm anyway. It could not be reattached.

Of course he knew it could not be reattached at this late stage—he had come to terms with that—but what distressed him was that he could not remember it. His old arm was all a blur. Had there been freckles. Yes. But in what constellations. He had never paid attention. There was a scar on his left hand from a mis-adventure on the Lopper (a roller coaster). He would never see that scar again. He had simply *lost* a whole section of himself.

Nor was he experiencing the phantom limb syndrome so many amputees boast about. How he would have welcomed a phantom limb! But he had no sense that his arm still existed, here or in Dublin or anywhere. It was simply gone.

He came to believe that the freckles on his lost arm had been a code to himself that he might have cracked if he had paid attention. But he had never paid attention. He spent a lot of time staring at his right arm and then staring at the space on the hospital bed where his left arm should have been.

His old life was over. He would never handle baggage again. His co-workers visited and brought gifts—usually objects left behind on airplanes—and told amusing stories of air disasters to cheer him up. They expressed concern about his future. What would he do now, a one-armed baggage handler with no baggage to handle.

They offered to raise money, through bake sales and other means, to pay for a new prosthetic arm, a top-of-the-line model, since the airline was refusing to pay damages.

Uncle Thoby thought about this, and he thanked them very much, but he did not like the idea of a generic arm that wasn't his attached to a shoulder that was.

What.

He didn't like the idea of someone else's invented arm pre-tending to be his own.

Oh.

I should have said earlier that Uncle Thoby's arm was cut off here. (My dad makes a sawing motion above his left elbow.)

Ouch. Yes, you should have.

Okay. Uncle Thoby decided that he wanted to make his *own* prosthetic arm. He had heard that there were special camps where amputees could go to learn how to do this. Of course, people who attended such camps had to accept *temporary* prosthetics not of their own making while they made their own. You can't make a new hand with one hand. You need two. And even then it is hard. You can't expect to rebuild yourself overnight.

But when an amputee leaves one of these camps after months, or sometimes years, they take with them an original limb of their own making. Now that is pretty special.

So it was that the baggage handlers and airplane mechanics and aircraft groomers all rallied and contributed money to send Uncle Thoby to the Leg and Arm Reconstruction Camp in that piratical, picturesque town, made famous by the operetta: Penzance. So off Uncle Thoby went.

Penzance was lovely by the sea. Uncle Thoby made slow progress on his arm. Naturally progress was slow. Imagine building your own arm from scratch, using one hand that belongs to you and another that doesn't, and the one that doesn't is stupid and unresponsive, more a piece of wood with some tweezers stuck on the end than a real hand and arm. And the arm you are painstakingly trying to build yourself with these imperfect tools must look like your original limb, must be electronically jiggered to perform all the movements of your original limb, must maintain a body temperature of 37 degrees Celsius. Etcetera. It boggles the mind.

Not surprisingly some inmates get frustrated and give up. This happened to Uncle Thoby. He fell in with a shady Penzancian crowd not affiliated with the LARC who were all missing body parts and celebrating that fact. After a little spree in Penzance, Uncle Thoby returned to London and told everyone, including himself, that he was content to be a one-armed man.

His friends from the airport were furious. Had they not baked cookies and auctioned off the contents of thousands of unclaimed bags so that Uncle Thoby might attend the LARC and be a two-armed man once more.

Uncle Thoby apologized and scuffed his feet. The arm-making process was too *hard*. He didn't have the technical skills.

But surely the whole point of the LARC was to acquire those skills.

Yes. But. He didn't have the patience. It was hopeless.

Bollocks, said his closest friend, an aircraft groomer. Whereupon she shoved him into her car, strapped him in tight (knowing he was prone to falling out of moving vehicles), and drove him back down to Penzance herself. He was not to give up, she said.

They sat together on the LARC deck and he showed her what he had made so far. It was only a shell of what his future arm might be. It had no wires in it. But it was skin-coloured, and the aircraft groomer thought it was beautiful and he should keep going, even if it took years.

She said, Someday you will lift baggage with that arm.

Uncle Thoby smiled sadly. He knew this was not true. Or at least, he knew he would not lift baggage again in a professional capacity. However, maybe there were other things to be besides a baggage handler. Other lives that could be lived.

Let us pause there.

Was Uncle Thoby at the LARC when Grandfather died. Is that why he wasn't at the funeral.

My dad looks up from his cereal. Biographies are not usually discussed at the breakfast table. They are like dreams that way.

Grognard Man nods.

Why didn't Grandmother pay for the camp.

Grandmother didn't know.

Did you know.

Only recently.

Is that why you went to England.

Wait for the end of the story.

The arm he's building sounds an awful lot like Luke Skywalker's in *The Empire Strikes Back*.

Does it.

Remember how Darth Vader slices off Luke's hand with the light sabre and the hand falls into outer space, lost forever.

Vaguely.

Vaguely!

Uncle Thoby has finished his arm. It is a work of beauty. A masterpiece. So much so that it is indistinguishable from a real arm. With one exception. It is bigger than a real arm. Substantially bigger. But that is because of all the technology Uncle Thoby crammed into it. Because of all the hardware and wires, plus a heat generator.

How much bigger.

Well, big enough that when people see it they are sometimes afraid. They see a monster's arm. And they think, Only a monster could be attached to an arm like that. All they see is the arm. It's as if I looked at you and saw only your ponytail, sorry hairnet.

That would be okay.

No it wouldn't. Because I wouldn't bother to see the rest of you. And what if I had a fear of hairnets. Which I actually sort of do, by the way.

Why!

They're spiderwebby. But anyway, my aversion to your hair might stop me knowing your true story. And when people see Uncle Thoby's arm, they don't know his true story. They don't know what he has suffered and lost and how hard it was for him to rebuild himself. They think a man with an arm like that couldn't have a good biography of his own. They think he must be a thug in someone else's.

Poor Uncle Thoby. I would never think that.

I hope not.

Does the arm come off.

I don't know.

All biographies have a big obstacle. But even though Uncle Thoby has overcome this big obstacle of losing his arm, this is not *the* big obstacle of his life. There is a bigger one to come. That is what I feel.

Wait for the big obstacle.

I find myself thinking about him all the time. It is like on TV when they want to show two things happening at once, so they split the screen in two, an upstairs and a downstairs. I am in the downstairs part, riding Rambo, being tucked into bed by my dad, while in the upper part Uncle Thoby is working on his arm. He is clumsy and often hammers his right thumb by mistake (the temporary arm has various attachments, tweezers, hammer, etcetera) and then he curses a series of symbols (<£‰Ö%@#^). Or he is walking along a beach, one arm much bigger than the other, and people are staring, and he wants to go swimming more than anything but salt water isn't good for the mechanism. Or he is helping to paint the deck at the LARC and some brown paint splatters on his new arm and he can't get it off, and this small splatter is enough to make him cry. All his fellow LARCians gather round with their mismatched limbs in various stages of construction and say, Don't worry, a little nail polish remover will take that right off. What is the matter.

What is the matter. Where is his family, that is the matter. All he's been through, and where are they.

He looks at his new arm and there are freckles now.

· · ·

Instead of working on Jim Ryan's biography, I work on my arms. I map out my freckles in a notebook so I will have a record. I even use a ruler and measure distances. When my dad sees what I'm doing, he says I need a protractor to measure angles. He shows me how to use a protractor.

Why don't you use a protractor on your own arms, I tell him.

I connect the dots on my arm with blue pen. Triangles. The letter W, over and over. Then I copy the shapes onto paper. It is easy to map the freckles below my shoulders because they are sparse, but my shoulders are impossible because there are millions of freckles up there. It is like when you look at the sky and see four, maybe five stars, but then you turn off the porch light and holy, there are millions behind the ones you first saw.

The nail in the coffin of Jim Ryan's biography was when he started painting his deck with a known carcinogen. My dad went outside and had a fight with him. Sorry, a tête-à-tête. He went out there and warned Jim Ryan of the dangers of that substance and said he did not appreciate being downwind from it. Jim Ryan waved his paintbrush around and told my dad to stop being so foolish. My dad cited various studies. Jim Ryan called my dad a rude word. I did not hear it or I would not withhold it. But my dad came inside and said Jim Ryan had called him a rude word.

Goddamn it. I threw down my pen. Jim Ryan's biography is over. Rule Number One of Biography: Never be rude to your biographer's father.

Good rule, said my dad.

And Rule Number Two, for the fathers of biographers: Do not get into your kid's biography.

Is that what I did, said my dad.

My dad knocks on my door and says, Sorry to bother you.

I put away my Audrey's Arms notebook.

How's it coming, he says.

Good, good. How can I help you.

It is fun to talk like this when you're sitting at a desk. Try it.

My dad sits on the little square ottoman. He is too tall for it and his knees are up near his chest.

I have some information to share with you, he says, playing along.

Please, I say. Which means: Share that information.

Uncle Thoby is coming to visit.

I lose all composure. Glee. Glee is what I feel. It's like hearing that a famous person is coming to town. It's like getting mail on Saturday.

I jump up and put my hands on my dad's knees and do a little dance.

What are you doing, doofus, he says, which is his new favourite word. He bounces his knees awkwardly, which is the most dancing he will ever do.

I'm glad you're glad, he says after a moment. Because it will probably be a long visit.

I write down a list of questions about Uncle Thoby and over breakfast I make my dad answer them. Interviews are not normally conducted at the breakfast table. They are like dreams and biographies that way.

Me: I have some questions for you. Are you ready. Here they are. Where will he sleep.

Dad: Who.

Me: Uncle Thoby.

Dad: Oh. In the guest room for now.

Me: Can you clarify what you mean by "for now."

Dad: I mean that if Uncle Thoby stays longer we might turn the basement into an apartment.

Me: Can you clarify what you mean by "we."

Dad: No. What are you writing.

Me: Your answers.

Dad: Looks like scribbles to me.

Me: It's code.

Dad: So now you're, what, a journalist.

Me: Perhaps.

Dad: Perhaps. What happened to a biographer.

Me: You ruined that career.

Dad: Come on, Audrey. I ruined *one* biography. And I apologized for the Jim Ryan brouhaha.

Me: Laugh all you want. Ha ha. Brew. Yes. Does the arm come off.

Dad: What. Haven't we covered this.

Me: I'm just wondering if you've obtained any more information on the arm.

Dad: No, I have not. Next question.

Me: Will Uncle Thoby be able to do the Northwest Shove. Considering his arm, etcetera.

Dad: We'll teach him.

Me: Can you clarify what you mean by "we."

Dad: Jesus.

Me: Okay. Moving right along. Does Uncle Thoby like Clue.

Dad: He adores Clue.

Me: What character does he like to play.

Dad: Mr. Green.

Me: How does Mr. Green feel about Miss Scarlet.

Dad: You mean Miss Sarcastic.

Me: Brew ha ha. I mean *moi*, Miss Scarlet.

Dad: Ah. *Toi.* He finds Miss Scarlet very jumpy. The way she jumps around the board without rolling the dice. That alarms Mr. Green, who is afraid of flying.

Me: Is Uncle Thoby afraid of flying.

Dad: Wouldn't you be if your arm had disappeared in a plane.

Me: Holy Lada, yes.

Dad: Can I drink my coffee in peace now.

Me: What's his favourite food.

Dad: Shepherd's pie.

Me: What's that.

Dad: You want the recipe.

Me: No. Does Piety make it.

Dad: Unlikely.

Me: Will you still read after dinner.

Dad: Unless Uncle Thoby objects.

Me: Do you think he will.

Dad: No. But he might object to Shirley MacLaine.

Me: Shirley he won't object to her holding up the window.

Dad: Shirley not.

Me: Does he know about me.

Dad: Of course he knows about you.

Me: Have you been telling him my biography.

Dad: More or less, yes.

Me: What do I sound like.

A week before Uncle Thoby is scheduled to arrive, my dad and I head to Julian-Brown's Furniture. We are in the market for a coffee table. We are in the market for a bed for the guest room. We are not in the market for a cheval glass.

But the cheval glass steals the showroom!

Yes, well.

Apparently a mirror, if it can stand by itself and take a bow, becomes a glass horse. Of course I'm in love with it. Of course I want it. Try this. Stand to the side of a cheval glass and move one arm and leg in front of the mirror so that your reflection appears to be floating.

My dad does not try it. He is trying out beds. Fine.

There's a baby on the floor who belongs to the store. He's mesmerized by my floating trick.

Bonjour bébé, I say, and wave to him in the mirror. He reminds me of Beaker on the Muppets, the mute scientist with a tuft of upward-growing red hair. Imagine growing up in Julian-Brown's Furniture, with fifty rooms crammed into one. And every room like a set from a TV show. You can be in a sitcom or a love scene or a murder. The baby can choose the room he grows up in. He can choose his show.

He toddles into a floral-printed living room and crawls under a coffee table. He looks up at me through the glass. This is his trick. Maybe I can float in the mirror, but he can crawl under a table.

I press my fingers against the glass like a spider doing push-ups.

My dad says, Is that our coffee table, then.

I would not say no to a cheval glass in the living room instead of a coffee table.

My dad makes big batty eyes at the baby. I would, he says. I am. Saying no.

I point out that a cheval glass could double as a table when swivelled sideways.

My dad points out that such a table would see-saw precariously.

I point out that it would not see-saw if it were properly supported at both ends.

My dad points out that he would rather not have to concern himself with converting a cheval glass into a coffee table when he could just buy the coffee table.

I concede that point.

A few days later the new bed and cheval glass are delivered.

By which time Uncle Thoby's arrival is imminent and there is much tension at number 3 Wednesday Place. My dad has become an uptight Modern Major General, like the one in the opera, sorry operetta, who wields a protractor and has many cheerful facts about the square of the hypotenuse. He takes a weird geometric delight in arranging the furniture in the living room like a gnomon. Which means a clock, not an idiot. The furniture is now arranged in a circle with Wedge overseeing. All feet, when people are seated in here, will now point to the centre.

But will there be room to sit in here. *Bien sûr,* because my dad is saying adieu to the stacks of Lionel de Tigrels with their—what *is* this, Audrey—ice cream sandwich stains. That's disgusting. But I did it for you. Oh, well, thank you. Welcome. Anyway, no more Lionel de Tigrel articles or bizarre gifts from Patience. All this stuff is being cleared out, and when the sun comes through the window it will tell the time on the floor, using the furniture.

The room also tells infinity because the cheval glass is across from Wedge, and behind Wedge, on the wall, is another mirror, so the two mirrors play tennis, with Wedge as ball, and make a tunnel of Wedges into forever.

My dad looks at all the Wedges and says either that is his worst nightmare or his dream come true, he doesn't know which.

The Pirates of Penzance plays on the stereo. It is a pretty good story. You can follow it, even with the songs interrupting. There's a guy with my birthday who has a big obstacle to overcome. He gets in with the wrong crowd who turn out to be the right crowd. The pirates have huge hearts and all you have to say to make them love you is: I'm an orphan. My dad's favourite song is the one about the hypotenuse. He chuckles to himself every time he hears it. There are thousands of jokes in *The Pirates of Penzance*. Naturally I only get twenty percent. But I get that Frederic was supposed to be apprenticed to a *pilot* and was mistakenly apprenticed to a *pirate*, all because someone mispronounced a word. That is pretty funny.

Also that he is twenty-one, but really only five and a little bit older.

As for the tension. Right. The tension arose when I was first recruited by the Major General to clean up the living room and we pulled back the sofa and found a card shuffler, which my dad said was a gift from Patience. An idiotic gift, he said. Who can't shuffle cards.

I pointed out that a one-armed man could not shuffle cards.

My dad looked abashed. You're right, he said.

We also found a mushroom-growing log. It was in a box that said SHIT on the side. I laughed at the word *shit* until my dad told me to stop being such a doofus. It's shiitake, he said. It's a log that grows shiitake mushrooms. Also a gift from Patience.

Shit cake, I pronounced. Log.

My dad was not finding me funny. He was throwing out the shiitake log and the card shuffler and a mug with the Charter of Rights on it. Good riddance.

Wait. I grabbed the card shuffler. I have a home for this.

No, my dad said. It takes a nine-volt battery.

So.

So it will be noisy.

So.

We don't have any nine-volts.

I think we really do.

Not the fire alarms.

I went off in search of a nine-volt. I found one in a fire alarm. I dragged over a stool. It is really not hard to disable a fire alarm. Then I took the card shuffler and battery to my room. As I passed the living room, my dad said, Hey, I need some help in here.

Yup, I said.

I installed the nine-volt. I love nine-volts. I love saying nine-volt. I love how they are rectangles. I would like to keep one in my pocket just to show people. Or not show them. Just to have on hand. What's that you've got there.

Oh nothing. A nine-volt.

Did she just say nine-volt.

The card shuffler came with a deck of cards, which was nice of it. I tossed out the instructions. I mean, come on. You'd have to be an idiot. You split the deck in two, put half the cards on one side, half on the other, and then push the red button. A racket ensues. It sounds like a lawn mower hitting a rock. And then, ta-da, cards all over your room.

My dad called up from downstairs, Is that the shuffler.

No comment.

Where'd you get the nine-volt.

And so I am yelled at because we could have burned alive in our beds and terrariums without an alarm to accompany our burning.

Speaking of beds, there is a brouhaha over the new bed. The new bed has circular knobs on the four posters. I have drawn happy faces on those knobs. To make Uncle Thoby feel more welcome.

My dad sees the happy faces and makes an unhappy face. He shakes his head.

I shake my head too. What.

Those knobs are not very nice.

Yes they are.

You've vandalized his bed.

I kick the bed. Bad bed.

Go to your room.

And so off to my room I go, viciously kicking cards out of my path. Later I will take a marker and return to the guest room and make all those smiles fangy.

The day Uncle Thoby is scheduled to arrive, my dad buys plants. This is maybe the weirdest thing. We have never had plants in the house before. But now we have to rush out to Canadian Tire and buy plants that look like slices of somebody's hedge and put them in the corners of the living room and on the stairs and in the upstairs hallway.

Uncle Thoby likes plants, my dad says. What's next.

We are in final countdown mode. The guest room is ready. Wedge has been combed and fluffed. I have been combed and netted and hard-hatted. I stand, looking over my shoulder into the cheval glass.

Mirror mirror nowhere near the wall, who is the fairest of them all.

My dad walks by. Stops. Points at his own head. We're going to the airport not the stable.

The airport is across the runway from the stable.

So.

So.

Fine. He carries on into the kitchen. It's two thirty. Let's go.

Does your tooth hurty, I ask as we get in the car, but he doesn't even smile at our favourite Christmas-cracker joke (when is a good time to go to the dentist). He just says, Seatbelt, and starts the car.

We are forty-five minutes early, so there is time for soggy fries at the Bite-to-Eatery. My dad doesn't eatery. Every so often I wave a fry near his mouth and he swats it away.

Ladies and gentlemen. The flight from London has arrived.

My dad jumps up. He is a gentleman. I am a lady. I shove the five remaining fries in my mouth and race after him.

I hop aboard the baggage carousel as soon as I see it and am promptly lifted off. What does that sign say, my dad asks.

NO RIDING THE BAGGAGE CAROUSEL EVEN THOUGH IT'S CALLED A CAROUSEL.

My dad is wearing jeans with a dapper white shirt. His hair is fluffy. I hug him hard before he puts me down. I burp gravy.

A few ladies and gentlemen smile at my headgear. I salute them.

Okay, I've decided not to ask Uncle Thoby about his arm in case this causes him trauma. I'm not even going to look at it. Much.

The passengers from England will not be coming down the usual brick hallway with velvet ropes at the end to corral them. They will emerge from behind a wall once they have successfully cleared customs. I forget what customs is. Customs, says my dad, are police who make sure you aren't carrying dangerous items from non-Canada in your luggage.

Like what.

Oh. Like meat.

Meat! We have meat in Canada.

Right. But we only like our own.

Oh.

Speaking of meat, did we take the shepherd's pie out of the freezer.

Yes.

I've asked you that already, haven't I.

Yes.

The wall protecting us from non-Canada is just a flimsy wood board. You can see the nails holding it up and everything. I knock very discreetly on that wall.

Audrey.

What.

Stop that.

I knock again, smiling up at my dad.

No one knocks back. But I can hear them talking. At first I think they're making fun of my dad. I clench my fists. Then I remember, no, that is how people talk in England.

Bags plop down onto the carousel.

The carousel is laying eggs, I tell my dad. This is a joke, sort of, but he doesn't smile.

Those eggs are from another flight, he says.

Oh.

He shoves his hands in his pockets and watches the place where the wall ends and Canada begins. So far, everyone who has stepped out from behind that wall has two arms the same length.

Meanwhile people are leaning in sideways and picking bags off the carousel, like, no big deal, plane, carousel, home. They roll away.

I pull my dad's hand out of his pocket and hold on to it. I do a half-spin and push my face between his arm and his side. He smells Daddish.

Don't glom on, Audrey.

We wait. Finally we sit on the edge of the carousel, even though this is not allowed. There are only three bags left. I check the tags. None says Uncle Thoby.

He wasn't on the plane, I say.

He might be tied up in customs.

With ropes!

No, not with ropes.

But wouldn't his bag be on the carousel.

Didn't I say those bags are from *another flight*.

Ok*ay*. Jeeze Louise.

My dad pushes up his hair. What is this Jeeze Louise. You can say Jesus Christ.

I'm beginning to feel like we are dumb. Like someone is playing a joke on us. I want to hug my dad and protect him. But I also
want to kick him.

I hear laughter from behind the wall. Which is unacceptable.
I decide to march right over there into non-Canada.

Wait, Audrey.

Two men in uniform. No ropes. What a good laugh they are
having.

Ha ha, I bark from under my black visor.

Their mouths close.

Are there any more non-Canadians left to come.

They exchange looks.

No my duck, says one, bending down. You missing someone.

My uncle.

Audrey, says my dad from behind me. He apologizes to the
customs men.

Quite all right.

Takes my hand. We're going home.

In the car I rearrange my feelings. I want to hug my dad. I want
to kick Uncle Thoby. Why wasn't he on the plane.

My dad is quiet. He's driving slow, which is not like him. He's
driving like there's a rubber band on the bumper still attached
to the airport, and although we can stretch that rubber band, we
can never break it.

Dad, shift into fourth for the love of God.

He looks at me, like, what is fourth.

Gear.

He shifts.

I didn't know Jeeze Louise was short for Jesus, I say, staring
out the window.

It's not short for Jesus. It's a euphemism for Jesus.

Oh.

Don't be sarcastic. A euphemism—

I know what a you-fizz-em is.

No you don't.

I bet it's when you say one thing and mean another.

Well, yes.

So like sarcasm.

No.

Now he's tangled up. This is good. Keep his brain on this.

I 'm not sure how many times Uncle Thoby failed to show up. It feels like five. But maybe it was only three. Out to the airport. Knock knock on the who's-there wall. No answer. No Uncle Thoby. Back home in excruciatingly low gear. No shepherd's pie for dinner.

In my mind Uncle Thoby becomes a cross between a shepherd who loves pie and a black sheep. A black sheep, I decide, is a euphemism for the son who is loved less.

My dad spends hours on the phone after I've gone to bed. I can hear the annoying phone voice through the vent. In the morning he tells me that Uncle Thoby has the flu. That's why he didn't fly. He was about to get on the plane at Heathrow, but then he was sick in the bathroom.

Heathrow-up airport.

My dad laughs and sips his coffee. Apparently I am funny again. For days I have not been funny.

He can't fly because of flew, I say and kick Uncle Thoby's chair under the table. I think about how I would like to cut down the legs with a saw and make that chair really low. So that when and if Uncle Thoby ever shows up, only his head will be visible over the table. I recall the fangs on his bedposts and smile a fangy smile of my own.

What are you smiling at.

Does the arm get a fever when he does.

My dad wants me out of his hair. Thus I am sticking around. I go with him to the Before Building. Verlaine offers to take me out to the stable but I say no. I will not leave my dad. The most I will do is put on my hard hat and ride my bike around the wraparound porch. Around and around I go, practising my posting trot even though there is no beat. I ride down the steps and pretend they are jumps.

Every so often we go out to the airport and return without an uncle. It is humiliating. We are humiliated. Humiliation is being left like an uncollected bag on the carousel.

Remember when Big Bird tried to introduce Mr. Snuffleupagus to the rest of Sesame Street. Remember how he never showed up.

My dad and I are playing Clue. Clue is not really a game for two people, but I don't know that yet.

Remember when Big Bird—

I suspect Colonel Mustard with the Revolver—where is the Revolver—in the Billiard Room.

I check my cards. Nope. Remember in the old Sesame Street how Mr. Snuffleupagus never showed up.

My dad marks something on his scoresheet. Uncle Thoby is not Mr. Snuffleupagus.

Yes, but he is. Why doesn't he call *before* we go out to the bloody airport for the millionth time. Is he trying to humiliate us.

The Revolver is missing, my dad says, lifting the board. Where is the Revolver.

After my dad has gone to bed I sneak back downstairs. Wedge's wheel stops. What are you doing.

Neveryoumind.

The wheel starts up again, but more slowly.

It is easy to solve a crime. You just pick up the phone and push the redial button. Then you wrap yourself in a curtain to muffle your voice.

All the beeps sound like that pirate song. Pour, oh pour the pirate sherry.

Hello.

You, in your deepest pirate voice: Is this Thoby Flowers.

I'm sorry.

I said is this Thoby.

Who is this.

I think you know who this is.

Yes. I think I do.

Listen, don't bother getting on that plane tomorrow or the next day or whenever. I don't care if you come here. Neither does my dad. You and your homemade arm can stay where you are. I've got a Revolver. I might shoot you if you come here.

Silence.

Do you understand me, gnomon.

Gnomon. Well. I'm sorry we had to meet like this, Oddly.

What did you call me.

I want to hang up now. I try to hang up. But I am caught in the goddamn curtain. I try to push the receiver away, but it's holding on to *me*. I kick at the curtain until I find the opening. Wedge has stopped running. He is watching me. It is dead quiet. I put the receiver back in its cradle.

The shadow I make on the wall is monstrous.

Wedge's hands press the glass. Want a hug.

I shake my head, no.

Actually, Walter, I was all set to board the flight this time—I'm feeling much better, thank you—but then I got a call from your daughter at six o'clock in the ante meridiem, my time, telling me to stay put if I did not want to be murdered upon debarking from the plane.

You must be mistaken, dear brother.

That is how I imagine the conversation going. I am sick with dread. I ride my bike in slow circles around the porch. My dad is upstairs taking a nap. He is tired from being on the phone so much.

I hate the phone.

Uncle Thoby's flight is scheduled to arrive at three thirty. Will he or won't he be on the plane this time. At two o'clock I'm supposed to wake my dad. What if I don't wake him. What if I let him sleep straight through the arrival time. Then, if Uncle Thoby does show up, *he'll* be the one humiliated for a change. He'll be the one waiting on the baggage carousel like an uncollected bag.

But then I remember his biography and I have hurt feelings. Because what if this is the big obstacle in his biography. Getting on a plane and coming here. And I just made the obstacle bigger. Of course he is afraid to get on the plane. Of course he is.

Inside, the house is quiet. I take off my sneakers. Pad into the kitchen. Drink some milk. Take off my hard hat. Scratch my head. Put it back on. Stare at the table with its three chairs.

A fruit fly bobs by. En route to the hedge in the living room. Excuse me.

I move out of its way.

That chair, Uncle Thoby's chair, looks empty. It didn't used to look empty. How can it be empty now. How can someone have his own chair when he's never been here.

Pad, pad upstairs. I pass the slice-of-hedge on the landing. Three fruit flies bob in formation over it. Onward to my dad's bedroom. Open the door. He's asleep on his side. How can he sleep in the early post meridiem. This is unacceptable. But while he is sleeping I will steal some chocolate from the pie-shaped drawer.

My dad has a desk from Denmark that holds itself together without nails or glue by some miracle of gravity. The drawers are circles that swivel out. I swivel out the top drawer where the dark chocolate lives.

Why is his breathing so stupid and deep when he sleeps, like he doesn't care if I steal his chocolate. I creep over to the bed and lie down beside him. I push the chocolate against the roof of my mouth. Overhead, Sylvester Stallone is looking mighty muscly.

I put my ear against my dad's back, between his shoulder blades, because maybe I will hear what he's dreaming. He's wearing a blue shirt that was dapper this morning. Now it's a little bit damp. I listen. Nothing.

Just when I'm about to give up, he rolls onto his back. I yelp. Good thing I'm wearing my hard hat.

He sits up and says, Christ Audrey.

Hi.

What are you doing.

Having a bit of a lie-down.

He scratches his head, which is the first thing he does when he wakes up. I call it waking up his hair.

What time is it, he says, suddenly anxious.

One thirty.

He flops back down. You've got something here.

Where.

He points on his own face. What have you been nibbling on.

Nothing. I swing my legs off the bed and bend down to adjust my sock. I spend a long time adjusting it.

Ready to go to the airport, he says.

I keep my head down. Now is the time to tell him: Dad, I called Uncle Thoby at tooth hurty in the ante meridiem and pointed the Clue revolver at the phone and told him not to come. I was mad. I'm sorry.

But I don't say this. Instead I keep adjusting my sock. Yup. Ready.

And lo and behold, this time, when I knock on the wall, someone knocks back.

It's him!

I canter to the edge of non-Canada and peer around the corner. He's talking to the customs guy. It's definitely him because he does not have two arms the same length.

Holy Lada. I spin around, my back to the wall.

My dad looks at me, like, what is your problem.

It's him, I say.

Are you sure.

I close my eyes. Yup.

He steps out from behind the wall and it is true love. He looks around, eyebrows up. Well, you can only see one eyebrow because the other is hidden under a flop of hair. Also, he has a short scruffy beard. He's dragging a suitcase behind his long arm.

He sees us.

Then my dad is saying, So you made it, did you have any trouble, good flight, etcetera. And Uncle Thoby is saying, Customs. Bloody customs was terrifying. He laughs. He scratches his beard.

Their voices overlap. They both make their words bounce in the middle.

I hide behind my dad.

Oddly. A knock on my hard hat.

I look up. There he is, under my visor.

The knock becomes an open palm. Finally we meet, he says.

So. He will not give me away.

When I grab his hand, his left hand, to take him on a tour of the house, it feels like a normal hand. It feels 37 degrees Celsius.

He smells sweet, like perfume.

I introduce him to Wedge. Hello little man, he says. Wedge proceeds to drink from his bottle and look very winning. When Wedge drinks he holds on to the bottle with two hands. Uncle Thoby is very much won. He asks about the number 18 on his ear. That is from his lab days, I say. That is Verlaine's doing.

Of course, he says.

I can ride a horse, I tell him. But you knew that from my biography.

And from your hat.

Oh. Right. I'm in full riding regalia. Also, I'm wearing a white blouse with buttons all the way up the sleeves that can't be undone. There's a Bite-to-Eatery stain on the ruff.

I show him the infinity of Wedges in the cheval glass.

Yikes, he says.

Then I show him my floating-in-the-mirror trick. Now you try, I say, because I am generous with my trick.

Uncle Thoby stands to the left of the mirror and moves his right arm and leg in front of the glass. His flop of hair disappears. He has two arms the same length. He is not himself in the mirror. He is Symmetrical Uncle Thoby. I pull him away. Okay, that is my trick, I say, not yours.

We head upstairs. I do a sort of dance in front of the fangy bedposts, to distract him.

He joins me in the jig. Why are we dancing.

Supper's ready, my dad calls from downstairs. He sounds so happy that I feel instantly afraid.

Let's go, I say. I grab the hand.

As we turn to leave, Uncle Thoby's eyes alight on one of the bedposts.

Yeah. Sorry about that.

It is love. But it is one thing to love someone at the airport, or when you are giving him a tour, and another to love him in the presence of your dad, who is talking solely to him.

So there will be conversations now that do not include you.

You sort through the mail, loudly. Rudely. You wave an election flyer. Byrne Doyle, you announce to your dad and roll your eyes and don't explain to Uncle Thoby who he is.

You mention Jim Ryan. You casually mention your biography-in-progress, even though it no longer is.

Your dad relates the carcinogenic creosote episode. He tells how Jim Ryan waved a brush dripping with creosote right in his face. Did that really happen. Your dad makes the story funny. Uncle Thoby is laughing and leaning against the fridge.

You say, Move, because you want to get milk.

Later, forever, you will remember how he stopped laughing, how politely he moved out of the way, and how he looked unsure of where to move to.

Over dinner Uncle Thoby asks about my biography. I tell him it's actually on the back burner.

The back burner.

He and my dad make twinkly eye contact. So I am amusing behind my back now. This will be another new thing.

My dad tells more Jim Ryan anecdotes. Wasps. Crescent driveway. Pull in forward, pull out forward. My dad does a killer Jim Ryan imitation. Since when.

That is not very nice, I say.

And they stop.

I make my fork stand up in my shepherd's pie and go to the fridge for ketchup. Why couldn't I write a funny biography like my dad's, full of jokes and imitations. Maybe put in a few car chases.

We sit at the table for a long time and forget to turn on lights. The colours go out one by one. Uncle Thoby props an elbow on the table and rests his cheek in his hand. Pushes his hair back. He looks happy.

I try to keep my eyes open. Their voices seem very far away. I hear Uncle Thoby express surprise that Shirley MacLaine is holding up the window.

Then suddenly, thump. I am on the floor.

Gasps from above.

Are you okay, sweetheart.

I scramble up, lift my arms, like, ta-da! But then I feel confused and for a moment I can't remember who Uncle Thoby is. I push my face into my dad's stomach. Someone is exhausted, he says.

He picks me up and carries me upstairs. Straight into bed with my frilly blouse and fake buttons and the Bite-to-Eatery stain.

Good night Oddly Wobbly Flowers, he says.

So that is who I am now. I snuggle in. Am instantly asleep. Or almost instantly. I can feel him tugging at my hairnet. I turn my head to make it easier.

And somehow I discover, by turning my head and corkscrewing my arms so that the backs of my hands touch, a new sleeping position that is the best one yet. When the backs of your hands touch, they feel like someone else's hands, but not in a bad way. They feel like you, from the outside. My legs are in a leaping position. I am falling asleep in a corkscrew-leaping position. The last thing I think is, remember this position so you can find it again tomorrow night.

The next morning he is gone. There is a note on the counter. Out for a stroll. See you anon.

Grognard Man is having trouble with the coffee filters.

I run to the window. It's raining sideways. The range hood is whistling. Oh no. He's run away.

He's still on English time, says my dad. Like that explains something.

Let's go find him, I say.

No, let's not.

Who the hell is anon.

Anon means soon. Anon means *bientôt*.

There's an orange cut into sixteen pieces at my place. I climb into my chair. A fruit fly bobs like a helicopter over my plate. I swat it away. It comes back. It crashes into my orange.

Goddamn it.

What.

Fruit fly.

Do we have a *Drosophila melanogaster* problem, says my dad. Can you. He hands me the filters.

The flies came with the hedges, I tell him.

Don't call them hedges.

I separate two or three filters from the stack. What should I call them.

Indoor plants.

Yesterday, when I gave Uncle Thoby the tour of the house, he said he'd never seen hedges indoors before.

They're for you, I told him.

They're lovely.

The fruit flies live in the hedges but make daily reconnoitring trips into the kitchen for food. They also like toothpaste, which is gross. At least one fruit fly lives in the bathroom. I can't believe my dad hasn't noticed this. Nine times out of ten, when I look in the bathroom mirror, there's a fruit fly doing a jig over my shoulder.

Are you going to be brushing your teeth any time soon.

No. Get away.

Okay. Let me know.

Bob, bob.

Look at you, I say. You with your little antennas parted in the middle. You with your toothpaste addiction. Sad. Truly sad.

I clap my hands over my shoulder, but he always bobs to a safer altitude.

The rain sounds like it's chewing the window. I slide off my chair. There he is! On the other side of the pond. Having an argument with an umbrella. Look, Dad.

A moment later I'm on my bike, bumping down the porch steps. I pedal hard, keeping my head down like a jockey with aerodynamics in mind. The bike is Rambo, pretend. I am soaked in two seconds. The path has rocks that must be dodged. Mud. A few snails with portable rooms go crunch. Oh sorry, sorry, sorry.

Me to the rescue. This is my pond. This is my rain. You should have consulted me on the subject of umbrellas in Newfoundland. You should have waited for a proper tour.

He sees me. Lifts a hand. The umbrella is inside out. I put on the brakes. Be casual. Hi, I say.

He points at my feet. You're not wearing shoes.

Forgot.

His cheeks are red and wet and raw. His flop of hair is plastered like an arrow. He looks different from last night.

I point at my own chin. What happened to your—

Shaved it off.

Why.

Itchy.

I walk my bike beside him. Careful of the snails. Don't your feet hurt. No. He carries the umbrella like a dead friend. Stupid Newfoundland, killer of umbrellas. I stomp a bare foot on Newfoundland.

He laughs.

I laugh too.

I was chased by one of your swans.

Those swans are not native to our province. Look how bright their beaks are. You should have waited for a tour from me.

He watches my feet worriedly. A smack of rain hits us hard from behind and we fall forward a bit. Mother of God, he says.

Don't take it personally.

When we get back my orange has five dead *Drosophila melanogasters* in it. Uncle Thoby says, Poor little guys.

Poor. Stupid. They get stuck in their own food.

My dad points out that we share ninety percent of our DNA with the *Drosophila melanogaster*.

Uncle Thoby says he will cut me a fresh orange. Do we have any Alka-Seltzer by the way. The coffee burbles. My dad says yes, there is Alka-Seltzer upstairs.

It all feels incredibly normal.

I race upstairs to get the Alka-Seltzer. Back downstairs. Pause on the landing. I can hear my dad whistling along with the range hood.

B-flat, he says.

A-sharp, says Uncle Thoby.

At my place at the table there's a work of art. It's called an Orange in a Castle. All the slices lean out over the parapet.

Start at midnight and eat clockwise, says Uncle Thoby.

Why.

Because if you go counter-clockwise the orange will peel itself back up.

It turns out an orange has eleven slices. Five on one side, six on the other. It's missing an hour. I've never noticed this because my dad always cut the orange into sixteen pieces, which I then sucked off the peel. But this is what an orange really is, underneath. Not symmetrical.

After breakfast, Uncle Thoby devises a trap for the fruit flies, which he calls the Drosophila Melanogaster Detention Centre. The DMDC is a glass with a piece of orange at the bottom and some cellophane stretched over the top. There are little fruit-fly-sized holes punched in the cellophane. The flies crawl through the holes to get to the orange. They celebrate at first. They do the tango. But then they can't figure out how to get out. So they stay in there, bouncing, out of breath, perplexed.

When the DMDC is full we have an emancipation ceremony on the porch. Go forth and be fruitful, says Uncle Thoby.

We take him on a tour of the city and finish at the top of Seagull Hill. The wind makes our jackets rattle like they might explode. The seagulls hang suspended. They never have to flap. This is their hill. There are signs that explain about Marconi and the first passenger seagulls. I tell Uncle Thoby that the seagulls have learned a thing or two since then. They don't fly back to England anymore.

I see, he says. He puts a hand on my head.

Seagull Hill has a square parking-lot top. On one side you can see Newfoundland clearly. On the other side you can see England unclearly. I try to keep Uncle Thoby on the Newfoundland side.

I point out my school. GOLEM, I yell.

What.

God of Light and Eternal Mercy. See the corkscrew Jesus on top.

Uncle Thoby laughs. His pirate patch of hair blows straight up.

My dad wants to show him Cape Spear, which means going over to the ocean side. Cape Spear is the most eastern point in North America. See how the lighthouse blinks. Do not look at the ocean, which is a wide blue road to England. Look at the lighthouse. That is the farthest east you can go, okay.

Uncle Thoby nods.

No easter than that.

Right. No easter.

I climb onto the rock wall. He holds my hand as I walk along. I'm sending you a secret message, I tell him. Are you getting it.

He gives me a funny look. Then he says, Yes, Oddly.

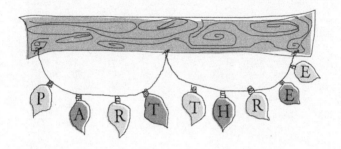

PART THREE

THE PLANE IN THE BASEMENT

C huck holds me in the palm of his hand and says, Alas, poor Yorick!

His face is so exaggerated that I have to look away. Infinite jest. Etcetera. And smelt so? Pah!

I ponder the irony of being cast in the role of a skull when I will likely outlive Chuck by a century or more. Unless of course he makes good on his threat to throw me in the Willamette.

A knock at the door. He puts me down.

Maybe it will be Julius, the UPS guy, with another gift. A fire extinguisher. A road map with directions to Canada. Something that tells me she hasn't forgotten. She is thinking of me. I am not off the radar.

But it's not Julius. It's Chuck's actor friends. The thugs are here to rehearse.

This summer, the official Shakespeare in the Parkers are putting on three Antonio plays: *The Merchant of Venice, The Tempest,* and another one I can't remember. Chuck's plan is to stage *Hamlet* on the other side of the park. Wherein there are no Antonios. That is how he will advertise it. *Hamlet:* No Antonios!

I head for my pool. One thing I have learned. If my plastron is wet, then I'm off bookmark duty. Chuck won't go so far as to *dry* me. And today, as far as I'm concerned, Shakespeare can kiss my ramparts.

Mission aborted. I am picked up en route by Lucius, who is particularly ripe.

I withdraw my head. And smelt so? Pah!

He calls me W-W-Wanda and pretends to eat me. This is apparently funny. The others slap their knees. Then they get down to business. Lucius has been out canvassing for the Heart and Stroke Foundation. Only he does not represent the Heart and Stroke Foundation. So far he has raised four hundred dollars. Renard and Dick's all-weather discount roofing business is prospering. They specialize in flat roofs where they can't be seen from the ground.

They used to be a travelling troupe. Those were the good old days. They used to travel to parks all over Oregon, California, and Nevada. Recently, however, due to diminished funds, they have only been lowering the bard locally, venturing no farther than Oregon City, Boring, and Bend. But things are looking up, and there is talk on this rainy solstice of perhaps heading south to Ashland next season, to Shakespeare country, where the plays run frothy all summer long and are not of the in-the-park variety. Ashland is in the Shakespeare *business,* with shops that sell gloves and gauntlets, and several theatres.

Chuck concedes that he might even say yes to an Antonio role in Ashland. An Antonio in Ashland equals a Hamlet in Boring, he explains.

I slide into my pool. Read the recipe on the bottom, even though I know it by heart. I love the word *whisk*. Whisk, I sometimes say as I slide into the water. Whisk the egg yolks.

We drove through Ashland once. I remember men in armour. The flash of weaponry. Chain mail. We stopped for gas and a man was fencing with a gas pump.

I stared at him through the bug-splattered windshield.

How do you like his épée, Audrey said, getting back in the car.

I dropped a piece of lettuce.

Nevermind.

We were heading south. She had packed the tent. Come, thou portable room, she'd said, referring to either me or the tent, not sure which. We were charging up Cliff's credit card. Credit card purchases are like bread crumbs. You leave a trail. But had you asked me then if such a tactic would work, if our racking up gloves and gauntlets, motels and mileage, would act as a Cliff magnet, I'd have said not on your life.

I rode the dashboard through Shakespeare country. She had a stye in her eye from the stress of Cliff's absence. She was a mess of freckles. We crossed into California, the radio rattling my plastron. We saw windmills. Hundreds, thousands of windmills. It was late afternoon and Audrey said, I don't see any cliffs.

No. These were rolling hills.

I think we should spring for a motel.

Good. Yes.

We pulled into the Inn Stead, a two-storey motel with cheap rates and a pool. Our room was on the second floor. She carried me upstairs under her armpit. The room was cool and dark, and there was a gap under the door high enough for a tortoise to crawl through. She dropped her bag and said, Come on, Win.

The pool was a bright blue rectangle in the fading light. She sat me on the edge and stripped down to her underwear. I looked around. We were alone. She dove in. Splash.

She swam like a fish. She came up beside me. Curled her fingers over the rim. Grinned. Because *she* was in a pool. Ha. I got it. She was playing me. I looked down into her eyes. Wet eyelashes. Was the chlorine good for her stye. The windmills turned like plane propellers in the distance.

Where are we going.

She put her head underwater.

Two nights later we camped at a KOA outside Las Vegas. She roasted potatoes from Idaho. I ate iceberg lettuce from a grocery store called Skagway. The fire crackled. The sun set. Las Vegas rose shining out of the desert.

The family camping next to us had four kids. The littlest ran around with no pants and was called Wiggle Worm. She told Wiggle Worm that I was a snapping turtle and he kept his distance. I was allowed to walk around the campsite, sorry Kampsite. I ate an upside-down beetle. I felt bad because this can happen to tortoises too. We can be tipped.

The tent had a ceiling that could be unzipped so you could see the stars through a screen. Look, Win.

We were not allowed to be sad. We were not allowed to think about Cliff.

The sky was not unfamiliar to me. I had crossed the desert a century ago, before I became an object human beings could not say no to. I had seen many stars. The sky at night looks a lot like the inside of my shell. But of course she would not know that.

We hit New Mexico. Look, Win. The Rio Grande. There were people walking with long sticks like pilgrims. There were red cliffs with graveyards at the bottom. We crossed a mountain pass into a town called Angel Fire. There was only one road into Angel Fire. Population 1,000. Why were we in Angel Fire. Because Cliff had mentioned it once. There was a ski hill there.

We were behind a school bus going 30 miles per hour. She passed it just as its stop sign was extruding. Guess who was behind us. The only cop in Angel Fire. Who followed the school bus every day because what else is there to do. He pulled us over. He said, What you just did. And shook his head and looked over the roof of the car like he couldn't find the words.

She said she was an excellent driver. She had never had a collision. She would have seen the little sneakers under the bus.

You might have decreased our population to 999.

I would never do that. I would never decrease a population.

Nevertheless, he said. The fine was astronomical.

After the cop left, she said she needed to sit down.

You're already sitting down.

So she got out of the car and sat on the shoulder, which in some states is called the berm. I waited on the dashboard. When she got back in, she said, I might not have seen the little sneakers under the bus. I was busy looking at the ski hill with no snow on it.

The Grand Canyon was a hologram. We camped at the top. It was cold. A bitter wind. I guess we should go down into it, she said. Meaning the canyon. But we didn't, not at first. We sat on the edge. It looked fake. Then we went back to the tent and boiled water. Ramen noodles. Brown lettuce.

What was the plan. I don't think she had one, beyond just driving and spiralling, hoping Cliff would catch up to us, intercept us, or we him.

Let me explain about breakups, how the first one never sticks. I used to live in Texas, in a shallow river. The river was a favourite strolling place for couples. The couples who came in the daytime were breaking up. The couples who came at night were getting back together. They were usually the same couples. I can't tell you how many times I saw two idiots running into each other's arms, one from the left, one from the right. Or sometimes, if they were on opposite sides of the river, they would use the tortoises (the largest of which were the size of dinner plates) as stepping stones. We were pretty good sports about that.

No, I am not as big as a dinner plate. I am as big as your fire alarm. If you hold me in your palm, my legs will dangle over the edge. Unless you are Cliff. Who has hands like an orangutan. Then my legs won't dangle.

Speak of the ape, here he is.

Audrey hasn't seen him yet. She's stirring the ramen noodles. I'm surprised she hasn't heard him. The whole campground is looking. It's the Harley. He's on a loud Harley with a tank the colour of a flame. Angel Fire. That is the colour. No helmet. No helmet law in Arizona. Yellow wavy hair. Sunburned nose. Humungous hands.

Audrey is crouched over her tiny stove. Heels popping out of her sandals.

I drop a piece of lettuce. Ahem.

She looks.

He's picking his way through the campsites. And it's just like by the river. How their eyes meet and then she is running towards him. Well, stumbling. She loses a sandal. And I am forced to concede that the credit card ploy was a stroke of genius. We have been found.

Everyone watches.

His arms wrap around her like five times.

Show's over, Cliff says into her ponytail.

The guy in the next campsite tends his fire. Well, that was oddly moving, he says.

Cliff had to buy the Harley to come find her. Find us. Hello Iris, he says to me. He is not sad about buying the Harley. He goes on and on about the Harley. Which is called a Fat Boy.

That night in the tent she says, I had to pretend you didn't exist. That's how much it hurt.

I'm sorry.

It is all very touching.

The next day we decide to go down into the canyon. Well, they decide. Cliff says it would be funny to pretend to fall into it. The ultimate stunt. She says, Please no.

So the canyon is not a hologram because we are in it. It is the inverse of a mountain, the sign says. What does that mean. It means you should keep in mind that, unlike a mountain, you will be performing the ascent later, when you are tired. It all feels like a dream right now, as you skip down the switchbacks into warmer climes. But remember that, at the end of the day, when you are tired, you will be schlepping your butt back up to the top.

Cliff scoffs at the warnings. I'm a rock climber, he says and smacks his chest.

I'm wearing sandals, she says.

I'm being carried.

The people we pass going the other way are huffing and looking for any excuse to stop. They lean against the cool canyon wall. Oh my God a tortoise. Did you find her in the canyon.

Yes, says Audrey stupidly.

Well, you can't take her out.

I'm kidding. She's a pet.

If she's part of the ecosystem, they say, getting all strident, you can't take her out.

Oh boy, says Cliff.

She's not part of the ecosystem.

The tired hikers inform her that they will be reporting a tortoise stolen from the canyon. When they finally reach the top.

Be my guest.

We carry on down.

We pass a donkey convoy. The riders are loud and stupid. The donkeys have black eyes and wrinkled nostrils. The path is narrow so we pass quite close. One kicks out at Cliff. Cliff just laughs and slaps him on the rump.

Of course she falls in love with the donkeys. She walks in tandem with one and holds me up so I can look in his eye. Look, Win.

I see the Grand Canyon upside down and me in it.

By the time we got back to the top, the sun was setting. She had very bad blisters. Cliff had an empty look like he missed his Harley. We clambered over the rim and met the park police. Lights flashing.

Is that tortoise native to the canyon.

This tortoise is native to me, she said.

We were remanded into custody.

In a beige building we were separated. I was examined by two park rangers in beige. Everything in Arizona is beige so as not to offend the beigeness of the canyon.

They turned me upside down.

I am not native to Arizona. I am native to Texas. But are beige people smart enough to realize that.

They were. It just took them awhile. When I came out of the examination room, she was sitting there alone, waiting. Where's Cliff.

Cliff had gone to Colorado. And taken his credit card.

I wake with my arms in a double helix, the backs of my hands touching. Rule Number One of Real Sleep. Are you in a corkscrew-leaping position. Then you have really slept.

The first thing I see is the tree on my wall, its bare branches ribcaging around me. It is not quite daylight. I shift my legs out of leaping position. I feel like I've finally landed. Like I'm home. Maybe you don't really arrive at a place until you've slept and woken again. Quick montages at the kitchen table don't count.

The tree's upper branches bend onto the ceiling like a spoon in a glass of water. What is the word. *Refracted.* Uncle Thoby painted the tree with his left hand. The brush was very far away. He said he had an advantage over painters with short arms because he could see the big picture while he painted. The branches forked and forked and forked. The tree sprang up in a single afternoon. He glued on the Velcro buds. Then he made the accessories: green leaves for summer, red and yellow leaves for fall, snowflakes for winter, pink blossoms for spring.

Here is the rule, he said. You can only change the tree on an equinox or solstice.

Right.

Do you know, he said, that if there were no leap days, the seasons would wander all over the calendar and pretty soon we'd be having Christmas in July.

So it's because of me that we have Christmas in December.

It's because of you that we have December in *winter*.

I stuck a leaf in my hair. I keep the seasons in place. *Moi.*

. . .

I unwind my arms and roll over to face the window. It is the solstice. Today or tomorrow. If you are born on a leap day, you can always tell. It is like a superpower. Not a very exciting one, but there you have it. You can recognize a solstice by the end-of-tether quality of the light. The sun is about to rein us in. I can tell an equinox too. Just by the light. When the sun is smack dab at the equator.

It is almost the solstice and that is why the sun left the funeral early yesterday. That is why it is so dark. That is why it is so quiet.

Wait. Why is it so quiet. I lean off the edge of my bed and say Uncle Thoby's name into the heat vent. No answer. Something else I can tell. When a place is empty.

I get up. Call Uncle Thoby's name. Still no answer. Call it again. I keep calling as I go downstairs. Are you there. Do you feel like answering. I pause at the top of the basement steps. Uncle Thoby.

He's not down there.

On the kitchen counter there's a note. I stare at it from a distance. Oh no. A sinking feeling. Read the note. I can't. Yes I can. No I can't. I don't know how to read. My heart starts to pound.

The note makes no sense. Stupid stupid brain. I turn on the range hood light but only certain words resolve. It is scratched in Uncle Thoby's worst handwriting. *Sweetheart* might be *sweatshirt*. I don't know. I decipher *clipart*. What the hell. I decipher *stroll*. I decipher *anon*.

Oh. I look up. He is out for a stroll in a sweatshirt. He will see me anon.

At the bottom of the page he has printed the word *Toff*. That I can read. Followed by a phone number and address. A London address.

The word I thought was *clipart* is *airport*.

Grab note. Grab keys. Grab coat. Run outside in unlaced boots. Hurry, hurry. Turn the ignition. My breath is everywhere. As I back out of the driveway, I remember Uncle Thoby on the porch last night. When he thought he was alone. When he thought it was okay to not be okay.

What did Toff do to him.

I gun it out to the airport. I drive badly, stupidly, with Uncle Thoby's note open against the steering wheel. Trying to read while driving. Occasionally I look up and there is no one on the road. No one, no one, no one. This is a desert island. I carry on through red lights.

Does that say London or Lebanon. London. And he does not say why. He does not say goodbye. He says anon.

I glance up and I am on the Parkway. I am high above the city. On my left the Confederation Building is shaped like a staircase going up and coming back down. On my right, far away, Seagull Hill wears a bright star like a sheriff's badge for Christmas. Merry Christmas, can I see your licence and registration.

Flashing lights behind me. Shit. I pull over.

Merry Christmas, can I see your licence and registration.

Good morning, sheriff. I'm afraid I'm without licence.

I'm not a sheriff.

I do have one. Somewhere.

The wind fills up his jacket. He glances at the note pressed against the steering wheel. You were driving very erratically, he says.

But I'm an excellent driver.

You might have killed someone.

I didn't think there was anyone left to kill.

He looks uneasy now. Anyone *left* to kill.

I mean, I thought the roads were empty.

So you decided to catch up on a little reading.

We both stare at the note. I decipher the word *sorry*. And once I do, I see it everywhere. It is all over the note.

I look up at him.

He has seen the word too.

I'm trying to get to the airport, sheriff.

He nods and thumps the roof. Go on, he says. Git.

Suddenly I have a thought. The note is not a Goodbye-I'm-off-to-London note. Of course it's not. It's a See-you-anon-I'm-seeing-Toff-off note. Because Toff is leaving this morning. That's right. *Toff*. Toff is going to London. Not Uncle Thoby. Uncle Thoby is seeing Toff off. Toff off. I like the sound of that.

Except why would he do that. And why the sorrys. Why Toff's address.

Sweatshirt, I'm sorry to live for the clipart like this. Something something stroll something London. See you anon.

I hang on tight to the word *anon*. Because that is Uncle Thoby's word. And he has used it many times, when he is going down to the basement, when he is going across the pond, when he is going out to do an odd job for someone like shovel their driveway or replace a hard-to-reach bulb. He has never used it when going to London. Because he has never gone back to London. Never. The farthest he has gone is the Civil Manor. And whose fault was that.

I can't get into the airport because it's been evacuated for a grenade. People are milling about outside, eating Timbits. Stand back, she's gonna blow.

What, the whole airport.

Just them revolving doors would be nice.

I scan the crowd. No sign of him. Someone with a similar build, but symmetrical, tells me that the passengers who were already through security have been evacuated elsewhere.

Oh. I stand next to him because he is the closest thing.

If Uncle Thoby is not in the parking lot, that means that:

a) he is a passenger who has already gone through security, or

b) he is not a passenger but has already said goodbye to Toff and taken a Clint's cab home, or

c) he is buying clipart at a store that is open twenty-four hours.

Twenty minutes later we are given the green light. Not a real grenade after all. A grenade-shaped belt buckle in someone's checked baggage. All is well. Proceed.

And so we pour en masse into those ridiculous slow-revolving doors. They immediately seize up. Oh my God is there a limb caught somewhere. Let us pause. Indefinitely.

Who's touching the goddamn glass, someone says.

We all scrunch together. We're stuck.

All because of a grenade-shaped belt buckle purchased at the mall in that cheap little store next to the food court. The cheapness of a store is directly proportional to its proximity to the food court, someone says. We all stare at that someone. Really. Anyway, this grenade belt buckle was obviously not so cheap as to not fool security personnel at St. John's International Airport. Who have been waiting their whole careers for a moment such as this. And now look how it turns out. Humiliating.

At least they're scanning checked baggage for grenades, someone says.

Good to know.

I feel safer.

The door moves. We are in.

I rush upstairs. I will penetrate security, temporarily, sans boarding pass. Make my day, burly man with weapon and Santa hat.

At the top of the stairs there's a sign that says COMING SOON: SNIFFER DOGS.

Burly man picks me up and carries me back through the free-standing rectangle, setting off an alarm. Because he is armed.

What's wrong with this picture. He, with gun, is allowed through. I, without gun, am not.

Get yourself a boarding pass and we'll talk, missy, he says.

But I just want to say goodbye to someone.

Wave your soundproof, bulletproof goodbyes from upstairs.

There's an upstairs.

Observation deck.

I take the steps two at a time.

He is at the gate. He is standing at the window looking out at his plane. I am filled with love for his asymmetrical outline.

I knock on the glass. No one looks up.

Then I see Toff. He is sitting closer, right under me in fact, reading a newspaper.

They are on the same flight.

There is a feeling I get called the feeling of Foul Play, and I am getting that feeling very strongly. It is a bad feeling, but it is also a little bit good. Toff is behind this. Toff has arranged this. I nod to myself.

This is not a see-you-anon kind of trip. This is not across the pond. This is across the ocean. Via Montreal. But for now let's not dwell on the stupidity of Air Canada. Uncle Thoby is crossing the ocean via Montreal. Why.

Because the word I thought was *stroll* is *stroke*.

Your grandmother has had a stroke. She is waiting for me to open her eyes. Must depart.

Oh. Is that what this is about. Grandmother's stroke. Of bad luck. Of genius. It's a trap. A plot. To shuffle us apart.

I knock on the glass. No one looks up. Pound, pound.

The observation deck has an outward-sloping window, so you can lean your whole body out over the boarding area and pretend to be parachuting into. it. Of course there is a sign that says not to do this.

Also waiting to board flight 623 to Montreal: Three guys

in military fatigues, laughing into cellphones. No doubt they are relating the grenade-belt-buckle debacle to fellow military personnel. Or maybe one of them is the owner of the belt. That would make sense. I mean, if grenades are part of your daily life and have killed a few of your enemies, maybe you develop an aesthetic fondness for them and want to showcase one over your groin.

I envy them their cellphones. Uncle Thoby and my dad are, were, against cellphones. My dad for the obvious reason: They make *people* ring. And Uncle Thoby is against them because they are a way of not seeing people in public. But it occurs to me now that a phone is like a heat vent between two people. And I desperately want a heat vent to say Uncle Thoby's name into.

Toff looks up. Slowly. Like he has known all along that I was in the ceiling and was just finishing a paragraph first. I point at Uncle Thoby. Get him for me.

He rubs his beard. Goes back to his paper.

I smack the glass. Why. Why would he do that.

A fellow observer on the observation deck says, Excuse me, should you be leaning on the glass like that.

No, but this is an emergency.

Oh. Okay, carry on.

I sidle along the window. Movement will make me more noticeable. I feel like a tap dancer. Turn around, Uncle Thoby. Turn around.

He does not turn around. They are boarding now. Uncle Thoby picks up his bag with his long arm. He looks like an extradited prisoner. Or like someone whose brother just died. He and Toff do not stand together. The Canadian army is between them.

Sniffer dogs will brighten the place right up, someone says behind me. A few yellow Labs.

I watch until he disappears. Is disappeared.

I drive home in second gear. I stop at all the red lights, and the green ones too. What just happened. Was Uncle Thoby kidnapped. Or did he decide on his own to go see Grandmother. Why didn't he wake me. Because he knew I wouldn't have let him go. I would have made going impossible. That was why he left for the Civil Manor in the middle of the night too.

Yes but the Civil Manor is not London.

What was said on the porch last night in lower case voices.

A knock on the window. I jump.

Merry Christmas, can I see your licence and registration.

Good morning, sheriff. How have you been.

He looks at his watch. Afternoon.

Is it.

Any reason why you're stopped at this intersection. Car trouble.

I shake my head. I'm just gathering my thoughts.

He glances at the note, now on the passenger seat. You have a lot of thoughts to gather, I gather, he says.

Actually just one or two. Two, really.

Okay. Well. Can I suggest you put on your hazards if you plan to block the intersection.

Of course. Thanks, sheriff. I turn on my hazards. I start rolling up my window.

He knocks again. Hi.

Hi.

Where you trying to get to, he asks.

And so he escorts me home. Which is really sweet of him. Because all I have to do is follow his tail lights and stop when he stops and go when he goes. All I have to do is keep up. And without him I might not have made it home before midnight.

But not so fast. Because when I do get home, finally, and perform the Northwest Shove on the front door, the brass knob comes off in my hand. I try to screw it back in, but it is not screwable. I kneel on the porch. Keep it together. The door, I mean. Keep the door together. I give it a shove. It doesn't open. You need the knob to perform the NWS.

Was I rough with it. Did I push to the east instead of the west. I pound the door, briefly.

Jim Ryan, who is out "touching up" his crescent, calls out, What's the matter.

I lift the doorknob.

He waves me over with his shovel. He says to come inside. He'll call Murph's Turf, Lock, and Key. He'll have her fixed up in no time, Murph will.

Her is the door, I take it.

I don't realize how dark it is until I am sitting in Jim Ryan's kitchen and he opens the fridge and the light makes me squint. How can it be dark already.

'Fraid we don't have much in the way of refreshments, he says. How about olives.

Okay.

And coffee, he says.

I brighten. I would not say no to some coffee.

Jim says Mrs. Ryan is out right now remedying the emptiness of the fridge.

On the table, the brass doorknob looks amazed to be reflecting the inside of someone's house. It lies on its side like it has fainted.

Murph is an old friend, Jim says.

Murph made my Flower Shovel™.

So you said. Jack of all trades is Murph.

The coffee burbles. Just the smell makes me feel hopeful. In the doorknob I look nosy. A convex surface will do that. The window behind me is slanted and gold. Snowflakes fall sideways.

You in some kind of trouble, Jim asks me.

Sorry.

I saw a patrol car—

Oh. The sheriff. He was just escorting me home.

The sheriff, Jim says.

I nod.

The inside of the Ryans' house reminds me of one of Mrs. Ryan's floral-printed dresses. It is a bit like being up her skirt. Why don't we have flowery wallpaper, and why don't I wear floral-printed dresses. Because that would be too much. Yes. But the Flower Shovel™ is not too much. No. Why. Because it's not like I carry the shovel around like a trademark. Well, even if I do, there is a limit to how much attention you should draw to your own name. Most of the time you should not be thinking about it.

Of course my dad did sometimes refer to us—the three of us—as the Bouquet. I think the Bouquet should hit the sack, he'd say. The Bouquet is wilting. Or at least one Flower is. Speak for yourself, Wilter.

Jim puts two steaming mugs of coffee on the table and two forks. The jar of olives opens with a hiccup.

Olive olives, I say. Get it.

He nods. You love olives.

Jim has a big ring on his right middle finger. What is that about. What does Jim Ryan do for a living. Or did he do. He's retired. But from what. That ring looks like a bishop's ring. But he couldn't be a bishop. I'd have heard about that. Or maybe not. How can I be his biographer, sorry lapsed biographer, and not know if he's a bishop. We stab our olives and it feels cosy like fondue. He'd have to be an Anglican bishop since he's married.

Meanwhile he is discoursing on locks. He can't believe we've never locked our door. I tell him the door seemed locked to people who didn't know better. He says a thief would be one of those people who knew better. Now your double deadbolt, he goes on. Jim Ryan is a fan of the double deadbolt.

Apparently with a double deadbolt you have to use a key to get *out* as well as *in*. This is not something I want. To unlock myself from the inside. Or do I. Would it make me feel like I owned the outside if I had the key to it.

It took Uncle Thoby three months to perfect the NWS. My dad put him through an intensive training process. You have to hold the knob and stand with your toes on the threshold. I mean, right up on the step. You have to be at eye level with the door, he said. What eyes, Uncle Thoby said. Well, where the door's eyes would be if it had them. Then you have to thrust up and to the left, jabbing your left knee into the door's groin to give it a little encouragement.

Uncle Thoby fell back off the step, laughing.

It was not easy to get into our house, but it was easy to get out. Which, now that I think about it, is what you want in a house. The double deadbolt poses an obvious safety hazard. What about fire. Imagine looking around for your key when you're trying to get out of a burning house. Where is my key to the outside world that is not burning. Where oh where. Sizzle.

I have been well-drilled in fire safety. Uncle Thoby made sure we had four different fire extinguishers in the house. Each for a special kind of fire. One was for hair and fur. Necessary because I had once caught my ponytail on fire while trying to see my aura in the bathroom mirror with a candle. The hair and fur extinguisher became known as the Oddly extinguisher. Then there was one for ice cream and fat fires. Another for curtains. One for indoor flora (Christmas trees, hedges).

Ice cream fires, said my dad, reading the instructions. What am I missing.

When you deep-fry ice cream, said Uncle Thoby.

Which we do regularly.

Nine times out of ten when you deep-fry ice cream.

What.

House burns down.

If I refused to go to bed, my dad would pretend to look around for the Oddly extinguisher. Where is that extinguisher. I want to put you out. Now.

Anon.

Now.

Anon.

Uncle Thoby also organized drills. Sometimes in the middle of the night his harmonica would "go off." I was responsible for no one but me. I just had to get out of the house, fast. My dad was responsible for Wedge. Uncle Thoby blew the harmonica. Only when we were all safely on the front lawn did he take a breath. Does Jim Ryan remember those drills. Do you remember us all out on the lawn in the middle of the night, Uncle Thoby's harmonica blaring like a siren.

Oh yes, he says. God yes.

Mrs. Ryan comes home with her hands full of bags and says why are we sitting in the dark.

Audrey's doorknob came off.

Yes, but why are you sitting in the dark.

Didn't notice.

How are you, honey. She touches my cheek. The snowflakes on her coat are disappearing.

Good.

Did you call Murph, she asks Jim over my shoulder.

Yes.

Mrs. Ryan unzips her boots. She has one tone for Jim and one tone for me. I prefer my tone. When she straightens, her face is flushed. Where's your uncle, she says.

He had to go to London.

Jim stops mid-transfer of bags to the kitchen counter.

London, says Mrs. Ryan. England.

I purse my lips. Nod.

Turn on a light, Jim, for the love of Christ.

So he does. It is of the overhead variety.

When did he leave.

I look at my watch. Um.

But it's *Christmas,* Mrs. Ryan says, her voice all whispery. Which makes me feel like crouching down on the floor. Don't say that. Don't say anything against him or I'll have to hate you. I explain that Grandmother had a stroke. And the stroke caused her to fall. She's on her last legs, I say, even though I don't know this for sure.

Oh. I'm so—

Can I use your bathroom.

Of course.

I take the doorknob with me. Is that weird.

Last legs, I think, as I climb the stairs. As if we have several sets and then arrive at the last pair. I stop on the landing. There's a picture of a young Jim Ryan in a cop's uniform. Well. Mystery solved.

In the bathroom I tighten my ponytail. Itch my left eye. Pee. Stare at myself in the doorknob while I pee. My eye is red. Look around for the toilet paper. It's behind me, under a Barbie doll's flared skirt. Her legs are down inside the roll and her skirt is poufed out over it. So you have to lift up her skirt to get some toilet paper.

Sorry about that.

Barbie's teeth are bared. Is that usual.

As I come down the stairs I hear Mrs. Ryan say, She's all alone. And Jim says, She's got the Russian, sure.

How can it be dusk already. It's like the sun came on for a few minutes—when Uncle Thoby's plane was leaving—and then went out again.

I was standing by the chain-link fence. His plane was pale blue with a crumpled maple leaf on the tail. Since when is Air Canada pale blue. Like a candy wrapper left in the sun.

The sun came out, came on like an overhead light, bright and ugly, and my eyes teared up. It makes no sense that your eyes tear up in bright sunlight because the tears act as magnifiers. What kind of naturally selected trait is that. I thought about climbing the fence and blocking the runway. Can you stop a plane once it is taxiing. Once it is gathering its thoughts and thinking of England. Or Montreal. Can you hang on to the wheels and keep it on the ground.

Do not go easter. This is as far east as you can go. Remember.

A pigeon waddled over and stood beside me, watching the plane. Then it looked over its shoulder, like, did I leave my lights on. Which made me wonder if I had. So I looked, and I hadn't.

You could fly over this fence, I told it.

Not easily.

Pigeons fly.

Stomach's full of Timbit.

Oh.

My dad told me once that flying animals—birds, bats, and the like—have smaller genomes than non-flying animals. Like part of their genetic code is missing. And it is this *missing* part that allows them to fly. You would expect the opposite. You would expect a flying creature to have a larger genome. Some extra code tacked on that says: You Can Fly. But no. It is we who have extra code. And the extra code says: You Cannot Fly. A whole section of our genome devoted to keeping us down.

Uncle Thoby's plane reached the end of the runway and turned slowly around. Now it was girding. Oh please please please. Be Qantas.

M urph arrives with sparkling eyes and overalls. He crouches down to knob level and says the old hardware has to go. He'll put a metal sleeve on her. He skips back to his van and returns with the metal sleeve. Industrial grey. I shake my head. We like brass. We like the old hardware. Which was not a sleeve.

I put the old knob in Murph's hand. Let it speak for itself. Look at it. Look at yourself in it. Fix me.

Murph says there is no fixing. There is only replacing. The old door hardware is at least forty years old. The parts required to fix it are scattered nether and yond.

Pardon.

They are unfindable.

I explain how my dad and Uncle Thoby are away right now, and how they are used to the old door, which could be opened only by a secret family shove, and so my concern is that when they return and discover new door hardware, they will not be able to get in. I would like to keep the old hardware, if possible.

Murph, without looking at me, says, I was sorry to hear about your father. Jim told me he passed away.

I sit down on the steps.

You got a back door.

No.

Snow falls. The sound of the old door hardware coming off makes a dental crunch. I start crying. Because of this sound. Murph pauses and looks over his shoulder. I get up and walk around the porch to the back. I look through the window into the kitchen. The phone is blinking. A message.

I make a loop. I check the mail. There's another recall notice for my dad and something from the War Amps for the previous owner, Mr. Rowe, who is dead. Who is *also* dead.

Murph tells me Jim Ryan used to be in the Stab. The what. The Constabulary. Oh. Murph has helped out the police on several occasions. With what. With home invasions. He can't be more specific. That's how he knows Jim. He also put a double dead-bolt on the Ryans' front door.

That's not a double deadbolt you're putting on now.

No girl.

I relax against the railing. I tell him how I once wrote a biography of Jim Ryan. It was two sentences. I didn't know then that he was a retired cop. My biography could have been three sentences.

Murph finds the idea of a biography of your neighbour pretty funny.

Why.

He shrugs and paws around for a tool. You should write one about me. I got interesting kids.

I'm done with biographies.

Well, put me in the next thing you write.

That will be a cheque.

He laughs.

The house smells like something gone off. Funeral food. I track sawdust into the kitchen. Please let the message be from Uncle Thoby, saying: I'm in Montreal. It was all a mistake. I'm coming home.

But no. It is from Judd Julian-Brown, my local Christmatech representative. He is recalling the D-534 Christmas lights. So that's a double recall. To be clear: Neither the D-434 nor the D-534 models are safe for indoor use. Outdoor, maybe. Indoor, definitely not. So if you wouldn't mind returning both models, we'd be happy to issue you the newly minted D-634 model.

The royal we again. Come on, Judd. It's just you in a basement somewhere, isn't it.

No more messages. I kick off my boots. Sawdust from the door surgery all over the place. The metal sleeve looks like a hand clamped over the door's mouth.

The previous owner, Mr. Rowe, probably installed the old door hardware. He was a carpenter. A not very good one. He built the porch, which is a bit dodgy. Anyway, my dad never met him. Mr. Rowe came to an untimely end, which necessitated the selling of his house. So we don't know if Mr. Rowe originated the Northwest Shove, or if he had some other method of getting across the threshold.

Here is how Mr. Rowe died. He was building a rock wall and he ran out of rocks. He had heard about an island off the southern shore where there were some excellent rocks to be had. So off he went in a little boat. Yes, a rowboat. Mr. Rowe rowed to that island and loaded up his boat with rocks. Then he tried to row back, fool of a man, and the boat sank. He drowned.

Of course we laughed. Old Mr. Rowe who couldn't row fast enough to get his boat full of rocks back to shore. It felt like a parable. It felt *deserved*. So we laughed. It was okay to laugh. The man was a cartoon. A stupid cartoon. Who had to die so that we could get his house. Because it was always really *our* house. Or waiting to be.

But Uncle Thoby did not laugh when we told him the story. Poor Mr. Rowe, he said. Stop it you two.

But the name, the name!

Stop it you two.

Okay, I'm stopping now. Mr. Rowe was a real person. Whose hand turned this brass knob many times. Whose body was reflected in this knob as he approached and left the house. His house. Mr. Rowe met an untimely end. There is no lesson. He did not deserve it.

Filling up a boat with rocks is something I'd do for Chrissakes.

I sit in the living room with my feet pointing at the centre and roll the brass knob up and down my chest. Someday will a different family sit around in here, laughing about the untimely end of Walter Flowers, mown down by a Christmas tree. Untimely for him. Timely for us. Our house now.

Over my mown-down body.

Or—I sit up straight—is there a family right now sitting around the Christmas tree that killed him. Holy. Right now, this very moment, sitting around the tree that killed my dad, laughing about the untimely end of a man called Walter Flowers who was, of all things, in the *longevity* business. Ha ha. I press the knob to my forehead. Of course. There are murderers. For the first time I am looking these people in the face. Or trying to. Who are they. Where are they. The Foul Play feeling hits me like a ton of rocks.

Which feeling is compounded when I look up and see an empty terrarium in the cheval glass. The black ribbon still tied to the wheel. I get up. Slowly.

Wedge is gone.

My first thought: Someone stole my mouse!

Who would steal your mouse. Come on.

Well, he is not in the terrarium. Therefore.

The grid roof is not exactly ajar but it is not properly fastened either. He might have got out by himself. He might have been swinging from the roof—building his upper body strength, as he is wont to do, the wheel not being good for that—he might have been building his upper body strength and found the roof not properly secured and pushed himself out through a tiny space.

How did he get off the mantel. Jumped. Fell. Oh God.

I sit down on the floor and call his name. He was probably dying for a run. Poor Wedge. I left the ribbon on and he was dying for a run, so he escaped.

Or did he.

When was the last time I saw him. After the funeral. Looking very stressed. All those people milling about his terrarium. Let's call them suspects. All those suspects.

Let's rule out that he is somewhere in the house. Search the house and rule it out. Then compile a list of suspects.

There are people who, when they lose something, immediately assume it is stolen. As in: Someone stole my glove. Those people are ridiculous. On the other hand there are people who, when they discover their car missing from the driveway, think they've misplaced it. The trick is to strike a happy medium.

If I sit quietly, maybe I will hear scurrying.

I do not hear scurrying. I begin the search. It is not a systematic search. It is more like a panicked stomping about and falling flat on my stomach to look under furniture and calling his name, all of which will probably paralyze the little frigger with fear. He is huddled in a corner somewhere, biting his nails. Behind the fridge probably. Okay. I will move the fridge. And somehow I do. I marvel at my own strength. The Force is with me. Wedge is not behind the fridge. I leave it out from the wall at an angle. Why does a fridge have to be flush.

A knock at the door. I pause in my frenzy. My ponytail is gone. I mean, it is out. When did that happen. I am all staticky like a Muppet. I get a shock when I touch the new door hardware. Goddamn it. It is Byrne Doyle with a Piety pie. Not lemon. Blueberry. Still, that's nice. Come in.

Jim Ryan told me, he begins.

My mouse is gone.

He told me your uncle is gone.

Him too. I carry the pie into the kitchen.

Byrne shuffles after me. Jacob Marley. Encumbered by a coat instead of chains.

You'd have a longer stride if you wore a different coat, I tell him.

It's warm.

The pie.

No, my coat.

Yes, but at what cost.

I can see by your hair that you're stressed, he says. Sit down and have some pie.

So I sit. Byrne shoulders off his coat. Looks askance at the fridge. Sniffs. Garbage needs to go out.

Yeah.

There are no clean plates so he washes two from beside the sink.

Thanks Byrne.

Your servant, he says.

I watch him eat. With the side of his fork, he cuts away geometric sections of pie, starting with the pointy end and working his way back towards the crust. Like he is shovelling a driveway. Whereas I eat my pie in layers. I lift the lid with my fork. This could take an hour. Look at all the blueberries.

Did you see anyone take Wedge out of his terrarium.

Hm.

My mouse. After the funeral.

He shakes his head and swallows.

Then it occurs to me: Did someone break into the house. Is that why the knob was loose. Did someone with an imperfect knowledge of the Northwest Shove come into the house and take Wedge.

Whoa, whoa, says Byrne, putting down his fork. Don't get ahead of yourself.

Right. I tighten my ponytail.

He says he will help me look for Wedge. But he cautions me against shifting into what he calls everyone-is-screwing-me-over mode. There is no coming back from that. He's a politician. He knows.

Who has been screwing him over, I wonder. The Poles.

I grab a bag of Licorice Allsorts and head upstairs.

How would a mouse get upstairs.

Running boards.

Oh. Byrne says he will take out the garbage.

Upstairs, I check under my bed. Listen for scurrying. The heat vent. Oh no. If Wedge got into the ventilation system. Calm down. The ventilation system is a maze like any other. Put an Allsort at the exit and move on.

I pause in the hall.

It would not be necessary to look in my dad's room if there weren't a mouse-high space between the bottom of the door and the floor.

I open the door.

The room still smells Daddish. I turn on a light. The bed is made but has a dent in it. Don't look at the dent. The dent is where he sat down to put on his socks. Sylvester Stallone is still on the wall, but is curled at the edges. The book beside the bed says *Repulsive Gravity: The Big Bang*. That sounds sinister. The Danish desk holds itself together in the corner.

Wedge, I call softly.

Mice don't come when you call them, gnomon.

Under the bed: A stack of old Lionel de Tigrel articles holding up one corner. The old red cot I slept on when Grandmother and Toff were visiting, its legs folded like a dead beetle's.

On the desk: Laptop. Rubik's cube.

Did he know. Did he feel it coming. I mean, when you sit on your bed for the last time and put on your socks and the future you are so used to stepping into will soon *not* be there. Do you sense it.

Hold it together, Wobbly.

The Rubik's cube is solved. It would be. Focus on this. A Rubik's cube requires you to see six sides in your head at once. My dad could do this. Not me. I could only solve one side at a time. When have you ever solved even *one* side of a Rubik's cube.

Okay, never. But I have wedged a knife down in between the squares and broken the thing apart and put it back together. There. Solved.

Doesn't count.

I lift the cube in my palm. Imagine being able to see all the sides at once. To turn it around in your brain. As opposed to feeling trapped inside it.

I put it back on the desk.

Why did I come in here.

For Wedge.

Well, that was stupid. He's not here. And now you have made your dad dead in this room. And you will keep doing this. Every new room you enter, you will make your dad dead in it. Now he is dead on the second floor. He is dead on the ground floor. There is only one floor left.

Byrne Doyle calls up from downstairs, Find him.

No.

It occurs to me that Uncle Thoby had no floors left.

The red Christmatech van is parked outside Julian-Brown's Furniture. Otherwise there's no Christmatech signage. I check the address on the recall notice and push open the door. It is almost exactly as I remember it. All the magical rooms within a room. A set for every scene you could want to act out. Love, crime, comedy. A bit more black leather than I remember. No cheval glasses. No customers either. I ring the bell, my box of D-534-model Christmas lights tucked under my arm.

If I had to choose one room to be my own at this moment, it would be that kitchen with the country-and-western theme. Check out the horseshoe handles on the cabinets and the cowboy hat on the coat rack. That is a nice touch.

I would not say no to a cowboy hat.

I put on the cowboy hat and take a seat in the kitchen. Drum my fingers. I think this is what is called a ranch-style kitchen. On a ranch, a stove is called a range. Thus *range hood*. Or is the whole ranch called a range. As in home on the. There is also something called a ranch-style house, which is one sprawling storey. Hard to believe that people actually live in stairless, one-storeyed places.

Now there's a clumpety-clump and here comes the Judd. I bet. A door swings open at the back of the store.

The same grey sweater. Straight red hair. Lumbering walk. Towards the counter.

Howdy.

He turns.

I hold up my recycled pizza box or whatever it is. I'm answering your recall.

His whole face brightens.

I plugged in the D-534 model last night, indoors, even though I was not supposed to. I plugged in the lights, in my room, and it was like flying over Vegas. They were like Vegas from above. They left an imprint on my retinas that I will not soon stop seeing. I fell asleep with them across my bed. I know I should not have done that. What is in these lights, Judd, that is so hazardous. Do they catch fire or do they blind you. Well, whatever. I did not catch fire. And if my retinas are damaged, if I am radioactive, so be it.

The other model, the D-434, I don't know where they are. Probably in the basement. My dad will be returning them to you soon. If that's okay with y'all. But I have brought these lights back. And I would like to exchange them for the D-634 model. I am ready for the next model.

Judd sits across from me at the table. Half-smiling because of the cowboy hat. Though he frowns at the thought of me sleeping with the D-534 model.

So do you own this store.

My parents do.

I nod. And you run Christmatech out of here.

Christmatech is upstairs.

I look around. We bought our cheval glass here.

Your ice horse.

Our standing mirror.

We're all out of ice horses.

You knit that sweater yourself.

Why yes.

It turns out Judd went to GOLEM and was Frenchly submerged like me, but he was four years behind me, so we didn't really overlap. We both had Miss Daken for math. Lordy. Miss Daken, with the high heels and the braids. Judd remembers that he was quite smitten with Miss Daken. Remember how she put her students in her math problems, he says.

Her math problems were little biographies.

I was always weightless in a rocket, he says. Or I was climbing twenty flights of stairs.

I was always a Russian farmer trying to convert versts to kilometres. What was that about. Did she have a Russian connection.

Judd doesn't think so. But there were messages in her math, he says.

What kind of messages. What was she trying to tell me, putting me in a Siberian field trying to calculate the distance home.

I don't know. But she was trying to tell me to go on a diet.

And still you were smitten.

I loved how she walked around on tiptoes, he says.

Because of the high heels.

She'd stopped wearing the heels by the time she taught us, but her calf muscles had developed in such a way that she couldn't walk flat-footed. So she tiptoed.

He gets up and turns the CLOSED sign on the door to say OPEN. Open on our side. Closed on theirs.

Someone who tiptoes either loves you or hates you, he says.

I think about this. Is that true.

Come on.

Up some metal stairs. They are porous, and they shiver. Judd's boots clump like castles. We come to a door at the top. Still no Christmatech signage. He opens the door.

Welcome to the Christmatech workshop. Watch where you step, please.

I step into a small square room. Rolls of green wire on the floor. Dark bulbs. Stacks and stacks of pizza boxes. But they are not pizza boxes, he says, offended. I mean, they never contained real pizzas. Yes, they are recycled cardboard. Yes, they were originally

intended for pizzas. Nevermind that. They are not pizza boxes
now. They are Christmatech boxes.

Got it.

The only furniture in the room is a round table with no top.
There is a metal grid where the top should be with wires hanging down.

What's that.

A table.

Doesn't look like a table.

When it's finished you'll be able to see stars in it.

He crouches down and wraps some wires around the base.
He smiles up at me. Seriously, he says.

As in famous people.

As in constellations. He gestures with his chin. There's a star
map on the wall.

Oh.

So Judd is putting the sky into a table. Well, if anyone can do
it, the inventor of the D-534 Christmas lights can. The blue in
your lights, I tell him.

Yeah.

Better than anything I've seen.

Thanks.

Bunsen-burner blue.

I love Bunsen burners.

Me too.

The Christmatech workshop has a single window with a sliding pane. The sun is going down fast, like someone's got a finger
on a dimmer switch.

Judd prepares a package of the new-model lights.

How did my dad find you.

Find me.

Where did he get the D-434 model.

Canadian Tire.

Canadian Tire sells Christmatech lights.

He is kneeling on the floor surrounded by bulbs and pizza boxes. He looks up at me. Twinkly eyes. Okay, their parking lot does. When I'm in it.

I laugh. I ask if he remembers my dad. He says no. I kneel down beside him. Sure you do. British guy.

He is twisting a twist tie. Really twisting it.

Okay, that's good. I stop his fingers. Think. You remember him.

British guy, okay, yeah, maybe.

Good. This is all I wanted. I sink back on my heels.

One last thing. When Judd was at the party the other day—

I wasn't exactly *at* the party.

Did you see anyone leave the house with a mouse.

Like a computer mouse.

No, like a real mouse. A Christmas-coloured mouse.

Christmas-coloured.

White. Red eyes. A number 18 on his left ear.

No.

He hands me a pizza box with D-634 written in black marker across the top.

As we descend the metal staircase, me first, Judd behind, I look down through the steps (because they are more air than metal, really, just hollow metal circles all shivering together like enlarged atoms) and I think about what my feet are doing. Which you should never do if you are Wobbly Flowers. You should never think about what your feet are doing, or not doing, on a staircase.

I stumble.

I feel myself fall like in a dream when falling turns into flight. Slow like that. You know how in a dream, when you fall, it is slow motion and you end up floating or flying. I have often wondered why this would be, why we would have such dreams, if our brains were not *remembering* how to do it. If we were not recalling a time when our genomes were smaller and we learned to fly by falling slower and slower from trees. Staircases are just modern-day trees.

But I don't fly. I fall down sixteen stairs. Then: impact.

A staircase made of air should not hurt this much.

Wobbly Flowers has had too much coffee today and not enough sleep, and she is made dizzy by airy-fairy staircases, and her retinas are burned, and her imagination is the inside of a Rubik's cube, and she is trying to solve six mysteries at once, five of which she can't even bloody see. No wonder she fell.

And Judd comes tumbling after.

No, he stays on his feet. But he is rushing down the stairs.

Oh my God. He puts his hands under my arms. Steady.

There's a cowboy hat on the landing. I forgot I was wearing that.

To my left, Jim Ryan is pulling frontwards out of his crescent. He rolls down his window. I roll down mine.

Everything okay.

I give him a thumbs-up.

What in Christ happened to your face.

Neveryoumind.

I'm sitting in the LeBaron, in the driveway, not moving. I guess this is unusual behaviour.

Haven't pulled the new knob off, have you.

Nope.

Sure you're okay.

Yup. Carry on.

He carries on. Reluctantly. What was he implying. That I pulled the old knob off on purpose. I look at my face in the rearview mirror. My left eye has the beginnings of a stye. As for the rest, it is best not to look too closely.

Uncle Thoby has not called. Wedge is still MIA. There are no bite marks in the Allsorts I left by the heat vents and the basement door. I have put down saucers filled with water. There is nothing to do. I stare at the dark house. Go on in.

Anon.

What if, when it comes to people I love, I am the straw breaking the camel's back instead of the camel driver who removes the straw. Or whatever the expression is. What if I make things worse, not better. And now Uncle Thoby is in

England with his back broken, being held hostage by Toff and
Grandmother. Or maybe he's tied up in customs with ropes and
unable to get to a phone. And it is my fault because I increased
his stress level instead of decreasing it.

Also because I fell asleep on the job and didn't stop him.

And isn't this what I always feared would happen, and what
my dad always feared too, although he never said so: that Uncle
Thoby would go back. That we would lose him. Because he felt
like a prize we had won by accident. We had just lucked out after
a third trip to the airport.

One day when my dad was at work, I asked Uncle Thoby to
drive me out to the stable. I knew he couldn't, wouldn't, drive
the car. But I asked anyway. Why. Because earlier he'd been
talking about how efficient the London tube was, and by impli-
cation how inefficient our Metrobuses were, and that was not
acceptable. Didn't we have Clint. The Qantas of cabs.

Oh yes. Clint was a jewel. But you would love the tube, Odd.
Secret tunnels. Like heat vents. Take you anywhere you want to
go. Someday when you travel you'll see.

I don't want to travel.

Now he was lying on the sofa reading a book about people
in London. Again, not acceptable. So I put on my riding gear
and stomped into the living room and asked him to take me out
to the stable.

He put the book down on his chest with its wings open.
Maybe Verlaine will take you after work.

You take me.

I can't.

I threw the car keys into his lap. They landed below the belt.
Ouch. The book slid off his chest.

I can't, Odd.

Fine, then I'll ride my bike.

Of course I couldn't ride my bike to the stable. The stable

was out by the airport for Chrissakes. But I marched out to the porch and got on my bike, which was Rambo, pretend.

Let me call Clint, Uncle Thoby said. If you really want to go.

I looked up from under my visor. I want *you* to take me.

I can't drive you, sweetheart.

Yes you can.

I'm saying no.

Okey-dokey. I pedalled down the steps.

Oddly.

He kept talking.

As fate would have it, Jim Ryan was pulling out of his crescent. He didn't see me. I braked at the end of the drive. His bumper passed within arm's reach. It practically scraped my tire. My first impulse was to reach out and punch that bumper. My second was to reach out and hang on. Hey, free ride, I thought.

I heard Uncle Thoby say, Don't.

So I did.

I was hanging on and I didn't have to pedal. The hardest part was keeping my balance. One hand on the handlebars, the other curled around Jim Ryan's metal bumper. Datsun. Bronze colour. We turned at the end of Wednesday Place. That was a trick. Lean into it. Then we turned again. Now we were whizzing down Blackbog Drive, past the Civil Manor and the Piety factory. Whiff of pie. I'd never gone so fast on a bike before. The street was rolling backwards the way it did under the hole in Verlaine's car.

I got down all aerodynamic.

Cars were honking. Jim thought they were saying hi. He honked back.

They pointed at me.

He pointed back at them.

You've got a lapsed biographer hanging off your ass, Jim. In an English riding hat.

Faster and faster. It now occurred to me to wonder where
Jim Ryan was going. Um. Probably not the stable. No, probably
definitely not the stable. Had he ever been to the stable. No. He
was heading for the Trans-Canada probably. Which did not go
across Canada because this was an island. So it went to the airport,
almost. If Jim Ryan was going to the airport, maybe I could ride
my bike across the runway to the stable.

My hand began to hurt. I thought of Uncle Thoby lumbering down the driveway after me. The way he had yelped, Don't.
I began to hurt inside. I assumed a crash position. Which is not
very different from getting down all aerodynamic.

A pickup truck passed by on the left and a boy yelled, Let go,
you retard.

I hated him.

I hated Jim Ryan. There were no red lights on Blackbog
Drive. We kept going and going. We would never stop. I couldn't
unclench my hand even if I wanted to. It was freezing for one
thing. When had it got so cold. My hand was stuck to the bumper.
I felt tears streaming.

Suddenly there was some prolonged and familiar honking. I
knew that honk. I looked sideways. Guess who. Uncle Thoby in
our little brown LeBaron! Windows down. His face exaggerated.
Pull over. Pull over.

I think at this point Jim finally checked his rear-view mirror.
No doubt he had got out of the habit of using his mirror, never
having to back into or out of his crescent. Rear-view mirrors
were for people without crescents.

He braked hard and swerved to the right, which was not a
smart move and might have been accidental.

Ambient Vehicle Distraction. That's me. I went flying. I was
riding my bike sideways through space. Then the bike was gone.
Then it was just me sliding sideways. I went splat into the space
between the street and the sidewalk. Not the gutter. Well yes, I
guess the gutter. I fit into it quite nicely. Face first, I went into

this space. For a moment it felt cosy and quiet. And guess what protected my face. My black visor. And guess what protected my whole brain. My hat. I had torn the black velvet on the left side. I had heard it, or felt it, tear.

Soon there was swearing. Jim Ryan on the sidewalk. I was rolled onto my back. Uncle Thoby was poking my legs. Cars were slowing down. It was sunny, but there was no warmth. I couldn't remember for a moment what season it was. Is it summer.

Can you feel this.

I nodded.

What about this.

I fell off my bike. Where's my bike.

Uncle Thoby thought I was paralyzed. I was not paralyzed. I stood up. I was wobbly like someone who has just broken a world record for speed.

Uncle Thoby, driving slowly home, hugging the shoulder of Blackbog Drive, said, That was not the kind of travel I meant.

Me: I know.

Uncle Thoby: Adventures are good, but not that kind. I want you to have great safe adventures.

Me: I know.

Uncle Thoby wiped his eyes with his sleeve.

Me: Why are we going so slow.

Uncle Thoby: We're not. You're velocitized.

Me, after an interval during which I made Uncle Thoby explain velocitized: I don't want you to go away.

Uncle Thoby: I have no plans to go away.

Me: Ever.

Him: No.

Me: No what.

Him: No, I will not ever go away.

Me: Promise.

Him: Yes.

Me: Don't you want to go on great safe adventures in tubes.

Him: This is my great safe adventure.

Me: What is.

Him: You. Your dad. This.

Verlaine answers the door, hair like a serrated edge. What happened to your face.

Are you referring to the gouge in my chin or the stye.

You look like that ex-president of Russia.

Oh, right. The bruise on my forehead. Also my teeth feel like they're jammed deeper into my jaw. I fell down some stairs.

She looks unsurprised and asks if I want tea.

Verlaine's living room is cold and drafty. There's a window divided into fifty-four diamonds. What's the word. Mullioned. There are no Christmas decorations, as such. Verlaine's idea of decorating is to put little antlers on the horses already prancing about on all her flat surfaces.

I call out that I have a list. And I take the Clue scoresheet out of my back pocket. Dr. O'Leery. Patience. My dad's grad students. Lionel de Tigrel.

She comes back with two mugs of tea. I sit in the rocking chair. She sits on the sofa. My mug has a weather system. I blow it away. It comes back.

Pretty chilly in here.

She is wearing a T-shirt, of course. It says PSYCHONEUROENDOCRINOLOGY. The OLOGY disappears under her armpit. She says it was a gift. From who. Some idiot in the building.

I rub my stye. Okay, so the suspects.

She knows Wedge has disappeared. On the phone I told her I suspected Foul Play. She had no comment. So I said, Can I come over.

She listens to my theory. Which is actually several theories. Either: Dr. O'Leery, who is now working with mice, decided he needed an extra one. Or one of my dad's grad students, besotted with him, decided to slip away with a living memento. Or Patience. I don't know. I just suspect her. Or Lionel de Tigrel.

Who.

My dad's arch-enemy. Remember all those articles in the living room.

Vaguely.

Vaguely!

Your father had no enemies, Audray.

That's nice of you to say, but trust me. Lionel de Tigrel. I fold my list.

Verlaine says she has a theory too.

Okay, let's hear it.

The little croque monsieur is somewhere in the house.

I've searched the house.

Audray.

What. I acknowledge that my case is weak for Patience. But as for the others, not so weak. My plan is to rule out the local suspects and, once I've checked them off my scoresheet, expand my investigation to include non-Canada.

Non-Canada.

England.

You haven't heard from your uncle.

Blink.

Audray.

What. Lionel de Tigrel is my strongest case. I've been doing some research. There's a laboratory at Cambridge called Humouse House. It's sponsored by Duracell and run by Lionel de Tigrel. If he can make a mouse live for—

A mechanical mouse.

No, a real mouse.

But it runs on batteries.

No. Humouse House is *sponsored* by the batteries. Lionel de Tigrel works with knockout mice. Which is probably one of the reasons he wanted Wedge. For his upper body strength. But that is beside the point. His real motive is Wedge's *longevity.* Not to mention his lifelong vendetta against my dad.

Verlaine scratches her head with both hands. Where did *this* come from.

Are you asking me or yourself.

She looks up. You.

I did some research on my dad's laptop. I know what you're thinking. You're thinking how did Lionel de Tigrel kidnap Wedge if he's at Cambridge.

She raises her eyebrows.

Good question. Remember the Belgian.

What Belgian.

At my dad's post-part-him party.

At the what.

The guy who called me a leapling.

Oh. Yes.

Who was he.

I don't know.

Exactly. I lean back.

She says nothing.

Exactly, I say again. He came here to kidnap Wedge.

From Belgium.

From England.

From England. To steal a mouse.

Yes. Because my dad had been successfully engineering negligible senescence and Lion the Tiger knew it. And maybe my dad had plans to start his own Humouse House and win the two million dollars and the trip to Stockholm.

The what. Wait. You're saying this man at your father's funeral was the Humouse man.

Yes.

Lionel de Tigrel.

Yes.

So Lionel de Tigrel is Belgian.

Probably. Remember how big his eyes got when I said we'd had Wedge since I was a kid.

For a moment Verlaine seems to be entering into the spirit of the thing. Then she gets a balloon-bursting look. Audray.

What.

She hesitates. The average lifespan of a mouse.

I rock in my chair. I know.

Do you.

Four years, I say.

Try two. That is a far cry from twenty.

You're telling me. Rock, rock. What is she getting at. That Wedge is not Wedge. That Wedge could not be Wedge. That is what she is getting at.

Does she think I wouldn't know my own mouse. Having nursed him back to health after a near drowning in a Canadian Tire garbage can and lived cheek by jowl with him for all, or most, of my life. That would be like Verlaine not knowing Rambo from, I don't know, Sylvester Stallone.

The day we brought Wedge home, he was cold and shivery, so we put him in a small box banked with Kleenex. He burrowed in. Then we shone a desk lamp on the box to keep him warm. He wouldn't eat, so I fed him milk from an eyedropper.

My dad warned me that he didn't seem right. There was something not right about him.

Wedge liked being held. So I held him a lot. My dad said there had been some research (not his) that showed that mice who were cuddled when they were young lived longer. He wasn't sure he believed this. He disapproved of cuddling lab animals. Drying them gently with a towel behind the ears and making them go all dreamy with happiness, that was one thing.

What was it.

Not cuddling.

Sometimes the drops of milk would be more than Wedge could swallow and there would be overflow onto his whiskers. I remember how his nose looked when damp. I remember how his eyes looked when closed. I remember how he didn't have eyebrows.

After two weeks he was better. He started trying to climb out of his box. So we moved him into the terrarium.

He overlooked the living room and scratched his head and had ideas about how to rearrange the furniture.

The way he held his water bottle for balance. The way he ran with his hands in the air. The way he fluffed up his bangs if we had guests. The way he played violin if we mentioned Byrne Doyle.

I would know if Wedge were not Wedge.

Plus, the 18 on his ear.

I need you to get me into Dr. O'Leery's lab, I tell Verlaine. So I can rule him out. The first step is to rule out the local suspects.

She looks leery. Remind me of the second step again.

I mean, remember how fit he was. A typical mouse's heart rate is around 700 BPM. Wedge got his down to 500. Astounding.

Mine is 61. At rest. When I wrapped around the wraparound porch at full speed it went up to 75. My dad taught me how to calculate BPM, and for a while I was all about BPM. Mine and other people's.

What is your resting BPM, I would ask people at rest. Would you like me to check.

My dad said that Wedge's genes and ours were very similar. For instance, there is a group of genes called the tinman genes and guess what they build. Hearts. Picture a guy in a construction hat. Picture him standing at your very core and saying, Build a heart here.

In the case of Wedge, the construction guy says, Build a mouse heart here.

In the case of me, he says, Build a person heart here.

My dad said it was not inconceivable that the guy with the construction hat could be tricked or relocated.

We share most of our genes with mice. We are closer to mice than we are to cats or dogs or horses. And yet if I were rolling-pinned flat—I mean all my heart, my brain, my cells, everything, rolling-pinned to a thickness of a millimetre—I would cover 200 acres and Wedge would cover one. Still, one is nothing to sniff at.

My dad said that my heartbeats were like whole notes to Wedge's eighth notes. I didn't understand. He said, Think of it this way. Wedge's heart fills in the gaps in yours.

I liked that idea.

Then there are other animals with very slow hearts, he said.

Like.

Tortoises.

Tortoises!

My dad said that in London he once went to a performance of "Ode to Joy" slowed down to last twenty-four hours. Ode to Slow Motion. That is like a tortoise, he said.

What did it sound like.

Like a planet rotating.

All I'm saying is that Wedge could run 20 kilometres a day on 2-centimetre-long legs. He was fit. He could light a light bulb for Chrissakes.

And Uncle Thoby fed him Licorice Allsorts, which he claimed had special anti-aging properties.

And I cuddled him.

It occurred to me at some point that the slower your BPM the longer you could put off your LHB. The irony was that whenever I thought about my LHB, or the LHB of anyone I loved, my BPM increased.

My dad asked where had I heard about such a thing as an LHB.

I don't know. I made it up.

He said, Assume your LHB can be put off indefinitely.

• • •

Verlaine says Dr. O'Leery has all the mice he wants and can get more just by asking her, so why would he steal Wedge.

Retaliation against my dad.

She stares at me. Retaliation against a dead man.

For sending him on that long sabbatical.

Come on, Audray.

Come on where.

She says I am off my rocker.

I look down at my rocker.

You know what I mean. She says do I really believe. And stops. Makes a hand-tossing gesture. Like she is giving up. Like this is not her problem. She takes my mug into the kitchen. You didn't drink your tea, she says.

It hurts my teeth.

She returns and leans in the doorway. She folds her arms across PSYCHONEUROENDOCRINOLOGY. She says I am not seeing the leaves for the trees.

What.

All her words are tiptoeing now. She hesitates. I respected your father very much.

I nod.

But death is not *evitable,* she says, pronouncing it Frenchly. And to cast a spell on your child and make her believe it is, that is a form of cruelty.

Which gauntlet I did not pick up. She closed her eyes for longer than a blink, which usually means people are looking inward and regretting what they have just said. Yes, well. Look inward and regret much, Verlaine. I took my list and left.

Audray.

I left without saying anything. Which is a form of picking up a gauntlet, I guess, and running away with it.

The airport is crowded with Christmas travellers. There are more flights coming in than you can shake a lead marshal's wand at.

Miss, we're asking greeters to wait outside the Arrivals area.

This from a man not exactly in uniform, but he's got a badge pinned to his tie.

Greeters.

You're greeting someone, he says.

That would be nice.

Okay, in any case, please stand back. It's mayhem in there.

Of course.

But the next time the sliding doors open, I slide through. Where is the carousel. I thought I would wait by the baggage carousel in case someone showed up. But it's gone. Gone is the merry-go-round carousel and in its place is a low-riding conveyor belt shaped like this

with a door at each end. I walk along in tandem with a bag wearing a green tag that says YOU DON'T LOOK LIKE MY OWNER. That makes me a bit sad. I carry on towards the Arrivals escalator where a crowd has gathered. Apparently I am not the only determined greeter. Here they all are with their antlers and their banners. Well, a few of them are wearing antlers. And no one is waving a banner. But such is the overall impression. Festive. It's Christmas and people are coming home.

I lean against a Hertz counter. This is new too. All these car rental booths. I help myself to a candy cane from the counter.

You want a car.

I've got a car. A brown LeBaron. Stick shift. I'm a greeter.

Greeters aren't supposed to be in here.

Yes, but it's an emergency.

Oh, well then, carry on.

It's amazing how many people are carrying strollers on the escalator. Big strollers with mountain-bike tires. Surely that's a safety hazard. I look for someone I know. No one, no one, no one.

People hug and wave their banners and sing and run in circles. It is mayhem, like the man with the badge said. After a while they calm down and wander over to the baggage belt. There will be another new flight any moment, and then another, and another.

I scan the horizon for the wall to non-Canada. Where is the plywood wall. There must still be a wall. But the closest thing I can find is a non-plywood wall with artwork on it. I knock on that wall.

No answer.

I take a seat on an unattended bag.

The floor is not brickish anymore but smooth and white. Good for rolling bags. Was the new floor here when I arrived. Yes. The new airport. I remember. No more carousel. No more Bite-to-Eatery. But already my arrival feels like years ago.

I remember the old floor and how the metal buggies made your teeth hurt when you pushed them. If I was pushing the buggy, my dad always said, Hey, you're driving me buggy.

The day I left, he pushed the buggy and said, Am I driving you buggy, but I was in no state to joke around. We checked my luggage. Uncle Thoby carried my carry-on bag. We went to the Bite-to-Eatery but I didn't feel like biting. I was excited and sick.

Now I wish I had laughed at the buggy joke. I wish I had paid attention to my dad instead of girding my loins for the flight. Why wasn't I funnier. Why didn't I point out the resemblance of the woodcut on the wall to Han Solo when he gets frozen by Darth Vader. Didn't I *always* point out the resemblance of the woodcut to Han Solo. But not that time.

Brave Miss Scarlet, Uncle Thoby nudged my dad. About to leap clear across the board.

As is her wont, said my dad.

They both looked so proud.

I was going to Europe. Verlaine had arranged for me to stay with her aunt in Switzerland. From there I would branch out, travel on TGVs (*trains à grande vitesse*) to wherever my rapidly beating heart desired. The sound barrier was the limit!

Terrified Miss Scarlet, I said.

Fear is the mark of insufficient curiosity, said Uncle Thoby. And you are too curious to be fearful, Oddly.

Curious inquisitive, or curious odd, said my dad.

Ha ha.

Are you sure you don't want something. Fries with gravy.

I shook my head. I'll need the sick bag.

At home the tree on my wall was bare and would stay bare until I returned. There would be no Changing of the Tree. Time was supposed to stand still while I was on my great safe adventure. Nothing was supposed to change.

Don't picture them waving from the chain-link fence. And my dad sitting down on the pavement. And Uncle Thoby putting his hand on his shoulder. And them both thinking it wouldn't be forever.

There are no bags left on the conveyor belt except YOU DON'T LOOK LIKE MY OWNER. Should I take you home, I ask it. Even though I'm not.

The man with the tie and the badge is en route.

Miss.

Yes.

Are you missing someone.

What a nice thing to ask. I thought you were coming over here to kick me out of the Arrivals area.

Well, that is next on my agenda.

Oh.

He offers me a hand. I take it. He pulls me up. It's not so bad as all that, is it, he says.

Actually it really is.

He escorts me out, hands in pockets, like we are just taking a stroll together. Have a good night now.

Is it night. Yes, it is.

The night is bright, the taxi queue long, and the short-term parking lot runneth over. I can't remember where I parked. I walk up and down the rows, rubbing my stye. This constant looking for something that is missing is becoming tiresome. It is my new default setting. Where are you, LeBaron. Where oh where. Then I see it. Its eyes are dimly lit. Very dimly.

Oh shit.

The LeBaron looks the way I feel. Low on battery power.

I turn the ignition and it makes a sound that would break your heart. Okay, I won't put you through that. We need a jump. I will go back inside and kill two birds with one stone. I will get a coffee to jump-start me and I will call—who, Verlaine—to jump-start you. No. Even if I wasn't still harbouring a gauntlet, the Lada couldn't jump-start a mechanical mouse. So what are my options. Do I leave the LeBaron out here and take a Clint's cab home. Do I sneak back into the Arrivals area and rent a car from Hertz. I can't leave the LeBaron in short-term parking for a long term. I can't leave it to watch other people come and go, thinking, You don't look like my owner. Where is my owner. Your owner will not forsake you, little LeBaron. She will get coffee and think of a solution.

At Tim Hortons, when I reach into my pocket for change, I pull out the Christmatech recall notice, full of concern for my electrical safety, the phone number big and bold.

While I wait for Judd, I wander over to the chain-link fence and watch a plane land. The windows of the plane are dark, not because there is anything wrong with its electrical system, but because the pilots have turned off the lights during landing. On the tarmac a lead marshal stamps his feet and waits, hands all aglow.

The plane touches down, back wheels first, then the front wheel. The edges of the wings flap up. Slow down, slow down. What is the word. Career. When you skid off the path. Also when you are gainfully employed. But no, the plane is not careering. The plane is under control. Now it's behaving just like a car, en route to the gate. Dum-de-dum. You'd never know it had just been airborne.

On the phone I said, Is this Judd Julian-Brown, Christmas light inventor and electrical wizard.

Speaking.

I explained my predicament.

He said, I never turn down an opportunity to use jumper cables.

Really.

Really.

I hang on to the fence. Across the runway, I can make out the shell of the old hangar, a bumpy moon on its roof. I was in that building once. I *rode* into it. I came across it on one of my hacks with Rambo. I was riding by myself by then, and I'd been searching for weeks for a way onto airport property. You had to scrape through a tight forest, and when you came out on the other side (a little bloodied), you were in a field beside the runway. The first thing I saw was an old building with a hole in its side. A hole big enough for a horse to walk through. So walk through it we did.

It was dark. Rambo's hoofs made a crunching sound. I waited for my eyes to adjust. That's when I saw them. Old airplane seats. Not in audience formation. Just tossed down by God. And broken beer bottles on the floor.

I turned Rambo around carefully. You never walk a horse on broken glass. The undersides of his hoofs are like exposed hearts.

Outside the wind blew and Rambo did a little dance.

My ultimate goal: to race a plane down a runway.

We waited. Rambo showed no interest in eating the grass. His ears were pricked. Finally a plane pulled away from the terminal. Reluctantly. Pushed by its little car. Go on now, said the car. Go on.

Don't make me fly, said the plane. We are not meant to fly.

Actually you are.

Rambo and I trotted forward. Posting trot towards a plane. You have not lived until you've done this. And when you post you are of necessity calm.

We got close enough that I could see astonished faces inside the oval windows. The plane was girding. I pointed a finger down the runway. On your mark. Get set.

The noise was tremendous. No fear from Rambo. So he really had been faking all those times. He was all prancy readiness. I had to turn him in a tight circle. Two tight circles. When I let him go, he didn't believe it at first. I can go. Yes! You can go. We kept to the grass. Because you don't gallop exposed hearts on pavement. Rule Number One of Galloping.

We raced the plane. All four hoofs left the ground. We flew.

The conversation in the cockpit: Merle. Yeah. Girl on black horse at two o'clock.

. . .

Judd arrives in the Christmatech van. He takes one look at my face and winces. Oh right. I am bruised. From his staircase. Does it hurt, he says.

Yes.

Judd parks the van hood to hood with the LeBaron. He busies himself with the jumper cables.

I look inside the van. Boxes of lights. A ball of wool. A ladder. Hey, my cowboy hat!

Is the cowboy hat for me.

He looks over his shoulder. Nope.

I open the door and grab it.

Were you greeting someone, he says from under the LeBaron's hood.

What is it with the word *greeting*. No, I was dropping someone off. I was dropping off my dad. And my uncle.

He stops doing whatever he's doing.

What, I say.

Nothing. I just have to think about this. Plus on plus. Minus on minus.

Sounds right to me.

Where they off to.

England.

He straightens. Looks me straight in the stye. What, I say again.

Nothing. Hop in. Wait till I give you the sign, then fire her up.

Okay.

And so I'm in the LeBaron with the cowboy hat, and he's in the van. He turns on the van and lets it run. We sit there like that for a while. Just watching each other through the windshields.

You're lying about your father and uncle.

Yeah.

Why.

Because it hurts.

Why not tell me that.

I did.

Okay. But why not really tell me.

Because I'd like to keep someone in the dark.

He nods. Meaning, okay, I'll be that someone. Meaning, okay, start the car now.

I start the car. Thank you, thank you.

Welcome.

Another slow drive home in excruciatingly low gear.

I have two plane crash dreams: a ground one and an air one. In the ground one, I am watching a plane from the ground, and the moment I think the word *crash*, it starts to. In the air one, I am inside a plane and it's a party—we're all having a grand old time—when I notice that the pilots are at the party with us. In the cabin. Um. And the moment I think the word *crash*, we start to.

These dreams stopped for a while after Uncle Thoby came to live with us. But they started again after I'd found the hangar with the airplane seats all thrown down like a bad hand by God.

My dad's way of dealing with a bad dream was to explain to me, at great length, that night terror was an evolutionary adaptation.

It would be.

Imagine two men asleep in the woods. The sound of a branch breaking startles them awake. They sit up, look around, listen. Nothing seems amiss. One man shrugs and goes back to sleep. The other man lies awake, feeling afraid. Why is he afraid. He doesn't know. So he invents a reason. Or two. Or three. He imagines all the terrible things that could happen to him tomorrow. Maybe the other man will abandon him. Or meet someone he likes better. This worry keeps him awake and alert. Half an hour later when the lion, whose coming was foretold by the breaking branch, arrives in the clearing, the man whose adrenalin is already pumping leaps into a tree and survives. The sleeping man gets eaten.

But I didn't have a dream about a lion.

Go back to sleep. No—in your own bed. It won't be scary in the morning.

But the guy who fell asleep got *eaten*.

Sure. But we don't live in the woods anymore. Your body is just remembering a time when we did.

This was not comforting.

My body is just remembering a time when it was in the air. Don't ever do that again, is what it's telling me.

Uncle Thoby's bad-dream procedure was different. He said I should go back and *change* the dream. At first I didn't think that was possible. A dream feels too real. It feels true and unchangeable, and the reason you are still so afraid when you wake up is that your body secretly knows that the crashing plane *is* real, and this being safe in your bed is the dream.

Uncle Thoby said, Remember the montage. How it is true, but also fast and mixed up. You get to choose what you put in and leave out.

So like a biography.

Sort of. Uncle Thoby said real life was packed with stuff that didn't matter. Whereas in a montage, you only saw the stuff that mattered. If this were a dream, he said, I wouldn't see the horses on your blanket or Yoda on the shelf. I wouldn't look out the window and see a car parked in the driveway. *Unless* all those things were going to matter soon. Unless someone was going to get in the car and drive away. That's the thing about a dream. You get to decide what matters. You get to decide the outcome. Hold the plane in the air from the ground. Fly the plane yourself while the pilots have a party in first class. Take the dream in a different direction.

Okay. This worked for a while. But then I found the hangar.

Uncle Thoby, I said into the heat vent. My bed is crashing.

Two seconds later he was in my room. What's up.

I found a building with a plane crash in it.

A what.

He sat down on the ottoman and listened. Then he asked where was this building and how many seats were there and what on earth was I doing riding Rambo on airport property.

Don't tell my dad.

He said he wouldn't, but he did. Not to get me in trouble but because he had this idea. He had this idea for a plane in the basement.

Apparently he and my dad were more worried than they'd let on about my fear of flying and my insistence that I was never, ever going to get on a plane again, for as long as we all three shall live.

That is a bit extreme, said my dad.

Uncle Thoby agreed. There are too many great safe adventures to be had.

And so they devised this plan, to help me get over my fear.

The basement had already been converted into an apartment for Uncle Thoby. Well, a bedroom with a bathroom. It was bigger than it needed to be. Essentially it was a long rectangle with a bathroom at one end. What does that remind you of.

Oh. And it was painted the colour of iceberg lettuce with the sun coming through.

They rented a truck and went out there. I was not with them. I knew nothing about it. It was a surprise for me on their joint birthday. I got a present on their joint birthday. A plane in the basement.

They had stolen the seats, and a beverage cart, from the hangar.

Holy, I said, when they took off the blindfold. Sweet Jesus in the garden!

They looked at each other. That's a new one.

The seats were arranged in audience formation, facing the short end of the rectangle. They were navy blue with a diamond pattern. They were bandaged (duct-taped) where necessary.

A plane, a plane!

I did a little jig of happiness. Uncle Thoby joined in. My dad tapped his foot.

But that wasn't all. At the front of the plane was a "cockpit" consisting of an old desk with knobs and dials glued on. Some of them actually lit up, don't ask me how. I think they were part of an old stereo. A steering wheel was bolted to the front of the desk. Where did the steering wheel come from.

Someone's front lawn on Logy Bay Road.

Much laughter.

I stared at them. They were burglars. They were pirates. They were amazing.

Captain, said Uncle Thoby. And he gestured at the pilot's chair. I sat. My dad assumed passenger status. Uncle Thoby sat beside me. My co-pilot.

I looked over my shoulder at my dad. I don't think I've ever smiled so big as that.

A plane. In our basement.

Welcome to Qantas flight 123. This is your captain speaking.

Okay, so we just stared at the pale green wall when we were flying, but we were *flying* for Chrissakes. We flew all over the world. We flew to China and France and I played with the knobs and said, Ladies and gentlemen, we will be experiencing some turbulence. When we were out of the turbulence, Uncle Thoby headed for the beverage cart. My dad said, Anywhere but London. Uncle Thoby, when he walked down the aisle, pretended to lose his balance. Steady on, Airbus 320.

This is a 747.

Sorry. Do you mean it has two floors.

Yes!

We are not converting the whole house into a plane, said my dad, who was reading the *Telegram* in seat 1C.

Uncle Thoby sipped his beverage in 1D.

I turned the seatbelt sign on.

No reaction.

I just turned the seatbelt sign on.

Oh.

That's something we need to work on, said Uncle Thoby, fastening his.

Sometimes I felt like being a passenger, and so my dad and Uncle Thoby flew. If my dad was flying, we went to places like Ouagadougou, Shanghai, and Dubai. If Uncle Thoby was flying, we usually went to Corner Brook.

Since when does Qantas fly to Corner Brook.

Since Australians began immigrating en masse to that lovely city.

Oh. Okay.

We never went to England.

The flights were always more eventful when my dad and Uncle Thoby were flying because they'd had more in-flight experiences and could think up all sorts of (near) mishaps. Whereas for me there was only ever a) turbulence or b) trouble with the landing gear.

When my dad flew, we often lost altitude. Inexplicably. Crap, we're losing altitude again.

What is it with you and altitude, said Uncle Thoby, flipping a switch.

I'm going to drop fuel.

No, you're not.

Yes.

No.

Into the ocean. It has to be done. Sorry marine life.

Bloody hell.

Three seats only had their flip-down tables intact. I always sat in a seat with a flip-down table. So I could flip it up and down, up and down. Ad nauseam.

Speaking of which, we sometimes had our meals in the basement. All three of us facing forward, in our different seats. None
of us in the cockpit.

What is this barfy airplane food. Please pass me a sick bag.

Hey.

Who's flying this plane! my dad would ask suddenly, leaping
up. Oh my God who's flying the plane.

Much laughter.

I stopped having plane crash dreams.

Before a flight, Uncle Thoby would load our baggage. The cargo
hold was under his bed. We were allowed only one item. I usually brought Wedge in his ball, who inevitably rolled out of the
cargo hold with his hands in the air like there was some great
emergency. Evacuate!

My luggage has gone astray, I said, looking over my shoulder.

If only we could train him to push the beverage cart, Uncle
Thoby said.

When Uncle Thoby flew, there was fog. Visibility is bad, he
would say. I can't see a bloody thing. I'm waiting for clearance
from the tower. The ground could be anywhere. We may have to
go back to St. John's. Yes, I think we will have to go back to St.
John's. No Corner Brook tonight. Just a big old circle in the sky.

Let me fly, my dad would say.

No.

Yes.

No.

Punch on the shoulder.

Smoke in the cockpit, said my dad. Can you smell that. Sniff.
Yes. That is a bad sign. Land immediately.

Did you see a horse on the runway, I asked co-pilot Thoby.

No. I was busy turning these knobs.

There was a black horse on the runway.

He looked at me. I don't like the sound of that, Captain Oddly.

I winked at him. Neveryoumind.

Over time the plane was embellished. The cockpit got new lights. I liked to fly in the dark. Oval windows lined the walls with a sun-setty sky beyond. The cockpit got a windshield. In the distance, if you looked closely, you could see other planes flying.

All this courtesy of Uncle Thoby's long arm and a paintbrush.

But what I wanted, what he couldn't paint, was an actual glittering city to descend into. A New York, say. Or a Las Vegas. Captain Oddly flew into Las Vegas a lot. She had seen it on TV. The lights were bloody dazzling. Like a campfire when it is just embers. She was developing a taste for great safe adventures.

Ladies and gentlemen, we are beginning our final descent into Las Vegas International Airport. Can I ask you to ensure that your seatbacks are in an upright position and your seatbelts—

Only gentlemen back here, said co-pilot Thoby, sipping something strong.

It was all practice. So that I would be brave enough to be curi-ous. Or curious enough to be brave. So that I would be able to get on board to new places. And when I finally did get on board, I would sit calmly but alertly in seat 12A or 14A or 21F. I would have a table of my own, or I wouldn't. I might or might not have a secret compartment in my armrest. But I would not assume a crash position prematurely or don a life vest without due cause. And if things went terribly wrong, I would not sit idly by in audience formation.

And in the event of the very worst thing happening—and by worst I don't mean a plane crash, I mean, say I was left alone, really alone, on a desert island—well, I would just have to build a plane of my own, wouldn't I. And I would practise taking off and landing. Just like in the basement. And I would make big circles to Corner Brook and back. And then I would widen the circles. I would widen and widen until I had crossed the ocean. Because maybe across the ocean there is another person, also on a desert island. And he thinks he is alone. But surprise, surprise. Here comes my Boeing 747 with a big maple leaf like an open hand on its tail. *Bonjour, bonjour.* And this other person looks up and makes his hand a visor. Sweet Jesus in the garden, he says. I am not alone. No, you are not alone. And I land my homemade plane expertly and dismount, sorry debark, and there he is on the runway, waiting.

ANTONIO: In sooth,[1] I know not why I am so sad.

> It wearies me, you say it wearies you;
> But how I caught it, found it, or came by it,
> What stuff 'tis made of, whereof it is born,
> I am to learn;
> And such a want-wit[2] sadness makes of me
> That I have much ado to know myself.[3]

I find Shakespeare's use of exponents curious.

I am on bookmark duty while Chuck stares out the window. He has been wearing the same boxer shorts for three days. Again he mutters something about the Willamette looking inviting. Well. That is getting a bit old now, isn't it.

Sooth to the power of one means what.

When Chuck rehearses he does not say the exponents out loud. Nor does he say, I have much ado to know myself times myself times myself. In fact, today he is not saying much of anything. He looks pathetic over there from behind. Of course all humans look pathetic from behind, but Chuck especially so.

You can't be Hamlet every day. Or maybe you can. Maybe part of being Hamlet is not knowing if you are Hamlet. Maybe part of being Hamlet is being Antonio. Some days, anyway.

Today he is Antonio. But he will not lower the bar so far as to play a Salarino, Solario, or Salerio. He has his standards. A moment ago, when he plopped me down on the Antonio passage, he said, The reason you're so sad is because you're a chump.

Who, me.

The way Chuck stands at the window waiting for someone to pick him up and hold him under their armpit—that is pretty sad. He is waiting to be told he isn't a chump. He is waiting to be told he matters. That there are other roles in his repertoire besides a sad-sack Antonio who doesn't know who he is because he is three different people in one (himself to the power of three). And if he has to die—today, tomorrow, someday—at least his death will not be a stupid one, let us hope.

According to Chuck, Shakespeare gave all the characters he didn't care about roughly the same name. But Hamlet. Now there's a name. And wasn't Hamlet roughly the name of Shakespeare's son whose premature death the Bard never got over. That is mentioned somewhere in *Lowering the Bard*.

Outside it is raining and what is Chuck thinking. That it is just Bend and Boring from now on. He opens the window. He stands atop the radiator and leans out. Hey. I do not have a piece of lettuce to drop. Hey. Do not be stupid to the power of two. Get back in here.

Oh. He is just smoking. He is just breaking Linda's rule and smoking with his torso out the window.

Fine. Still, it seems to me that if you are going to lean out a window like that, and if you are not shaped like a tortoise (i.e., the rest of your body could also fit through the window), and if you are four or five storeys above ground, you should probably be wearing a harness. You should be what is called anchored in. Even Cliff, whose prime directive was not safety, was never so repelled by the role he had to play in life that he failed to anchor himself in properly before he rappelled off the fire escape at great speed. But of course Cliff was what is called a gearhead. Which means someone who loves gear for its own sake. He often slept in his harness.

Sometimes of course it is necessary to sleep in a harness if you are leapfrogging up a tremendous cliff with another climber.

If the cliff is so tremendous that it takes more than a day to climb, then you must bolt a special hammock into the rock and sleep 37,000 feet or thereabouts above ground with your harness on and eat nothing but Power Bars and wait for the sun to wake you in the morning when it hits your hammock. Cliff has done this on several occasions.

Not that I have ever accompanied Cliff on a real rock climbing adventure. But I have, on one occasion, been part of a rock climbing *day trip*. That was when we all piled into Cliff's car (Cliff and Audrey in front, Chuck and Linda in back, me on the DB) and spent the day at Lake Soupçon, which when Audrey pronounced it meant a little bit of suspicion, and when the others pronounced it meant supper's ready.

In any case, the reason for the trip was so Cliff could teach Chuck the basics of rock climbing. Really I think Chuck just wanted to learn to rappel. He had visions of rappelling into productions he was not cast in.

Lake Soupçon is a shallow lake shaped like a soup bowl with sides that can be climbed by novices. These sides are not so tall that you have to leapfrog up. Rather, you can anchor a single rope at the top and practise climbing up and rappelling down, ad infinitum. Cliff could have climbed the sides of Lake Soupçon in his sleep. What was a soup bowl after the Yelps. But Chuck, with his scrawny arms, not so easily. Even though Cliff said arms don't matter in rock climbing, they sort of do. I mean, an armless guy couldn't climb a mountain without some pretty fancy prosthetics. What Cliff meant, of course, was that your legs are what matter most in climbing. You've got to *walk up* the rock, even if it's vertical, not haul yourself up by your hands. Comprendez.

Meanwhile, Audrey, Linda, and I bobbed in a rented boat in the middle of Lake Soupçon. Linda kept her head tilted back because she was trying to get freckles. Audrey already had freckles enough. She was holding the oars. I was on the dashboard, which is not called a dashboard in a boat but nevermind. I was on the dashboard, taking a bow over the edge and admiring my reflection in the still brown water.

Careful, Iris. Will you grab her.

Linda grabbed me and plonked me down in Audrey's bare lap. I turned slowly around. It was hard to see Cliff because he was wearing his beige STEREOTYPES ARE USEFUL T-shirt—which is a joke, but one I don't find particularly funny—so he blended into the rock. Mostly you could only see the pink rope and Chuck at the bottom, standing beside the cooler.

Cliff was, I think, demonstrating a traverse. A traverse is when you move sideways along the X axis.

Chuck was belaying. Belaying is when you hold the rope that is attached, via a pulley, to the climber. To nutshellize: Chuck was holding Cliff's life in his hands, a situation that, judging from the tension in Audrey's upper legs, did not sit well with her.

Cliff started up the Y axis.

Chuck decided he was thirsty. You could tell he had decided this by the way he suddenly had eyes only for the cooler. Audrey's legs tensed so much that I nearly tipped off. Why. Because Chuck was breaking Rule Number One of Belaying, which is: Don't take your eyes off the person whose life you hold in your hands.

And then he broke Rule Number Two, which is: Do not let go of the rope when you are holding someone's life in your hands.

Followed by his breakage of Rule Number Three, which is: Do not partake of a cold one while you are holding someone's life in your hands.

Audrey started rowing swiftly back to shore.

Linda said, What the.

But really, why was the cooler there if not to tempt him. And shouldn't Cliff have known better. But, as I say, safety never was his prime directive. It was Audrey's. Although the chances of Cliff falling during that brief interval when Chuck was not looking at him, when Chuck had exchanged the life he held in his hands for a beer—well, the chances were pretty slim because, as I said, the sides of Lake Soupçon were not so slippery as to foil an expert climber like Cliff.

Audrey continued to row powerfully. Which is something you do need strong arms for.

When we arrived on shore, or near enough that Audrey could splash out, she deposited me on the dashboard and bolted towards the base of the cliff.

What is going on, said the clueless and freckleless Linda.

Audrey scrabbled. She hip-checked Chuck and grabbed the rope. She yelled something to Cliff, who looked over his shoulder and started back down the rock. Now there were four hands on the rope and all eyes were on Cliff. When Cliff reached the bottom, he turned around—his T-shirt making its stupid statement—and Audrey dropped the rope and walked away. Stomp, stomp, scrabble, splash, she came back to the boat, picked me up, and headed for the car. For a moment I thought we were going to drive off into the sunset together. But we didn't. Stranding is not her style. We sat together on the hood and looked up at the sky and waited for the others to pack up the gear. This took a long time. The sky got darker. The hood got colder. She put me under her T-shirt. Warm enough, she said.

Two weeks later she came home with six boxes of climbing holds and proceeded to turn our flat into an indoor mountain. So that the walls became cliffs. Sorry, Cliff's. So that if he fell, he fell six feet to the floor, max.

Since the fall down the stairs I have been having some dental issues. What does *impacted* mean, because I'm pretty sure that's what has happened to my teeth. They are impacted, I tell the receptionist in Dr. Overli-Domes' office.

She pauses in her typing. All of them, she says.

Yes.

Please have a seat.

I sit. *Reader's Digest* has an article about introverts. They are being interviewed and forced to tell their secrets. This will be good for them. I feel a longing to be an introvert. To have an extrovert draw me out. Where is my extrovert.

Dr. Overli-Domes appears bald and white-clad from behind a closed door.

Audrey Flowers!

I stand up.

Sweet Jesus in the garden you're all grown-up.

I try to make myself seem smaller.

Come.

I follow him to the orange chair. Ah, the old orange chair. The examination room is the same except now there's a TV embedded in the ceiling, showing cartoons. Just watch and relax, he says and disappears.

Charlie Brown's Christmas. I yawn.

I sit up. He'd better not be leaving the room so he can turn on the X-ray machine. Dentists do this. Leave the room and X-ray you. Just let me rest this piece of equipment against your cheek—

I'll be right back.

No, no X-rays. He is just getting my file from Ingrid.

So what, he says. You only come round here once every blue Christmas.

I've been away.

Yes. You and everyone and his brother.

I explain that I had a fall and my teeth are now impacted.

Fall from a horse, he says, still looking at my file.

No.

It was a horse last time.

Yes. But not a fall.

I have written here: Kicked in the face by an equine.

He looks in my mouth. Gasps. Hand to chest. Oh yes, the Swiss bridge. I'd forgotten the Swiss bridge. What a thing of beauty. Your dad paid a pretty penny for that piece of hardware, as I recall.

He snaps on his gloves.

I look up into his glasses. The amazing thing about sitting in a dentist's chair, if you are not distracted by the cartoons in the ceiling, is that you have a singular opportunity to look deep into someone's eyes for a long, long time, without them being able to stop you. Their eyes are almost, but not quite, meeting yours. Their eyes are meeting your mouth. They are so absorbed by the Swiss bridge. They are so in love with the Swiss. They don't notice you noticing.

Impacted where, he says.

Dr. Overli-Domes patched me up when Rambo kicked me. He kept humming that song "All I Want for Christmas Is My Two Front Teeth" and winking at me. Later my dad thanked him profusely for coming in on a holiday. And Dr. Overli-Domes said, What in God's name was she doing getting kicked in the face by a horse on Christmas morning.

Dr. Overli-Domes is one of those doctors who is really nice to kids but as a rule dislikes their parents.

My dad hung his head.

He and Uncle Thoby and Verlaine all hung their heads in the waiting room.

I was cleaning out Rambo's hind hoof, I told him. And I was singing "O Tannenbaum" a little too close to that hind hoof.

Dr. Overli-Domes smiled down at me.

He didn't mean to kick me, I added.

The temporary bridge felt like a highway overpass. Concrete and huge. He said, Don't you worry. We'll order you a nice new one from Switzerland, won't we Dad.

My dad nodded.

Verlaine perked up. All things Swiss are indeed superior.

Later, when the new bridge was installed, I thought about how weird it was that my teeth had been somewhere I hadn't. Which led me to start flying the plane in the basement to Zurich.

Now Dr. Overli-Domes says, That a stye.

So he has been sneaking looks at my eyes.

Yeah.

He rolls his chair over to the sink and washes his hands. Antibiotics clear that right up.

I would not say no to some antibiotics, were you to prescribe them.

I'm a dentist. Not an oculist.

So.

That would not be ethical.

Oh.

But I can tell you not to touch it. Leave it alone. Don't drain it.

I drained it already. I like draining it.

Styes happen when you're run down, he says. You been run down.

My dad was run down.

He looks over his shoulder.

A chain-link fence holds GOLEM prisoner. In case it tries to sneak away before they can tear it down. It looks blindfolded and beaten. It looks small. New condos gnash beyond the fence. You're next, they taunt. You're next. Some of the condos say *hotel* in sly lower case letters.

Meanwhile the school walls say THUG LIFE, all upper case. Some thugs with difficult lives have scaled the fence with spray paint.

My eye waters.

Judd is burly and beside me. We hold on to the fence and lock our elbows against a wind that would like to make a chain-link impression on our faces. The only colour is the red of Judd's hair. And his van. And the syncopated hazards.

Hey. Jesus is still stuck like a corkscrew in the roof.

What happened to Catholic. It used to matter so much.

Judd and I share many fond GOLEM memories. We share the boiler room/cafeteria. (He shows me his scar from a pipe.) We share Principal Pouvoir, whose real name turned out to be Dave Power. We share Miss Daken, with her math biographies. We share the song "God Is a Surprise!" (Surprise, surprise! God is a surprise! Right before your eyes! He's baffling to the wise!)

We share the red parachute.

Oh the red parachute. The red parachute was the best. How it billowed and filled the gym and you could run under it and pretend the red ceiling would last forever. Judd says he once tried to steal it, but was caught red-handed. Ha. He'd had this idea of taking it up to Seagull Hill and unfurling it.

Holy Christ. You'd have been carried out to sea.

I'd still be out there.

I look sideways at him. It's almost Christmas. Isn't there somewhere he has to be.

Family's in Florida, he says.

They left you alone at Christmas.

We don't celebrate Christmas, he says.

How come.

We're Jewish.

Since when.

Since always.

But you went to GOLEM.

So did you.

I thought I was the only non-Catholic.

Nope.

But I'm an atheist, I say. I'm a Frenchly submerged atheist.

So am I. A Frenchly submerged Jewish atheist.

Interesting. With a business called Christmatech.

He smiles. That's right.

The furniture store, which may seem magical to some, is a kind of hell if you hate overhead light. Which Judd really, really hates. Yes, there are rooms within rooms, but the light in each room is the same.

Imagine living in one room that pretends to be many where it is perpetually high noon and people are always coming through the door and you want to have gunfights with them but you are not allowed. Also, you are not allowed to eat on the furniture.

Judd very early developed a love for the dark, for chocolate, for stoplights.

He remembers being in his car seat, eating a Milky Way bar, and loving the green of Go. The red of Stop. The yellow was weak and needed more pixels. He invented, while still in his car seat, a new stoplight that incorporated the whole spectrum. A red light that graded slowly to purple, then to blue, then finally to green. So you knew when green was coming. And a green light that faded to yellow, to deep orange, to red.

Apparently he used to say to whoever was driving, The light is blue. Get ready for green.

He says birds and some reptiles have four kinds of cones in their eyes for seeing colour. We only have three. Which means they can see colours we can't.

Imagine what a peacock looks like to a peacock.

If he were a superhero and could have one power, that would be it. He would take the extra cone.

Even his hazard lights make him happy.

So do traffic jams at dusk on a highway.

And Christmas lights.

Upstairs in his room above the store, he works for as long as he can without turning on a light, so that the room fills up blue. That is the only way to invent Christmas lights.

Okay, he does have a single halogen desk lamp. But he keeps it on the floor.

What is it about overhead light. He doesn't know. But it is soulless. Think of the interior light of a car. Think of noon on a sunny day. Soulless.

I nod. I have to agree.

The light outside GOLEM is white, even though it is dark. A stretched, baseball-stadium kind of light. It makes our faces bright and our eyes dark.

The van that thinks my dad is alive continues to blink the rhythm of its heart.

Judd says he remembers my dad now. He, Judd, had his D-434-model lights plugged into the van's cigarette lighter outside Canadian Tire. My dad came out of the store with a dancing snowman, the kind that shakes its hips. It was still dancing in the bag.

It is like the van has this gravitational pull for some people.

My dad came over and introduced himself and stared at the lights. He asked if they were LED, and Judd said, Light-emitting diodes are so last year.

Which made my dad smile. Christmatech, he said, reading the van. He bought three strands.

Are you cold, says Judd. *Viens ici.*

I move my hands in a sideways climb (what Cliff would call a traverse) along the fence until Judd's right arm closes behind me like a gate. The wind dies down.

Why are we here. Because the school soon won't be. Because we have a memory that needs feeding.

When I tilt my head back, my ponytail bunches on his shoulder and his cheek touches my cheek. We have cold cheeks. He says into my ear, how is my chin, my forehead, my teeth, my eye. He is so sorry I fell down his stairs.

My dentist prescribed antibiotics.

All I have to do is turn around and a new chapter begins. You know that feeling. When all you have to do is let go and turn around.

I left a tortoise in Oregon, I say.

That can change, can't it.

Christmas Eve and Uncle Thoby has not called. Other people call and impersonate him. Well, not on purpose. But the Hear Ye 3000 rings in his voice: Are you there. Yes! Do you feel like answering. Of course!

Rush to pick up. And then I am stabbed in the heart when it is not him. It is Murph asking how I like my new door hardware. Really, some people take customer service to an extreme.

I get a shock every time I touch it, I tell him.

Then it's doing its job.

Right. Well, thanks for asking.

There must be a way to disable this ring.

Verlaine calls with an apology—or with what for her amounts to an apology. She says that since Uncle Thoby has *foutre le camp*, I should not be alone.

Foutre le camp. I always confuse that with *coup de foudre*. *Foutre le camp* is what Cliff did. *Coup de foudre* is what I feel when I look at Judd's hair.

Uncle Thoby has not bolted from the campsite, I tell her. He will be back anon. And I'm not camping alone.

I'm wearing my dad's CRYNOT bracelet and I jingle it, loudly, while Verlaine says she did not mean to upset me when I came over with my Clue scoresheet of suspects in Wedge's disappearance, but—what is that noise, Audray.

Nothing.

Sounds like bells.

I have an investigation to carry on. I should go.

But it is Christmas Eve.

Yes. Well.

And she reminds me of the Christmases-past tradition whereby she would pick me up on Christmas Day (after the Flowers had opened their stockings and watched and ridiculed the Queen's address on TV), and we would head over to the Before Building to feed the lab animals and then out to the stable to groom Rambo. And when I got home, if my teeth were intact, I would find Uncle Thoby and my dad asleep on the sofa because I had been such a bundle of energy since six o'clock in the ante meridiem and they were exhausted. Wake up! Wake up!

I cut her off. I don't want to visit my Christmases past. Not today. Not with her. In fact, I am thinking of not capitalizing Christmas anymore. That is how much it hurts. So can we wait until Boxing Day to do the Before Building.

But Audray.

Gotta go.

And I hang up.

I reread the bracelet. What is Heparin. It says we were supposed to inject my dad's body with Heparin.

My legs ache. I sit down at the table. They ache from waiting. They ache from wanting to run.

The phone rings again and I assume it's Verlaine so I don't answer. But it's Patience. She leaves a message. I half-expect her to say, I have your mouse. How much are you willing to pay. But no. She says, How is the Grief Bar working out for you.

Oh. I had forgotten the Grief Bar. I head upstairs. It is one of the things I pack and take to the Civil Manor. Where I will be spending Christmas.

I am the only guest. *Quelle surprise.* Doreen is still watching TV, the same old TV, deeper than it is wide. I check in during *A Christmas Carol*. The real one. Starring Alistair Sim and Byrne

Doyle. When I mention to Doreen the resemblance between Jacob Marley and our local Conservative candidate, she looks over her shoulder and says, Blessed Christ, you're right.

It is early on in the movie, in the Christmas Past, when Scrooge and Marley are acquiring more than half the shares in Fezziwig's company and Marley says, Your servant, Mr. Scrooge, and bows his head.

Dead ringer for Byrne Doyle.

What room would you like.

Can I have 205.

Yes, honey.

No. 203.

Her hand moves to the left.

How has Doreen made a go of it all these years. The place looks the same. The orange carpet with the part down the middle. I drag my carry-on bag down the path.

I have tried to call Toff's number, but I get nothing. Not even a recording. Just dead air, or a siren sound. Now I try again. And again. I flop on the bed. The ceiling still reminds me of his beard.

I imagine them, Toff and Uncle Thoby, in a prolonged fist fight. It began at the airport in Montreal and has now alighted in London. It is the kind of fight that in cartoons is represented by a cyclone with the occasional fist or leg flying out. That is why Toff is not answering his phone. He has lost his phone in the cyclone.

But of course none of this makes sense because Uncle Thoby would not hurt a fly. And Toff would snap like a stick if you pushed him.

Meanwhile Grandmother is playing solitaire in her hospital room, in no real danger.

I fall asleep and have a quick montage of Uncle Thoby with a *Drosophila melanogaster* bouncing over his shoulder. He turns his head and regards it with fond exasperation. You again.

I wake up to the phone ringing. It's Doreen. There's a young man here to see you.

Does he have red hair.

Does he ever.

Kissing on the bed, all that.

Sweaters off.

Judd's white T-shirt glows in the light of the PIETY sign and the D-634-model lights, which are heaped on the table like a distant Zurich.

His hand on my ponytail. His lips on my cheek. His Christmas gift the red parachute. How did he get it. He went back to GOLEM and cut a hole in the fence. He can be a thug with a life too.

My fingers curl over his collarbone.

I am kissing someone who believes my dad is alive. Only I'm not. Because Judd had to refit Clint's dispatch office with the new-model lights, a project that took an entire day, and Clint told him. Clint told him my dad is dead, so now there is no one who matters who doesn't know.

T-shirts off.

He doesn't ask me why I lied.

Cassiopeia on my shoulder. He maps the constellations. Cassiopeia is shaped like a W. Here, here, here, here, here. He connects the freckles. He will put my shoulders into his star table, he says.

Speak astronomy to me.

Class G2V yellow dwarf.

What's that.

The sun.

Come hither.

I am hither.

Come hither closer.

I have a strong sense of déjà vu around you, I tell him.

If you want a feeling of déjà vu to last, you should keep very still.

Really. Is that true.

• • •

In the shower Judd notices the Grief Bar. I try to hide it but it slips out of my hands and then, in my attempt to grab it from between his feet, I slip and fall. Actually I don't fall right away. I flail around. Judd tries to catch me. But I am too slippery. I crash at the bottom of the tub.

I'm humiliated, I say.

Oh no. Judd kneels down.

Don't read the soap.

Baby, I already know.

Is it weird to love someone for selling your father Christmas lights.

No weirder than loving someone for falling down the stairs and putting a cowboy hat back on, even though she is bleeding from the chin and her eyes are tearing up.

We eat takeout Swiss Chalet. He asks how the investigation is going. I tell him about Humouse House and my dad's arch-nemesis, Lionel de Tigrel. I have a few local suspects too. Verlaine thinks I'm off my rocker. She says I have no motive.

A mouse worth two million, Judd says, licking his fingers. And a trip to Stockholm. I think you've got motive.

It is so refreshing to hear someone say that!

We drink milk from matching blue cartons.

Cheers.

Did you get your GOLEM file in the mail, I ask.

Yeah.

My IQ was a bit disappointing.

Mine too.

But you're a Christmas light inventor!

I know. I sure showed them.

Twinkly eyes.

Well, mine was more than a bit disappointing.

That's because they can't measure what you are.

I stop chewing. Really. What am I.

I don't know. But I wish there were more of you out there.

Judd has big arms on the table. And I am allowed to touch them whenever I want. And he is allowed to touch mine. And I am allowed to pull him by those arms back onto the bed.

I call home to see if there's a message from Uncle Thoby. There isn't. The power flickers. The wind sings B-flat. Judd says the wind is tugging at the wire on the isthmus.

The what.

The isthmus.

As in have yourself a merry little.

As in the skinny strip of land that connects us to the rest of the island. It is always windy on the isthmus. And all our electricity has to cross it. On one wire.

One wire!

That's why you feel a gust of wind a long time after the power flickers. That's how long it takes the wind to get here from the isthmus.

We lie still and listen.

Judd says the sound of the wind is the sound of the earth moving through space.

I think I will sleep tonight. My head on Judd's stomach. My hair still damp. He is knitting something blue. I watch the distant city on the table. You deserve a trip to Stockholm for your lights, I tell him.

The needles pause. Hand on my shoulder.

Thank you for my parachute, I say.

There are tiny battery-powered Christmas lights strung around my ramparts. Nice touch. I examine the nine-volt battery in the corner of my castle and, when no one is looking, try to eat it. No. That won't be happening.

Chuck and Linda are having a Christmas party. Lucius, Dick, and co. are invited, plus their insignificant others. Linda is already dressed and jingling. The footfalls of actors will soon be heard on the stairs. Chuck bloody Stanch, she yells. Are you ready.

Anon, good nurse.

She rolls her eyes and pours herself a shot of Baileys. What the hell, she says, and pours me a shot too. Merry Christmas, Winnifred.

Okay, maybe I am warming to them. Earlier, when Chuck was decorating my ramparts, he said, You have a beautiful castle, Winnifred.

I dropped a piece of lettuce. It has a name. Papier Mâché.

And it is a beautiful castle, only sometimes I get tired of reading the same old stories through the wash of purple paint. For instance, that story about canine acts of heroism on the north wall. Sigh.

I sip my beverage and reminisce about Christmases past.

Speaking of dogs, there was the Christmas we spent in Boring with Cliff's parents who own a Seeing Eye dog training facility. Cliff's parents have twenty acres of land in Boring and more than a hundred golden retrievers. On the way out to Boring, Audrey expressed some concern about meeting Cliff's parents and so many canines at the same time.

From the dashboard I seconded that concern.

Cliff said, They're really very boring. You'll see. We'll watch *Lawrence of Arabia* and you'll want to put a gun to your head.

Audrey said there is a rule that goes: If you own a dog, you are sad. So what does owning a hundred dogs mean.

You're suicidal, I offered.

Cliff said, My parents aren't sad about anything except that their elder son climbs rocks and wants to be a stuntman.

Audrey patted his leg and looked out the window. She remarked on the abundance of ivy.

Cliff said that if you grow ivy on purpose in Oregon they throw you in jail.

Go on, she said.

It's true, he said.

So if I cut off a sprig of ivy and put it in a glass of water—

I'd have to report you to the authorities.

Which made her smile. All was fine. She relaxed.

We arrived at the ranch and the Seeing Eye dogs were everywhere and golden. Mother of God, don't open the door. She opened the door. I could tell by the way the dogs sniffed the air and turned somersaults that my presence was intoxicating, that I would be fulfilling a lifelong dream if I were to consent to a quick romp around the yard between clamped canine jaws. I withdrew halfway into my withdrawing room.

They bounded around us. They tried to trip us up. What kind of Seeing Eye dogs try to trip people up.

On the porch stood Cliff's mother, father, and brother Ridge, none of whom were blind. I expected one of them to be blind. Audrey carried me like a dish over her shoulder.

Cliff's father made a joke: Is that dessert.

The actors have brought a tomato plant. For some reason this is funny. Chuck chuckles. Merry Christmas. Also there are girlfriends.

Are the girlfriends real or are they actors. One is definitely not an actor because she is a nurse and she has just got off duty and is still wearing her nurse's uniform, which looks to me like pyjamas. In fact, the cartoons on her pyjamas are very similar to the ones on my castle floor. I would like to show her my castle floor, if she would look my way. Her name is also Linda (confusing) and she works on the maternity floor. She helped deliver a Christmas baby today. They named the baby Poinsettia. You're kidding, says Linda. No, says Linda.

In the living room Chuck is waxing on about Kenneth Branagh, of whom he is not a fan.

Fuck, who got him started on Branagh, says my Linda, depositing the tomato plant on the counter.

Cheers, I say to no one in particular.

Two Lindas and a Twyla bend over my castle.

Wow, she liked the Baileys, says Linda.

You gave a tortoise Baileys.

I gesture at the floor. Yes, they nod. They have noticed the cartoons and they are indeed a match for those on Linda's pyjamas. Charlie Brown never gets old, remarks Twyla.

There were no adults in Charlie Brown, says Maternity Linda.

Wasn't there a teacher, says Twyla.

She was just a squawking voice, says my Linda.

Distance education, says Twyla.

I've always found Charlie Brown creepy, says Maternity Linda.

I back into my shell, which is involuted like a galaxy. Involuted means spiral-shaped but also raised to the power of. As in an exponent. As in, I have much ado to know myself times myself times myself. In short, the underside of my shell is both infinite and cosy. How can infinite space be cosy, you ask. Clearly you are not a tortoise.

In the living room, Chuck says, Don't be such a want-wit.

Space swirls above me.

· · ·

Kissing on the porch, all that.

I was on the railing. The dogs had closed their eyes. From inside came the sound of *Lawrence of Arabia*. It was warm. No wind. She said how excruciating the beginning of that movie was. How long it took the bloody man on a camel to arrive.

It's filmed in real time, said Cliff.

Kissing on the porch.

The sky was clear and full of stars.

Cliff said about Switzerland, about going back to the Yelps. Madame Mourou had warmed to him in the end, hadn't she. She had stopped calling him Hollywood. Maybe they could stay with her.

My shoulders sagged. Would this be another Dubai. Would I be left behind for the next tenant. Would I be left.

She stopped calling you Hollywood in order to call you something worse, said Audrey.

Oh, he said. Right. What did she call me again.

Ivrogne.

Cliff, who had climbed in French but not spoken it much, said, Which means.

She hesitated. Stuntman.

Cliff's parents wanted him to go into the Seeing Eye dog business. They were tired of supporting his stunts. Now Cliff was thinking a good compromise might be to go back to the Yelps and train sniffer dogs to rescue people buried alive. Be an avalanche technician.

Audrey said, But wouldn't an avalanche technician have to go what is called *hors piste*.

Well, yes.

I think I would say no to you going *hors piste*.

The thing about life in the Yelps is, it isn't boring. Remember, said Cliff, how I came to your rescue on top of Mont Dieu. You fell on your ass and lost both skis, remember. And—

And you sat beside me and shared your trail mix.

Yeah. Good times.

I knew this story. How he came to her rescue, retrieved both her skis, and said he was from Boring, Oregon. But I think you'll find I'm not, he'd said.

True enough.

And they'd come down from the mountain and she'd introduced him to Madame Mourou, who'd said what kind of name was Cliff. A *Bold and the Beautiful* name, she'd said, which was a soap opera she watched religiously and with much scorn.

And Audrey had said, He is very bold and very beautiful. And she had sneaked Cliff into her room, which was directly above a bar named Pauvre Jean-Jacques! after a famous French philosopher known for his whining. She sneaked him into her room, and the music from Pauvre Jean-Jacques! came up through the floor, and they danced until their clothes came off, and she said things like, You are so sculpted, Cliff.

And Cliff could do this thing where he fell downstairs but never got hurt. He called it waterfalling. It was a stuntman's trick, he said. Stuntmen have to know how to fall and never get hurt.

Yes, but if you are climbing a mountain and you fall, it is curtains. And if you are buried under an avalanche, it is also curtains, even if you are a stuntman.

Now he kissed her. And I wanted to move along the railing to give them some privacy, but I could not. My feet were straddling the beam. Plastron flat against the wood.

Earlier, when Cliff's brother Ridge had called me a turtle, Audrey had pointed at my feet and corrected him thusly: A turtle is to a tortoise what a mermaid is to me.

That hurt a little.

I looked away. I stared up at the moon with all its goddamn ski hills.

Ridge poked his head out to say, Opening scene's over. Camel's arrived.

B oxing Day and I'm sitting on the steps of the Before Building with my fists clenched. The wind punches me in the face. Jesus Christ I could beat the crap out of the guy who designed this campus to increase wind speed. My eyes water. My stye itches.

Here comes the Lada.

Verlaine sits for a moment and looks at me through the windshield. I wave.

Of course she's not wearing a coat.

Guten Morgen, I say as she comes up the steps.

She gives me a dark look. *Non.*

Please. I scramble to my feet.

She unlocks the door. I'm not a tour guide.

You used to be. In Christmases past. Is it because I hung up on you.

Non.

I just need to see Dr. O'Leery's torture chamber so I can cross him off my list.

I follow her inside. She glances at me over her shoulder. You look better, she says.

Really. I fluff my bangs.

But you sound as *détraquée* as ever.

Détraquée.

Off the rails.

Yeah, I know. I follow her down a corridor. Just give me thirty seconds.

I'd have noticed if your Wedge was in O'Leery's lab.

Did you look.

Bien sûr I looked.

I don't think you really did.

In my experience Verlaine does not look closely at the animals in her care. She looks closely at their water levels and food pellets and sawdust.

We stop outside a door that reads her thumbprint. Wow, that's new. Why is security so tight.

Because it can be.

Oh. She doesn't say I can't follow her. So I do. We pass my dad's lab. His name is still on the door.

Thirty seconds, Verlaine says as she unlocks Dr. O'Leery's lab.

The mice in Dr. O'Leery's lab have crushed spines. I walk up and down the rows. The spines have been crushed but the mice are alive. They drag their lower bodies around.

A mouse-sized sob rises in my throat. What is this research for.

Didn't I say this was a bad idea.

I thought Dr. O'Leery was a psychologist.

I don't know what he is these days. Look, Audray. If you really believed Wedge was here you'd have beaten down the door five days ago. He's not. Let's go.

The mice have alphanumeric codes on their ears like licence plates. No simple numbers.

How do their spines get crushed.

No response. She is holding the door open. Big arms folded. Okay. Moving right along. Who tattoos their ears. You do, don't you.

Sorry.

How many mouse ears have you tattooed.

It is not exactly tattooing.

How many.

She turns off the light. Over the years, I don't know. Too many to count.

What did I expect to find in there. I don't know. If not Wedge, then maybe a picture of my dad being used as a dartboard. Something. I stop outside the door of my dad's lab. Can I.

Verlaine hesitates, then takes her keys out of her pocket.

It is empty but it still smells brainy. Hey. The cauliflower brain! That brain is a person. My own brain still trips over that. What will happen to Mr. Cauliflower. Will he find a home. I take him down from the shelf.

Don't, Audray. It is toxic.

I'd like to keep it.

She sits down in my dad's chair. So is that what this is all about.

What what is all about.

Why didn't you just say you wanted to visit your father's lab.

Because I didn't know I wanted to.

You can't keep the brain. It is not yours to keep. But you can visit it.

Which idea, visiting the brain, makes me laugh.

She watches me.

What.

What is the English word for *oeillères*, she says. When you— and she cups her hands around her eyes.

Blinkers.

Yes. Blinkers.

I turn away from her.

I spoke to my aunt, she says. She scolded me for leaving you alone at Christmas.

I wasn't alone.

Non.

Non. Remember the Christmas light inventor.

The boy who was looking for your father. Please put the brain back, Audray.

Anon.

You spent Christmas with a Christmas light inventor.

Who better to spend Christmas with.

Indeed.

I turn the brain around. Where is the medulla oblongata. Where.

Verlaine slaps her thighs. Okay, she says. *Allons-y*.

I have a question for you.

She's at the door, hand on light switch.

Uncle Thoby said you went to the hospital.

She drops her hand. Don't look at her.

My question is: Did you make a moving speech at my dad's bedside.

A moving speech.

Did you talk to him.

I might have talked.

About me.

Non.

Did you secretly talk about me.

I don't know what that means.

Did you secretly talk about me and pretend that you didn't.

Non.

Secretly. I sneak a look at her.

No response.

I just mean. Talking about me might have made him open his eyes.

He didn't open them.

But you tried.

I tried.

I nod. I put the brain back on the shelf. On the way out, I notice my dad's stopwatch hanging from the coat rack. It's stopped at 10:02:48. My dad pushed the stop button at 10:02:48. Can I keep this, I ask.

That you can keep, yes.

. . .

Back at the Civil Manor, Judd is asleep with his arms over the covers. I lie down on top of him. His arms close around me like a gate. Outside, the wind dies down.

Did you find him.

No.

That's good news, isn't it.

I nod into his neck.

The stopwatch digs into our chests. What is that, he says.

I shift. The clock is counting forward again. I'm down one local suspect, I say.

I meet Patience for lunch at the Snark, the faculty lounge, and interrogate her about Humouse House and Lionel de Tigrel. Has she ever heard of them.

She rolls her eyes. Don't get me started.

So you have.

No. But just the names are enough.

I tell her that Wedge, my valuable childhood pet, has disappeared. And I mean *valuable*. Two million dollars valuable. I raise an eyebrow, like, are you sure there's nothing you'd like to confess to.

She listens to me with her feet tucked under her. The chairs in the Snark are big and leather. She asks if I've heard of a Victim Impact Statement.

I'm still so focused on Wedge that I think she means on his behalf.

It might be good for you to write one.

Then I realize she's talking about my dad. And the people who mowed him down. And me.

At the end of the day, she says, you need to carry on.

I nod. I study my list of suspects. By the end of the day, I tell her, I need the email addresses of my dad's grad students.

. . .

My dad used to say I was chalant. A lost positive. Nonchalance, he said, is indifference to mystery. Nonchalant is one of the worst things a person can be. You hang on to your chalance.

Right. Patience is a bit nonchalant. But I am not discouraged. Indifferent to mystery is the last thing I am.

Later that afternoon I send my dad's students a message. Subject line: Si Difficile Outbreak.

> This is to alert you that the antibiotic-resistant superbug known as si difficile has been discovered circulating among laboratory rodents in the St. John's area. If you have been in direct physical contact with a laboratory animal, especially a mouse (including domestic pets), during the past seven days, could you please report to the Student Health Centre tomorrow morning at 10 a.m. for treatment.
> Sincerely,
> Denise Cavalier-Smith
> Director of Student Health

I rub my hands together. I think this such a clever little mousetrap. It is all *si facile!*

Until I get one reply, then another, then another.

It's *C. difficile,* you idiot.

This is what happens when your suspects have higher IQs than you do.

Still, the next morning, I wait outside the Student Health Centre, hoping someone will show up, hands in the air, confessing, It was me. I loved your dad and wanted his mouse. I've been taking excellent care of him.

I'm sure. But he's not yours to keep.

I wait and wait but no one shows up.

I t is amazing how *si facile* it is to get the names of the people who killed my dad. I ask Jim Ryan and he tells me. He already knows. He has been holding on to this information since the collision occurred. One of the first things he did when he heard about my dad was call a friend at the Stab.

The names: Gill and Tina Tilley.

It's for a Victim Impact Statement, I tell him. Emphasis on *Impact*.

Is that a good idea.

Don't you worry.

And so it is that Judd and I end up in the backyard of the Tilleys out in Mount Paler, swinging on their swing set, waiting for them to come home.

I just assumed they'd be home.

While we wait, I read my Victim Impact Statement out loud to Judd. Who cries.

I jump up and stop his swing. Oh no. That wasn't my intention.

You're going to kill these people, Judd says, wiping his eyes with a blue mitten.

Okay, that *is* my intention. But not to make you cry. I hug his head. He lets me.

My VIS talks about how my dad loved Christmas and elections. How, because of the Tilleys, not only is my dad dead and deprived of his democratic right to vote, but we are all now robbed of our potential *immortality* because Walter Flowers was a *ground-breaking scientist* who was *this* close (and here I will mark off a tiny space between thumb and forefinger) to figuring out how to keep us all alive forever, barring accidents and murder (pointed look at Gill Tilley, who was driving).

The immortality part may be an exaggeration, I tell Judd, folding the statement.

It is starting to get dark. We crunch through the snow to a back window where there are no curtains. Judd lifts me up. Through an archway I can see the tree.

Is there a dent in it.

My dad would not approve of all that tinsel on his murder weapon. Holy hell. I start laughing.

Judd lowers me.

I turn around and lean against the house. I can't stop. He puts a mitten over my mouth. A car has pulled into the driveway.

I hear a woman call out, Reenie, take your Dora inside.

A little girl with mittens dangling and corkscrew curls comes racing around the corner of the house. She notices the boot prints first. That lead to her swing set. She has been planning a quick swing before dinner. Now she turns her head, slowly. Judd waves the hand that is not over my mouth. Reenie (short for what, Sabrina, Marina, Irena) Tilley's eyes get very wide and I know I will not be able to read a VIS that turns her tinselfied Christmas tree into a cudgel decorated with clumps of my dad's hair and skull and brains. That is not the kind of brave I am.

She screams.

My shoulders sag. Judd drops his hand. Gill Tilley comes running around the corner.

He is so not a killer. Look at him.

Hi, I say.

Hi.

He is not even suspicious. He smiles a bewildered half-smile that is more like, welcome to my yard, than, who the hell are you, potential home invaders.

We were just admiring your pink siding, says Judd.

Gill glances up at the house.

I wish I had not thought the word *brains,* plural. Because now they are all over that tree in my imagination. Which is of course not possible. My dad's head was not split open. Or was it. Do I need to know.

No.

And it is probably not even the same tree. The Tilleys would not keep, and decorate, a tree that had killed someone. They would not put their daughter's new Dora the Explorer doll under such a tree. They are not that morbid. Think of the girl's hair for Chrissakes.

We get in the van.

That was a complete waste of time, I say.

No, I don't think so.

I crumple my Victim Impact Statement.

The thing about clue-finding mode is that you cannot turn it off. I look out the window and there, parked in the Tilleys' drive-way, is the pickup truck. I walked right by it without seeing it. Hang on, I tell Judd.

The truck is a Ford, an old one. Navy blue with square head-lights. I make one complete revolution and return to the van.

Okay, says Judd.

Okay.

We are on the Harbour Arterial when I say, Shouldn't there be two side mirrors. I mean, you have two side mirrors.

Judd glances at me.

The Harbour Arterial has metal strips embedded in the pave-ment that make your tires beat like a heart as you drive over them. Thump-thump. Thump-thump.

And would a tree hanging out the back of that truck be level with a medulla oblongata. Thump-thump. I'm just asking.

Depends on the height of the medulla oblongata, says Judd.

I nod. Thump-thump.

Should I turn around, he says.

I nod.

As a rule I am against people who throw out their Tannenbaums right after Christmas. But today I will make an exception. We head back through Mount Paler and within fifteen minutes we find a Christmas tree lying prostrate on the curb.

Is this a good idea, says Judd as we load it into the van. Maybe we should pause and think about whether this is a good idea.

I look at him. Okay.

So we sit in the back of the van with the tree between us and gather our thoughts. Why would this not be a good idea.

Maybe because you are about to cross the line between investigation and re-enactment.

I nod. I study my list. Yesterday I was out of local suspects. But now Gill Tilley has been added. Granted, he is a suspect in a different case. Or is he. I'm confused.

I fold my list.

Warm enough.

Yeah. I breathe deep. Smell the tree.

It smells amazing.

Judd tells me how when he was a kid he once rescued a Tannenbaum that was blowing down the street the day after Christmas. His parents let him keep it. Even though Christmas trees, you know, are not kosher.

You rescued a Tannenbaum.

It was still green and alive, he says. Just thirsty.

Did you put lights on it.

Did I ever.

I stare out the back of the van. It's dark. I don't know what to do next is the problem. I mean, we can go back to the Tilleys' and we can put that tree in the back of their truck and we can imagine it sneaking up on my dad's head from behind. And I can look closely at the missing mirror. And maybe Judd can stand next to the truck for scale. Because his medulla oblongata is about on a par with my dad's. And maybe Gill Tilley will come out of his pale house and realize that we are not just admirers of his siding. He will realize what we are up to. And even if he says, Look, your dad was whacked by a side mirror, not a Christmas tree, or He was whacked by both, or Yes, the Christmas tree is a little higher than a medulla oblongata but your dad was on a snowbank. And I didn't realize the tree was hanging out of my truck in murder-weapon stance. I didn't bloody realize. It was an accident. Accidents do happen. They do.

I know they do.

Even then, I will be no closer to solving anything.

Let's go home, Judd says.

Can you clarify what you mean by home.

Room 203.

What about the Tannenbaum.

I'll take it to the store.

Because no way could we throw it back on the curb.

CLUE SUSPECTS	
DR. O'LEERY	X
PATIENCE	X
GRAD STUDENTS	X
LIONEL DE TIGREL	
TOFF	
GRANDMOTHER	
GILL TILLEY	X

All remaining suspects are non-local. Still no word from Uncle Thoby. I take a deep breath and decide to call Grandmother. I mean, what can it hurt. I push the numbers. No answer. Nothing. Just like when I call Toff.

I slump forward on the bed.

Did you dial the country code, says a weary voice.

I sit up. Hello.

This is the operator.

There are still operators.

The country code, she says. And she sounds fed up, like she has witnessed all my failed attempts to call England and has finally thrown up her hands and intervened.

Um. The country code. I don't think I've ever dialled a country code, no.

Well, that's your problem.

I have a low IQ, I tell her.

I'm sorry to hear that.

I don't expect her to be there. Only I sort of do. And she is. She sounds winded, like she has just climbed stairs, but otherwise fine.

Hello. Who is this. Speak.

What do you say at such a moment. Oh, I thought you were at death's door, in a coma, or at the very least playing solitaire in a hospital bed. But here you are at home. Hiking up stairs. What a stroke of luck. I'm so glad. By the way, where is your least favourite son. The one who is still alive. Have you seen him. Did you spend Christmas with him.

What have you done with him.

She now lives in London. Her eyesight is bad. She has a nurse who apparently does not answer the phone. I remember my dad saying she had to sell the Clue-board house because it was too much to manage. When was the last time I spoke to her. I don't even remember. There have not been many calls between St. John's and London. I wish I'd written up an agenda.

It's Audrey, Grandmother.

Silence.

Catch your breath, I say, upbeat.

I don't need to catch my breath.

You sound—

I just knocked over a table.

—huffy. So how are you.

Still alive.

Oh. Good.

Now, whom do you wish to speak to. Not me apparently.

Oh boy.

Uncle Thoby, I venture. Is he there. Have you seen him.

Who.

Okay, this is bad.

Uncle Thoby, I repeat.

Long pause.

Listen, whoever you are. I am confused. I am old. I am too old to remember what you ought not to know.

Right. Well, if you see Uncle Thoby, will you have him call me.

Of course. I will write that down.

•   •   •

The bed is unmade. I crawl under the covers. This has to be one of the worst feelings in the world: being under the covers in jeans. Get up and take off your jeans then. No.

Okay, here is a worse feeling: that Grandmother and Toff are the only family you have left. That the people who matter, the people you love, have been disappeared, and the people you hate, and who hate you back, are your family.

What I feel now is that the fight I have been imagining between Uncle Thoby and Toff is real, but that Uncle Thoby has already lost it. And that the mystery I have been trying to solve is the wrong one, but the real one, or ones, so far exceed my deductive/detective powers that not only will I never solve them, but I will never recognize them as mysteries that need to be solved.

I am too old to remember what you ought not to know. What the hell.

I remember one night when Toff and Grandmother were staying, I woke to a house that had only them in it. Uncle Thoby was at the Civil Manor. I knew that. Toff was sleeping in his bed in the basement. I could hear Grandmother snuffling in the guest room. But where was my dad. My dad was not in his room.

I went downstairs.

I asked Wedge, Have you seen him.

Wedge bit his nails.

I took a flashlight from the kitchen cupboard and crept down the basement steps. I could hear Toff breathing stupidly. I shone the flashlight around the room. On the walls there were five NO SMOKING signs. Courtesy of yours truly.

It was not yet a plane. It was just an embryo of a plane.

I shone the light on Toff. He was sleeping on his back with his beard laid over the covers. Ugh.

No sign of my dad.

I went back to his bedroom. I checked under the bed. I began to get scared. I began to cry into the heat vent. Where was he.

Where *are* you.

I went back to my own room and crawled into bed. It still smelled of the Lysol I had used to disinfect the Toffness. I pulled my blanket with the galloping horses over my head and tried to think about galloping. How one day I would do it and no hoofs would touch the ground. Finally I slept.

The next morning my dad was in the kitchen, being unsuccessful with the coffee filters, as per usual.

Could you. He pointed at them.

No.

I felt like kicking him. Instead I pushed my face into his stomach.

What's this about.

I stepped on his foot, which had only a sock on it, hard.

Ow.

I had a montage last night about being an orphan.

His hands came down lightly on my head. Oh sweetheart, he said.

I call Verlaine. I tell her I saw the people who killed my dad but they were not killers.

Silence on her end.

I tell her I am no closer to solving the mystery.

Which mystery, Audray.

Exactly. Which mystery. There are so many. I tell her what Grandmother said.

Can I make a suggestion.

Okay.

Go find him.

Wedge.

Your uncle.

You mean get on a plane.

I mean get on a plane.

D own I go. I pause halfway and sit on a step. Tighten my ponytail. Gird my loins. Carry on down into the plane in the basement.

It looks the same. Empty seats. Painted oval windows. Beverage cart parked in the aisle. The only change is a new pilot's chair. The new chair swivels. I stare into the distance as Uncle Thoby envisioned it. All those other planes, far away but on our path. I turn some knobs. *Noli me tangere.*

I swivel and face the empty seats. Wedge, I call. Because maybe he will miraculously appear, running towards me with his hands in the air.

This is your pilot speaking. Um. Where are my passengers. Where are you, Wedge. Uncle Thoby. Dad. Where.

You don't solve a mystery by adding information. You solve a mystery by subtracting what you think you already know. You just subtract your assumptions one by one until you are left with the truth. Then you ask again, Where are you.

And from the most unexpected corner will come a voice. Over here.

I open the beverage cart door. Bottles, bottles, everywhere. In every drawer. Empty and sideways. Pour, oh pour the pirate sherry.

Poor, oh poor Uncle Thoby.

Somewhere there is a bag. Uncle Thoby told me there was a bag of my dad's "effects" in the basement. I didn't know what this meant. Apparently "effects" are what my dad was carrying and wearing at the time of the collision. The CRYNOT bracelet was in this bag. The night I arrived Uncle Thoby had to look through the bag for the bracelet. Why did I make him do this. So I could call Darren Lipseed and listen to him tell me that there are degrees of dead.

The bag of effects is tucked under an airplane seat. Stowed away. A carrion bag.

Don't look inside. Just reach in. Wet. The clothing is still wet. I pull my hand out. How is that possible.

It hasn't been that long.

Yes it has.

No it hasn't.

I reach back in. Grope around for my dad's wallet. Will it be there. Yes. Because this was something we were supposed to iron out but never did. The effects were never ironed out.

I take the wallet, stow the bag, and head down the aisle to the bathroom. I need to throw up. I need to lean over the toilet and throw up. The stopwatch around my neck gets in the way. Get out of the way. I'm going to throw up now. Oh, sorry. Finally, after having ingested soap and WD-40 and gallons of coffee and God knows what else, I'm going to throw up.

But I don't. No doubt most people would throw up when confronted with a bag of their dad's effects. Most people would throw up when they entered the last storey of the house and made their dad really dead in it. But whatever I've ingested is not throw-up-able. Or maybe I am just not a thrower-upper.

I sit down on the bathroom floor. The stopwatch counts forward but it can only count so far before returning to zero and starting again. Over and over. It moves forward in circles. I've got my dad's watch and bracelet and wallet. I'm going to England. Make me brave, plane in the basement. Make me curious.

Through the door I can see Uncle Thoby's bed and under it,

among other things, what looks like three pizza boxes. The D-434 lights. Well, that's one mystery solved.

The bed has the look of a bed that has not been slept in for a long time. And I wonder, while I was not sleeping at the kitchen table, was he not sleeping down here in an airplane seat.

Poor, oh poor Uncle Thoby.

Subtract what you think you know.

I get up. Beside the bed there's a framed photograph of my dad. The quality is not good. It's a Polaroid. The frame has one of those inner borders that makes a tight oval around the face like an airplane window. My dad looks irritated about the oval. But also full of love for me. Because I took this picture. I know I took it. He's reading. At the bottom of the oval I can see the white of a page.

When did I take it.

I took lots of pictures with that camera. For a while I was all about Polaroid.

Where is he. I try to see beyond the oval. This picture has been here for years and I have never looked beyond the oval.

Something I've learned: You can take a picture *out* of a frame. As a kid, I would never have done this. Once a picture was behind glass, it lived there. To take it out, you had to go behind the picture's back. And behind the picture's back was complicated. There was a mechanism and how did it work. You weren't smart enough. You would probably have to use a weapon, like with the Rubik's cube, and pry the whole thing apart. But while you would gladly take a weapon to the Rubik's cube, you would rather not take one to your dad's back, or Uncle Thoby's back.

But that was silly. A weapon is not required. Yes, each frame is different. Some are velvety with tabs that swivel. Some are cardboard with little nails you have to pry up. But whatever they have, you can figure it out. A frame is not *si difficile* as that.

After removing the back, you will probably find other layers of stuff before you reach the picture. Crinkled cardboard, maybe, or some very thin foam. A glossy picture of a yellow Lab that came with the frame. Or a folded piece of paper that has text on one side and on the other a crude map of Wednesday Pond with an arrow pointing at your house. A note in your childish handwriting. A plea not to crash. A plea to write back. Because you knew that if someone got this message, you were alive. We were alive.

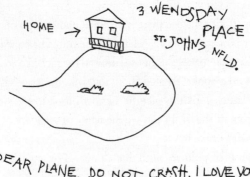

The other side is the first page of an article. "Slow Mortality Rate Accelerations During Aging in *Mus musculus* Approaches That of Humans." Author: Lionel de Tigrel. Well, he is one of the smaller authors. Probably if you look closely at *any* article, Lionel de Tigrel is one of the authors.

Moving right along. I peel the picture away from the oval. My dad is sitting in an airplane seat.

Well, that is hardly surprising.

But he is not sitting in the plane in the basement. The seats are not the same. The seats in the basement are blue with black diamonds. The seat in the picture is without diamonds.

He is on a real plane. I took this picture. Remember. But how did it get here. I left it on the plane. I left this letter and two pictures in my armrest.

Where is the other picture.

Up and down the aisle I go. Jiggling every armrest. No, no, no. First row, window seat. Left side. The armrest opens!

Well, it opens after twenty minutes, with the help of a screwdriver.

And lo and behold, a secret compartment. And it is not empty. No, it is not. Here is the other photograph, the one of my dad throwing up in the sick bag. And there are letters. Maybe fifty letters with a rubber band around them. I sit down. Fasten my seatbelt. Pull out the first letter.

> Wilfred Moss
> 138 Welkin Way Road
> London W12 2RU
> United Kingdom

> Dear Mr. Moss,
> You understand why I might intercept a letter to my
> daughter from "The Plane." What message are you
> referring to. No doubt you are well intentioned.
> I am sorry for your circumstances. What I infer are
> your circumstances. What are your circumstances.
> What an odd missive. Are you describing some
> form of hemihypertrophy.
>> Forgive a protective father and please explain.

> Walter Flowers

For a while I don't move. Then I fold the letter and put it back in the armrest. Close the armrest. Undo my seatbelt. Put the screws back in. This is not my secret compartment.

Come on, Audrey.

Come on where.

Get up. Go.

Part Four

COME, THOU TORTOISE

Once again I am Shakespeare's doorstop. Sorry, bookmark. While Chuck makes a tomato sandwich with all the remaining tomatoes from the thugs' Christmas gift. Linda will not be pleased.

My eyes close. My head droops. I have not recovered from my Christmas libations. I am thirsty as hell. My only thought is of my pool, inaccessible while I am on bookmark duty.

Heads up, Winnifred, says Chuck and drops a piece of lettuce on the page.

You are too kind, Mr. Stanch.

Can a bead of moisture be extracted, I wonder, from such a pathetic, wilted piece of greenage. We shall see. I take a bite and drag the leaf towards me. As it moves down the page, it uncovers the following words:

Come, thou tortoise![60]

Which words stop me mid-bite, I can tell you. Were they there before. How could I have missed them.

I toss the lettuce to one side and point at myself. Me.

Yes, you.

Come where.

I want to keep reading but I can get only so far before I risk falling off the book and possibly the table too.

Fuck.

I look hopefully at Chuck. Totally absorbed in dilapidating the tomato tree.

I turn back to the words between my feet.

Come, thou tortoise to the power of sixty!

I *am* a pretty powerful tortoise. I walked across the desert once, about a century ago. All the way from Texas. Slow like the camel in *Lawrence of Arabia*. Talk about thirst. No Lemon Pie pools back then. All along the way I passed overturned tortoise shells, picked clean by birds. Pretty discouraging. But I kept going. Why. Because I had heard stories about trees a hundred feet tall. I had heard about rain. And why should a tortoise not have rain in her life. I was curious. I was youngish. I was adventurous.

Come, thou tortoise!

I can't believe there's a tortoise in Shakespeare. This changes everything.

Anyway, I remember waking up on my fiftieth or so morning in the desert, having made imperceptible progress the day before, and thinking to myself, Oh God, will I ever see colour again. Because there was only brown for as far as the eye could see and the hot stretched blue of the sky, which does not count.

I despaired. I would never see trees. I would never feel rain. Put me out of my misery. I shook a fist at the sky. I even tried to flip myself over. But just as I was heaving myself sideways, a red butterfly alighted on a rock in front of me.

The wings beat slowly like a fan.

Why, hello.

I could have eaten that butterfly, it was so beautiful, so red. I stood very still (not hard to do) for a long time, drinking in its colour. What did those sunglassy eyes see. A brown tortoise. I felt ashamed of my blandness.

I am ashamed of my blandness, I said.

Me too, she said.

I was astounded. What! But are you not aware of the art you carry on your back.

What art.

Well. That was an enlightening moment. Because if the butterfly could carry such art on her back and not know it, what might a tortoise carry on *her* back.

Apparently art enough to inspire Shakespeare.

A century later I made that same trip through the desert on the dashboard of a car. Which is definitely the way to go. Takes two days. Two leisurely days.

The tomato plant has been dropping tomatoes. Sometimes they fall surprisingly far from the tree. And earlier, when Chuck was playing Prospero, a tomato fell *really* far from the tree. I mean, it heaved itself at Chuck. Which Shakespeare's tortoise found very amusing indeed. She laughed and laughed. She finally got the joke of the tomato tree.

Now Chuck is exacting his revenge on that tree by eating all the tomatoes in one sitting, even the green ones.

He will make himself sick, the fool. What an Antonio he is today.

There's a knock at the door.

Chuck pauses mid-bite. Wipes his hands on his bare chest. Which is gross. Opens the door.

I've come for the tortoise, says a familiar voice.

I look over my shoulder. Cliff!

I n the middle of London a white horse canters out of the fog and almost runs me over.

That's the horse path, miss.

There's a horse path!

And not five minutes ago I was in the Starbucks quarter, asking for directions.

London is all crowds and Starbucks and startling handbags. And a horse, cantering through the middle of it. The fog is white. If you get very close to that rose bush you can see some tired yellow roses. Very pale.

Uncle Thoby once said I would love the tube. Boy was he wrong. The map, I love. At Heathrow I bought a map that opened like a flower with six petals. You could open one petal or two or all the petals. I loved what a cat's cradle the underground was, on the map. I loved the word *underground,* as a noun. But I was not loving how packed it was. I could barely open one petal of my map.

It was morning rush hour. What did I expect. I expected the claustrophobics to unite! I expected someone to acknowledge that this was a mighty tight squeeze. No one did. And just when I thought not one more person could possibly fit in here, there was absolutely no way, ten schoolgirls in grey uniforms piled in. Three stops later, nine schoolgirls got off. One girl was not going to school. One girl had other plans.

This was my first impression of London.

And that everyone looks at your bag, at what you are carrying, not at you.

I burst with glee from the train and saw a sign that warned: 195 STEPS. It was either 195 steps or a lift so crowded that people were being slotted in horizontally near the ceiling. A no-brainer.

When I got to the top of the steps, I had to sit down. A cop hovered. I expected him to say, No loitering with a carry-on bag that big. But he only offered me his hand. Upsy-daisy, he said. Now where are you trying to get to.

I looked at my map. One of the petals was gone. The one with Toff's house on it. Goddamn it. Did someone on the tube steal that part of London. I stopped at a kiosk and bought another. This one was fluted like a coffee filter. It began in a tight whorl shape and then exploded in your hands.

I crossed a street without looking, because I was studying exploded London, and a car neighed at me. The horn was a neigh.

I found Toff's house in a mews. On a mews. I expected cats. I saw none. All the houses were white, like teeth. I checked the address. Then knocked. No answer. I knocked and rang the bell and knocked some more.

I pounded my fists, briefly.

Somewhere in London bells started ringing. Someone was taking big careless swipes at a bell.

I sat down on Toff's stoop. It was sunny at this stage. A horrible white sun that hurt my eyes.

A woman with wet hair stepped onto her stoop. She was on the phone. The word *brilliant* snapped down the mews. She noticed me and did not seem amused. She watched me while saying into the phone that she was not inviting what's his name because he'd been trying to quit smoking for too long and was, frankly, more addicted to his stressed-out persona than to cigarettes. So you'll bring the—brilliant. Yes, brilliant. Okay.

She looked at me and it was like a staring contest, so I got up and walked.

•   •   •

I walked along Oxford Street and saw all the startling handbags.
I stopped at Starbucks where small equals tall. I found Hyde Park
and the fog rolled in. I was run over by the white horse. At home
the fog is grey, not white. This is like dry ice.

There is a black clump in the fog that turns out to be Peter Pan
with all his crew. I circle the statue, looking for the Newfoundland
dog, because isn't there a Newfoundland dog in *Peter Pan*. No dog.
The statue would be better if there were a Newfoundland dog.
And if it were in colour. The boy at the top looks bossy.

Onward. There is a man-made river, more a rivulet, that if
seen from above spells PRINCESS DIANA. There is a golden Prince
Albert sitting on a throne. He is rumpled and reminds me of Judd.

What am I looking for. The stable that horse hailed from.

It begins to hail. Huge white golf balls of hail. Is this usual.
I look up and one smacks me in the eye. Hard. Not the stye eye.
The good eye. For a moment all I can see is white.

I find a tree near the pale yellow roses with its branches bent
like a birdcage. I crawl inside. The branches have no leaves. I sit
on the ground near the trunk and keep my head down. Then I feel
the ground shake. The white horse is galloping by, its nose tucked
in against the weather. He and his rider are galloping home.

The flight over was uneventful, except that I did see, I think, a piñata
in the cockpit when I boarded the plane. I said to my neighbour in
34J, What is the last thing you would ever want to see in a cockpit.

A terrorist, she said, struggling with her seatbelt.

How about a piñata.

She let the seatbelt go slack.

Yeah, I said.

The plane took off and felt like it was travelling west. Which
of course it wasn't. It was travelling east. But west is how it felt,
and I couldn't turn the plane around in my brain. I thought about
how, when you are in audience formation, your brain wants you

to be facing *something*. And so it invents a direction. That direction is arbitrary and has nothing to do with real geography.

34J was reading a book: *Don't Fall Off the Mountain* by—surprise, surprise—Shirley MacLaine. On the back cover Shirley was on a beach, as per usual, but the shot was taken from above, like maybe she already *had* fallen off the mountain but had landed on her feet. There was a quote from Shirley that said: "After two months on a picture my car seemed to veer toward the airport of its own accord." I hear you, Shirley.

34J was not turning the pages.

You're not an air marshal, are you.

Sorry.

Nevermind. Carry on. I tilted my chair back and watched an episode of *Sherlock Holmes*.

I felt remarkably calm. Why. Because I had a mission. To bring Uncle Thoby and Wedge home. It was a matter of Sherlock-Holmesian step-by-stepness. It was a matter of exercising my deductive powers, however weak, to eliminate what is false until only what is true remains.

Also, I had packed the red parachute.

There were two scenarios that were fun to play out in my mind while everyone else on the plane napped.

SCENARIO 1:

I go to Cambridge and wait outside Humouse House in the early ante meridiem. Hopefully there is a Starbucks across the street. I wait for Lionel de Tigrel to turn up. When he does, I pounce on him. His lion's ears twitch. The leapling, he curses. That's right. You have something that belongs to me, *n'est-ce pas*. He tries to block my path, but I, abuzz with caffeine, leapfrog over him and directly into his lab. There I find a terrarium bathed in a shaft of golden light. Wedge! He stands up, ribcage rattling. Here I am, Audrey!

SCENARIO 2:

I go to Toff's house and wait outside in the early ante meridiem.
Hopefully there is a Starbucks across the street. When Toff exits
his house, I pounce on him. His wolfish eyes flash. The leapling,
he curses. That's right. You have something that belongs to me,
n'est-ce pas. He tries to block my path, but I, abuzz with caffeine,
leapfrog over him into his house. There I find Uncle Thoby tied
to a chair, bathed in a shaft of golden light. Uncle Thoby! I
remove the gag. Oddly!

There was nothing to see out the plane window until, after many
hours, the pilot said, Ladies and gentlemen, we are flying over
Belfast. It was still dark, though the horizon had a pink edge.
Belfast was a sprinkle of lights. Belfast should be more than a
sprinkle, I thought. But we were very high up.

The pink edge widened and widened.

My window shutter was an eyelid half-closed. Wake up, little eye. In the bright pink distance I saw other planes. So many I
couldn't count them. Okay, I could count them. Eleven. I counted
eleven planes out my window. Was that normal.

34J said, This is the busiest airspace in the world. Of course
it is normal.

Noli me tangere, all you other planes. They were circling. So
were we. We were making what was probably a pretty pattern of
interlocking circles. Just biding our time, waiting for our turn to
land at Heathrow-up Airport.

Planes from all over the world. As we taxied, I saw a real live
Qantas plane. Which I took as a good omen. I saw Hemus Cutis
Air. All Nippon Over Air. Click Air. Curly Air. Straight Air. I
couldn't help but feel a little excited. Despite the seriousness of
my mission.

I tightened my ponytail. I was on the ground. New ground.

We arrived at our gate. I fidgeted in my seat and watched the
baggage handlers. They were all symmetrical.

When I wake under the tree, the fog has lifted. The sun is going down. Holy hell. I try to jump up but my limbs say, Wait. We are frozen in a fetal position. We must unfold slowly. Like a flower. Fuck that. No time. My jeans and my legs inside them make a creaking sound. I hobble out of the birdcage, dragging my bag.

And it is a whole other park. The sun streams bright gold. The skyline is ridiculously ornate. I feel like crying when I think of the long walk back to Toff's mews. My legs won't make it. They climbed 195 steps today. They are frozen. They are still very much resenting the long flight via Montreal. They have had it up to here (my waist) with me. Let's sit on that bench for a while.

No.

It is dark by the time I reach Toff's. There's a light on. I can see into the living room. Sorry, drawing room. It is a sad underwater green. I suspect an overhead light is the culprit.

Toff appears in the window. There he actually is. On the phone. An open, very open collar. No cravat. He taps his clavicle while he speaks. So he actually has a clavicle. And a phone that works.

He's about to get the surprise of his life.

Knock knock on the glass. He leaps back. I wave.

The leapling, he curses.

That's right. You have something that belongs to me, *n'est-ce pas.*

We stare at each other for a moment. He has the look of someone who is seeing the bane of his existence through his own reflection. Finally he gestures at the door. I traverse the front of the house to the stoop.

He is beside himself with not exactly joy. Audrey, Audrey. I am ushered in. What happened to your face. Lord, what are you doing here. When did you arrive. Etcetera.

I park my carry-on bag and look past him. Where is the chair and the shaft of golden light and the ropes.

What about my face, I say.

He points. To my left there's a cloudy mirror and I have a black eye in it. And a stye. Which was clearing up until I forgot my antibiotics at home. Not to mention my other battle scars.

Did someone hit you.

A hailstone.

You were out in that. He scratches his head fiercely.

I stare at his chest. It is so. Visible. He looks entirely different with a chest.

How did you get here, he says.

I extend my arms. Flew.

No, I mean—

Air Canada.

No, I mean—

Uncle Thoby left this address. Why didn't you answer my calls. And don't pull the country code excuse.

The what excuse.

There's a dark staircase behind him. I look up that staircase.

Have you eaten, he says, taking my coat. I have cheese, he says. I will put out cheese.

I grab his arm. Is he here.

He looks blank. Who.

Uncle Thoby.

No.

.   .   .

The drawing room is divided in half by a sofa. On the other side of the sofa, Toff busies himself creating a cheese skyline on the dining-room table.

Are you hungry, he says when he's finished.

Not so much.

Oh.

So he gets me a glass of orange juice and something stronger for himself and we sit facing each other from opposing sofas.

You haven't seen him at all, I say.

Not since the airport.

Which airport.

Montreal.

Not Heathrow.

We were on separate flights.

Why.

What is this, an interrogation.

I look up. It is indeed an overhead light. With a frosted glass shade. A recipe for ghoulishness. Toff looks very pockmarked and ghoulish. But probably not as ghoulish as me. Is he lying.

Yes, I say.

Yes what.

This is an interrogation.

He looks so helpless over there with his clavicle.

I know Grandmother isn't at death's door. I spoke to her. So the game is up.

What game. No. Don't tell me. You've got the Clue revolver somewhere on your person.

Ha ha. I tell him there are many games. Many many games I am currently solving. Okay, two. He is the prime suspect in one. Lionel de Tigrel is the prime suspect in the other.

Lionel de Tigrel. The wolfish eyes flash.

So you know him.

No.

You look like someone who knows him.

What does someone who knows him look like.

Like you. Listen, Wedge is missing.

He seems perplexed. Not that Wedge is missing, but that it matters. I'm sorry, how is this connected—

Lionel de Tigrel kidnapped Wedge from my dad's funeral. Much the same way you kidnapped Uncle Thoby.

Audrey.

What.

Settle down. And listen to me.

I lean back. Okay. I can settle. I can listen to my suspects. Speak.

Lionel de Tigrel was not at your father's funeral.

I think he really was. Big guy. Belgian. Lion.

Lionel de Tigrel isn't Belgian.

I think he really is.

He puts down his drink. Leaves the room. Comes back with a magazine. Was *he* at your father's funeral.

The magazine has a picture of a man with a long Rumples*toff*ian beard and a Hawaiian shirt. The caption says: Maniac or Messiah.

I don't recall seeing that man, no.

That's Lionel de Tigrel.

I laugh. It is not.

It is. Look. Read.

I don't like to read.

Audrey.

Okay, so it is Lionel de Tigrel. That's funny. He looks nothing like the Lionel de Tigrel from my dad's funeral.

I think it unlikely there are *two* Lionel de Tigrels, says Toff, and he returns to his sofa.

Fine. Doesn't matter. He's still a suspect.

In what exactly. Look, Audrey—

A noise in the hall pulls him up short. A measured click, click, click. Footsteps. On tiptoe.

Well, says Toff. Someone has decided to grace us—

A face appears in the doorway.

I scream. Sort of. I yelp, more like it. Because I do not register at first that this is not a person. The face is so serious. Plus, the face is at human height.

But it is not a human. It is a dog. A Great Dane.

I climb slowly down from the back of the sofa.

The eyes regard me calmly. I thought I heard a visitor. He clicks into the room on stilt legs. Stops beside Toff. The horsiness of him. My God.

This is Hamlet, says Toff. Sit, Hamlet.

Hamlet sits. When he sits, his back legs plié out like a ballerina's in a way that is a bit, okay very, indecent.

I know what you're thinking, says Toff.

I don't think you do.

You're thinking how many Great Danes have been called Hamlet.

That's really not what I'm thinking.

As we talk, Hamlet's face moves right to left, listening. His face is so narrow and serious. I want to laugh. He is all grey. His ears are perfect folded triangles.

Come here, Hamlet, I whisper.

Hamlet looks at Toff.

Toff nods.

Hamlet walks with great dignity across the floor.

I feel very small on my sofa.

He sniffs my eyes. He blesses my forehead. His upper lip droops wetly.

I put my arms around him.

Later, in the cab to the Atomotel, I realize what a bloody distraction that dog was. What a master stroke on Toff's part. Because for the rest of my time in the house, I had eyes only for Hamlet. I tried to concentrate. I tried to extract information from Toff about his connection to Lionel de Tigrel, which he continued to deny. About Grandmother's health, which he admitted was not as bad as he'd thought (a minor stroke, a broken wrist). About Uncle Thoby, whose whereabouts he insisted were unknown to him.

Meanwhile, behind him in the dining room, Hamlet was slowly dismantling the cheese skyline.

A whole Camembert down the gullet.

A whole ham. Silently, stealthily.

And every so often he, Hamlet, would glance over as if to implore me, please, mum's the word.

Toff, facing me, was oblivious.

You can bet Sherlock Holmes would not have allowed himself to become so besotted with a dog that he compromised his investigation. I did manage to get one valuable piece of information: directions to Grandmother's.

Can I recommend you call her first.

I don't like calling her.

Call her, he said. And see her in the morning not the afternoon.

Why.

Because she's lucid in the morning.

Then he said I was mad to stay at an Atomotel miles outside the city. The cab fare would cost more than the room.

I am a loyal Atomotel patron, I said. And thanks for offering.

Offering, he said.

By the glow of the interior light, in a cab paid for by Toff, I skim the article on Lionel de Tigrel. I begin to feel carsick. My investigation is unravelling. The article says Lionel de Tigrel is ten years away from curing aging. Spelled ageing in England. Ten years! My dad already had the cure. Why wasn't my dad featured in this magazine—what's it called—*Hourglass*. Why hadn't my dad been interviewed on *60 Minutes*, as apparently Lionel de Tigrel had been earlier this month.

And how could I have missed seeing Lionel de Tigrel's face, which is apparently everywhere. Insufficient research. The story of my life. Nevermind. So Lionel de Tigrel did not kidnap Wedge. Directly. But since he is so famous, he might have hired an accomplice. The Belgian. He might have hired the Belgian to kidnap Wedge. Because Wedge is so old and yet so young. And because Walter Flowers is the real McCoy and Lionel de Tigrel is a fraud who has always been fiercely jealous of my dad's success.

I nod to myself and look out the window to quell my carsickness.

And wasn't it weird how Toff's face went all ashen when I said I was going to Cambridge anyway, to interrogate the lion himself.

Atomotel is a chain. Cliff and I stayed in one in the Alps. Atomotels are reasonably priced because the rooms are so tiny. Some have bunk beds. Everything is clean and white. I booked my room using my dad's credit card. No questions asked. Welcome, nucleus, said the receptionist when I checked in. Because that is Atomotel's motto: The customer is the nucleus! Pretty catchy.

A computer voice in the elevator said the floor numbers on the way up, I guess in case you are blind or blindfolded. I got off on the eleventh floor. Room 1106.

My atom doesn't have a bunk bed. Too bad. It has a small electron-shaped bed with a white duvet. The pillow is puffed up into a pyramid. Interesting.

I call home. Two messages. One from Linda. She says Cliff turned up and took Winnifred. Am I okay with that. She hopes so. Because they're gone. They went back to the old apartment, apparently.

Hang on. What. Replay the message.

Well. Isn't that why you left her. So that she would be there if Cliff came back. So that someone would be there. You invited him to come get her, didn't you. Yes, but that was when I thought I'd be going back.

And you won't be.

No.

This is news. I won't be going back to Portland.

The second message is from Judd. A recall notice. Thought you might like to know that someone is recalling you fondly. Also that someone is tracking your flight online. Hey, you're over Ireland.

I turn off the light and climb into bed. Punch the pyramid. Put my head down. So Cliff is back. Safe in the old apartment. With Winnie. And I won't be going back.

I am bruised and exhausted. My eye throbs. This is not unlike how I felt the last time I stayed in an Atomotel, after a day of "skiing" in the Alps. How many times had I fallen.

The bunk bed in our room was a novelty. I learned to be sexy in that bed. You could brace yourself against the ceiling in all sorts of interesting ways.

We went to dinner and what I remember is Cliff's vaporous drink, how the vapour curled over the lip of the glass as he told me tall tales about Oregon. Its Alice-in-Wonderland forests and high deserts and low mountains and tepid rain. And then later, in the bunk bed, he said, Would you say no to coming back to America with me.

I would not say no, no.

But I would say no now.

I start to shiver. My atom is cold. And then I remember that in Europe when you turn off the lights, the heat sometimes turns off too. So you can be warm in the light or cold in the dark. Sleep well, nucleus. I get up and put on my jeans. My legs are so, so fed up with me. I pull the parachute from my bag and spread it over the duvet. Thank you, Judd.

He tracked my plane across the ocean.

You can't just "come for the tortoise."

Chuck and Cliff face off. This is flattering. Who'd have thought Chuck had it in him. Well, he's a pugilist, so of course he has it in him. But I mean, over me. A mere tortoise. Correction: Shakespeare's tortoise.

I turn slowly around.

Chuck has put his naked torso between me and Cliff. She's not yours to take, he says.

Cliff gently swings his motorcycle helmet. He doesn't want a fight. Audrey said it was okay, he says.

You've talked to her.

She sent an email.

I'd like to see something with a signature.

Cliff laughs. Come on, Chuck.

I'm serious.

Cliff peers over Chuck's shoulder. Hey, little buddy, he says, and waves his free hand.

Are you talking to me, Chuck says.

I'm talking to Iris.

Her name's not Iris.

Since when.

Since you left. I'm calling Linda. He picks up the phone.

Cliff approaches, bends down. Winks at me. He looks a little worse for wear. His jacket has one of those tags on the zipper that means he's been skiing. It says ANGEL FIRE.

You're using my tortoise as a paperweight, he says.

Bookmark, says Chuck. Last time I checked, that didn't qualify as cruelty to tortoises.

Cliff lifts me off the page, the page I'm on—and *in*. The page with the tortoise to the power of sixty. He holds me up in his big flat palm. She looks thirsty, he says.

How perceptive you are, Cliff.

Hey, Chuck says, presumably to Linda. You won't believe what the cat just dragged in.

Wanna take a ride, Cliff says to me. On a Harley.

Hang on, says Chuck. Stop right there. Talk to Linda.

Reluctantly, Cliff exchanges me for the phone. Chuck carries me back to my castle. Don't you worry, Winnifred.

Do I look worried.

Unless they make helmets for tortoises, you're not getting on a Harley. Jesus fucking Christ.

He deposits me in my pool. I put my head underwater. Drink. When I come back up, Cliff is saying, She didn't say. She just said the apartment was free. She said the tortoise was here and the apartment was free. And her dad—

Silence.

Oh man.

I climb out of the pool. Stick my head out the window. Cliff is slumped on the sofa. He pushes his hair back. No, I didn't know. Yeah, okay. He looks over. His eyes get big. He points at me.

What, says Chuck.

That is the most adorable—yeah, okay, he says to Linda, and gives the phone back to Chuck.

He circles my castle. So she built it, he marvels.

I look up at him. Of course she did.

Chuck agrees to let me go, but not on the bike. On that score he is putting his foot down. He'll take me and my castle in his car. He'll follow Cliff. Okay.

Cliff says okay.

Chuck puts on some clothes. Cliff puts on his helmet. Chuck grabs his smokes. Cliff grabs me and Papier Mâché. We descend four flights of stairs. When we get to Chuck's car, Cliff says, She likes to sit on the dashboard.

I know what she likes, says Chuck.

Fine, says Cliff.

Fine, says Chuck.

Chuck puts me on the dashboard. Through the windshield I watch Cliff get astride the orange Harley. There's a bit of blond hair hanging down below the helmet. The helmet is sparkly blue.

Am I really going home. To the inside-out mountain.

I look over my shoulder at Chuck. He's got a cigarette hanging out of his mouth. He squints as he starts the car.

We turn off Taft and I start counting down the presidents. Cleveland, Harrison, Cleveland, Arthur. When we hit Washington, Oregon City will be over. Taylor, Polk, Tyler, Harrison. I see the bridge. So many presidents, so few names. How are drivers supposed to keep them straight.

Cliff's hair flutters in the wind. It's overcast but not raining. Traffic slows down at the second Adams. Then we're on the bridge. And I see, down below, the Willamette. Far below. Looking very *un*inviting. And I have a sinking feeling. I look back at Chuck. Is he about to give Shakespeare's tortoise the old heave-ho. Hasn't he been waiting to do this for weeks.

He glances at me, then back at the road.

I begin to discreetly traverse the dashboard.

Where do you think you're going.

And then he rolls down his window! But oh. He is just tossing his cigarette.

What, he says and rolls the window back up.

Traffic moves slowly over the bridge. Chuck's face looks pinched. I think about how, when he's naked, you can see where his rib was broken. I think about him looking out the window.

And I have a new kind of sinking feeling. And this feeling continues all the way into Portland until we reach the old building.
Chuck puts me in Papier Mâché and hands me over to Cliff. Her
name's Winnifred, he says. Not Iris.

Cliff nods. Sorry about the paperweight comment.

No sweat.

And for a moment we all just stand there on the sidewalk.
Then Chuck says, Godspeed, Winnifred. And he bows. Not
something he normally does. Or is he just hiding his face. I stick
my head out the window and watch him as Cliff carries me away.

Cliff climbs the walls. It is the same but not the same because
there is no Audrey. The flat feels colder and mouldier. Cliff dis-
covers the heat lamp and sets it up like a second sun over my castle. Be warm, Winnifred, he says, trying out my new name.

He gives me my dinner and sits on the floor to eat his own.
His hands are chalky from climbing. Mr. Noodles in one hand. A
tiny spoon in the other. Big bottle beside him. He admires my
castle and says, She could really build things, couldn't she.

We are both thinking about how she turned the flat into a
mountain. I drop a piece of lettuce. Remember how she arranged
all the climbing holds on the floor and said they looked like
Utah from the air. Yeah. Remember how she tried to bolt the
first holds into plaster and they just fell away in her hands.
Yeah. And then she got the idea of putting up plywood. Everywhere. So the whole flat got smaller by an inch in every direction.
The walls closed in. But they could be climbed. Yeah. They could
be climbed.

Why did you go, Cliff.

He slurps his Mr. Noodles. His third Mr. Noodles.

Here are a few things you won't remember. The night before
you left, you banged your head on the overhang, a not unusual
occurrence, frankly, and you bled. Your forehead was bleeding.
And she got a tissue and put it on the wound and then you both

sat on the futon and she pressed her forehead against your forehead and said, Are you okay. And you looked so pathetic there,
both of you, with your foreheads pressed together, a Kleenex
between them. And she said, Move and I'll make the futon. So
you moved, and she turned the sofa into a bed, something I have
always found fascinating to watch.

I was not in the Panasonic printer box. I was on the coffee
table because when you banged your head she was in the process
of changing the comics on the floor of my yet-to-be castle. I was
on the coffee table, and I could see your reflection in the TV. The
dark grey glass of the TV that made the room look weirdly
convex and all the climbing holds like so many teeth.

And the second the bed was made, you crawled in and you
were out like a light. But not her. Know what she did. She went
out and moved the car somewhere where you couldn't find it.
She was gone for maybe half an hour. This wasn't the first time
either. She came back soaking wet. So she must have hidden it
good. She came back wet and took off her wet clothes and saw
me on the coffee table keeping watch, and said, Oh shit, Iris.
I'm sorry.

That's okay.

And she put me back in the Panasonic printer box with the
new comics on the floor and finally the lights went out.

Because you had this tendency to wake up and drive the car.
You had this tendency to leave.

And okay, so the next morning you left anyway, but you
didn't have a getaway car this time. So I guess you walked or
hitchhiked or called Ridge. I don't know. You stood in the kitchen
and said the mountains were beckoning. You had your harness
on. Ropes at the ready. And she did not say, What about me. She
said, What about Iris.

Long pause.

And you said, Would you like a tortoise. Which was your
way of saying, I'm going for good this time. Because it was what

the last tenant had said to both of you before he moved out: Would you like a tortoise.

And she had said then, I would not say no to a tortoise. And now she said it again.

And even though we both knew you were a previous tenant, we waited and waited for you to come back. But you didn't. You didn't. And she climbed the walls waiting for you. And I got cold because, oh by the way, this heat lamp tends to set castles on fire, and she had to remove it.

And you know the rest of the story. How she went out looking for you but called it a vacation. How you showed up at the Grand Canyon and then decamped. Left her sitting there in the waiting room of whatever that building was where they examine tortoises to see if they are native to the canyon—you left her there, and you know what she said when we went back to the campground. She said, How can there be no helmet law in Arizona. Don't Americans care about the brains of their citizens.

She was still thinking of your safety.

Grandmother lives in Knightsbridge. Near Harrods, according to my exploding map, on which Harrods pops up three-dimensionally. In fact, Grandmother's street lies in the shadow of Harrods.

I thought Harrods sold shortbread in double-decker bus tins. But in the display windows everything is Egyptian. Or lower case egyptianized. Chairs with sphinx armrests. Mannequins with embryo eyes and broken wrists. Pyramid doorstops.

Grandmother has a flat, not a house. So no stairs to climb. On the ground floor there's an old elevator operated by a man with gold buttons called Hillings. Hillings says he adores Mrs. Flowers and Hilly.

Who.

Hilly, her nurse.

And you are.

Hillings.

As we ride up, I can see the outer wall going down. Most elevators protect you from seeing the outer wall.

He cranks open the gate. Thank you, Hillings.

Your servant.

When I called from the Atomotel, Grandmother said, Yes, by all means. Come. And hung up.

Hilly answers the door. She is tiny and bowlegged with a bald patch. Her eyes are very bright. She straightens the mat outside the door and says (to the mat), Trying to escape again, little devil.

I step into a dark antechamber.

She takes my coat. Your grandmother is in the drawing room.

It occurs to me that Hilly might be a more reliable source of information than either Toff or Grandmother. I touch her arm. I'm trying to find my uncle, I tell her.

Have you tried the directory.

The drawing room has mint-coloured carpet and a white pillar in the middle. The pillar is shaped like one of those Greek women. She's got the ceiling on her head. This pulls me up short. It's not the kind of thing you expect to see inside. All around the pillar are spindly tables with legs that end in paws. The tables are cluttered with *objets d'art*.

Watch the tables.

Grandmother is sitting by the window. A cast on her right arm. Come, she says, not looking at me. She can't see, I remind myself.

Come and let me see you, she says.

I negotiate the tables and take a chair opposite hers. No hug. No kiss.

Audrey.

Hi.

She has aged. But of course she has aged. Her floppy hair is gone. Now she wears those backwards combs that rake your scalp. But she doesn't look any smaller. She looks like, if she stood up, she'd be a match for the pillar.

I need the light to see, she says. Come a bit closer.

I lean forward. Her eyes flash. Like a nocturnal animal's. Tapetum lucidum, it's called. When the retinas reflect light. There's a mother-of-pearl backdrop in there.

You look just the same, she says.

Which confirms her blindness, because my face is an accident scene.

Hilly brings tea on a tray with biscuits. I vaguely remember

the biscuits from the Clue-board house. Powdery. Hilly guides
Grandmother's hand to her cup. Yes, I've got it, she says.

How's your arm, I ask.

Broken.

But otherwise you're doing well.

She scowls.

I dislodge biscuit from my molars. We sit in silence. I remark
on the beauty of pillar. Look at those muscles.

It's hideous. I'm glad I'm blind.

Well, this is going to be fun.

It's called a caryatid, she says after a moment.

What is.

The column.

Oh. Presumably *tid* is another word for ceiling. Interesting.
How about I sign your cast. In Canada we sign casts.

I don't want my cast signed.

Sure you do. I look around for a pen.

Is it true what they say about your father, Audrey.

I freeze. What do they say.

They say he was hit by a car.

Yes, it's true.

I was hit by a car. Isn't that funny. She sips her tea.

Hilly, who has brought napkins, says, You fell off the curb
into a parked car.

Happens to the best of us, I say. Do you have a pen, Hilly. Or
a marker.

She nods.

Don't listen to a word she says, Grandmother whispers to the
window. She is a consummate liar.

But a good nurse, I hope.

Grandmother makes another face.

My plan is to work Uncle Thoby into the conversation casually. Like this: So, did Uncle Thoby stop by to see you. Thanks
Hilly. Here, give me your arm.

She resists at first. Then relents.

Who, she says.

Thoby.

Oh. Yes.

When.

I don't know. Yesterday. Two days ago. More.

Where did he go. Did he say where he was going.

Home, I think.

I lean back in my chair. He went home.

That is my recollection.

Did we cross paths over the Atlantic, then. I have an image of us watching the same *Sherlock Holmes* episode, "The Mystery of the Dancing Men," except his episode is playing backwards as he flies home.

Is he at home right now, trying to Northwest Shove the door open and finding it locked against him. Where's Oddly. Oddly's in London, investigating something, rescuing someone, but she is a bit confused.

I drop Grandmother's arm and look up at the tid. Where to now. What's next.

Did he seem okay.

No answer.

Grandmother.

Yes.

Did he seem okay to you.

Who.

Uncle Thoby.

She nods. Your uncle was here.

Yes. And he said he was going home.

Tapetum lucidum eyes. Unreadable.

I try again. Did he seem upset.

She makes a *comme-ci-comme-ça* gesture. He came to apologize, she says.

What for. Why would he.

Long pause. He would have to tell you about that, she says.

I feel like breaking her other arm.

Audrey.

What.

I'm tired and I think you should go.

You're my grandmother. You're supposed to want me to stay indefinitely.

Well, but I don't.

Did you forgive him.

Who.

You know bloody who, I say.

The word *bloody* startles her. No, she says after a moment.

No, you didn't forgive him.

No.

I stand up. Rest a hand on her shoulder.

Ow.

I'm going now.

I love my sons, Audrey. Both of them.

As I put on my coat I hear Hilly say, She wrote Oddly on your arm.

I take a taxi back to the Atomotel. The cabs here do not have big Napoleon hats. They have little flat caps perched on their foreheads.

She doesn't, though, love both her sons.

London speeds by. We neigh at pedestrians. I think about how a Clint's cab with its hat all aglow is one of the most reassuring sights in the world, and what am I doing in London if Uncle Thoby is back in St. John's.

He isn't, though, back in St. John's.

Up ahead there has been a collision in front of a church. A man in a white truck is arguing with a man in the street. The man in the street is wearing black. He is a chauffeur or he is in mourning. The man in white is a deliverer of some kind.

Traffic stalls while this resolves itself, or fails to resolve itself.

Lorry should stand down, says the cabbie, rubbing his forehead in frustration.

Funny how I know they are fighting, even though I can't hear what they're saying. It's all in the posture. This seems simple—of course there is such a thing as body language—but how do you really know two people at a distance are arguing. How does the brain know.

The same way you know from far away that someone is a threat. You know by the shape they cut against the sky.

And you can tell how long two people have known each other just by observing them walk down the street together. Give or take a year, your brain knows.

There are so many clues your brain picks up without you realizing.

The man in black is contorted. His face. Don't look at him. He has been at a funeral. And now this. The white truck, sorry lorry, hitting his car. It is too much. Today of all days. He sits down on the church steps. Lorry man is writing something on a piece of paper. Lorry man is resisting feeling pity. His pen strokes are jabby.

I remember Uncle Thoby saying something about an olive branch. To be extended towards England. And my dad saying, Bugger that. Which word was full of venom and made Uncle Thoby sit down. My dad didn't usually take sides unless there was an election. But now he was taking sides. Our side of the Atlantic against theirs. And it wasn't for himself he was doing it. It was for Uncle Thoby. I looked up from the floor where I was playing with Wedge.

He'd forgotten I was in the room.

Uncle Thoby glanced at me.

My dad shrugged, like, let her hear it.

What's an I-love branch.

Olive.

Olive you too.

There was no rule in our house about rude words, but there was a rule about hurting people with rude words. You didn't do it. But my dad hadn't broken that rule because his rude word had been on our behalf. We were safe because my dad had pointed a gun at England and said, *Noli me tangere*.

I nodded to myself.

But Uncle Thoby did not nod. And I suspected he would like to be sending whole olive trees to England.

England was another word for Grandmother.

I open my coffee-filter map and ask the cabbie if he can take a quick detour.

At the next red light he looks at the map. That's hardly a quick detour.

Yes but can we swing by anyway.

Yes we can swing. He puts on his indicator.

Good. I lean back.

He looks in his rear-view mirror. You sure that's where you want to go, he says.

Why.

He shrugs.

I put my feet up on the jump seat. That is one thing I like about English cabs. The living-room seating arrangement.

Half an hour later we turn onto a road lined with rundown little shops. Everything is closed except an auto parts store. The cab slows.

Number 138 Welkin Way Road is a Vacuum Repair Shop. Someone has spray-painted NATURE ABHORS A on the brick wall to the left of the sign. The windows are blank. Maybe it used to be a residence, but not now.

Don't you say *hoove* in England, I ask the cabbie. Don't you hoove the carpet.

We hoover. But we also vacuum.
I see. My dad always said hoove.
What do you want to do.
Nothing. Keep going.

I'm sure it's an accident of the chimneys, but here is the general outline of Humouse House.

What does that remind you of.

Cambridge has a sprinkling of snow. People ride bikes with those metal clamps around their pants. Their front tires wobble because they are smoking or reading while they ride. If you stop to ask someone where Humouse House is, they answer in your dad's accent that they haven't the foggiest. Or they say it is over there, across the Cam. Oh yes. The Cam is the river that only comes up to Toff's waist. Thank you. It is all very agreeable but grey and you are struck by the intense colour at the end of a cigarette.

There is no Starbucks across from Humouse House.

Is Wedge in that building.

When I called Lionel de Tigrel I was told by his secretary, Michael, that Lionel is all booked up until May.

I glanced at the agenda in my hand. Um. Tell him whose daughter I am.

Whose daughter are you.

Michael put me on hold. The hold music was an advertisement for Duracell.

So now I am meeting Lionel de Tigrel at the pub where Watson and Crick discovered DNA. Most people don't know that DNA was discovered in a pub—or the important role beer played in that discovery.

I wanted to meet him at Humouse House, but he said no, he couldn't take me inside the building because he had a rotten cold, or possibly an untreatable strain of tuberculosis, and many of the mice have human immune systems.

How convenient. By the way, I too have a human immune system.

But we could meet at his favourite pub, where he has a liquid lunch every day.

Okay, I said.

He sounded hyper. And congested. And not at all Belgian.

In the article it said that Lionel de Tigrel's diet consists mainly of beer and Kit Kat bars. So I have brought him a Kit Kat bar. I put it on the wood table in front of me and order coffee. Then I look over my revised agenda.

1. Audrey Flowers, daughter of.
2. Wedge, astounding age of.
3. Wedge, heart rate of, upper body strength of, knockout potential of.
4. Belgian man, accomplice of.
5. Walter Flowers, your vendetta against.
6. Toff, your acquaintance with.

I should be able to remember six items, right. Right. I fold the list and put it in my pocket.

Aside from a plaque on the way to the bathroom, the pub does not advertise its claim to fame. I try to imagine what the discovery of DNA looked like. Did they bring microscopes to the pub. Or is it all math. Sorry, maths in England. Did Watson and Crick just solve an equation on a pub napkin. Or was someone opening a bottle of wine at the next table and, upon seeing the corkscrew disappear into the cork, they had a double-helix moment. Aha!

To my left is a table of knitters. Two girls and a guy. Students. They chat while watching their needles. They pause to sip beer or tug on their wool. In the pub where DNA was discovered, students are knitting. In the pub where Lionel de Tigrel, maniac, messiah, whatever he is, has a liquid lunch every day, students are knitting.

The richness of life blows my mind.

Here he comes, blowing his nose. I wave. He lifts an elbow in greeting. Goes straight to the bar.

He is wearing a thin grey sweater over a Hawaiian shirt.

Rotten cold, he says, sitting down.

Yes, you said on the phone.

I'm sorry about your father.

He has a ponytail that looks like it hasn't been brushed in a month. And a beard that looks like it was brushed on the stoop before he came in. He does not bat an eye at the knitters. But he does bat an eye at the Kit Kat.

For you, I say, sliding it across the table.

How thoughtful.

He is very thin. The article said that he practises calorie restriction. Apparently if you keep the body not-quite-starving, it will keep going and going. Fuelled by hope. Also, the body will become more active. You will discover stores of untapped energy. This is because the body wants desperately to forage.

Rapacious is the word for his eyes.

He puts the Kit Kat in his bag.

So this is my dad's arch-nemesis.

He tells me that, yes, he used to know my dad quite well. They were students together. They dressed up as Watson and Crick for Halloween one year. That was long ago.

And did you keep in touch.

Through publications. I followed your father's work.

Really. He didn't follow yours.

He squints at me like I amuse him. Okay, Audrey. So, what's this about a twenty-year-old mouse.

On the phone, when I mentioned that I had a mouse five times the age of the oldest mouse in Humouse House, he did not guffaw. He did not say anything except to invite me to lunch.

Now I tell him all about Wedge. How low his heart rate. How strong his upper body. How he could light a light bulb. How a Belgian man, possibly his accomplice, showed up at my dad's funeral and now Wedge is missing.

He nods like this is just what he expected. Then he says, A twenty-year-old mouse is impossible, Audrey. Wait—he lifts a hand—let me rephrase. Twenty years ago the technology did not exist to prolong a mouse's life twofold, let alone five- or sixfold. Twenty years from now we will have twenty-year-old mice.

My dad had the technology.

He couldn't have.

Say he did. Say a twenty-year-old mouse came into your hands, via a Belgian accomplice, could you tell how old he was.

A gleam in those eyes. Like a Kit Kat has appeared on the horizon. Yes, he says.

Humouse House began as the Drosophila Melanogaster Centre.

We had one of those.

But alas, fruit flies do not capture the public imagination.

I beg to differ.

Well, they do not capture corporate funding. No one cares to prolong the life of a fruit fly. Believe me, I flogged that dead horse for years. On the other hand, if you talk directly about human immortality, I mean *on the ground* human immortality, people get very nervous. But a mouse. A mouse is okay. A mouse is cute. There's Mickey. There's Mighty. There's Wedge, he adds, tipping his glass in my direction.

Beer number three.

To answer your question, he says—even though I haven't asked one—it's understandable. I mean, consider how much we've invested in quote unquote coming to terms with death. Thousands of years worth of religion and art. Now here's this bearded bloke who says it was all for naught. All those mental somersaults over the abyss. Unnecessary. Or, to put it another way. Imagine you've been chased to the edge of a cliff by a man with a gun. You can either jump or be shot. You decide to jump. But the moment you do, even as your legs are uselessly windmilling, someone on the edge of the cliff—not the man with the gun, but a benevolent bearded bloke—says, By the way, you needn't have done that.

He pauses.

I'd feel like shooting the bearded bloke, I say.

Lionel de Tigrel laughs and extracts some tissue from his sleeve. Okay, I was going to say you'd tell the bearded bloke he's full of shit. But okay. You want to shoot him. But now. Enter the mouse. The mouse hurries you along to the *of course* stage. The *of course* stage is when you realize—or remember—that *of course* you don't have to die. Haven't you always suspected a loophole. Remember being a kid and feeling that some technology would come along in your lifetime to prevent your going where billions have gone before. *Of course* there is a magic formula. *Of course* there will be a bearded bloke. Because if such a miracle as being alive is possible in the first place, then why shouldn't the miracle of *staying alive* be equally possible. Indeed, the second miracle should be more easily negotiated than the first.

He pauses to blow his nose. He is talking quite loudly. Maybe his ears are plugged.

And we are quite right to feel this way, he resumes. Being alive is what the body knows how to do best. More than that, the body remembers being young. Having been young once, that knowledge—of *how to be young*—is stored in our every cell. We need only jog the memory and persuade the cells to resume an earlier state.

Yes, but what if the body also remembers how to be dead.

He leans back with a thud, like, now you have really wounded me, Audrey Flowers. How can the body remember not existing.

I vaguely remember not existing.

Bollocks. Nevermind. I know what you're saying. You're saying that to die is natural. And to prolong life is unnatural.

Is that what I'm saying. I don't think that's what I'm saying.

And I'm saying if I'd lived five hundred years ago, I'd already be dead. My body would have "remembered" how to die at age forty. Today it "remembers" at age eighty. What has happened. Has our memory of how to die deteriorated. Or has our memory of how to live improved.

At the next table the knitters have stopped knitting. Cheers, Lionel says, lifting his glass.

I lean on my cheek and listen to him. My coffee is cold. It is a bit like meeting an exaggerated version of my dad. The palm trees on his lapels, framing his beard, are freaking me out. I try to steer the conversation back to mice, specifically Wedge, and he launches into an explanation of the derivation of the word *muscle*. Which comes from *Mus musculus*. Because apparently the Romans thought the muscle in the upper arm, when flexed, looked like a little mouse trapped under the skin.

Oh God please don't let him show me.

This is beer number four.

Yes, he is removing his thin grey sweater, under which his Hawaiian shirt is short-sleeved. His arms are very thin. Don't look at them. Still, he can make a small *Mus musculus*, by god. Look. The Romans thought this tendon looked like a mouse's tail. He points to a ropey business running along the inside of his elbow. See.

Okay, I see, I tell him. Put your sweater back on. Don't get cold.

He puts his sweater back on and stares into his beer. A mouse that is in pain or dying will hide, he says after a moment. Will burrow.

What.

Your father and I used to stay up all night arguing.

About what.

Nothing metaphysical. Methods. He didn't believe in calorie restriction.

Probably a good thing for me, I say. I look over my shoulder. I would not say no to more coffee if someone should come by to offer it.

Then he went into psychology of all things.

So you two were close.

I wouldn't say close.

But you dressed up as Watson and Crick.

There were many Watsons and Cricks.

I wonder what this means. Literally, on Halloween. Or how. I picture two men intertwined in a double helix. Would I know a Watson and Crick if I met one on the street.

Lionel heads back to the bar. He promises to bring me coffee.

One of the knitters leans over and says, That the guy from *60 Minutes*.

I nod.

I told you, she says and kicks her friend under the table.

Click click go the needles.

My hands around a steaming fresh cup of coffee, I feel instantly better. I sit up straight. Meanwhile, on this side of his fifth beer, Lionel seems to be sobering up. He seems to have just noticed me.

Walter Flowers' daughter, he says, shaking his head.

I lift a hand. Hi.

He looks at my chest. What's the stopwatch for.

It's an heirloom.

He seems unsurprised. Well. He looks at his own watch. Time to get back to work.

Work.

He chugs the rest of his beer.

Did you know my dad's brother, I ask.

He wipes his mouth on his sleeve. Nods. Met him a few times. Law student.

No.

Tall lanky bloke. Fancy dresser.

Thoby.

Yeah. He points at me. Except he went by another name. A diminutive.

H ow long does it take to catch tuberculosis, because I'm pretty sure that's what I have.

On the little toy train from Cambridge to London, I sit beside a window that won't close, and instead of changing seats, I wrap myself in the red parachute, which other passengers seem to interpret as a show of solidarity with a sports team. Fists in the air. Slaps on the shoulder.

Down the aisle a Seeing Eye dog wears a sign that says PLEASE DO NOT DISTRACT ME.

My eyes feel hot and my neck aches. I stare at the sky. Overhead, the wires tangle and miraculously untangle. That is sort of pretty.

When I wake, I don't feel a future. I don't know where I am. Piccadilly Circus or Paddington Bear. I hate these toy names. I disembark in a dark corner of a dark terminal. Pigeons jog by like business travellers. Excuse me, excuse me.

I take long strides in my red parachute. But long strides to where is the question. This is what a little sleep will do to you. This is why you should not nap in the middle of the post meridiem. This feeling of horror. King's Cross. With who. With you.

A voice over the intercom says, Have you left your bag unattended. Because if you have.

Shit. My bag. I hurry back to the toy train where my carry-on bag is waiting with a very worried expression. Where is my owner.

Here. Sorry.

Back out into the terminal. Long strides towards the pay phones with their oversized receivers and heavy directories. The intercom voice says, If you have left your bag unattended, we will remove it and the king will torture it.

A pigeon rides by on someone's suitcase.

Something Hilly said. When I told her I was looking for my uncle, she said, Have you tried the directory. Which I thought amusing at the time. Ha ha. If only it were that simple. Silly Hilly. How little you know about the complicated existence that is mine.

But maybe it is that simple. What are directories for if not to direct you. Because I am alone in London and I have found no one, no one, no one.

I open the directory to the Fs. Flowers, T. There are six T. Flowers. One lives on Toff's mews. In Toff's house.

The funny thing about solving a mystery is that the closer you get to the solution, the more it feels like you are remembering rather than discovering. Like you are just jogging your memory.

Of course. Toff has been impersonating Uncle Thoby. Of course.

I jog down Toff's mews, unamused. Parachute billowing. I don't bother knocking. I burst in.

Toff, I yell. Or whatever your real name is.

Except it's not Toff's house. It's the brilliant woman's. I recognize her even though her hair is dry. Oops. My apologies. These houses all look the same. Like teeth. Don't they.

Get the fuck out.

Of course. But you should lock your door if you do not want overseas visitors.

Slam.

Toff's house is three doors down. Jog, jog. My parachute is creating some wind resistance. Which is what it was designed to do, of course. But it is a bit of a drag.

Burst open the door. Toff! Or whatever your real name is.

Hamlet trots down the hall, a growl dying in his throat. Oh, it's you. Yes, it's me. Be nice. He blocks my path. Looks over his shoulder.

Toff appears with a dishtowel, drying his hands. He looks like he was expecting an overseas visitor. So you've been to Cambridge, he says.

Yes, I've been to Cambridge. What's your point.

No point.

Goddamn it. He thinks I'm a better detective than I am. He thinks I know something I don't. This is like a red flag to a bull. Speaking of which, he's back to cravats, and this one is red. I lunge for the cravat and get a grip on his clavicle. Is it because you always wished you were my dad's brother that you are now pretending to be him. Is it because Uncle Thoby was in Newfoundland that you thought you could get away with it.

He backs into the wall. Jesus God, Audrey.

What.

You're upsetting the dog for one thing.

I look down. Not that far down. Hamlet is practically at eye level, and snarling. I release his master's clavicle. The tail wags. Dogs are so simple.

Toff arranges his cravat.

I back up. Sorry.

This is off the wall, even for you. What's with the cape.

It's a parachute.

Oh, well that makes much more sense.

I push my palms into my eyes. I feel not good.

A dry hand on my forehead. You've got a fever.

I nod. Possibly an untreatable strain of tuberculosis.

Look at me, Audrey.

I look. At first I see only black spots. Then I see red. What. Why would I do that.

Do what.

Impersonate your uncle.

Because you loved my dad and wanted to be his brother.

Okay, that is true, he says. That is true.

Toff brings me a warm beverage. When I ask what it is, he says,
Remember the advert with the St. Bernard dog.

The what.

Nevermind. It's for cold and flu. And tuberculosis.

I take it in two hands.

We sit together on the sofa. He asks how my meeting with
Grandmother went.

Poorly.

And Lionel de Tigrel.

Poorly.

Oh Audrey.

I look at him. You're all I've got left, Toff. You've got to tell
me the truth. Where is he.

I don't know.

You look like someone who does know.

Has it occurred to you that he doesn't want to be found.

Bollocks. Don't act like you know him better than I do. Don't
you dare.

Hamlet puts his head into the conversation. Toff pushes him
away.

Grandmother said he went home.

Then he probably did.

Home with his olive branch. A tear drops into my lemon
beverage.

Oh don't, says Toff. Cry. Please.

It's my stye. It's my black eye. It's this potion that's making
me weepy. I'm not crying.

He pulls a Kleenex out of his pocket.

Thanks. Too kind.

I've been an ass, he says after a moment.

Yes. Well. It's not too late to stop being one.

He looks at me. Slowly he nods.

Where is home. His home.

Cornwall. Forgive me, dear brother.

Toff's guest room is warm. I climb under the covers. I am so sleepy. Possibly he has poisoned me. He said that tomorrow he would go with me. To the bottom of England. Tomorrow. But there are no trains tonight. And I need to sleep. Take off that parachute.

I have left the door ajar.

I do not know Toff's last name. I have never known it. I have never noticed that I don't know it. Is that usual. Will I remember in the morning that I don't know it. Or is my noticing just a side effect of the hot beverage. I am sleeping in the house of someone whose last name I do not know.

I close my eyes and see Uncle Thoby in the imaginary chair, in a shaft of gold light, tied up with ropes. Oddly!

I will find you.

And in my usual delayed way, I process something that Lionel de Tigrel said, the only thing he really said, though he spoke non-stop for two hours. I finally hear it, ten hours later: A mouse that is in pain or dying will hide. Will burrow.

The door creaks open. Enter Hamlet. I was hoping he'd visit. Is he going to climb on the bed. Because that would be awkward. No. He just stands there and rests his chin on my chest. And sleeps this way.

England is a rumpled landscape with the seams of the blanket showing. Hedges belong outside, Dad. How could you not have known that. Ponies canter in the shadows of clouds. There are bursts of sun and rain. The train makes its slow way south to the foot of the bed.

Destination: Penzance.

When Toff first said Penzance, I thought he was kidding. Penzance. As in the pirates of.

Yes.

But Penzance isn't real, is it.

Across from me Toff wears a yellow cravat with small blue specks. We are in the dining car. When he looks out the window he is a playing card. A jack, sorry knave, cut off at the waist.

My head feels stuffy. We order coffee. Across the aisle, a man talks loudly on a cellphone.

Toff has been writing a letter. He seals it in an envelope and doesn't address the envelope. Is it *pour moi*. No. *Pour qui*. It sits there on the table between us.

The man with the phone is giving his credit card number. To the entire dining car. I grab Toff's pen and write it down on my napkin. Will he give the expiry date. Yes. What a fool.

Audrey.

What.

Accent-grave eyebrows.

Might come in handy, I say.

We should talk about money at some point.

No.

You have plenty.

Do not bust out another Hellvetica will or I will spill my coffee on it.

Fine.

A strong wind buffets the train. We are close now to the foot of the bed. Who knew there were palm trees in England. We roll to a stop in front of a yellow brick wall that says St. Erth.

Toff says, Just popping out for a cigarette.

Oh no you don't. I reach across to grab his cravat but instead knock over his coffee. Shit.

Come on, Audrey. What am I going to do, run away to the ends of St. Erth.

Ha ha.

He leaves the car.

I mop up the coffee. He took his briefcase. Left the envelope. Wait a minute. I stand up.

Outside he is lighting a cigarette. He's making that hand-cupping gesture all smokers make. His cravat flaps in the wind. I pull down the window. Get back on.

He looks up.

Get back on.

I'll wait for you here.

What do you mean you'll wait for me here.

In St. Erth, he says.

For how long.

Indefinitely.

That's sweet of you, Toff. But get back on.

The train starts moving.

But I don't know where I'm going.

There's only one stop left, he calls. Get off at the next stop.

I sit back down and watch him get smaller. I lift the envelope. *Pour moi.* Of course it's for me. So now we are getting to the bottom of it. Are you ready to get to the bottom of it.

Dear Audrey,

You asked me if I had kidnapped your uncle, or
threatened him, or at the very least said something
to make him leave you. I assured you I hadn't. But
it's possible I did say some things—some unkind
and threatening things that I now regret. Please tell
him when you see him that I am sorry, that what I
did for him and Walter I would do over. He will
know what I mean.

I am here to help you.

Always,

Toff

Penzance is at the bottom of England. You leave St. Erth and
alight in Penzance. There are white beaches with palm trees like
inverted umbrellas. The ocean throws white pearls at your feet.
Welcome, welcome orphan.

So Penzance is real. I have arrived in my dad's biography
of Uncle Thoby. And surely Uncle Thoby must be here, must
be in his own biography. Surely this is one of the rules of
biography.

I walk the cursive streets that spell PENZANCE from above. I
make my hand a visor. I scan the beaches for an asymmetrical
outline. The wind is strong and cold. The sky darkens. Where.
Where oh where do I look.

I come across a pub called 'Tis Mabel's. It reminds me of
Bebe's at home. There's a fire in the hearth. The woman behind
the bar has puffy sleeves. She's drying a glass. She puts the glass
down and looks at me. Poor wand'ring one, she says.

Sorry.

You look lost.

Well. I'm looking for someone.

The bar is empty but there's a second room, through an arch,
where a group of men are playing darts. I drift towards that

room. Pour, oh pour the pirate sherry. Fill, oh fill the pirate glass. They all sound like Uncle Thoby. But none of them is him.

Something dawns on me: If everyone in Cambridge sounds like my dad, and everyone in Penzance sounds like Uncle Thoby, and if the people in Cambridge do not sound like the people in Penzance, then my dad and Uncle Thoby do not sound alike. This is what is called a syllogism.

Mabel, I assume 'tis Mabel, comes up beside me. Who're you looking for, luv.

A man with one arm longer than the other.

She tilts her head. Wilfred.

I sit at the bar while she draws me a map. Here, eat this. She puts a bowl of soup in front of me. 'Tis a long walk, she says, and there's snow on the way.

Snow. How can there be snow if there are palm trees.

Five whole centimetres, she says. And we've only got three ploughs.

Won't that cover it.

Three for all of Cornwall, she says.

Oh.

I look at the map. Tremorden Lane. It's at the very edge of the E in Penzance. Up on a hill. Overlooking a beach.

I pay for the soup without touching it.

Outside it is starting to snow. Big beautiful flakes. When will I ever see snow falling on palm trees again. Unless I buy a Penzance snow globe. But then, how would I get that snow globe home.

It's dark. Street lights come on. My shadow wobbles on the cobbles. My bag bounces. A black flag flaps over a store. To keep my spirits up, I hum my dad's favourite song, the song of the Modern Major General.

> About binomial theorem I am teeming with a lot o' news
> With many cheerful facts about the square of the hypotenuse.

And I start to feel cheerful. I'm going to find him, Dad. He's here. He's been burrowing, but it's not too late. I pick up the pace.

It's a steep climb up to Tremorden Lane. At the top there's a stone wall and a row of dark cottages. Summer cottages. Are they even heated. There are no numbers. I will have to knock at the door of each one.

On the other side of the stone wall, far below, is the beach. The ocean is throwing its weight around. Snow swirls.

It feels impossible that Uncle Thoby, *our* Uncle Thoby, could be inside one of those dark cottages. That's just it, though. It is possible. He is. He will be. I knock on the first door. No answer. I move on to the next. No answer. And the next. There are eight cottages in all and no answer at any of them.

Do not be discouraged.

I return to the first cottage and try the door. Locked. The next. Locked. The third. Unlocked. I give the door a shove and step into a kitchen. Bottles clink underfoot. I wait for my eyes to adjust. A pair of orange gloves on the counter. Uncle Thoby, I call.

I step into a living room. He is on the sofa, asleep. Very asleep. But breathing.

I sink down beside him. In the dim light he looks bluish. Beaten around the eyes. I push his hair back. He looks like a pirate. Or like someone whose brother just died. Or like someone whose true love is dead.

Uncle Thoby. I'm sorry it took me so long to get here. Open your eyes. Please. I'm sorry. I was having an adventure. I was solving a mystery. I was afraid.

Don't be like a mouse burrowing and dying. Don't be like the pilot who flies away from a populated area in order to crash his plane alone on a desert island. Be Qantas. Be Uncle Thoby.

Wake up.

Okay, I have a question for you. Are you ready. Here it is. Why did you leave me. Was it because

a) I was a straw breaking your back, or

b) Toff said enough is enough, the game is over, or

c) you wanted to make amends with Grandmother, or

d) you had to run away to a place that did not have my dad dead in it, or

e) you were afraid to crash in front of me.

Answer my question.

It's because of me, isn't it. I grab his left hand. It's my fault.

Of course if it *isn't* my fault—if I am making a false statement—you should wake up right now and correct me. You should wake up and tell me it isn't my fault.

Mr. Green, remember when we played Clue and my dad would accuse someone—say Mrs. White—and then he'd look in the envelope and it wouldn't be Mrs. White, and he'd get all annoyed and start accusing one of us of having Mrs. White and concealing her. Remember that. But no one had Mrs. White. No one had cheated. Okay, sometimes I cheated. Sometimes your long arm made it easy to see your cards. And sometimes I left the room on business and glanced at a scoresheet en route. But it was all above board. And I did not do too badly at Clue, considering I refused to roll the dice and visit the five rooms I could not leap to.

Remember that.

But sometimes a card went missing. Sometimes a card fell on the floor. And we were so absorbed in the game on the table, in the rolling-pinned-flat house so like the one my dad had escaped in England, that we forgot there was a floor, and a real house around us, and an under-the-table world where other mysteries might be unfolding.

At least I forgot.

Because I was on the board. I was leaping. And okay, I was cheating, a little.

And where was Mrs. White.

I slipped off my chair and there she was, on the floor. I crouched down to pick her up, and as I did, I saw my opponents holding hands under the table. Outside the game.

I grabbed the card and sprang up with this surge of happiness. What was the source of this happiness. I thought it was because I'd found the lost card. Look! Look what I found! But it was not because I'd found the lost card. Do you hear me. That was not why I was so happy.

I shake my head. Do you know, when I first read your note, I thought you'd gone out to buy a sweatshirt or clipart. Isn't that funny. I mean, who buys clipart. Your handwriting is really bad. Or it has its bad moments. But I could make out *anon*. That I could make out. But how long is anon. How long before you were going to come home. Or was coming home not on the agenda.

How could coming home not be on the agenda.

I look out the window. Snow polka-dots the air. Check out the snow falling on palm trees. Check it out, Uncle Thoby. Have you ever seen anything like it.

No response.

How can you not be responding.

I watch the rise and fall of his chest.

There's an old saying that goes, Fly the plane in a different direction. Fly the plane in *my* direction. Remember that.

You won't believe this, but Wedge is missing. Wedge is gone and I've been conducting an international search that has put me very much in harm's way. I'm bruised and battered. Look at me. Look at my face. I look almost as wrecked as you. Look at me. Please wake up.

Okay, last card.

I know who you are, Mr. Green. Mr. Moss. I know it was because of me that you met my dad. I know you answered my letter. Thank you for answering my letter. Thank you for loving my dad. Thank you for coming to live with us.

This is the moment when you are supposed to open your eyes. Open your eyes, Uncle Thoby.

He doesn't open his eyes.

I fall asleep on the floor beside the sofa with my chin on his arm, a position not unlike Hamlet's of the night before. I can feel his pulse in my jaw. Cold air pours through the walls. There is no heat. No heat vents. Is that why you didn't hear me calling.

I wake to the sound of a snowplough scraping cobbles. Pray you never hear this sound.

Uncle Thoby shifts his arm. Opens his eyes. Closes them. Opens them again, wider. We stare at each other. He doesn't say anything. Then he scrambles up the back of the sofa.

Hi.

Holy Christ.

You're awake.

I'm having a montage that Oddly Flowers is here.

It's not a montage.

Miss Scarlet in a red cape.

Parachute actually.

How on earth.

I get up and hug his head. I tell him I made a moving speech at his sofa-side. Does he remember.

He shakes his head.

I think you really do.

I think I'm going to be sick, he says. And he gets up and goes to the bathroom. I listen for the sound of him being sick, but all is quiet.

Sun pours through the front window and glints off all the bottles. If they weren't so scary they'd be beautiful. I look around. There's a bedroom off the living room. The bed hasn't been slept in. There's an electric heater on the floor, the kind with coils that glow orange. I look up at the ceiling. No fire alarm.

Uncle Thoby.

From the bathroom: I'm okay.

When he comes out, his eyebrows are all up and worried. Oh Odd.

S'okay.

You shouldn't be here.

Were you ever going to call me.

When I wasn't like this.

Like this. But how long can someone be like this. How long can someone carry on like this. Doesn't he know that I'm a caryatid. A what. A caryatid. A pillar of strength. Oh, I know that sweetheart, I know. Let me carry the tid then. The tid. The ceiling.

He sits down next to me. Puts his hands over his eyes. Oddly. Yeah.

What happened to your face.

A stye.

But who punched you.

London.

Oh, sweetheart.

Don't cry.

I'm not crying.

Yes you are. Plus, I have tuberculosis. But don't worry.

I'm sorry, he says. I'm sorry I wasn't there to look out for you.

And what about you, I say. Who's looking out for you in this tinderbox without a fire alarm.

Penzance is lovely by the sea, my Dad said in his biography of Uncle Thoby. He was right. The beach beneath Uncle Thoby's cottage is deep and white. Five centimetres of snow covers the sand. The palm trees flap black. We walk along Tremorden Lane, then follow a trail down to the beach.

He asks how I found him. Deductive reasoning, I tell him. Or possibly inductive. He looks at me. What, he says. Nevermind. I'm a sharp antler, let's leave it at that. True, he says. Okay.

It is windy and cold. I am wrapped in my parachute. Uncle Thoby wears a coat I don't recognize and his bright orange gloves.

The beach has two boulders like giant tortoises with their middles carved out. You can sit in them like armchairs. They are smooth like the ocean. But today the ocean isn't smooth. Today it is green and churning like an upset stomach.

Uncle Thoby clears the snow from the boulders and we sit.

His legs are shaking. His pirate patch of hair blows up. He looks thinner. Has he been eating. When we stepped out of the cottage, there was a basket of food on the stoop. 'Tis Mabel again, he said. They take care of their pirates in Penzance.

Maybe. Maybe they try. But who is Mabel. Not me. Not family. And this is not home.

Hey look, I say, gesturing at the horizon. Look, there's Newfoundland.

France actually.

Whatever. I knock my boots together.

Oddly—

This feels like the end of a Shirley MacLaine memoir.

He nods. Then: Have you ever finished a Shirley MacLaine memoir.

No. But I'm sure it ends just like this. It ends on a beach after I rescue you. Then we go home.

He pushes his orange gloves down over his knees. Oddly.

Of course there'd be a dog. Ears flapping in the wind.

Odd.

Don't say what I think you're going to say.

I'm not ready to go back.

Then I'm not either.

Odd.

I'm not leaving you here to burrow on Delirium Tremens Lane.

·   ·   ·

Years ago my dad arrived here just like me, minus the red cape. Overnight. Because Uncle Thoby was in a spot of trouble. Remember that. Yes. Well, it was more than a spot. He had lost his job. At Heathrow. Yes, at Heathrow. And there was some trouble with the law. What kind of trouble. Well. He had lost his licence. Let's leave it at that.

He was living in London, trying to put his life back together. And for a while it seemed to be working. For a while he thought he could do it. He was corresponding with my dad, and this correspondence kept him afloat.

But then he had a relapse. He crashed. He came back to Penzance. He was sleeping indefinitely. And so my dad arrived here overnight. And when the right person arrives at the bedside of the sleeping person, the sleeping person opens his eyes. Rule Number One.

My dad rescued you.

You both did, he says. It was both of you.

The shadows of the palm trees lengthen. We sit and watch the water. Weird that a boulder can be comfortable.

You have to come back with me, I say, because Wedge is missing.

Uncle Thoby's eyebrows fly up.

Yes, I tell him. Wedge is missing. Someone kidnapped him. Lionel de Tigrel was my last suspect, and he turned out to be not who I thought he was. I thought he was that lion guy at my dad's funeral.

What lion guy.

Exactly. I don't know.

Uncle Thoby says he is sure Wedge is in the house.

But I searched.

Is Verlaine checking the house.

I look at him. Nod.

He'll turn up.

Will you, I ask. Will you turn up.

He gets to his feet. Come on, he says.

Anon.

He starts walking. Come on.

No.

I sit in my boulder and wait for him to come back. But he doesn't. He doesn't. He keeps walking. And I can't stand it, so I jump up and run after him. But now the wind is against me, and my parachute billows. Help. It wants to pick me up and carry me home without you. Don't let it carry me home without you.

I reach out and grab his arm. Is it because of Toff. Because if it is, he's sorry. He told me to tell you he's sorry. He's waiting for us back on St. Erth.

Uncle Thoby stops. What.

He's waiting in St. Erth with an olive branch.

Toff is in St. Erth.

I nod.

Since when.

I check my stopwatch. Um. I don't know. Yesterday afternoon.

Oh Oddly.

Oh what.

You have to go back and accept it.

Not without you.

He adjusts my parachute around my shoulders.

I look into his face. I hang on to his arms. You came here to disappear.

He shakes his head, no.

I nod my head, yes.

He stops shaking his head.

Why, I say.

He doesn't look at me.

Okay. I know.

I just need some time, Oddly.

I look at him. Really look at him. I won't let you be disappeared. Promise me you'll come back. You have to promise me.

We go back to the cottage. My carry-on bag is parked in the
corner of the living room. Through the front window I can see
Uncle Thoby sitting outside on the rock wall, waiting. What if
I refuse to go. What if I chain myself to the coffee table. Will
that work.

That is not what he needs me to do, though. He needs me
to go.

My dad came to Uncle Thoby's rescue, but then he left. He
left and let Uncle Thoby arrive in his own time, didn't he. We had
to wait.

I open the outside pocket of my bag and pull out the piece of
paper I've been carrying since I left St. John's. I leave it on the
coffee table, map side up.

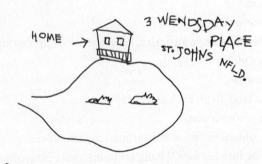

There are degrees of invented. My dad's biography of Uncle Thoby feels like a montage we invented together. It was made up. But it was also true. It was fast and true and mixed up. There is no Leg and Arm Reconstruction Camp in Penzance. But there are palm trees and snow. There are kind-hearted pirates. Penzance is not just a biography. It is not just an operetta. It is a real place.

I figured out pretty early on that Uncle Thoby's arm was not made up. It was not true that he had lost a part of himself and then rebuilt it. But it *was* true. With much effort and pain and falling down and getting back up, he had rebuilt himself.

Here is a walk down a memory lane. Walter, Uncle Thoby, and Oddly sit on the wraparound porch. It is September and the sun has already set its sights on the other hemisphere. The air is cool, but not so cool that we cannot sit outside after supper and eat Piety pie in the fading light. There is no wind. A mosquito hovers. It has already bitten my dad, who brushed it away. It has already bitten me, who did not notice until the evidence bumped up on her ankle. Goddamn it. Mosquito bite.

Now it hovers over Uncle Thoby's shoulder like an exponent. He looks at it. It looks at him. It lands on his arm. His left arm, mark.

Meanwhile I have been tasked with calculating the midpoint between Uncle Thoby's and my dad's birthdays. So they can celebrate a joint one. What is the midpoint between July 14 and September 10. I am counting forward on my fingers.

I am about to invent the Doozoo.

And I am watching the mosquito on Uncle Thoby's arm. Of course he does not swat it. He lets it bite him.

My dad says, Like Donne's flea.

Whose flea, I say.

Nevermind.

And I suppose I know in that instant that Uncle Thoby's arm is flesh and blood because a mosquito is biting it. I know that we are all mixed together in the mosquito. I know that we are all mixed together in the twelfth of August. But there is no *aha* moment. I don't jump out of my seat and say, I've got it, by Jove. I've figured it out. Because you cannot figure out what you already know but don't know you know.

The train pulls into St. Erth and there he is, leaning against the yellow brick wall. Like no time has elapsed. I pull down my window. Toff.

He lifts a hand.

Get on.

He gets on. Looks around the empty car.

He's not ready to come home, I tell him.

I see. But is everything okay.

More or less.

He sits down across from me. Adjusts his cravat.

Did you sleep out there, I ask.

On the bare Erth, he says, smiling. No. I waited till the last train and then checked into a B & B.

Oh. Good.

The train rolls forward. A triangle of sunlight appears on the table.

I brought you a snow globe, I say.

How kind.

Palm trees and snow.

Yes. Lovely.

Thank you, Toff.
You are most welcome.
Do you know what I'm thanking you for.
Looking out the window: Yes.

Epilogue

• • •

THE GRAND FINALLY

A cold night in May and we are on our way to the airport. She has said three times that we should not get our hopes up. Judd takes another mint from the bowl on the dashboard and says there is nothing wrong with getting our hopes up. I look over my shoulder at him. His face is green in the light of the GPS readout. We're early, he says.

Audrey says we need to allow time to get through the revolving doors. People get stuck, she reminds him.

This is true. The day I arrived we were stuck for ten minutes in the airport revolving door with a man and a mandolin. The man immediately started playing a mournful tune. It was cold and Audrey put me inside her coat while we waited. I poked my head out. The coat was new. Otherwise she looked just the same. The coat said CLINT'S CABS and was black leather, quilted on the inside. An announcement came over the intercom that a man, a mandolin, a woman, and a tortoise were trapped inside a revolving door and would someone from Facilities please proceed directly. Soon a crowd had gathered to look. This was my first impression of Canada.

I was tired and dizzy from having travelled most of the trip upside down in a louvred crate with a note from Cliff taped to the inside. The note was two sentences. I read it many times. I know you will not say no to a tortoise. I am really sorry about your dad. Love Cliff. Okay, three sentences.

At customs they couldn't figure out what I was, which was humiliating.

Then on the flight to St. John's I was tucked into a compartment behind the cockpit and I heard the pilot say to the passengers, We have a tortoise on board but hopefully that won't affect our airspeed, ha ha. No doubt this was the metric sense of humour I'd heard so much about. It would take some getting used to.

Audrey was at the airport to greet me. Tears filled her nictitating membranes as she lifted me from the crate and pressed me to her chest.

I observed how professional she looked in the black jacket.

When we finally stepped out of the revolving door, a blast of cold wet wind shocked me straight into my shell. I have since learned to expect this. A shining black cab awaited. I was placed on the dashboard.

Look, Win, she said. Snow.

And indeed there were huge dirty banks of it, dwarfing the trees.

I looked over my shoulder at her. She was a cab driver.

The GPS readout in a Clint's cab not only shows you where you are going and if there are any snowploughs in the vicinity, it also tracks incoming and outgoing flights. Judd is mesmerized by this feature, and who can blame him. For Audrey now it is old hat. She concentrates on the road, which is her job. Judd says the plane is still an hour away. The readout shows the plane's path in green and our path in red, and it shows how, in an hour, the twain shall meet.

Audrey says again that maybe he won't be on this flight.

Judd says that the plane is shining a brighter green than usual, and this bodes well.

What Judd doesn't know, but what I know, is that for a few cruel weeks in March, when Air Canada briefly resumed its direct service between London and St. John's, Audrey went out to the airport every Wednesday at midnight to meet the overseas flight. Just in case.

And came home alone. And slept with the door unlocked so that it could be Northwest Shoved open.

Actually maybe Judd does know this. I have learned not to underestimate the power of Judd. When he is around she lights up like a Christmas tree.

Sometimes she looks into my new castle, which is 360 degrees of glass—a glass palace—she looks into my palace and her eyes seem very large and sad. But this might be a distorting effect of the glass. Then she looks into the castle next to mine, which contains a mouse.

The mouse is usually asleep during the day. At sunset he wakes and before long he is aboard his wheel. His wheel faces my palace, so that he seems to be forever running towards me with his arms open. Come, thou mouse. For one who moves so fast it must be frustrating to never arrive.

Apparently not long ago he disappeared, prompting an international search. Only to be discovered in the middle of the living room eating a Licorice Allsort when Verlaine came by to check the house. Cheeky *souris*. She put him back in his palace and locked the gate. Meanwhile Audrey was in England making an idiot of herself looking for him.

The mouse has an exponent on his ear. But it is a small exponent compared to mine.

Across the room is a mirror and in that mirror I can see many tortoises. Sixty, maybe more, receding in a tunnel of glass palaces. Come, thou tortoise![60]

I laughed at first at the mouse's exponent. And he laughed at me when I tried to eat the fly painted on the rim of my new water dish. I knew the fly was not real, but sometimes a bead of water would settle over it and the fly would seem to rise up off the rim, three-dimensional, and I could not resist trying to eat it once more.

As I say, I laughed at his exponent, until one evening when we were watching the sunset together and I saw his ear lit up from behind: The 18 became 81.

Shit.

We are not exactly friends, but we have reached an understanding. Our sleeping schedules are reversed, and between us we maintain 24/7 surveillance of the living room, which resembles a Druid timepiece. We cover the day between us and provide company to those who come and flop. This is usually Audrey and Judd, and sometimes a neighbour, or Verlaine.

There are countries that have both a president and a prime minister, and it is difficult to remember which office holds the real power. I like to think we are one of those countries.

Do I miss old Papier Mâché. Well, sometimes. But the purple prose had become a bit tiresome, truth be told. Besides it was a fire hazard.

It should come as no surprise that I looked up one night and saw the crenellated edge start to shine like an orange sun. It would have been beautiful except that it wasn't. There was smoke and a crisp sound. I put my head out the window and dropped a piece of lettuce. Kelp, kelp.

' Cliff was asleep on the futon. Passed out on the futon. Lucky for me Audrey had outfitted the flat with three fire alarms. One for curtain fires. One for ice cream fires. One for castle fires. There were three fire extinguishers to match. The castle fire alarm had a fresh nine-volt as of November. It could have woken the dead. And it did. Cliff jumped up and smacked his head on the overhang. I winced. By now the west wing of my castle was alight. Oh shit shit shit, said Cliff, and he actually ran in circles for a moment. I thought only cartoons did that. Finally he got his shit together and grabbed the extinguisher (the one for curtains, but nevermind) and fired the thing at my ramparts.

I withdrew my head in the nick of time, because the force of the spray could have decapitated a tortoise.

When it was all over, Cliff held me to his chest and walked with me around the flat. He didn't bother to mop up the kitchen.

Around and around the indoor mountain we went. I was feeling dizzy to begin with. Smoke inhalation, you know.

Finally he sat down on the futon and we had a heart to heart. I noticed he had a wet tortoise print on his chest. Yeah, he said. This isn't going to work, is it.

I blinked up. He blinked down.

God Iris, I mean Winnifred, I'm so sorry.

It's okay.

The next day he brought home a louvred crate filled with straw.

A few days after I arrived in Canada Verlaine came by a with a newspaper and announced that she had found *le belge*. His name was *not* Lionel de Tigrel.

No kidding.

His name is Gunter de Sitter, she said. He is the new president of the university and, of all things, a Swiss *allemand*.

That's him, Audrey said, sitting down with the paper. The lion from the funeral.

Bien sûr it is him.

It says he's refuting allegations of a *C. difficile* outbreak on campus.

Yes, said Verlaine. I am caught in the middle of that. They are blaming the lab animals.

How funny.

It is not at all funny. Oh, is that the *tortue*. She approached the mantel. *Ça va bien* in your new home.

Perfectly *bien,* thank you.

She was in short sleeves, even though it was winter, and her arms looked like they had mown a few lawns.

How could you not have recognized a compatriot, Audrey said.

A Swiss *allemand* is not a compatriot.

Verlaine walked through the arch into the kitchen. She stared at the pond with no bottom. Your politician is out for his constitutional, she said.

•   •   •

For several days I had watched the politician through the arch, circling the pond, deep in thought. The swans put their heads underwater whenever he passed, prompting me to climb into my dish and do the same. Then one day he dropped by to say he was leaving. He was sad to go, he said, but this was what he had burned the midnight oil for.

To go to Ottawa.

Yes girl.

Byrne Doyle approached the mantel and marvelled at the mouse.

He was in the house all along, Audrey said.

Well, I'll be. And doesn't the tortoise look cute in her sweater.

It's actually a cosy. Judd knitted it.

Nice of him. Keep her insulated.

She has no heat to insulate. But don't tell Judd that.

What. This was news to me.

You're not hurt that I'm driving a Clint's cab, are you.

He winked. No girl. I know you didn't vote for him.

Audrey turns onto the airport road. Immediately it is foggy. Shit, she says.

Fifty minutes, says Judd, consulting the readout.

We pull into short-term parking. There are very few cars. For a moment we just sit there, the car idling. Audrey studies the readout. You really think the plane is glowing brighter than usual.

I really do.

Or is it just darker outside.

Across the parking lot the short-term parking man is a blurry shape behind fogged glass. Audrey says he's been trapped in there for months.

Judd adjusts my cosy. Ready, he says.

So yes, I have warmed to Judd. Despite what Audrey says about my having no warmth to warm, I have warmed to him.

The adjustment was difficult at first. Because Judd is not Cliff. He is the anti-Cliff. Quiet, out of shape. When we were first introduced he called me a turtle and Audrey pointed out that I have claws not fins. She is not a mermaid, she said. Right, Judd said. And shook my claw. Then, when she told him the importance of keeping me warm, he promptly said he would knit me a tortoise cosy.

After he was gone, I dropped a piece of lettuce. What the hell is a tortoise cosy.

Judd likes to knit things, she said. And make Christmas lights.

The cosy materialized a week later. It was bright blue. Judd had taken careful measurements, bless him, and it fit snugly over my shell.

No swimming with the cosy on, he said.

Right.

I now wear the cosy on cold days and whenever we leave the house. Which is often, because I like to ride the dashboard of the cab, and more than once I have ridden the dashboard of Judd's van.

If I am scheduled to take a ride in Judd's van, he will leave it idling for half an hour so that it is warm enough for me (shocking, but thoughtful). Not long ago the three of us went up to Seagull Hill in Judd's van and watched the signals fly. The wind was so strong that the left tires came off the ground.

Look, Win. The ocean.

It looked like no ocean I had ever seen. It looked bloody cold.

Cars have been thrown out of this parking lot, she said.

Judd said, I had a montage last night that Winnifred was driving my van.

I looked over my shoulder. Yes, that happens.

But the real turning point for Judd and me was the night of the Grand Unveiling. I didn't know what was to be grandly unveiled, and when I dropped a piece of lettuce, Audrey would only say to hold my horses. She put on my cosy and off we went to Judd's Christmatech workshop, stopping en route to pick up Swiss Chalet.

At Swiss Chalet she left me in the car while she ran inside. A silver semi pulled up. It was the kind of truck that used to pass us on the highway in the desert. The surface was clear as a mirror and outlined in orange lights. I could see the cab with CLINT WON'T COST YOU A MINT spelled backwards, and I could even see myself and the bowl of mints on the dashboard. When Audrey got back in the car, I gestured at the truck. Look. Why drive a cab when you can drive something like that. Imagine carrying that on your back. We're a good driver. Something to think about.

We arrived at the Christmatech workshop and were greeted at the top of the steps by Judd, who was even more flushed than usual. Judd has red hair and brown eyes and no freckles. He is, I admit, lovely. He is what is called an Autumn. Audrey is what is called a Winter.

He kissed her, and for a moment I was perched on his shoulder like an exponent. Then we proceeded inside.

The workshop was tidy. The only furniture was a table with a single lamp that made a white moon on its black surface. The lights of St. John's sparkled through a small rectangular window.

I was put down on the table with a clink, my cosy removed. Thank you, it is quite warm in here.

The smell of Swiss Chalet filled the room.

Now for the Grand Unveiling, Judd said.

I looked around. There was nothing to be unveiled that I could see—besides me, and my cosy was already off.

Are you ready, he said.

Ready, she said.

The moon on the table went out. The room went black. And then, in a single dizzying instant, the universe burst into being under my feet.

Imagine standing atop the universe and having no piece of lettuce to drop.

The Coma Cluster, Judd said, pointing. The Tadpole Galaxy. The Tortoise Constellation.

There is more to Judd than Christmas electronics and wool, went through my mind.

Come hither, she said.

We all stood absolutely stock still for, perhaps, ever.

We do not get stuck in the revolving doors. We arrive in plenty of time. There is a yellow Lab in a black vest patrolling the floor. When Audrey tries to pat him she is told by the handler that the dog is *working,* the dog is *on duty,* and could she please respect that.

The vest says SNIFFER DOG in white letters. The dog sniffs in my direction. I am under Judd's arm. My smell is apparently not on the dog's list of smells to worry about.

We proceed to the food court. Nothing is open. We sit at a table anyway.

I still feel hopeful, she says.

Good, says Judd.

There have been phone calls. And he has promised he will be on this flight. He has said he is ready to come home. And Audrey has spent two days in the basement, making it different from the way it used to be so that he will find it less painful to descend the steps into it. The cockpit remains. As do the airplane seats. But the seats are no longer in audience formation. Now they face each other like seats on a train. Also, his bed is against a different wall. This, she hopes, will be enough. She wants him to remember, but she doesn't want the remembering to hurt him, and how do you achieve this. How do you achieve this when you find yourself crying in the cockpit, remembering.

I can hear the plane, she says and stands up, though how this is possible, I don't know. The plane is at least twenty minutes away according to the Arrivals screen. But Judd gets up and tucks me under his arm and follows her out to the escalator. The escalator is steep and empty.

I have a sinking feeling, she says.

Come away from the escalator, says Judd.

You don't know how many times I've come out here, she says.

Yes I do, he says.

And he's never on the flight.

I know. But this time he will be.

Why this time.

Because this time he said he would be.

Yes but he has said that before.

Judd looks at his watch.

Please let it land safely, she says. Please oh please oh please. I should be out on the runway.

You're fine.

Waving him in. Saying come hither Airbus 320.

The flight is announced. It has landed. Judd holds me up in the palm of his hand so I can see.

We watch the escalator.

How will I recognize him, I wonder. Will I know him by his arm alone.

The first passengers appear at the top and begin their descent. They are from first class and they are all symmetrical. They carry coats draped over regular-sized arms. They are not him.

Will I know him by his asymmetrical outline. Will I know him by the orange gloves.

No. I will know him by the way Audrey is right now running towards the escalator. The way she is flying up a sinking staircase. And by the way the man at the top says her name. Oddly.

ACKNOWLEDGMENTS

Thank you x 10^6 to the following people for all their help and support:

My editors at Knopf Canada, Angelika Glover for her wisdom and enthusiasm and Diane Martin for not saying no to a tortoise; Kelly Hill for the super artwork; my agent Anne McDermid, with special thanks to Vanessa Matthews; Aritha van Herk for her invaluable comments on early drafts, her generosity, and her humour; the University of Calgary for the gift of time to write; the Burning Rock crowd—especially Ramona Dearing, who nudged the book along its way.

Big thanks also to Aubrey de Grey, Helen Buss, Jeanne Perreault, Suzette Mayr, Rosemary Sullivan, and Henderikus Stam.

Thank you x 10^{100} to my parents for bolstering me when the novel was no longer novel, for reading and rereading, for telling me I knew what I was doing, for making me laugh, for finding me punny, for being the audience I write for.

Jessica Grant's first collection of short stories, *Making Light of Tragedy*, includes a story that won both the Western Magazine Award for Fiction and the Journey Prize. She lives in St. John's.